Margery Allingham's
Albert Campion returns in

MR CAMPION'S FAREWELL

Completed by

Mike Ripley

Severn House Large Print
London & New York

This first large print edition published 2015
in Great Britain and the USA by
SEVERN HOUSE PUBLISHERS LTD of
19 Cedar Road, Sutton, Surrey, England, SM2 5DA.
First world regular print edition published 2014 by
Severn House Publishers Ltd., London and New York.

British Library Cataloguing in Publication Data

Ripley, Mike author.
  Margery Allingham's Mr Campion's farewell.
  1. Campion, Albert (Fictitious character)--Fiction.
  2. Private investigators--England--Fiction. 3. Detective
  and mystery stories. 4. Large type books.
  I. Title II. Mr Campion's farewell III. Carter, Youngman,
  1904-1969 author. IV. Allingham, Margery, 1904-1966
  associated with work.
  823.9'2-dc23

ISBN-13: 9780727897664

Severn House Publishers support the Forest Stewardship Council™
[FSC™], the leading international forest certification organisation. All
our titles that are printed on FSC certified paper carry the FSC logo.

Printed and bound in Great Britain by
T J International, Padstow, Cornwall.

Author's Note

Philip ('Pip') Youngman Carter married his childhood sweetheart Margery Allingham in 1927 and collaborated with her on her famous 'Albert Campion' novels which appeared to great acclaim during and beyond the 'Golden Age' of English crime fiction, where her contemporaries were Agatha Christie and Dorothy L. Sayers. On Margery's death in 1966, Youngman Carter completed her novel *Cargo of Eagles* (published 1968) and two further Campion books: *Mr Campion's Farthing* and *Mr Campion's Falcon*. He was at work on a third, which would have been the twenty-second Campion novel, when he died following an operation for lung cancer in November 1969.

Pip's fragment of manuscript, which contained revisions and minor corrections but no plot outline, character synopsis or plan, was bequeathed to Margery Allingham's sister Joyce. When Joyce Allingham died in 2001, the manuscript was left to officials of the Margery Allingham Society (MAS) and published in the Society's journal *The Bottle Street Gazette* under the title 'Mr Campion's Swansong' in 2008–9.

As a guest speaker at the Margery Allingham

5

Society's annual convention, I learned of Youngman Carter's unfinished novel for the first time, despite being an avid Allingham fan for more than forty years and having lived within ten miles of Pip and Margery's home in Tolleshunt d'Arcy in Essex for more than twenty. Needless to say, I was intrigued.

In 2012 Barry Pike, Chairman of the Margery Allingham Society, took up my rash offer to complete Pip's manuscript as an affectionate conclusion to the adventures of Albert Campion, one of the brightest stars in the rich firmament of British crime writing. To this end, I suggested *Mr Campion's Farewell* rather than 'Swansong' and have attempted to follow Pip Youngman Carter's style and approach rather than try a pastiche of Margery Allingham at her sharpest and funniest, which would have been difficult if not impossible. Dedicated devotees of Pip's solo writings will recognise the influence of his 1963 travel book *On To Andorra* and his rather obscure 1960 short story *Humble's Box*, for which I have to acknowledge Barry Pike's detective skill in unearthing a copy. I must also thank Julia Jones, Margery Allingham's biographer, and novelist Andrew Taylor for their encouragement after reading early drafts.

I am immensely indebted to Roger Johnson, a Sherlockian scholar and Allingham devotee, not only for his astute editing skills but also for his map of 'Lindsay Carfax' which was Youngman Carter's fictional creation, but reminded me instantly of the beautiful wool town of Lavenham in Suffolk. It was Lavenham's history and architecture which were always in my mind as I wrote the book but nothing I (or Pip) wrote reflect the real people of Suffolk, or for that matter Cambridge, though the more astute reader will notice that St Ignatius College is inexplicably located on the site occupied today by Heffer's Bookshop.

I have set the novel in September 1969, as that would have been when Youngman Carter was drafting those early chapters. For the insatiably curious, or the collector of trivia, the full moon that month was on the 29th, which just happened to be my 17th birthday.

Mike Ripley,
Eight Ash Green, Essex.

Contents

One

Sequel to a Nine Days' Wonder

'I find it shocking,' said Clarissa Webster. 'Shocking, and, if you must know, rather frightening.'

She pushed back the papers on her roll-top desk, put down an empty glass and lit a cigarette. The back room of the shop called appropriately The Medley, once the kitchen of a Tudor cottage, was part office, part store. Canvases, framed and unframed, lined one wall; cardboard cartons of artists' materials, convex mirrors, bookends and tourist souvenirs were stacked in that curious disarray which suggests that it is part of a system understood only by its creator.

She was past fifty but still handsome and well aware of her sex, with an easy charm that beckoned and comforted. Her customers, particularly if they were male, found her as irresistible and as memorable as the setting which had attracted them into her net. Sweet, sly, pretty Mrs Webster, a natural saleswoman who could convince any buyer that he had acquired a bargain – a future family heirloom – rather than an overpriced painting of a scene better left to coloured postcards.

'Shocking?'

The girl who had been engulfed in an armchair too low to the floor pulled herself out of it and straddled one of the squat square arms. Despite jeans and the painter's smock worn for practical reasons, the results of which were smeared all over it, she merited more than a casual glance. Everything about her, from the short, almost cropped dark hair about a face which was just too rounded for classic beauty, to the tips of her small spatulate fingers suggested an expert in her choice of work whatever it might be.

'Shocking?' she repeated. 'Frightening? Putting it a bit high, aren't you? You might say it's crackingly silly publicity hunting. I'd call it a load of old codswallop myself.'

Mrs Webster picked a thin paperback book from one of the heaps on her desk. The cover, a pale puce, swore violently with strident orange and green lettering. She held it at arm's length.

'Get with the Psalms,' she read aloud, 'by the Rev Leslie Trump, vicar of Lindsay Carfax.' She opened a page at random. 'Get a load of this. "I was chuffed when they said let's make the God-bothering shop." That's the kick-off of Psalm 122, in case you don't know – according to Trump, the silly little ape.'

'I shouldn't have thought,' said her companion, 'that you were the religious type. You certainly never go to church. What makes you so hot and bothered?'

The proprietress of The Medley poured herself two fingers of gin, adding water from a lustre jug.

'How long have you been here, Eliza Jane?' she asked. 'Just over a year since you first appeared, I think. You're the wrong generation – miles too young. History doesn't mean a thing to you unless it repeats itself and bobs up to fetch you one across the chops. I couldn't care less about Trump – I don't even know him well enough to dislike him. What I don't want just now is trouble. We can all do without another Nine Days' Wonder which is what he's asking for. Have a drink.'

'Gobbledy-gook,' said Eliza Jane. 'Who gives a damn about what Trump says or does? He could blow till he burst without anyone paying attention. *What* Nine Days' Wonder?'

Mrs Webster moistened her lips from her glass and considered the slim figure perched on the chair through her convincing artificial eyelashes. She appeared to change the subject.

'Ben Judd,' she said after a pause. 'I suppose you sleep with him from time to time – I would if I were your age – but are you thinking of shacking up with him? I mean do you intend to stay here for keeps?'

The girl was clearly not embarrassed by the question.

'I might. Ben is rather too fierce for me just now. He's a real painter and my stuff drives him up the wall. Why do you ask?'

'Not out of bitchy curiosity.' Mrs Webster was thoughtful as she sipped her gin. 'I'm going to tell you something and you can believe it or not as you choose. It's always been unlucky to stick your neck out if you live here. That may sound

13

completely mad to you, but it's true. People who do anything which might tend to destroy our image have a pretty parroty time. Perhaps you haven't been here long enough to notice that.'

'You mean those deadbeats, the drop-out crowd, who thought they'd move in last summer?'

'Them – and others. They weren't the first.'

'The Nine Days' Wonder, then?'

Mrs Webster blew a smoke ring into the air and poked a plump forefinger through it.

'This village,' she said, 'as you very well know, is not a village at all – it's a very nicely organised money-making machine. You're part of it with your blissful trick of turning out old-world paintings of it by the dozen. I'm part of it with my arty-crafty racket. So is every man, woman and child in the place. We all live in and on Lindsay Carfax the unspoiled beauty spot of Merrie England as it never bloody well was except in Cloud Cuckooland. We could just as well be working in a film set and the drains would be less smelly.

'We've been a carefully preserved gold mine for at least seventy years and it has never paid anyone to step out of line. People who do become accident-prone. One of Trump's predecessors found that out in 1910 or thereabouts. He was the original Nine Days' Wonder – or one of them.'

'The dreaded elders of the village fixed him? The Gestapo in the form of Gus Marchant's grandfather? What was he up to anyhow?'

'My Aunt Thisbe, who raised me, always said

14

he was a very dull earnest man with theories above his pocket. His name was Austin Bonus – it's on the roll of clergy in the church – and he had an idea to establish a children's home here: East End slum children, waifs and strays and so on. There was a lot of opposition to the scheme on account of it might be noisy and dirty, and bad for the Lindsay Carfax image as a haunt of ancient peace. Bonus fought for a bit and even raised some cash for his scheme – not from the village, I promise you, but from distant do-gooders.

'Then one day he disappeared. It was just after Christmas and he was last seen at an old folks' party at the Carders Hall. He was gone for nine days and when he turned up again he dropped the children's home like a hot potato and carried on as if nothing had happened.'

'No explanation?'

'Nary a word. His wife was furious for a bit, they say, and some of the Church council weren't entirely pleased but it all blew over. They restored the church roof instead and bought a very good organ. No one explained where the money had come from, but it must have cost a packet. Johnnie Sirrah wasn't so lucky.'

'Who was he?'

Mrs Webster's eyes became soft. She smiled like a cat remembering a dish of cream.

'He was by way of being a boyfriend of mine – my first now I come to think of it. It was just before the war when everyone was clamouring for peace and yet doing nothing about it except going to Spain to join in the shooting there.

15

Communism, pacifism, anti-bloodsportism, anti-clericalism, anti-vivisectionalism – you name it, we had it. He tried to organise the whole thing into one vast wail of anger, starting from here because this was supposed to be the deep heart of England, and he had just begun to get himself noticed in quite a big way by the press. I was only eighteen then and quite a dish, though I say it myself. I didn't love him but I thought he'd do very nicely to begin with – he was a sort of challenge to any girl with growing pains. He taught me a thing or two and I never regretted it. Poor Johnnie.'

She emptied her glass to his memory.

'What happened to him?'

'He was found in the gravel pit at Saxon Mills with his head in the water and his neck broken. It's quite a fall from the top and they said he'd been drinking, which was probably true. What nobody knows is why he went there at all. The odd thing was that it took them nine days to find him. We seem to like that number hereabouts.'

'The ghastly Nine Day Festival of the Crafts?'

Mrs Webster sighed. She had not thought about Johnnie Sirrah for many years and the sudden re-appearance of memory brought a twinge of emotion: not pain but surprise.

'Nine oaks by the church, nine acres of the Common, nine steps to the Carders Hall. They used to say there were nine ways to Carfax but it's not true any longer – there's only one. The rest are just lanes leading nowhere in particular.'

She stood up and closed the bottle. 'If you're not going to have one I shall put this away before

16

I get a taste for it. By the way, could you knock me up a sort of Constable's *Haywain* job? About thirty by twenty? Make it a Morland if you feel like it. The pond, the church and the Prentice House. You know the sort of thing – plenty of thick dark varnish. I've got a very good prospect in mind who won't be over here for a month.'

The girl made a mental calculation before answering.

'It would take that long,' she said. 'Varnishes have to dry properly and then it has to be baked till it cracks nicely. I've got about four half-finished but they're all what I call quickies. They wouldn't suit.' She flicked a direct glance at the other woman. 'You wouldn't try passing it for real?'

'Just a sucker's price, my dear,' she said. 'I never guarantee anything as genuine except the wood carvings and anyone can see they're hand done. I shall get what I can for this one when I see how he shapes up as a buyer. I'll come clean about it with you: fifty-fifty and nothing to be agreed in advance. OK? Are you off now?'

Eliza Jane hesitated. 'Well, I was,' she said, 'but you've just reminded me of something I heard out of the corner of my ear this morning when I was talking to Ben in the Woolpack. Someone has been missing from home for a couple of days and his landlady is wondering if he's gone off on the toot and should she do anything about it. Or so they say.'

Mrs Webster turned her head sharply.

'Not little Trump, then. So who?'

'Someone I've never heard of. His name is

Walker – Lemmy Walker, I think they said – and he teaches at the Carders' school for Juniors. Has he been bobbing his head up, or speaking out of turn?'

'Now that is news,' said Mrs Webster.

The two men who were sitting in the hazy morning sunlight on the terrace of the Hôtel de Paris in Monte Carlo appeared to have nothing in common except for the fact that they were both English. The older, a shrivelled bird-like figure wearing a linen jacket and a discoloured panama hat which had evidently been preserved at the back of a wardrobe against the owner's return to the south of France, might have been a clergyman on holiday or the senior partner of a legal firm. Mr Marcus Fuller was in fact a house agent and a dealer in property.

His companion, a lump of flesh, solid as a sack of sand, favoured an overbright blazer and fawn trousers. An unkind guess would have placed him as a North Country man, possibly a butcher, but although Augustine Marchant owned several shops, including a butcher's, he had never handled a carcass in his life, and his voice in moments of stress betrayed his native Suffolk. He sat now, an arm on the balustrade, a John Collins in his hand, with his back to the hotel scanning the morning trickle of tourists into the Casino.

'As mad as a flaming coot,' he said. 'I've always known it. And now you can see it for yourself.'

The older man sniffed. He spoke in the dry

18

clipped tones of the true pedant.

'The Redcars have always enjoyed that reputation. They cultivate it, so to speak, as if it were a rare cactus or a special breed of Siamese cat. Her ladyship is no exception. Eccentric, if you like. But not mad – or only nor' nor' east in my opinion. There's method in it, Gus, if you take the trouble to look for it.'

Marchant grunted dismissively.

'Trotting into that clip joint at this hour in the morning regular as clockwork is mad if you ask me. Stark staring raving nuts. Why does she do it?'

'Because she wins. Housekeeping money, you know – nothing very much, but enough for the morning shopping.'

'If she's got a system why doesn't she clean up with it? I spent a packet trying to get my own off the ground and came away with a hole in my pocket. That proves she's mad – if it needed proving. She's a fairly rich woman yet she spends her mornings – her *mornings*, not her evenings, you realise – in that dreary hole. Round the bend, like I said.'

Mr Marcus Fuller did not reply until his friend had turned back towards their table.

'Her system is almost infallible,' he observed casually. 'A lot of people here – mostly English women – live by it. It is extremely dull, foolproof, and tolerated by the authorities because it dresses the house – keeps a table going in the mornings when the coach parties come in and want to see real gamblers in action.

'You back on the column – a two-to-one

chance – and go on doubling your stake until you make a win. Then you come away with enough money – just – for the groceries or your hair-do or whatever your needs for the day are. All it requires is patience, a little capital and a total lack of interest in gambling. It wouldn't suit *you*.'

Mr Fuller sipped thoughtfully at his *paradis terrestre*, the brightly coloured fruit drink of the hotel.

'It's her health that interests me, if you recall, not her mental state.'

'Well?'

'I've made some enquiries whilst you've been disporting yourself. At eighty, you wouldn't expect her to be strong on the wing. She's frail, but still quite active, her concierge says. Sees a doctor regularly – a man who specialises in heart conditions, I'm told. A shock, I suppose, would be more dangerous than a chill. That fact may become important in certain eventualities.'

Marchant's full-blooded complexion deepened under his newly acquired sunburn. He looked back towards the steps of the casino where a fresh coach load of tourists was streaming towards the avenue of fruit machines which flanked the entrance to the gaming rooms. He shook himself, emptied his glass, and, after a pause, produced a sheet of folded paper from a notecase.

'This came yesterday,' he remarked. 'I didn't happen to use my room last night or I'd have had it sooner. As it is, I'd only just read it before you appeared. I don't like the sound of it.'

He skimmed the letter across the table.

'From Clarissa. She's a good girl – on the sharp side. I like 'em like that. In business, that is.'

Mr Fuller changed his glasses from a leather case in his breast pocket. He picked up the sheet and examined it with a professionalism which mysteriously transmuted it from a mere letter into a document. It was dated but without pre-amble.

I think you should know that Lemmy Walker the schoolmaster has just re-appeared here after being missing for nine days. There was no wild fuss about this because of the school holidays and he mostly looks after himself though he lodges, in two private rooms, with the Thorntons – the one who used to work in the store. Said goodnight to them on the Friday at about ten and told them he was going for a walk. *Very* strange, I thought. No toothbrush or pyjamas, says Mrs T., and didn't turn up to two meetings – Rate-payers Protection and Free Youth Club, who are a bunch of commies anyhow. Usually he shoots his mouth off at both, they say. Mrs T. says he walked in just before breakfast yesterday, unshaven and clothes torn, she thinks brambles, and face scratched. Not a word could she get out of him. *Nine days.* If you can take time off from being a dirty old man, do tell Mr F senior about it. He might know something, which is more than I do. Have fun.

C.

P.S. My favourite scent is *Ma Griffe.*

Marchant waited ponderously, allowing the information time to be digested. His voice had a belligerent edge.

'Well, what do you know about that?'

The older man doubled the paper precisely and unfolded it for a second reading.

'A question I might have asked you in other circumstances. If it is significant at all, it is rather disturbing.'

'Not you, then. Not me. Not Simon, surely? Who else? The new boy?'

Marcus Fuller considered the question and gave it unconditional discharge.

'More than improbable. He has no interest in the subject and even less information. We have all seen to that. But if Mrs Webster has her facts correctly co-ordinated – and despite her pulchritude I would describe her as an astute creature – then we are presented with a most peculiar alternative.'

'Meaning what? Take five from five and the answer is nothing, or it was when I was at school.'

'In that case,' said Mr Fuller, tilting his panama so far forward that it appeared to rest on his eyebrows, 'the original premise has been inaccurately stated.'

He peered through narrowed eyes beyond the line of American cars lounging opulently under the palm trees.

'Lady Prunella is leaving already after her morning stint. A single throw must have been productive. As you say, or infer, we can rule her out. You have no suggestion to make – no more of an idea?'

'I just don't like it. It's as simple as that.'

Mr Fuller consulted the slim golden watch on his wrist and a page of notes in microscopic writing at the back of a diary which he produced from his hip pocket.

'I could be back in Lindsay Carfax in time for dinner if I stirred myself. One of us at least should keep an eye open. Simon will have all the facts but he will not have gone further. He will feel guilty because he should have written to me, or called me, rather than leaving it to an inquisitive woman. My young brother is an idle man in some ways – he lacks my initiative.'

'You take it all that seriously? I do myself, but...'

'Yes,' said the elder Fuller. 'On reflection, I do. We're all getting old, Gus – reaching the tricky age when our guard is down and we are inclined to doze. Just the time for fresh blood to appear, and from an unexpected direction. If someone else is starting to play at Nine Days' Wonders then it must be taken very seriously indeed.'

He stood up.

'The delectable Miss Annabelle – I think I recall the name correctly – will have exhausted you and your pocket by the end of the week, unless you have a most improbable run of luck at the tables. By then I will know a little more about Walker's escapade. I may even persuade him to discuss it.'

'And supposing he shuts up like a clam? Others did in their time.'

'Then there is a new factor. If you were a

23

mathematician instead of a grocer you would call it X. We can't afford it, Gus, as you should know better than anyone. It will have to be identified and cut off before it develops. I shall catch the afternoon Caravelle. Give your inamorata my kindest regards.'

'I don't go for mysteries. You do. That's the difference between a policeman and a nosey parker in one word – well, say seven.'

Superintendent Charles Luke of the Criminal Investigation Department was indulging himself in a favourite relaxation, a perennial attempt to take a rise out of an old friend. He was sitting in the private bar of the Platelayers Arms, a cabin perched above the saloon with a long window looking down upon the general customers. The hostelry itself had survived destruction by a quirk of town planning and reconstruction. Outside there was devastation. Mechanical dinosaurs chewed vast caverns out of the London clay, drills rattled mercilessly and concrete pylons which would soon support an arterial flyover were already dwarfing the little triangle of Victorian dwellings which included the public house. By day, the whole area symbolised progress at its most repulsive; but by seven in the evening, the Platelayers Arms, as peaceful as it had been in 1898 when it was first opened, contained only a handful of regulars.

Mr Albert Campion provided a contrast to the dynamic energy of the superintendent. Few heads turned when he came into a room and his eyes, behind his large horn-rimmed spectacles,

24

suggested that whatever thought was in process it was nothing of immediate importance. Grey hair had brought a certain distinction to his thin face but those who did not know him dismissed him, sometimes to their cost, as a vague nonentity.

'A mystery to me,' said Luke, conjuring an amorphous shape into the air by fluttering his hands, 'is a pain in the neck, meaning leg-work; reporting in triplicate and prodding strangers until they don't know if it's Wappity Goorie night in Peru or the wife's birthday. Quite different for you. For you it's like a fat brown trout' – he made a cast with an imaginary rod – 'or a rare species of butterfly. If they get away, well, too bad. There's always the chance of better luck next time.'

Mr Campion smiled. 'I thought,' he said apologetically, 'that you didn't deal in mysteries as a rule. Safe-breaking, racketeering, swindling, confidence trickery – these things may be complicated but they're not mysteries to you?'

'Try telling that to the AC.' Luke pulled down the corners of his mouth and ran a finger along an invisible but well-clipped moustache. 'You'd find yourself top of the list for retirement. The only mysteries I like are those I hear about second-hand – nothing to do with me. Then I can sit back and let the next man do the worrying. Like the item I'm bringing you right now with a large Scotch and as sure as I'm riding this giraffe.'

'I thought you were leading up to something.'

'I was. None of my business, thank you, but it

25

concerns you in a way.'

'How?'

'We'll come to that. This is a piece of local gossip I picked up last week from an old pal called Bill Bailey who's head of regional crime, East Anglia. We were talking shop, or he was, after a conference of some sort at Cambridge. You know that area – we both do, come to that. He was talking about Lindsay Carfax. Ever been there?'

Mr Campion cast his mind back. 'In my youth,' he said. 'It's a show place, all old oak. Shakespeare's birthplace, Anne Hathaway's cottage and Cockington Forges by the dozen. Once a flourishing wool town in the days when monopolies were first invented, which is why it's nearly all Elizabethan rather than Tudor or earlier. Picture postcards and dainty cottage teas for the tourist trade. Have I missed anything?'

'Quite a packet.' Luke assumed the tone of a guide rattling out the phrases as if they had been worn smooth by parrot repetition. 'Birthplace of Esther Wickham, 1821 to 1872, bracketed by many critics with Charlotte Bronte and Jane Austen, author of *Jonathan Prentice* whose fictional home may be seen on our left as we drive by the Carders' Hall, central architectural gem of the village containing many unique features. On our right the residence and workshop of Josiah Humble, died 1794, inventor of Humble's Box, admission two shillings. The tour will be resumed after a short interval for refreshment. I thank you one and all for your kind attention.'

He paused to empty his glass. 'You get the

picture? You should. I went there myself to take it.'

'Vividly,' said Mr Campion. 'There must have been a strong magnet to draw you there. Not a mystery by any chance? I thought you didn't go for them.'

Luke eased the inside of his collar and shrugged his formidable shoulders.

'Not when they're dumped on my plate,' he admitted. 'But I had a couple of hours free after the conference, so I drove back that way. Bill Bailey made me curious – like a gossipy old woman.' He parted invisible curtains and peered through the gap with avaricious eyes. 'I couldn't resist looking over the other chap's fence. Not that he's preserving the game there, if you follow me. If I must come clean, I'm interested because he isn't – he's only got two pairs of hands he says and they're both full.'

'And what did you find?'

'Quite a basinful.' Luke carried two glasses to the little bar where Mrs Chubb, the landlady, was presiding and refilled them. 'This isn't classified information, you know. Nothing that anyone couldn't discover in a good morning session at the Woolpack, which is the name of the local at Carfax. Ancient history most of it.'

He sat down as if he were chairing a meeting, opening a folio and straightening an imaginary paper with the flat of his hand.

'Carfax isn't run by the parish council, the rating authority, the sanitary inspector and the local rozzer as you might suppose. They're there all right and consider themselves pretty fancy.'

27

His cheeks inflated to create a multi-chinned worthy. 'The real bosses are the Carders – something to do with wool, four hundred years back. They wound stuff on cards, I suppose; hence the Carders' Hall and the Carders' School, now a primary. All tied up with heredity and tradition and no doubt enough mumbo-jumbo to keep the Antediluvian Order of Emus happy for a year. Turn to the East, bang your head on the floor and repeat "Ichabod is my Uncle" three times after me.

'All very comical if you've a mind to it but these boys are very fly customers – they're right on the ball. Boiled down, it comes to this: they're a syndicate who run this place – which makes a packet – with their own rules. One way or another they probably own most of it. You couldn't sell a twopenny postcard in Carfax without their written authority. Any undesirable publicity, anything to spoil the image and you're out – bingo – slap on your backside.'

'You destroy my fondest illusion, Charles. Sordidly commercial, perhaps; but not criminal.'

'Wait for it.' Luke was beginning to glow. 'Listen to this little lot. Apart from old wives' tales and a little item thirty years or so back I'd have treated as murder if it had cropped up in my manor, they're still active – or so the locals think. Last year there was a summer invasion of longhaired deadbeats, and not the best of the species. There's an arty colony down there and it started innocently enough with a group of swinging Morris dances, pop versions of "Blind Man's Turnip" – that sort of thing. What with it being

28

fine weather for sleeping rough and the group being quite well known in their way, the real hippy locusts descended and began to make the place look like Piccadilly Circus on a Saturday night. Not quite demanding with menaces from the innocent tourists but as near as a toucher. Damned bad for business, according to the Woolpack.

'They say in Carfax – or they did in the couple of hours I was there – that things in those parts go by nines. Nine acres, nine crows, nine pins I shouldn't wonder. Say a word out of turn and you vanish for nine days and come back not knowing what year it is. The tale is that the word got round that those layabouts had been given nine days to clear out – or else. None of them took the slightest notice until the ninth day when a couple of them were found dead in a barn. Overdose of drugs apparently. They were most of them on LSD or pot or stronger stuff but this was something very strong indeed and no one knew who had peddled it. Three more were carted off to hospital. Bill Bailey's boys came down in strength, and within a week there wasn't a hippy for miles. It didn't make headlines because some other tale was getting all the silly season billing – a two-headed monster in the Serpentine or a flying saucer seen over Tunbridge Wells.'

'The Carders got the credit?'

'That's the idea – or it was Bill Bailey's anyhow – but he didn't get to first base with it. For a start, they don't really know who the present Carders are. They were always a secretive

29

lot, doing quite a bit of good in their heyday –
the school for example – but as autocratic as the
bosses of a closed shop in the Censors' Union.
The only figure they are sure about is Lady Prunella Redcar, over eighty, reputed to be bonkers
and living in the south of France.'

'All the Redcars are mad,' said Mr Campion
unemotionally. 'I'm distantly related to them.'

'Are you, chum?' Luke was unabashed. 'I can't
say I'm surprised. I haven't finished yet.'

'Some stop-press news?'

'That's just about the size of it. A chap by the
name of Lemuel Walker, a schoolmaster who
sounds a right chip-on-the-shoulder merchant,
had started to shoot his mouth off. "Get with it,
boys! The twentieth century is nearly over!" Not
a popular message in Lindsay Carfax. He disappeared through a trap door as if he was being
shaved by Sweeney Todd.'

'For nine days?'

Luke snapped his fingers.

'Give the gentleman a coconut. Exactly nine
days. He turned up last Monday week looking as
if he'd been dragged through a hedge backwards,
resigned from a couple of trouble-mongering
societies where he'd been a ball of fire and
refused a blind word of explanation. Bill Bailey
who got the story from the local copper sent a lad
to see him. He stuck to it that he'd decided at ten
o'clock one night to go off on a walking tour and
he reasoned that a man over twenty-one and a
taxpayer was entitled to do as he bloody well
pleased. He'd a black eye and sticking plasters
all over his face to prove it.

'Now that, chum, is what I'd call a mystery. By all the rules there's an ordinary little anti-establishment runt – an issue job – who's been presented with a solid-gold hallmarked 25-carat grievance on a plate. A perfect chance to scream blue murder and "Follow me, comrades! To the barricades!" What does he do? Tells someone he's very sorry, sir, and he'll never break bounds again. It's funny ... not ha-ha but super-peculiar.'

Mr Campion pushed his spectacles back on to the bridge of his nose and took a long drink as an aid to rumination.

'The Hooded Brotherhood descended on him with their black grabbers, held him in a secret dungeon until he'd seen the error of his way and then returned him to his landlady not quite as good as new? An old-fashioned suggestion, but it fits. Do you have a better one?'

'If I – or Bill Bailey come to that – could improve on it I wouldn't be telling tales out of school. As it is, there's no complaint, nothing to make a song and dance about and will the arm of the law kindly keep its long nose off the private footpath. Message ends.'

'Not quite,' said Mr Campion. 'At the start of this gothic rigmarole you said it concerned me in a way. Apart from Prunella Redcar, who I think is my great aunt thrice removed and hasn't seen me since my Christening so far as I know, I can't see any connection.'

Luke laughed. 'You've got too many relations to keep track of them all. There's a girl living down there earning a comfortable living by turning out paintings of the place by the dozen. A very choice little item for anyone's notebook.' He sketched a well-curved figure in the air. 'Her name is Eliza Jane Fitton. Do you know her?'

Mr Campion raised his eyebrows and stared blankly into the saloon bar. 'Eliza Jane,' he said at length. 'My wife's – Amanda's – niece. She left home to seek her fortune about three years ago and nobody thought she'd have the slightest difficulty about it, whatever she decided to do. As I recall she is that sort of girl.'

Superintendent Luke looked at his watch and indicated that he would accept a final drink. 'I'm glad about that,' he said. 'Her boyfriend, Ben Judd, is the only other name I was given as a chap who might be a Carder.'

Two

Who Knocks?

It was apparent to Mr Campion as soon as he became acquainted with the white-coated barman
of the Woolpack at Lindsay Carfax that here was
a man who knew all about everything – an
accomplishment which he made no attempt to
conceal. He was a short man, a well-proportion-
ed miniature, with black hair receding from a
shining forehead and much of the repellent confidence of a television soap-powder salesman.

'They've put you in number eight, I see. Old
Draughty, we call it. I wouldn't stand for that if I
were you sir – not at the price you're paying. Tell
you what, I'll have a word with the guv'nor after
lunch and get you shifted into number twelve.
Twice the size, better bed, same charge and looks
over the garden. Leave it to me, sir.'

'You're very kind,' said Mr Campion with
proper humility in the presence of such importance, 'but I've unpacked and the fact is I like the
view down the street.'

The small bar in which he was standing had
been carefully designed to separate the sheep
from the goats in the matter of clientele. It was
intended for regular customers and those guests

who could afford the inflated prices which the hotel charged for food and accommodation, whilst the larger and more obvious saloon with its plethora of old oak and horse brass dealt with the ephemeral coach trade.

Mr Campion, who had placed himself at the end of the curved counter, had the advantage of a strategic position which made him almost invisible, for the sunlight from the window behind him reduced his thin figure to a silhouette. He stood for some time, sipping unhurriedly at his gin and tonic, surveying the half-dozen customers of which only two were identifiable by voice as local. The season was past its peak, it was just after noon, and trade lacked the urgency which precedes the sacred hour of one when the English eat by rigorous convention.

As he signalled for his second drink, he was aware that the barman delayed acceptance of this request by a fraction, waiting until he had caught the eye of the woman who was standing with her back to the man in the corner. She evidently acknowledged the glance, for the barman poured out both orders, placing them on the counter side by side so that both customers were forced to turn towards each other. It was not an introduction but an expertly contrived encounter.

Mr Campion found himself smiling apologetically into a pair of shrewd dark eyes set in a pleasant dimpled face beneath a froth of hair which he suspected had been assisted into premature whiteness.

'You're a visitor here?' said Mrs Clarissa Webster. 'I hope you're enjoying yourself?' She was incapable of speaking to a man without making him acutely aware of her sex and mildly ashamed that it should be the first thought in the presence of such an amiably unselfconscious stranger.

'Completing my education,' he said. 'I always regretted that the author of *Jonathan Prentice* was a woman. A very masculine mind, don't you think?'

She twisted her head, giving the question a more flattering attention than it deserved.

'Perhaps; but she was a poetess too, you know. "Sundials by moonlight telling lovers lies." Somehow, I feel only a woman could have written that. Would you agree?'

'Yet she never married.'

'You're old enough to know that isn't always important. She had her men – three or four if you ask me – and understood them very well. That's why you say she had a man's mind. You're a conceited lot. Bless you.' She emptied her glass, tossed him a smile that intimated that she had enjoyed the interlude and trotted out of the bar leaving a whisper of expensive fragrance tinged with regret at the approach of autumn.

The barman looked after her, washed out the glass and returned to the man in the corner. He had contrived the meeting by long-standing arrangement and hoped it would be profitable.

'A nice woman that,' he said. 'Runs an art shop just down the street. The Medley, she calls it. Her name's Mrs Webster, Mr Campion, and she's a widow. Mine's Don, by the way. Everyone calls me Don. Shall I get you another whilst you're

35

waiting?'

The thought that his intentions were transparent discomforted him.

'Not yet, thank you, Don. I'm waiting for a Miss Fitton.'

'Her?' For once, the fountain of knowledge was surprised. 'She'll be late, so I'd have a large one if I were you. She had an accident last night.'

He swished away pretending to have been summoned from the other bar, leaving Mr Campion torn between curiosity and a strong instinct to make an enemy for life by refusing to ask for details. The problem was solved by the sudden appearance of a girl who materialised in the open door propelled by a single hop. She rested on one leg, steadying herself against the upright, and scanned the few customers between half-closed eyes. Mr Campion moved swiftly to greet his guest.

'My dear Eliza Jane,' he said and bent a shoulder towards her. 'Use this as a crutch – the nearest table I think. The well-informed Don was about to tell me of your trouble, but I'd prefer your own version in due course. What sort of restorative do you use these days?'

She accepted his offer, putting an arm round his neck and hopping with agility to a wheelback chair with splayed arms.

'Dearest Uncle, could you run to a brandy and ginger ale? It's not a hangover cure – I'm on the weak and tearful tack this morning.'

She lifted a lock of dark hair with a hint of copper in it from her forehead to display a graze covering a considerable lump on her left temple.

'That means a lovely black eye before sundown, I'm afraid.'

Mr Campion examined the damage from behind owlish spectacles, noting with concern that her hand was unsteady.

'I agree,' he said. 'It could be a job for a piece of raw steak. In this old world set-up you might try a leech as well – they used to be highly commended. I'm sure the Apothecary stocks them.'

He did not attempt to press her for an explanation but piloted her adroitly by way of lunch, smoothed by banter and small talk, to a frame of mind in which the tension relaxed. Eliza Jane, it was clear, had suffered a shock and was mentally crouching inside herself until her strength returned. She ate dutifully at first, as becomes a well-brought-up niece in the presence of a favourite uncle, but with increasing pleasure. Coffee and a cigarette conjured her first genuine smile.

'Better now – much better. Come to think of it, I haven't eaten a thing since yesterday evening.' She put down her cup. 'I can feel you itching to know what happened to me, so I'll tell you the whole shooting match and don't stop me if you get bored; I want to get it off my chest, for my own satisfaction really. Then I'll know if it sounds a likely tale or not. Are you all set, or do you want to take Madeira or something with it?'

'I'll take it neat,' said Mr Campion. 'Start with Ben Judd.'

Her laugh held a tinge of exasperation.

'Ben? That's a bit of one-upmanship. I didn't realise the family knew anything about him. Or, have you been sitting around in this dump with your ears flapping? It doesn't matter. But you're right. It began with Ben.' She raised her head, looking beyond her host, conjuring a face into her mind's eye.

'Ben is a painter – quite a good one. He's got something to say and when he's a bit older he'll have even more to say and some of his things might even be important. I think so, but I'm not sure. I'm a slick commercial hack, and the awful thing is that I don't want to be anything else. I don't kid myself that I'll ever get a glimpse of the great soul-eating fiend who drives him along. It's not for me.

'The trouble is that I paint – I mean actually put the stuff on canvas – much more easily and rather more skilfully than he does. The business of technique tortures him – he fights with the bloody work down to the last flick of splatter.'

She considered her uncle over a gap of forty years.

'Are you with it, or am I talking jargon that's missing you by a mile?'

'The world is too much with it,' said Mr Campion regretfully. 'But I see your point of view – and his.'

'Good. Then hear this, dearest Uncle. Last night Ben and I had a flaming row. It was one of quite a few we've had lately, sex quarrels you could call them, I suppose. That's what they really are, if you want to be basic. But this was an epoch-maker. We didn't get to hitting each other with bottles – quite – but it came damned close.'

Eliza Jane grimaced as if the idea of using

bottles in Round 2 was a distinct possibility and lit another cigarette.

'The row began in his studio when I'd cooked up a meal and taken quite a bit of trouble over it. Not the easiest place for the Cordon Bleu technique. It's an old barn at the end of a farm track, and not very well converted. He has a bedroom up above half of it, which used to be a hay loft; and you can get to it by climbing a ladder inside, but it's much easier to go by an outside wooden staircase which leads to a platform and a perfectly good door. When we got up there the storm, which had been simmering all the evening, burst good and hearty.

'I was sitting on his bed gibbering and calling him everything I could lay my tongue to when it happened. Someone knocked on the door.'

She paused as if to recall the precise sequence of events.

'Was that odd?' asked Mr Campion. 'I mean, was it very late and therefore unexpected?'

'God, no. It was late-ish for these parts – about ten I suppose. It was a bit melodramatic because I'd just sworn that I wouldn't speak to him again and that I'd leap into bed with the first man who showed willing. Then there was this knock, dead on cue as it seemed. *Dada-Da-Da*.'

'Someone listening outside?'

She shrugged her shoulders.

'I don't know. The staircase creaks quite a bit when you tread on it, but then we weren't exactly paying attention. Ben shouted, "Get the hell out" and we got on with the row. After about five minutes when he'd run out of steam he did look out of the door but there was nobody there.

'About an hour later we were both in full blast again and I was working up to the farewell-for-ever scene when it came the second time. *Dada-Da-Da.*'

She rapped the table with her knuckles.

'As far as I was concerned it was just too good an exit line to miss. I said "My chum outside will see me home and he's welcome to stay" – or something equally damn silly – and flung the door wide open.

'Again; nobody there. It was a bit uncanny. The stupid part was that we were so obsessed with each other that we really didn't stop to think how queer it was. It was pitch black outside, but I'd swear nobody could dash down that staircase without making a noise, and if you tried to slide down the handrail it would drop to pieces. I left the door open so that I could see as far as the first step and started to trip down the rest, all hoity-toity. And trip is the word.

'There was a piece of cord stretched across the third step and I pitched straight down to the paving. I ricked my ankle, barked my skull and I suppose I'm damn lucky not to have broken an arm or a leg.'

'Or a neck,' said Mr Campion blankly. 'I hope Mr Judd came to your rescue?'

'Ben? Oh yes. He came tumbling after. Or rather, he didn't, because my weight had snapped the bit of twine, or jerked it away from the nail it was tied to. He didn't find it until this morning. He was rather good really. He picked me up, bathed my wounds, soaked my ankle and left me severely alone on a couch in the studio for what was left of the night. He thought I was a silly nitwit, probably making a bigger fuss than I needed to, just to get sympathy because I'd taken a toss. He changed his mind when he saw someone had fixed the whole thing up as a rather vicious booby-trap.'

'It sounds,' said Mr Campion, 'as if it caught the wrong victim. Apart from you, has anyone else been having a disagreement with Ben?'

His niece gave her mind to the problem, seeing it from an angle which was new.

'I can't think of a soul. He has everlasting rows with Tommy Tucker who shares the studio with him, but they're just about Art and who gets the space when they both want to do a big canvas. There was an inspector of drains or rates or whatever who got slung out on his ear and complained to the police, and a couple of lieabouts last year whom they'd lent the couch to for a night and who wanted to move in. That was just a simple stand-up fight. And a chap from a London gallery who got a bit patronising. Ben flung a can of paint at him and had to buy him a new suit. All trivial stuff, which could happen to anyone. Nothing serious.'

'No ghostly knocks before last night?'

'Not even a screech owl as far as I know. These were good sharp raps – *Dada-Da-Da*, just like that.'

Eliza Jane stretched her foot tentatively, wincing at the effort.

'And another funny thing,' she said. 'What brings you down here all of a sudden out of the blue? Your letter just said you'd be passing by, but the waiter just now said "You're number eight, aren't you sir?" So you're staying here, at least for the night. I hope you don't intend to keep an eye on me.'

'I came down here,' said Mr Campion, 'to oblige an old friend who says he doesn't like mysteries.'

Three

The Nine Carders

'If you want to see Mr Lemuel Walker, sir, your best chance is right now. You couldn't have picked a better time. He's giving the lecture in the Hall this very night – last of the season.'

The omniscient Don jerked his head towards the door of the bar.

'There's a card on the notice board giving the list, but the rest are finished. Once a month they have them during the summer, for the schools, the tourists and so on. Sometimes they get quite big shots to come down. At the Craft Festival Sir Philip Trumpington came over to talk about Esther Wickham. A hundred quid they paid for him and made money on it, so I hear. Walker will probably touch for a fiver if he's lucky but then he's small stuff, being local and just a school-master.'

It was early in the evening. Mr Campion had escorted his niece to her studio, a long room in one of the innumerable half-timbered cottages on the main street, explored the church, noted the sights he might wish to explore further and paid a dutiful visit to the exterior of the home of revered novelist the late Esther Wickham before

43

returning to the Woolpack in urgent need of refreshment.

His mentor skimmed a green paper ticket across the bar.

'Here you are, sir, compliments of the management. We get 'em for displaying the ads.'

'Is there a keen demand?' enquired Mr Campion.

Don laughed. 'Not that you'd notice it. Party of twenty having early dinner here – girls' school near Cambridge. Four of our residents have booked for the same service. There'll be quite a few from the village I'd say – a dozen, twenty maybe. Nothing to do here at night and Mr Walker's got himself talked about this past week.'

He cocked a beady eye at the thin man. 'You know about that?'

'I heard a rumour,' Mr Campion admitted. 'A nine days' wonder, I was told. What actually happened?'

The barman was not to be defeated by lack of information.

'If you ask me, sir, there was a female behind it. Now just to look at Mr Walker you wouldn't believe that was possible – he's not what you'd think of as a ladies' man, but you never know. I'd say he had an arrangement he wanted kept quiet with some little bit of nooky and it went wrong. She blacked his eye for him and gave him one or two across the kisser to be going on with. That's my opinion. It explains why he won't talk.'

'But he is talking tonight,' said Mr Campion. 'At 8 p.m. sharp, I see. What's his subject?'

'The Carders of Lindsay Carfax – that's what it

44

says on the bills. If you want to do it in style, sir, why don't you take the secret passage? Brings you right into the Moot Room where the action is. I could lend you a torch. It might give them something to think about if you popped up that way.'

He slapped a key on to the bar counter. 'Here you are, sir. It opens both doors – the one in the corner of this room, which you can't see because of the panelling – and the one at the far end.'

Mr Campion declined the offer. 'I think I'll drift along in the usual way. It sounds like a private entrance rather than a secret one.'

'Hasn't been secret for years. There are four of them – passages joining up under the Hall – and they have to be kept from flooding in winter or falling in when they change the drains and what-have-you. Todhunters, the builders – they belong to Marchants – do the work. No secret at all. It's in all the guide books. Sometimes we use it for guests when it's a bad night and there's a dance in the big hall. One starts at the Vicarage, one at Humble's and one at the Prentice House.'

'All the same,' said Mr Campion, 'I think I'll go by the street. Fresh air, you know.'

He wandered towards the dining room and at five minutes to the hour joined the trickle of seekers after culture which was moving by twos and threes towards the main architectural feature of the village.

The Carders Hall stood on an island site at the head of a gentle incline, a square tower of fif-teenth century brick to which had been added a portico supported by Tuscan columns above nine shallow stone steps. The Moot Room was solemn with black panelling; the rostrum still retaining traces of what had been a judicial bench beneath the painted heraldry of the Crown set between boards listing the names of worthies and benefactors. Apart from the twittering schoolgirls the audience was larger than he had expected. The central figure of the latest Nine Days' Wonder had attracted the interest of over a dozen residents, bringing the total to a respectable fifty.

Mr Campion sidled gently into a rush-bottomed seat near the back and settled to reading the rolls of the eminent departed: Jno. Marchant, Thos. Humble, Saul Fuller, Peter Willow Bt, Ephraim Wickham, Wm Kempster, Jed. Staples ... there had been no great changes through the centuries. A creaking chair beside him made him turn his head.

'Good evening,' said Mrs Webster. 'I thought I recognised you from the Woolpack this morning. I hope we're going to enjoy ourselves, but I doubt it. He's a horrid young man.' Her smile was intimate, conveying real pleasure at the encounter.

'What brings you here?' enquired Mr Campion. 'I would have thought you knew all there was to know about the Carders.'

'Curiosity. It hasn't killed the cat yet. I want to see if his adventures really have changed him.'

An upsurge of chatter and coughing followed by silence announced the arrival of the lecturer.

He was a tall man, nearing forty, walking with a scholar's stoop, a folder of notes under his arm.

46

The clerical grey suit hung on a gawky frame which no tailor could have fitted with pride. Spikes of dark hair projected obstinately from the crown of his head despite a recent haircut, and behind steel-rimmed glasses one eye was protected by a black patch. His hands were large and red, suggesting dampness, in contrast to a sallow skin marked with pits of bygone blemishes.

'He *has* cleaned himself up,' observed Mrs Webster. 'Cut off a very nasty moustache and pressed his clothes for once.'

The speaker reached the baize-covered table on the dais, sat down, opened his notes and rose again without any preliminary introduction.

'Ladies and gentlemen. The Carders or, more correctly, the Woolcarders of Lindsay Carfax. I propose this evening to tell you something about one of the most ancient associations in the history of English trading. Actually, no, not quite the oldest. That title belongs among the guilds of post-Roman origin, who...'

An indefinable accent marred the authoritative voice, the suspicion of a whine more suited to complaint than praise.

Mrs Webster mimicked him with malicious accuracy: 'Acktuallie, noew...'

'He suffers from loose vowels,' murmured Mr Campion, and was rewarded by a reproving tap on the knee.

The Carders, it emerged, began as a self-appointed body, neither a craft guild nor an association of masters, but containing elements of both. Their object had been the promotion and

47

protection of the local wool trade from the fourteenth century. Whether they served the same purpose today was open to question, since the present holders of the title were anonymous, their predecessors having incurred Oliver Cromwell's displeasure during the Civil War, and their proceedings since 1649 being held behind closed doors. The Carders School was perhaps the most important of many evidences of their benevolence in times past. As recently as 1820 they had...

The unhappy voice plodded along. Lemuel Walker was not an orator but he possessed the schoolmaster's gift of making his points clearly if without charm. Much of what he had to say was of true historical interest and he had evidently made a personal research, so that the lecture was not merely a rehash of guide book information. His tone belied his subject matter, implying resentment at past injustices.

Inevitably, there had been nine Carders at the inception in 1334. Three Woolmen or Clothiers, a weaver's Marchant, a tradesman or chandler, two landowners or lords of the manor, a taverner and the Abbot of Lindsay Carfax Priory which had been razed to the ground by Henry VIII in 1539 for persistent refusal to accept the royal edict. Most of the early records had been destroyed by Cromwell's men, but fragments of the ritual used at meetings in the fourteenth and fifteenth century survived.

Walker's accent did not help the archaic phrases.

'*So do I swear, to aid all good men of the*

gentle craft, be they shepherd or weaver, master or man, Marchant or clothier, having faith in God and being in fear that I shall answer at the dreadful day of judgement ... And to contribute to the Common Area...'

In the early days property had not been the only card which admitted to membership; heredity had its place, as did quasi-democratic election when a vacancy occurred which could not otherwise be filled. Whether or not this was still true today was a matter for speculation. The veil of secrecy, established for over four hundred years, remained impenetrable but the village never lacked a benefactor. In 1820 the chancel of St Catherine and St Blaise had been repaired. In 1870 the Carders Hall had been privately modernised despite the fact that it was parish property and at that time a magistrate's court. The school had been enlarged through an anonymous gift and in 1910...

The speaker paused, protracting the silence until he had aroused the curiosity of the entire audience.

'In 1910,' he repeated, 'the roof of the church was restored and the present excellent organ was added. Costly gifts, you will agree. The vicar, whose heart was set in other directions, was so overwhelmed by this munificence that he abandoned another and possibly nobler project. I think we may trace or infer the influence of the Carders here. Whether they are still an active body is a question I must leave unresolved. They alone know the truth.'

'They aloewn noew the trewth,' whispered Mrs

49

Webster venomously. 'Miserable little runt.'

Lemuel Walker sat down to applause which was respectful and gratifyingly prolonged. His face had reddened with pleasure, but a nervous tic was apparent as he lifted himself halfway to his feet.

'If there are any questions...?'

The offer halted the clapping, conjuring silence and embarrassment. Hopefully, the audience exchanged glances, each member unwilling to be the first to court attention. The tension was broken by a country voice, cocksure and deliberately impertinent, from a youth standing by the door.

'Ahhhr, just a little 'un. Where d'you get your black eye?'

This graceless vulgarity was not well received. It was greeted by a single laugh amid murmurs of disapproval. The lecturer winced as if he had been struck in the face and looked around – not without dignity – for support. The mistress in charge of the schoolgirl contingent came to his rescue, her clear academic voice commanding respect.

'Mr Walker, you said that the present activities of the Carders – and their identity – are wrapped in mystery. If they are a charitable body and they control funds then they are required by law to be registered. I can assure you that the Act of 1925 is quite specific, since I speak as the treasurer of a well-known charity. My books are always open to inspection. Can you explain that to us?'

The question was not entirely successful as a rescue operation. Walker avoided the woman's eye, opened his mouth and hesitated.

'I can only assume ... that is. I am guessing...' Unexpectedly he rounded on her. 'I do not think you can have considered my closing remarks. There is really no evidence that the present Carders of Lindsay Carfax, if they exist at all, are an active body. I have been trying to talk about history, not about archaic survivals, which are quite pointless in a modern world. That is all I have to add, madam.'

He closed his notes with clumsy fingers, a miserable man who had offered a needless snub to a would-be ally apparently by sheer ineptitude. The incident had ended on a sour note which he seemed incapable of softening. He examined his hands as if their presence surprised him, wiping them on a handkerchief which became limp in the process, and moved slowly towards the flight of steps which led from the dais to the floor. At the foot he paused, shook himself as if to be rid of a nightmare and strode out of the hall, his single eye glaring ahead.

The schoolgirls tittered, voices began to whisper, chairs scraped and somewhere out of sight a door banged. Mrs Webster stood up, gathering her purse and scarf.

'Well,' she said. 'That was quite a performance. Very peculiar really, don't you think? Did you get the impression that he was a bundle of nerves? He was sweating, you know, when he walked past us. I couldn't help noticing it.'

'I think,' murmured Mr Campion, 'that he had a very disagreeable experience not long ago and hasn't quite recovered.'

'He's frightened out of his wits right now,' said Mrs Webster brightly. 'Come along. If you're going back to the Woolpack you can be my escort.'

Four

Nightcap

Flattery is the most reliable weapon in any predatory woman's armoury. With Clarissa Webster the gift was as instinctive as the constant unobtrusive attention she gave to her appearance.

Mr Campion, a willing captive, ensconced opposite her in a high-backed Windsor chair in a corner of the bar considered her technique almost dispassionately. She was sitting with her head on one side, openly appraising him and clearly enjoying the sum total of what she saw and deduced.

'You know,' she confided, 'on closer inspection you're a surprise to me. A pleasant one or I wouldn't have dared admit it. I think you're far more intelligent than you seem at first glance. The truth is that I do a lot of business with men and most of them bore me – even my best clients. I don't think I'd ever be able to sell you anything you didn't intend to buy. Between you and me, it makes a delicious change.'

'You don't think you'll sell me a picture?' said Mr Campion. 'Most of them seem to be done by my niece. A talented girl but too wholesale for my taste. I saw some of them in your window this afternoon. Do you keep her busy?'

'She could work twice as hard and I could still handle the lot,' she sighed. 'You know, I wish I'd known you five years ago.'

'Why?'

'Because that was when I gave up selling really good antiques. If you'd been around then, I could have groomed you into becoming a very good customer once I'd discovered your particular taste. There's a lot of money in that business, but it's a full-time job and I like a bit of freedom. Besides, it's heart-breaking.'

'Indeed? The disappointments of the lost chase?'

She shook her head reflectively. 'Oh no, I never did my own buying at sales. It was simply a question over over-possessiveness. I used to fall in love with my best pieces and hated to let them go. It makes for over-charging and bad salesmanship. No good at all. I landed myself with a house crammed with beautiful pieces and hardly room to sit down. The Humble Box was the last straw. That was when I gave up.'

'Josiah Humble, 1725–1794,' said Mr Campion. 'I propose to visit his establishment to-morrow. Just at present I'm in a state of brute ignorance. You'll have to explain.'

She put on a pretence of being shocked. 'You shouldn't say such things aloud in these parts. Josiah Humble is our second-best celebrity attraction. He was an apothecary, a religious crank and a bogus old humbug if you ask me quietly. He invented or made a lot of herbal remedies. Humble's Universal Elixir, Humble's Infallible Body Unguent and Humble's Stomach Bowel and Wind Pills – they were for horses now I come to think of it. All this was tied up with the suggestion that he was in close touch with the Almighty. He also had a line in weather prophecy – long range forecasting you'd call it today. Hence the Humble Box.

'He was one of the first newspaper advertisers. You know the sort of thing – it sounds quaint today but I've got a copy of the *Morning Chronicle* for 1780-something which says *Mr Josiah Humble having perfected his miraculous device for the foretelling of storms, floods, droughts and every description of weather to be found in the Kingdom will demonstrate the machine to the Nobility and Gentry at his commodious premises...*'

She paused for breath and finished her drink. 'Phew! That was a mouthful. Thank you. Just one more very little one and tell Don to go easy on the soda.'

It was approaching closing time and the bar was crowded with Saturday night drinkers: young farmers and their girls, a group of late diners and a party of guns restoring their strength after much walking in search of partridges. It took Mr Campion some time to fulfil his companion's request.

'The Humble Box,' he enquired as he sat down. 'Why was it the last straw?'

'You'd understand if you'd ever seen one. They're beautiful and quite useless. Like a little spinet in faded mahogany with a bone inlay designed by Hepplewhite. Inside is a collection of dials, like barometers, showing Rainfall, Wind, Temperature, Earthquakes, Pestilences, and God knows what else. You're supposed to set them at nightfall and in the morning they'll tell you what's going to happen in a week's time. Nothing works, naturally, but it's a very pretty toy. They're collectors' items in these parts because there are very few of them surviving and most of those have been gutted so that only the box on its elegant little legs is left. There's one in his house, of course, so you simply must go round the Museum to see it, like a good little tourist.'

'I will,' he promised. 'Have you got one yourself?'

She wrinkled her nose, a curiously youthful gesture that brought a glimpse of the girl she had once been. 'No I haven't. I did once have a genuine one in the shop and couldn't bear to part with it because it was so attractive. I kept on putting up the price until the whole thing became ridiculous. I couldn't sleep at night thinking of the money I was throwing away and the pain I'd suffer if I parted with it. Believe it or not, I made myself quite ill. That was why I gave up that side of the business. Nothing but reproductions for me now, thank you very much.'

'But you sold it?'

'Oh yes, in the end. I had an offer from a dealer by post, one morning towards the end of a rather poor quarter. Not as much as I'd been asking but it was firm and I didn't have to behave like a saleswoman. I let it go and I've regretted it ever since. If only I'd known...'

She broke off, finished her drink and placed her glass slowly on the table in front of her as if she was selecting the particular spot for a purpose.

'Known what?'

'Who was behind the deal – the actual customer. He'd been in the shop enquiring on his own account and since I didn't care for him, I asked a crazy price to put him off. I simply couldn't bear to think of him having it.'

Mr Campion smiled.

'Let me guess,' he said. 'I'm chancing my arm as I stick out my neck to make a shot in the dark. Mr Lemuel Walker?'

Surprise flickered for a moment in Mrs Webster's expressive eyes, quickly chased by amusement.

'Quite right,' she said. 'I suppose my tone of voice gave me away. Now you know why I dislike him so. If someone really has scared him stupid by beating him up I couldn't care less. I don't feel the least bit Christian towards him.'

She stood up. 'I've enjoyed this bit of the evening. Come and see The Medley from the inside before you go. You won't be expected to buy anything – not even one of Eliza Jane's old masters, unless you insist of course. Good night.'

It was after the official hour for closing the bar, but Don was continuing to oblige the more important of his clients, investing each dram with the mystic quality which is added by mild illegality. Finally he closed his till, wiped his last glass and withdrew. The handful of overnight

57

residents determined to exercise their rights by taking a nightcap moved by twos and threes to the leathery depths of the lounge where the waiter on late turn carried out his duties at a pointedly discouraging pace.

Mr Campion sat where Mrs Webster had left him, spinning out a long whisky and water, listening to snatches of conversation as they drifted through the open door.

'Gus Marchant's back. I'm shooting with him on Wednesday.'

'Long Tye Farm?'

'And my little bit. And, of course, Buckram's – that's his now you know. Very useful bit of land. We used to lose a lot of birds down there when it belonged to Wilcox.'

'The bastard owns everything that's worth having from here to Saxon Mills. Greedy, like his old man before him. If you can't beat 'em join 'em. That's what I say. You ought to get yourself made a member of the club. Tell 'em thirteen is a lucky number and we'll all chip in.'

The sally produced a roar of laughter. Mr Augustine Marchant, it emerged, although a leading figure in the sporting and commercial life of Lindsay Carfax, was not one who courted popularity by the exercise of social graces.

A muffled scratching, followed by the sound of a key being turned in a lock made the eavesdropper sit up and look sharply round the empty room. The noise, repeated a second and a third time, came from somewhere behind the panelling in the far corner, which hid the entrance to the not so secret passage. In response to a determined thump, the concealed door rattled and quivered but refused to yield for reasons which were not hard to discover. Six sections of linen-fold panelling were held fast by bolts fixed flush with the woodwork at the top and bottom whilst the keyhole itself was covered by a small circular flap of wood which twisted aside on a pin.

Mr Campion rapped sharply on the woodwork by way of reply, but it had taken some seconds to locate the area and his knock was unanswered. The would-be intruder had either withdrawn or was waiting in silence for the next development. The bolts needed considerable persuasion before they could be moved. Stubbornly, grudgingly, they yielded. Mr Campion repeated his knock, but without Don's key there seemed no way of opening the passage from the bar-room side. As a precaution he closed the door leading to the lounge and moved his chair so that it faced into the corner, settling himself comfortably into its polished contours.

It was three minutes before a key scratched again behind the panelling, the woodwork swung back and after a perceptible pause a voice from the dark cavity broke the silence.

'This is the Woolpack, I suppose? Could I trickle in, d'you think?'

'Please do,' said Mr Campion. 'Have you come far?'

The man who stepped over the threshold was small and plump yet so nimble that he appeared to bounce. A fringe of curls surrounded a bald forehead above round protuberant eyes in a face which had once been cherubic but was now settling pouchily into middle age. A dark sweater worn over a soft white polo-necked shirt gave him a clerical appearance which was obviously deliberate.

'Sweet of you. Secret passages are really not my scene – not at all. So dark, you know – so short of couth.' He placed a large electric torch on the bar and skipped up beside it, swinging his legs as if he were supporting his entire weight by his hands.

'My name's Trump,' he said. 'Leslie Trump. I'm the vicar, the padre, the dog-collar dogsbody – take your pick, man. Have you been here long?'

'About twelve hours,' said Mr Campion. 'It seems longer now I come to think of it.'

'Oh, folly!' The tenor voice was arch. 'Not my drift at all. I mean have you been squatting around this grog shop most of the evening?'

'Only for the last hour. Is it important?'

'Could be, man, it could be. Provided you're not tanked up and you kept your peepers open. Did anyone happen to use this entrance during that time? If they did someone would have notic- ed, wouldn't you say? Any joy?'

'Not a soul. Not even the ghost of a Carder.'

Mr Trump considered the statement, his globu- lar eyes focussed shrewdly on his informant and his forehead puckered with surprise.

'A deliciously bad taste joke. So glad you're with it.' He frowned petulantly. 'It doesn't solve my problem, you know – makes a bigger mys- tery of it, in fact. If he didn't go this-a-way – and I'm damn sure he didn't go by the Prentice place or Humble's because they're locked and bolted – then he must have sneaked out by the Carders Hall. The caretaker will have gone now, so that means waiting until tomorrow before I can enquire. I find it very hard to keep my cool.'

'Forgive me,' said Mr Campion mildly, 'but I'm not quite sure what you're talking about. Has someone been exploring the underground?'

'Exploring it?' The idea seemed to amuse the newcomer and he tittered. 'Oh no, no, no. Not exploring. I think my caller knew his way very well. It suggests a parishioner, don't you think? Who else would drop in by our own special private entrance?'

Mr Campion contemplated the man from above his spectacles. He saw an odd tortured little creature totally unsuited to his profession, a mixture of conceit and self-suspicion, a misfit in almost any walk of life. At the moment, he was hovering between elation and fright, happy to confide in the first interested listener.

'Let me get this straight,' said Mr Campion. 'You have had a visitor, an intruder of some sort whom you didn't see, and you think he got in and out of the vicarage by way of the not-so-secret passage? Did he help himself to a souvenir, or leave you a message? How did you discover his existence?'

'You have got the picture in one blinding flash, dear man. Some intrusive personage has been blundering around in the vicarage and left the door unlocked behind him – the door to the passage. And not very long since because Mrs Duck, my housekeeper, leaves at ten and locks

61

everything up without fail. I came back at eleven, so that leaves rather less than an hour. Whoever it was must have heard me arrive and skipped off sharpish.'

'If fact, you've been burgled?'

Mr Trump continued to swing his legs. 'Burglary? Horrid word. I don't like to think in terms of mine and thine. I hold a few precious things in trust but if someone thinks he has a better claim he must be guided by the light as he sees it. Sometimes I doubt my own right to interpret the eighth commandment. The fact is, I don't even know if I have been robbed. The visitor may simply have been curious.'

'But the place was searched? Any serious damage?'

'Oh jiminy, no. No folly of that sort. Just someone who opened up my box – it's rather a good specimen or was – and left it with its poor little insides lying about all over the place. It looks terribly indecent in a perverse esoteric sort of way.'

Mr Campion sat up.

'Your Humble Box?'

'That's the scene, man. This joker unscrewed the board with all the dials and knobs on it, had a good look at the works, such as they are, and didn't bother to put them back. He may even have taken some of the parts for all I know. None of them worked in any case, except a sort of barometer thing which wasn't touched.'

'Had you ever looked inside it before?' enquired Mr Campion. 'I've never seen one myself, but they sound fascinating. What did the works consist of? Damp seaweed? The mummified toe of a gouty Chinese Mandarin?'

'I had just a peep when I first bought it.' The vicar made the admission as if it was slightly indelicate. 'Couldn't understand a thing. A lot of glass tubes with nothing inside them, a leather bag affair, quite rotted away, and some sort of hour glass effect with sand in it. None of it worked, I promise you. I doubt if it ever did and it certainly never will now.'

'I think,' said Mr Campion, 'that even if you haven't been robbed you should tell the police about your visitor. You may not mind what has happened, but other people may object if there's a chap wandering about the place breaking up antiques.'

'Police?' The little man was too shocked to remember his vernacular. He gulped, recovering himself. 'The Fuzz? Oh, folly, no. Not poor young Wilson, not even Sergeant James. I simply couldn't bear it. Not my scene at all. I must just hope that whoever it was will turn up again so that we can have a heart-to-heart.'

'You don't think that your visitor was making a nuisance of himself for some personal reason? He doesn't sound like an ordinary sneak thief.'

'Someone who's got it in for me?' Mr Trump cocked his head to one side as he considered the question. He lifted his body further on to the bar and crossed his legs. 'A non-taker for my efforts to bring a little new thinking into theology? Alack-a-day-dee! No, I think not. I had only one example of that, apart from the usual sheep noises from some of my flock. But it was very disappointing. The ghastly truth is I'd rather hoped for better things.'

'Your own Nine Days' Wonder?' suggested Campion.

Mr Trump hugged himself. 'Oh, you *are* quick on the uptake. A delicious sensation, finding someone who doesn't have to wait for a recap. Yes, that's what I meant. Like Austin Bonus, our twenty-fifth vicar. I think he was the first to be called a Nine Days' Wonder because of his adventure, you know.'

He glanced round the room, dropping his voice to underline the confidence about to be revealed. 'Between you and me, I've sometimes wondered if he wasn't a very clever man, who got what he wanted by threatening to make a nuisance of himself. A splendid idea but I'm afraid it's not really true, though I'd like it to be.'

'You think the Carders persuaded him to see things their way by a mixture of bullying and bribery which took them nine days?'

'I fear so. He got his roof replaced and a new organ, about five thousand pounds' worth in all and it could only have come from them – and he kept his share of the bargain, which was to cancel his children's home and keep his trap shut. I respect him for that, you know. It must have been terribly tempting, just to drop a tiny hint here and there. He must have known who most of them were, after his experience.'

'Perhaps,' suggested Mr Campion, 'he believed in keeping his word. Just now you said you were disappointed. Have you been *trying* to attract their attention?'

'I?' Trump giggled, lifted his body clear of the bar, supporting it on his hands, swung it back and forward and settled again. 'Me? I suppose you could say so. You wouldn't be wrong and you wouldn't be right. My little effort – my psalm book – is just to attract attention – anybody's. Religion needs a new image. That sounds pagan but it's true and rather witty when you come to think of it – I must remember to use it again. After it was published it did cross my tiny mind that if the Carders were still active, they might not approve, and if they tried to do anything about it, I might have a bit of a lark finding out who they are.'

'And did you?'

'Not a peep out of them. Well, just a tiny one, perhaps, but I couldn't be sure. Somebody sent me nine copies of my book in a parcel and they'd each been cut neatly in two. Still, I gather a two-shilling royalty for each one sold, so I can't complain – eighteen bob profit is not to be sneezed at. I'm happy to laugh at that sort of joke.'

'It doesn't sound much like the Carders, except for the number,' said Mr Campion. 'I suppose you haven't asked Mr Walker, the man I heard lecturing on the subject this evening, about his experiences? They say he had a nine-day adventure but he didn't mention it to his audience. He certainly didn't want to discuss anything that happened much after 1900.'

Mr Trump was not pleased at the suggestion. He looked away, shrugged his shoulders and beat a small petulant tattoo on the bar with his fingers.

'Lemuel Walker,' he said, as if the name was unpleasant. 'Why pick on him? What made him so important all of a sudden? I mean, we all know he's a nuisance and a bad influence on the young, but is he worth all that trouble? I've racked my brains and I can't come up with an answer.'

'Perhaps,' said Mr Campion diffidently, 'in the course of his researches for his lecture Mr Walker came up with some new facts about the Carders. For example, who the present ones are and what sort of funds they control.'

The little man pursed his lips as if he were about to whistle.

'Very acute,' he said when he had assimilated the suggestion. 'Very likely now I come to think of it. You're very knowledgeable for a stranger in our midst. You could be so right. If you are, would you think Walker was bribed as well as being given a black eye? I mean, I don't think I could put up with much pain if it came to a showdown and I find most of the martyrs a tiny bit off-beat, but if it was a question of corruption in a good cause that would be absolutely splendid. I'd love to co-operate.' He sighed. 'The trouble is, I seem to have missed the boat.'

Mr Campion stood up.

'If I were you,' he said. 'I wouldn't even wave it goodbye.'

Five

Crime Scene

The architectural glories of the Church of St Catherine and St Blaise (tower in flashed flint-work, fourteenth-century chancel, Carders' parclose and carved-stone chapel with wainscot) attracted a far larger share of the congregation than could be attributed to the ministry of the Rev. Leslie Trump. Wisely, he had refrained from obtruding his personality into the church and his Sunday morning sermon, upon missions and missionaries, lacked the customary castigation of colonial pioneers. Mr Campion wandered idly from the porch (fourteenth-century decorated woodwork, groined ceiling, clustered shafts), and skirted the pond, pausing like every newcomer to watch the ducks and to lift his eyes to the flawless charm of Tudor half-timbering and local pargetting which graced the gentle slope up to the Carders Hall and the Woolpack.

He had just drawn level with the bow window of J. Humble, Apothecary, established 1667, when a small open car drew up beside him.

'Good morning, Uncle,' said Eliza Jane Fitton. 'I'm better now, thank you. I've seen the vet and he says I won't have to be shot after all. I was just coming to see you. Hop in.'

Like Amanda, his wife, she had a heart-shaped face which was emphasised by the casual lock across her forehead and the fall of her hair beside her cheeks. A Dior scarf, in rich autumnal tones, loose about her neck, was her only concession to femininity.

'Where to?'

'To see Ben Judd, my intended. Don't mention the subject to him because he really believes he's fancy-free, and a natural polygamist in any case. You may hate his stuff, especially his big oils. If you do, say so. Admit your groove got stuck around Braque and Picasso. That will clear the air and we can talk about cabbages and kings.'

Mr Campion doubled his long legs into the car with commendable agility.

'And suppose I do like them?' he enquired. 'Would that be disastrous?'

'Watch your step about that. He hates being patronised. Ask him to be sure and send you a card for his next exhibition. That doesn't commit you and it shows willing. Otherwise, keep your avuncular trap closed.'

The studio, approached by a narrow lane off the main street, was one of three barns, its nearest neighbour surviving as some form of store house and the largest having been converted and expanded into a commercial garage. The ground-floor studio was an enormous room partly partitioned by a curtain of fishing nets decorated with corks hanging from a cross beam. It was comfortably furnished with two low sofas, long past middle age, and tables loaded with books and gramophone records. The air hung heavy with the scent of oil paint, which is exciting or repellent according to personal temperament. Canvases crowded the walls and a very large working easel stood with its burden ostentatiously angled away from any newcomer. A tall modern window provided the main light.

The man who greeted them seemed to have stepped from another century. He was tall, flaxen-haired and bearded, with the arrogance of a Victorian and the physical power of a Norseman. The fact that he was a painter appeared to confer unquestionable masculinity on the art. He lifted Eliza Jane by the elbows, held her at arm's length and deposited her on a high stool.

'Sit there, Fitton, and don't move until you're given leave. I thought I told you not to walk without a stick?' He greeted Campion with a jut of his beard. 'A vixen by nature, you know, but lacking the animal's intelligence. I can offer you almost any drink you care to name, having sold a picture last week to a man that carried folding money about his person.'

Eliza Jane slid to her feet. 'He does this to encourage me to work,' she explained. 'Get out of the way and I'll see what's on offer.' Deftly she dispensed the drinks, olives and small talk, splattered with the familiar routine of amiable abuse which betrays deep understanding between people of well-matched wits.

'Before I go and make omelettes,' she said at last, 'you can tell my uncle about the Carders. I know he's interested, because he went to a very dull lecture in the Hall last night and had a drink afterwards with Clarissa, who's fallen for him like a ton of bricks. Don't flatter yourself, Albert my darling, she falls very easily. Judd, you're one of them – the Carders, I mean. You admitted it to me in a drunken moment last year. Come clean.'

'Slut!' said Judd, grinning to show teeth. 'Only sluts, harridans and scolds fit for the ducking stool remember what a man says in his cups. And only the worst of them repeat it. The Carders are an ancient, secret – remember that, woman, *secret* – and as far as I know, benevolent society. If you, sir went to some dreary lecture about them last night, you know this already. What more is there to tell?'

'A very good question,' said Mr Campion apologetically. 'What indeed? For example, unless the answer is restricted information, how do you happen to be one?'

Ben Judd perched himself on the edge of a table and picked up a palette knife, twirling it in his fingers.

'Accident of birth,' he said. 'My mother was a Miss Dyer. Dyers have always been Carders, if you follow me, so there I am. I have what is called a Holding by Inheritance.'

He pointed the knife at arms' length directly at Eliza Jane as if he intended to transfix her.

'If you want the truth about the Carders, I will give it to you complete in one sentence. They are without the shadow of a peradventure the greatest bore this world has seen since the first committee was invented. Stultifying, abysmal, epoch-making bores, severally and collectively.'

70

He turned to Campion with a sweep of the knife. 'I happen to be one of those sentimental apes who believe in keeping their word if they've sworn to it, or I'd be more explicit. For example, I don't propose to give you any names I do know. But I will tell you this. The introduction ceremony takes an hour and a half, with the mug concerned either standing or kneeling. Like it says in the bit of ritual that survived and got itself into print – you swear by Yan, Tan Thethera, Methera, Pimp and all the rest of the old world ballyhoo. The Learned Clerk invests you in the Fleece of Jason, you drink from the golden cup – old Madeira, I'd say – and generally make of yourself one first-class medieval fool.'

'It sounds as if you've swallowed the medieval mumbo-jumbo in one gulp,' said Eliza Jane. 'Have you any idea what my darling jester here is talking about, Uncle?'

Mr Campion pushed his spectacles further back on to his face with a forefinger which remained poised and gently beating, like a conductor's baton keeping time.

'*Yan, Tan, Tethera...*' He chanted softly. 'It's the ancient way of counting sheep. Not to get yourself to sleep you understand, but real sheep out on the hills or in fields. Used by shepherds who were unlikely to be either literate or numerate, so they invented their own system of keeping track of the woolly beasts that were their livelihood. *Yan, Tan, Tethera.*' Mr Campion hummed again. 'When sung, it has a certain operatic quality, don't you think? Yet I would have said it came from a dialect found in more northern latitudes – Cumberland perhaps, or the Yorkshire Dales – I don't think I've ever heard the expression in Suffolk.'

'Hearing it once was enough for me,' snarled the angry young artist. 'I sent their infernal Learned Clerk what they call a Proxy in Perpetuity – had to do that because there's money involved and they vote on it – but never again will I endure such a farrago of long-winded, out-of-date balderdash. Not for all the tea in China. Never again.'

'Never?' said Eliza Jane, crossing his palette knife with a long paint brush as if they were fencing. 'I thought you told me...'

'Never is right. As it happens, I have never attended another meeting. What that gossiping Hecate is getting at is that I did make a half-hearted effort to put in an appearance last year. It was just after the great row about the drop-outs and the hippies and all that tedious jazz. There was a lot of chat about the Carders being behind the scenes in getting rid of them. I didn't believe it and I didn't see how it was remotely possible, but I thought I'd drop into the next Carders' get-together and just ask.

'They meet in the Carders Hall, as you would guess, and I was a few minutes late because I thought the more mumbo-jumbo I missed the better. If you went to that lecture you know what the place is like. You go through the main door into an outer vestibule with half-glass swing doors looking straight down the hall itself, facing the raised dais at the far end. I'd shown my invitation – the summons they call it – to the

72

caretaker who was very suspicious of me and delayed me before I could push ahead.

'It was really very odd. There was nobody there – nobody, that is, except the Learned Clerk, and he was sitting at the head of the long table reading a novel and making notes. I watched him for quite a bit – five minutes perhaps – to make sure he really was alone and then I barged in and wished him a merry Michaelmas. The old goat shut his book with a bang, looked up at me and laughed. The joke was clearly on me. "The council is closed, sir," he said. "The business of the day was concluded before your arrival. I have delayed my own departure in case you put in a late appearance." "What went on?" I said, "I wanted to ask some questions. You were damn quick getting through the hocus-pocus." "Our proceedings can only be discussed at our next assembly," he said in a ripe, sucks-to-you voice, "I suggest you attend it as a duty and a right."'

'And did you?' asked Mr Campion.

Ben Judd laughed, an uninhibited snort of genuine amusement. 'Not on your life. I had a very strong impression that if I did there would be nothing in it for me but another session worse than the induction ceremony and twice as long. I could tell by the look in that old dustbag's eyes. He won, hands down and no questions asked. And that, I'm afraid, dear uncle of a nitwitted vulgarian, is the way it's going to stay.'

He rotated his glare so that it fell on Eliza Jane: 'Get your frying pan, Abigail!'

'And just who,' demanded Eliza Jane, planting her fists on her hips, 'is this Abigail?'

73

'My dear young niece,' said Mr Campion with a shake of his head but also a smile, 'I will be reporting back to your aunt on the sorry state of your education. It was Abigail who cooked for King David and thereafter became his wife. She was both intelligent and beautiful, or so it says in Leviticus or Samuel, I forget exactly which. Perhaps both?'

'I think you might be right,' said Judd, 'and I am delighted to see there are brains in the family after all.'

'You are remarkably kind,' said Mr Campion with proper humility. 'If I asked how many Carders attended your first meeting would I embarrass you?'

'The answer is five, including me and the Learned Clerk. The other four had more sense and didn't turn up.'

The visitor considered this snippet of information carefully.

'Since there isn't any Abbot of Lindsay Carfax any longer,' he said, 'I wonder who represents him now?'

Ben Judd raised his golden beard and threw back his head in a chortle of delight.

'I can't tell you the answer to that one but it isn't Leslie Trump. I think he'd be more astonished than you if he ever found out.'

'Well he certainly gave no clues in his sermon this morning,' said Mr Campion wistfully. 'In fact he gave precious few clues as to what the sermon was supposed to be about.'

Judd laughed again and thwacked the flat of the palette knife against his thigh. 'He never does, which is why Saint Cats doesn't get my custom anymore and won't as long that little twerp claims the pulpit. He's even more pathetic when he tries to appeal to today's great un-washed youth. Have you read the little God-botherer's *Get with the Psalms*? An appalling, quite ghastly tome, not worth the paper it's print-ed on.'

'I have not had the pleasure of reading Trump's book, but he told me about it,' said Mr Campion, 'and that at least one reviewer seems to have taken exception to it by sending him nine copies neatly bisected, which strikes me as a rather violent mode of literary criticism.'

'Nine copies? I'm surprised they printed that many, but of course it had to be *nine*, didn't it? Everything happens in nines around here, it's part of the mythology of the place; everything comes back to the Nine Carders, so no doubt Trump will blame them.'

'Even though he does not know who they are?'

'Oh no, Mr Kindly Uncle,' said Judd, now waving the palette knife like a reproving finger, 'you won't catch me like that. I said I gave my word and my word stays given. Don't fish for clues about the Carders with me.'

Mr Campion nodded his head as if in graceful defeat.

'But can I assume that you don't blame the Carders for the little booby-trap that was laid for you the other night?'

'Excuse me!' Eliza Jane trilled from the tiny kitchen area where she was laying out bowls and pans like a grand master setting out a chessboard. 'This is supposed to be the age of equality for women. Why couldn't the trip trap have been meant for me?'

'Woman, know your place!' roared Ben grinning hugely, 'A man's home is his castle and if anyone is laying traps, then they are clearly aimed at the king of the castle, not the scullery maid!'

Eliza Jane began to crack eggs into a bowl with perhaps more ferocity than was absolutely necessary.

'Well here's a royal proclamation for his majesty,' she said loudly. 'If he wants to enjoy my *perfect* omelettes in their most *perfect* state and not cold and rubbery, then he'd better nip upstairs to the dungeons *now* and select a decent white wine to accompany them.'

Judd got to his feet and directed the palette knife like an épee towards the older man.

'We are, sir,' he announced grandly, 'commanded to do the queen's bidding, so allow me to give you a guided tour – it will not take long – of the only upstairs wine cellar in Lindsay Carfax, possibly the whole county. There is, I am told, a pub in Cambridge called the Snow Leopard which has its beer cellar on the first floor, but that is our nearest rival. Mere mortals, of course, would call it a bedroom "over the shop" but it happens to be where I store my wine and if you accompany me you will see where the booby trap tripped the delicate creature currently *perfecting* our luncheon, the scene of the crime itself.'

'A crime scene with a reward of wine,' mused

Mr Campion. 'Who could resist?'

Judd led the way out of the studio and into the narrow lane where Eliza Jane's small convertible was parked. As he strode past it, Ben patted the nearside wing with a paw of a hand and Campion had the fleeting impression that this Viking artist could, should the mood take him, pick the tiny car up and toss it over his shoulder if it were in his way. But with three loping strides he was beyond the car and at the corner of the converted barn where he swivelled on his heels and presented both hands to the right of his midriff in the classic 'Ta-dah!' gesture of the magician completing a trick.

'The staircase of doom,' he declared in sepulchral tones, 'or at least the staircase of a very pretty twisted ankle.'

Mr Campion perused the wooden staircase which rose up the side of the old barn at an angle of fifty degrees and counted eighteen steps to a small landing outside a door which he presumed led to the sleeping quarters above the studio. The dark planking and the handrail at waist height seemed to be of perfectly sound wood and the whole structure securely bolted to the wall of the barn.

'It's perfectly safe – now,' said Judd indicating that the older man should climb first, which Mr Campion did rather effortlessly for man of his age, or so he congratulated himself.

On the platform at the top, he waited for Judd, hot on his heels, to unlock the door and took in the view, such as it was. He guessed that at one time the narrow lane, which did not seem to be worthy of a name, had been the entrance to or accessible from a farm, but the only buildings left were three barns of brick and weatherboard. Ben's studio conversion was the furthest from the High Street (the only street) of Lindsay Carfax. Across the lane was a similar but smaller structure, although clearly used for storage rather than habitation, whilst a third, much larger barn to the left near the road junction was a going commercial concern.

On the roof, and presumably double-sided so that it could be seen from the High Street, was a large signboard in garish colours declaring that the barn was now the home of 'Sherman & Sons – Garage Repairs and Petrol'. Mr Campion thought the bright, crudely-executed signage (the second 's' in '& Sons' had obviously been added later) could not possibly be missed from the village, but in Eliza Jane's low-slung car he had managed to do just that. The original barn doors had been replaced with a metal sliding screen and in front of it, the corner of the lane had been concreted to form a forecourt on which two petrol pumps proudly stood guard. A free-standing swinging board like an inn sign advertised petrol at six shillings and sixpence a gallon, a price Mr Campion recognised from central London but thought rather steep for rural Suffolk.

Despite his elevated position, the lie of the land and the barn opposite meant he could see little of Lindsay Carfax itself other than rooftops and the church tower. The latter, and the easily identifiable roofs of the Woolpack and Carders' Hall,

78

seemed to be the only ones without a television aerial sprouting from them, and Judd read Campion's mind.

'Damned things, I hate 'em,' he sighed. 'Shouldn't be allowed on thatched roofs. They sprang up like nettles this summer when the Moon landing was televised; must have been the biggest boom in sales of goggle boxes since the Coronation.'

'They do intrude and rather spoil the chocolate-box image of the place somewhat,' said Mr Campion mischievously, watching Judd's expression.

'Don't talk to me about chocolate boxes!' he growled. 'I leave that sort of painting to your niece, who at least paints with a smile and churns out what the punters want for a fair price and never claims it's art, or else to piss-poor daubers like Tommy Tucker who takes up half my studio space for his picture-postcard landscapes. If only they were the size of postcards they might be bearable, but with him it's always a case of never-mind-the-quality-feel-the-width-of-the-canvas and he calls it "art", though, God knows, I've suggested he sells his work by the pound before now.'

He pushed a key into the lock of the door before them.

'Come on, the chef in the galley below will murder us if we're late with the booze. I don't really have a wine cellar up here, just a few bottles littered about, but I'm pretty sure a half-decent Chablis rolled under the bed the other night.'

'Was that the night of the big storm – both inside and out? And the mysterious knocking?'

'That's right, you've just walked right over the crime scene.'

Judd pointed to the stairs they had ascended. 'Just there, third step down. That's where somebody stretched a cord across, tied between the hand rail strut and a rusty old nail hammered into the wall at exactly the right height to catch a shoe or a boot and send the wearer arse over elbow, as they say.'

'A stupid question, I know,' said Mr Campion, 'but wasn't it obvious?'

'On a clear day and climbing up rather than going down, may be; but not in the dark during a storm. Good as invisible.'

'Did you keep the cord?'

'Never thought to. I was more worried about dearest nitwit and making sure she hadn't broken her neck. I just pulled it out of its moorings and chucked it as far as I could.'

'Was it any particular sort of cord?' enquired Mr Campion.

'Cord? Rope? Does it matter? It wasn't baling twine – which is what ties up most things in this parish that need tying – and it wasn't a length of clothes' line, it was much thicker and heavier. It felt like knotted hemp, but waxed? Does that make any sense?'

'It might,' said the older man pensively. 'When do you think the trap was set?'

'Well it wasn't there when we came up the stairs, but with the weather and the shouting match we were having, someone could have

80

sneaked up and done it and we wouldn't have noticed. It wasn't one of the Carders, though.'

'And you're sure of that?'

'I doubt any of them are nimble enough to climb up here in the dark without slipping and breaking their necks, or having a heart attack,' Judd scoffed. 'In any case, the Carders do things by nines, or so the fishwives would have it, and they would surely have booby-trapped the ninth step, not the third.'

'Nine is a multiple of three,' Mr Campion pointed out.

'Oh that's far too clever for the Carders! In any case, what have I done to upset them?'

'You refused to join their ranks,' said Mr Campion. 'They might have resented that.'

'Stuff and nonsense – no, just stuff them! I've given them their Proxy in Perpetuity, even if it is just a bit of legal mumbo-jumbo. Signed over my voting rights like a good little boy, so they no longer have any interest in me.'

'Somebody does,' Campion said thoughtfully. 'Somebody who can climb up here in the dark, knock on your door and run away before it opens.'

Judd peered over Campion's shoulder, looking down the stairs to the ground below as if judging the distance for the first time.

'Yes, that's quite a trick, isn't it?'

Six

Tourist Trade

'Today will be a day dedicated to tourism,' Mr Campion announced to the waitress as he finished his breakfast of Suffolk ham and eggs (only local hams served at the Woolpack), 'and that has set me up splendidly. I feel fit to face whatever rigours Lindsay Carfax can throw at the amateur explorer. Let me get my camera and my hat and do not tempt me with extra tea or toast, for I am, as our American friends would say, burning daylight!'

Mr Campion felt sure that his flamboyant address to the waitress – and the half-crown tip – would both find their way on to the news desk run by Don the barman when he came on duty, and thence into the ears of any of the Woolpack's patrons until an item of hotter news replaced him.

With a wide-brimmed soft grey fedora at a rakish angle and his camera case strapped over his head and left shoulder like a sash holding a sword and scabbard, he adopted the air of a wary Cavalier patrolling a village known to have Roundhead sympathies.

On his wanderings through Lindsay Carfax

over the weekend, he had already familiarised himself with the external geography of the place. Now, he decided, it was time to get behind the Tourist Board frontages, the pargeting and the wavy Tudor beams, and discover something – anything – which might ease Charlie Luke's unspecified worries. To date he had the makings of a stew – a stew of hearsay and rumour, its principle ingredients being nine 'Carders' whom nobody could, or would, identify or explain; to which he could add a spiteful booby-trap set for his niece's lover and an unpopular vicar who may have disturbed a burglar. However he spiced it up, it was thin gruel to offer a superintendent of detectives, and so he decided to retrace the tourist trail Charlie Luke himself had taken.

Being a Monday morning, the High Street bustled – as much as it ever bustled – with local shoppers, agricultural vehicles of every shape and delivery vans, rather than with gawking visitors and sightseeing coaches. Mr Campion politely returned the 'Good Mornings' of the inhabitants as and when they were offered and proceeded directly to that local shrine of literary fame, the house of the novelist Esther Wickham, whose name had once been murmured in the same quiet breath as Austen or a Brontë, and was still proclaimed in public lectures by distinguished academics such as Sir Philip Trumpington (for a handsome fee, according to Don the barman).

The oak plaque on the wall told him, in gold lettering, that this was indeed the house of:

Esther Wickham (1821–1872)
Social Novelist and Poet

and that it was open to 'visitors and the public' daily between 9.30 a.m. and 11.30 a.m. and between 1.30 p.m. and 3.15 p.m. 'during school term time'. Admission was 'free on purchase of a volume' but a shilling without a purchase. 'Academic researchers' were, however, welcome by appointment and could be accommodated at any time, although there was no indication as to where or how an appointment could be made.

Mr Campion decided that his particular researches were far from academic and steeling himself at the prospect of shopping for unwanted souvenirs, he lifted the iron sneck on the door and pushed it open. At first glance, he was stepping back one hundred years into a Victorian country parlour, but it needed only half a glance more to realise that discreet electric bulbs had replaced gas mantles and that whilst the leather-bound Visitors Book on a side table near the door could just possibly have contained a century's worth of signatures, the plastic ballpoint pen tied to the leg of the table by a length of string was unlikely to have written many of them.

Instead of the racks of faded postcards, over-printed tea clothes, pencils and India rubbers he had half expected to be on offer, Mr Campion was pleasantly surprised to find that the commercial aspect of the premises was of the gentlest ilk and the rampant capitalism openly on display was that of a dusty bookshop. Moreover it was a bookshop which only sold the books of a single author and, Mr Campion deduced, no title written after 1872.

There were numerous editions of that author's

most famous – or infamous, at least among those of school age, if set as a text for GCE – work, her novel *Jonathan Prentice*, published in 1854 (and probably overshadowed by Dickens' *Hard Times*) but set in 1812 during the Luddite riots. Surrounding that central work, as if guarding its flanks, were slim volumes of her poetry in numerous editions and colourful bindings, amongst which her most famous collection, *Sundials by Moonlight*, was most prominent.

Mr Campion's practised eye picked out what was clearly a companion volume, *Starlight at Noon*, of which he had never heard, and another substantial novel, *The Face of Diligence*, which he had never read, although he knew the title came from an earlier century and a commentary on rural life in Norfolk by Daniel Defoe.

'"The face of diligence spread all over East Anglia,"' he mused, thinking himself alone.

'Oi beg yours?' A female voice, and a local one, surprised him.

'Forgive me, I didn't see you there,' said Mr Campion cheerfully, 'and if I had I might have asked you to play a request.'

The small, wiry-haired woman sitting behind the mahogany piano-top davenport blinked rapidly four or five times, as though her eyes were camera shutters, as she took in the visitor.

'This ain't a piano, sir. It be a desk,' said the woman.

'And a fine example of what I think was called the "harlequin" style it is too,' Mr Campion said with false, but convincing, enthusiasm. 'Open the piano lid and there's a writing slope where the old black-and-whites should be; probably got several secret compartments for very private correspondence. Was it the very desk at which the talented Miss Wickham wrote?'

''Supposed to be, but Oi don't know nothing about no secret compartments. I do know half these 'ere drawers don't work, the handles being just for show; and that it's a bugger when it comes to dusting, Oi know that too.'

'I don't think the Victorians worried too much about dust; they had any number of housemaids to take of things like dusting.'

'I ain't no housemaid!' bristled the woman and Mr Campion imagined he could see static electricity sparking off the nylon housecoat she wore. 'I am the caretaker here, though Mr Spindler did have some daft idea about calling me a "concheeairge" or something. French I think it was.'

'I think it must be,' agreed Mr Campion vaguely. 'Do you get many visitors here, Mrs Spindler?'

'Get you on!' spluttered the housecoat indignantly. 'I ain't Mrs Spindler. There ain't no Mrs Spindler. Chance would be a fine thing. My name's Mrs Thornton. I look after the books during the day, in case of passing trade, and my husband, Mr Thornton, he keeps an eye on the place at night when Mr Spindler is away; which is more often than not – and him a man of his age gallivanting off all the time.'

'So this Mr Spindler lives here in Wickham House?' enquired Mr Campion, running a finger down the spine of a particularly dusty volume.

'Loike Oi said; he does when he's not swanning off on legal business. The rest of the house is his, only this parlour is open to *customers*' – Mrs Thornton emphasised the economic transaction which propriety demanded, – 'and anyway, it's known round here as the Prentice House, named after that there book Miss Wickham wrote. We had to read it at school in my day, though it was heavy going for us young 'uns. Nowadays I loike a good Georgette Heyer or a Jean Plaidy.'

Mr Campion selected what was obviously a modern edition of *The Face of Diligence* and flicked to the title page to discover it was more modern that he would have guessed.

'Still in print, I see,' he murmured. 'After one hundred and some years, that's impressive; a truly Dickensian achievement.'

'It's Mr Spindler that does the books. Always makes sure we have stock of everything Miss Wickham wrote, though I'll admit some of her poetry takes a bit of shifting these days. Still, it all helps with the upkeep of the house, so Mr Spindler says.'

Mr Campion set the book down on the piano-lid top of the davenport and drew his wallet to ensure the woman's full attention.

'A house like this must take some keeping up for a single man,' he observed. 'It not only has some age and a historic pedigree, but if this is the Prentice House, doesn't it have a secret passage? The upkeep on secret passages must be daunting, though I suppose the actual running costs must, by definition, remain secret.'

The small woman, who Mr Campion realised, was standing, not sitting, behind the davenport, snorted in soft derision.

'Secret passages my eye! How can they be secret when everybody knows about them?'

'Then what purpose do they serve?'

'Sheep,' said Mrs Thornton emphatically.

'I thought sheep preferred to gambol through meadows or perhaps jump over a fence as a favour to insomniacs. I had no idea they needed their own underground network,' smiled Mr Campion.

'Everything round here's to do with sheep,' the woman said firmly. 'Always has been. I reckon those tunnels were dug at the time of the Civil War, all the houses that have them are the right age. You put your sheep in there whenever there were hungry soldiers about – out of sight, out of stomach, they used to say. When it was shearing time, you'd always hide a few fleeces down there: fleeces you didn't tell the revenue men about, fleeces that somehow got across to Flanders where the weavers paid top price. You'll find it all in Miss Wickham's books if you read between the lines. Lindsay Carfax was a wool town with a wool church.'

'I have seen the church,' said Mr Campion, 'and marvelled at its size. It really is huge for a parish of this size. It must be difficult to fill.'

'That's true enough these days,' nodded the woman, 'especially with our latest *radical* vicar, but in the olden days, people were proud to go. Them that made their fortunes out of wool – and there were more than a few of them – put their money where their God was and built the biggest and best churches they could. Nowadays they spend their money in other ways. Foolish ways, if you ask me, though nobody ever does.'

'The owner – Mr Spindler – does he make his living out of wool?'

'There's no money in wool these days, least not round here. All that trade's long gone.' She narrowed her eyes and her voice adopted a tone of disapproval. 'Ain't you never read *Jonathan Prentice*? It's all in there; the last knockings of the old wool trade and all them Luddites smashing the machines. You should treat yourself to a copy. We've got a large-print edition somewhere.'

'I think I can manage regular print.'

'I was only thinking on those big glasses you are wearing and trying to be helpful,' Mrs Thornton said humbly.

'Absolutely no offence taken, my dear lady, and I would love to purchase a book, here at the shrine to the author.' Mr Campion turned his attention to the nearest pile but before he could select a volume, Mrs Thornton answered his unasked question.

'That one's five pounds, if you please.'

'Which one?'

'They're all five pounds apiece. Mr Spindler says it keeps things simpler that way, though you get more for your money if you go for one of the novels rather than the poetry. A bit slim, the poetry.'

Mr Campion let out a long slow breath and selected a copy of *The Face of Diligence*.

'Mr Spindler sounds to be a something of a sharp businessman.'

'He ain't no businessman, he's got no need to be in trade. He's a solicitor, ain't he – and an important one.'

'You mean a senior partner?' Mr Campion asked innocently.

'I meant he's the *only* solicitor in Lindsay Carfax. That way he's got a finger in every pie.'

On the High Street once more, Mr Campion clutched his recent purchase to his chest and surveyed his next port of call. His choice lay between Mrs Clarissa Webster's combination of art gallery and tourist trap called The Medley and the quaintly signed Humble Museum, which he optimistically took to be eponymous rather than descriptive. He was in no doubt that both emporia were likely to lighten his wallet further. Pseudo-science or fake art? It was a choice of the ages and one, he decided, which should not to be taken too seriously.

He opted for pseudo-science and crossed the road, rounding the Carders Hall, to the residence and workshop of Lindsay Carfax's second most celebrated inhabitant, Josiah Humble (1725–1794), apothecary, inventor and, more than likely, quack.

'It's two shillings' admission – for the upkeep – whether you make a purchase or not,' said a familiar female voice before the tinkle of the doorbell had faded away.

Mr Campion reformed his opinion of the late Josiah, who was surely also a magician.

'Why, Mrs Thornton, how nice to see you again – and so soon. My wallet was feeling quite forlorn and forgotten. How the deuce did you get here so quickly? No, don't tell me, the famously unsecret secret passages of Lindsay Carfax, unless I'm much mistaken, linking – let me see – the vicarage, the Woolpack, Carders Hall, the Prentice House and of course, here; the repository of all things Humble. The underground traffic locally seems more efficient than the Piccadilly line.'

'Oi saw yeuw heading this way,' said Mrs Thornton, blushing slightly, 'and thought I'd get round here straight off. There's only me on duty, you see, now the summer holidays are finished and there are no coach parties expected, so I cover both places.'

'Mr Spindler sounds to be a demanding employer,' Mr Campion observed.

'Oh, this ain't Spindler's business, well, not directly. It's the Fullers who run this place.'

'The Fullers?'

'Oh, they don't live here – nobody does – but the Fuller family has owned this place long as anyone can remember. Mr Marcus Fuller was the one who opened it as a museum but he's more or less retired since his divorce and his little brother Simon now runs the business. They're big property agents and are always picking up old stuff to put on display.'

The ubiquitous Mrs Thornton stood in a doorway across a room which strained at the seams with the amount of things packed into virtually every square inch of space so that Mr Campion took a moment to plot a path through the clutter.

His first impression was that he had stepped into a rag-and-bone man's junkyard in the Balls Pond Road but as his eyes took in the scene, he revised his opinion to one of a disorganised antique shop immediately after a burglary. As a museum, there seemed to have been little effort put into explanatory notices or descriptions of exhibits, but at least the exhibits did – Mr Campion thought charitably – attempt to reflect 18th century life, even if not the life of an apothecary in a small Suffolk wool town. Among the clutter, he noticed two long case clocks both silent and in need of restoration; wood-wormed malt shovels nailed to one wall; a brace of Brown Bess muskets hanging on another; there was an oak and pine trestle table and a folding coach table, both of which might have been genuine, and on them among other flotsam were piled painted silk fans, brushes, a wing compass, ceramic storage jars, metal skillets, a set of wick trimmers, a bronze pestle and mortar and a flint-lock Dragoon pistol. Smaller items – nails, handles, pin cushions and thimbles – lay in un-disturbed piles on the seats of four unmatched dining chairs and a Queen Anne-style wing-back settee whose upholstery was badly damp stained and somewhat mouldy.

Down both sides of the doorway which framed Mrs Thornton, hung small reproductions of paintings by Reynolds and Gainsborough and prints by Hogarth and all had small white price tags dangling from pieces of thread. As if reading his mind, Mrs Thornton slowly extended a hand, palm upwards.

'It's two shillings for the entrance,' she repeated. 'Postcards and guide books are available in the workshop through here.'

Mr Campion sorted out the appropriate coinage.

'Your two jobs must keep you busy,' he smiled, though he doubted that his charm would win him any discounts.

'Two? Hah! Three more likely,' the woman snorted, slipping the coins into the pocket of her housecoat with the speed and skill of a Western gunslinger holstering his revolver. 'I'm off at half-eleven to do the dinners at the junior school, then back here or the Prentice House depending on visitors and then I have to get home to cook the tea for my husband and the lodger; so you could say I have four jobs.'

Mr Campion looked suitably impressed.

'The devil has no need to make work for idle hands in Lindsay Carfax it seems. Caretaker, curator and now dinner lady at the school, you say? Would you happen to know one of the teachers there, Mr Walker?'

'Lemuel? Of course I know him. I not only serve him his lunch at the Juniors, but I cook his breakfast and his tea every day. He's my lodger.'

'What a small world! I heard his lecture on the Woolcarders on Saturday night. Some of the questions from the floor seemed to upset him.'

Mrs Thornton frowned in suspicion.

'Well, he's a very highly-strung individual. I knew he was upset afterwards, 'cos he woke me up banging about in kitchen making himself some cocoa when he got back, even though it was well after midnight. He should never have agreed to do public speaking, not after what happened to him recently.'

'Ah, yes,' said Mr Campion, 'he was what they call a Nine Days' Wonder round here, wasn't he? A disappearance without explanation *is* rather strange behaviour, don't you think?'

'Last time I looked it was still a free country,' Mrs Thornton stiffened, 'and Lemmy's a man of voting age *and* he was back before the school term started. Don't see why the poor man should be hounded in public. There might not be idle hands in Lindsay but there are quite a few idle tongues.'

'And what do those idle tongues whisper?' Mr Campion asked more in mischief than in anticipation of any insight.

'They say–' said the small woman sternly, glaring up into Campion's face '–that he wasn't minding his own business and I believe *your* business is to look round this here museum. You've paid your money, so you might as well get the good of it. There's this room and the workshop through here.' She indicated the doorway behind her. 'You get both in the price of admission.'

'Then I must take full advantage,' said Mr Campion blithely. 'Lay on, good lady, lay on.'

It was clear that Mrs Thornton's many job descriptions did not include museum guide. Not that there was much of a museum to be guided around, for the Humble house was a one-up, one-down building; the staircase to the upstairs cordoned off by a stout rope from which hung a printed sign saying: Stockroom – No Public Admittance.

The 'workshop' was a ground floor extension which might at one time have been a stable or a pig pen and had later been moulded on to the house. It was approached by stepping through the doorway previously guarded by Mrs Thornton and over a trap door with a large, inset ring for a handle. Next to it was a large battery torch.

'Is this the secret passage which allows you to pop up and surprise the tourists?' asked Mr Campion as the trap door creaked under his weight.

'It comes in handy when it's raining,' conceded Mrs Thornton. 'Now I'll leave you to enjoy the exhibits. I'll be in the front room so I can keep an eye on the Prentice House, just in case there are more customers about. If you wish to make any purchases, I won't be far away.'

'Is it permissible to take photographs of this Holy of Holies?'

Campion hefted the camera case hanging from his shoulder.

'Don't see why not; doesn't say anywhere you can't.'

'Then I'll take that as permission,' said Campion with a reverential bow.

The workshop of Josiah Humble was monastically furnished compared to the clutter which now filled his domestic quarters, the exhibits laid out on two long, thin wooden tables, giving the first impression that this was the workshop of a carpenter. Wooden-handled screwdrivers sat side-by-side frame saws, an elaborate brace-and-bit, sets of drawing instruments, set squares and smoothing planes in a variety of sizes. Along the tables the wood-working tools gave way to racks of glass tubes, ceramic storage jars and distillation equipment and primitive thermometers, presumably signifying Josiah's transition from artisan to scientist and to emphasise the point there was a rack of prints (reasonably priced) of portraits of Priestley, Lavoisier, Jenner and Watt though not of Humble himself. It appeared that his claim to scientific fame was promoted by association rather than achievement.

Finally, the *pièce de resistance* at the end of the room: the famous Humble's Box in all its mystic glory, along with a display of thin pamphlets declaring: 'The Famous Humble Box Explained. Price One Shilling.'

Mr Campion sighed and reached, automatically now, for his wallet.

'Eliza Jane tells me I should call you Albert. Perhaps she thinks we should have an affair.'

'I am certain, Mrs Webster, she meant you could call me your kindly Uncle Albert just as she does.'

'Oh well, you can't blame a gal for trying, can you?'

Campion had been caught in her carefully weighted net as he left the Humble Museum and now felt himself being hauled down the High Street towards The Medley just as a trawled cod – or should that be flounder? – is pulled in towards the fishing boat and dumped unceremoni-

96

ously on deck. With Clarissa Webster's sturdy right arm hooked through his left, Mr Campion decided further resistance was futile and allowed himself to be reeled in.

'I saw you meandering between Prentice and Humble and thought you needed guiding to the true centre of the Lindsay hive, which is of course the Medley,' announced Mrs Webster as they marched in step.

'And what might I find there: honey or a queen bee?' asked Mr Campion.

'Both, if you are lucky,' the woman flirted. She was dressed for flirting in a tight (a little too tight?) dress of red satin which ended an inch above very acceptable knees and was scooped low at the neck to frame an equally admirable bosom. She wore matching red shoes with impressive heels and had a short, brown jacket of soft leather hanging from two crooked fingers over her left shoulder.

'I simply assumed that after a double dose of Mrs Thornton – I'm guessing she did the tunnel trick which so impresses the Americans – you would be in need of rescuing. Was I wrong?'

'Did I need rescuing or was it perhaps my wallet?'

Clarissa Webster laughed and showed perfect white teeth haloed by her red lipstick.

'Should you have some disposable income left which needs disposing of, then the Medley is definitely the place for you. Far more interesting than those dusty old exhibits. What have they persuaded you to buy so far?'

Mr Campion raised the purchases he clutched.

'A nineteenth-century novel and an instructive pamphlet on the workings of the famous Humble Box.'

'I can do better than that, I could sell you a Humble Box.'

'You have one for sale?'

'Several. How many would you like? Or, as Mrs Thornton would say: how many can Oi do you for?'

Mr Campion looked down into her smiling face.

'Didn't you tell me you could no longer bear to trade in antiques?'

'Oh, I didn't say they were *genuine...*'

Clarissa Webster's eyes flashed like headlights and, if possible, her grin got even wider.

Seven

School Dinners

It was, Mr Campion decided, a half-decent piece of (reproduction) furniture, riddled with hocus-pocus rather than woodworm. The Humble box was a rectangular box the size, perhaps, of a small man's coffin, made from pale mahogany inlaid with bone, standing three feet off the floor on six legs which could have featured in Chippendale's Directory. The lid, maybe a quarter-inch thick, was secured with two small brass clasps but no lock and, when raised on a single sturdy brass hinge, revealed the innards of the box to be a collection of vessels seemingly unconnected and serving no particular purpose. There were glass bottles and spheres containing red, blue and clear liquids; a Fahrenheit thermometer and its predecessor, a thermoscope, lay side by side at one end of the box and at the other, a weather-ball barometer. Scattered randomly between them were glass-fronted dials marked 'Rain', 'Wind', 'Frost', 'Snow', 'Torrent', 'Earthquake' and 'Pestilence' which apart from their dramatic effect seemed to have no mechanical function.

Mr Campion looked as intently at the reproduction on show in the Medley as he had at the genuine article in the Humble Museum and mentally admired the quality and accuracy of the fake whilst simultaneously questioning why anyone should expend time and energy on bothering to forge such a thing.

'Any wiser?' asked Mrs Webster. 'About how it works, I mean.'

'Not really,' said Mr Campion, 'and the instruction manual I purchased is not exactly forthcoming. I'm not even sure *what* it's supposed to do, let alone how it goes about it.'

The Medley, although overcrowded with reasonably-priced saleable goods, was devoid of customers. Being a Monday morning at the fag-end of the summer season, this was not unusual – the proprietoress had volunteered the information unasked to explain why she had resorted, as she put it, to roving the High Street looking to kidnap someone. After a few moments admiring, as was expected, the oil and watercolour depictions of local scenes painted by his niece and signed enigmatically 'EJF' which adorned the walls, Mr Campion was confronted with a Humble box and, he feared, with the distinct feeling that he was being sold it.

'It forecasts the weather, or so old Josiah claimed, and he should know as he invented it,' said Mrs Webster cheerfully. 'I don't think it ever worked, though, and by all contemporary accounts his predictions were vague to say the least. I suspect he had an act, probably with a couple of stooges, which he put on to impress potential buyers. He would set the dials, show them the different coloured liquids and then pronounce that it showed there was a good chance of rain in the next week. No doubt he would have asked a local shepherd – red sky at night and all that rigmarole – what the chances of precipitation in the near future were. That's the way most people did it round here.'

'So the box didn't make Josiah's fortune?'

'Wouldn't have thought so. Suffolk's always been a superstitious county and they would have mistrusted any new-fangled inventions, preferring to stick to the old ways. Lots of Suffolk houses have dead cats buried under their front doorsteps. That's supposed to keep witches out, if you were wondering.'

Mr Campion allowed his eyebrows to rise but said nothing.

'These days they're bought as bits of furniture,' Clarissa continued, 'as conversation pieces. Or you can gut the thing and use it as a large sewing box, or a drinks cabinet, or keep books or sheet music in there. Some of the younger brigade keep LPs in there and put their record players on top.'

'So there is a market for them?'

'For the reproductions, yes, as long as we price them reasonably. The market isn't huge, but they do sell. We've shipped several to America and quite a few to Europe. People seem to get attached to them and even send them back for repair when they get damaged.'

'Who makes them for you?'

'A deliciously innocent young arts-and-craftsy type called Tommy Tucker. Put him in a leather

101

jacket and he could be a Soho tearaway; in a tie-dyed orange shirt he could be one of the hippy layabouts who besieged us last year. But Tommy's no idler; he turns his hands to anything going. Very supple, his hands ... a girl could...'

Mr Campion interrupted her reverie.

'I've heard that name before.'

'I should think you have,' said Mrs Webster opening her eyes again. 'He shares a studio with Ben Judd, though they often row about it and, I suspect, they've had words about Eliza Jane, though I don't think it's come to fisticuffs yet. If it does, you will tell me, won't you? Your niece is appallingly lax when it comes to passing on gossip and I don't think she has the remotest idea that Tommy is besotted with her. That's one of his.'

Clarissa pointed to a watercolour hanging at a slight angle on the crowded wall. It showed the High Street, in summer judging by the foliage and floral displays, down which travelled a single, open-topped sports car driven by a girl wearing a headscarf and huge, round sunglasses.

'Ben Judd doesn't have much of an opinion of him as an artist,' Campion observed.

'Well, it's not *art* is it? But, my goodness, it sells well enough to the tourists. That's why Ben doesn't rate it, but then Ben Judd has a pretty low opinion of almost anyone in Lindsay who isn't Ben Judd.'

'Why does he stay here?' asked Campion with genuine interest.

'Who knows? He has talent, that's for sure; but he's the sort of artist who thinks he has to suffer to get the best out of that talent. His late mother, Mrs Dyer, left him a few quid – enough for the essentials of life – and when that's gone he may well move up to London or go to Paris, if artists still go to Paris these days. But you can't really see Ben Judd starving to death in a garret, can you? Mind you, he probably would starve him- self to death rather than compromise his blessed artistic principles, whatever he thinks they are...'

Mrs Webster paused and looked over her shoulder as the first faint click of the front door handle being turned reached her ears. It seemed, Campion thought, that the woman's brain was equipped with radar.

'I spy you have some real customers at last.'

'You spy inaccurately, I'm, afraid,' said Mrs Webster. 'It's the third Monday of the month and that's when the rent man comes to call.'

It seemed that in Lindsay Carfax, the rent man came in threes, for when the door opened wide enough to trigger the shop bell, three be-suited figures entered and they were men of Campion's generation, unlikely ever to be confused with Soho tearaways or hippy 'layabouts'.

Their leader, once over the threshold, seemed to fill the Medley with his presence and when he flung his arms wide and advanced on Mrs Web- ster, she stepped daintily forward to surrender herself to his bear-like embrace.

'My darling Gus, how sweet...' she squeaked but her words were lost as she buried her face in an ample yardage of her visitor's pinstripe.

Mrs Webster disentangled herself and turned back to face Campion unembarrassed.

103

'We should think ourselves honoured, for we have the cream of Lindsay society gathered under this humble roof.' She returned to the broad, ruddy-cheeked bear who had hugged her. 'And just why, dearest Gus, is my landlord visiting me empty-handed?'

'Don't worry, my little vixen, I didn't forget your perfume. There's a half-gallon bottle of it in the back of the Bentley.'

Mrs Webster clapped her hands together once and squealed in delight, then planted a kiss on a bluff, red cheek, bending her right knee and raising her foot coyly as she did so.

'In that case, you and your henchmen are welcome, but why the three of you? Isn't there some ancient protocol about the three of you not travelling together in case of accidents? Or have you come to increase the rent and you're going to beat me up until I sign a new tenancy agreement?'

'Don't be ridiculous, Clarissa. We're going to try that new country house hotel called the Rosery – that's as in a place where they grow roses and nothing to do with rosaries and Catholics – over near Newmarket. It's supposed to have a jolly good restaurant and we thought you might like to have lunch with us to try it out. If you are busy with a customer, however...'

Clarissa pressed a red finger-nail to the centre of her chin, careful to avoid smudging her glossy red lipstick.

'You know Clarissa stamps her foot if she loses a sale,' she said in a little-girl-lost voice which would have sound hammy in the direst of amateur dramatics' productions, 'but then she'd positively *hate* to miss out on a free lunch with three gentlemen friends.'

'Let me ease the decision-making process,' said Campion with an extravagant bow in her direction. 'I have an errand to run and therefore must take my leave, but I leave only to fight another day. I will return and make a purchase, possibly two. I doubt they will be Humble boxes, but I feel strangely drawn to one or two of your paintings, if only for the sake of family harmony.'

'Do you promise to haggle over the prices? I love a good haggle.'

'Madam, I have haggled in casbahs and bazaars with the best of them, from Casablanca to Samarkand' said Campion returning Clarissa's smile, 'and I will give you a run for my money.'

Mrs Webster let rip a deep-throated laugh and then remembered her manners.

'But goodness gracious me, I am being so rude. It must be the presence of all these attractive men getting me all a-fluster. Let me to do the honours: Mr Albert Campion, distinguished visitor to this parish and favourite uncle of dear little Eliza Fitton, allow me to introduce the three most important men in Lindsay Carfax – a triumvirate of the ruling elite, if you like; Mr Augustine Marchant, Mr Marcus Fuller and Mr Hereward Spindler. If you ever think of buying property round here, Gus owns it, Marcus sells it and Mr Spindler will do the conveyancing. Now, talk among yourselves while a girl freshens her war paint, as she must do if she's being taken out on the town.'

'It's only Newmarket,' said Mr Marchant weakly, but Mrs Webster was a red blur as she disappeared into the back rooms of the shop.

Marchant thrust out a hand.

'Welcome to Lindsay Carfax ... Campion, was it? I'm Gus Marchant and I'm just a simple farmer. It's Marcus here who does most of the wheeler-dealing round here.'

Where Marchant's handshake had been as crushing as his bulk had implied, and had left Campion in no doubt that he had met a very sturdy son of the Suffolk soil, Marcus Fuller in comparison was a bird-like figure and his proffered claw indicated that it required only the briefest of contact to satisfy convention.

'Don't listen to my old friend Gus. He's far from being "just a simple farmer" though he can appear simple at times. Campion, did you say?'

'Well, I didn't, but it is,' said Mr Campion as a third hand was offered to him.

'Hereward Spindler,' said the man behind the handshake. 'I'm the local solicitor and my main job is to keep these two if not on the straight and narrow, then at least out of jail. You must be the Campion who married Lady Amanda Fitton ... and aren't you related to Lady Prunella Redcar?'

'Guilty on both counts,' said Mr Campion, 'though the Redcar connection is very, very distant. I think the last time Lady Prunella saw me, I was in a font having water tipped over me by an enthusiastic vicar and she was not much more than a girl. I am afraid I have not met the lady subsequently, at least not since I could walk.

106

She lives in the south of France these days, or so I hear.'

'Near Monte Carlo,' said Mr Fuller as if he resented the fact, 'where she visits the casino more regularly than the milk man – if they take milk in a casino, that is; I really wouldn't know.'

'You've got to admire her energy,' growled Mr Marchant. 'Marcus and I were down in Monte last week and we saw her troop in there every morning heading for the roulette tables like a guided missile, and God help any flunky who got in her way. And she must be eighty-two if she's a day.'

'Well if I wasn't related to her, I would certainly claim to be,' said Mr Campion with a smile.

Augustine Marchant put a stout finger in the air, signalling that a new thought had just occurred to him.

'Speaking of game old birds,' he said straight-faced, 'how long are you visiting for, Campion?'

Mr Campion allowed himself to look perplexed. It was a condition he was very adept at projecting, at least to the unwary.

'I am, as they say, a man of leisure these days, so my plans are flexible ... but game old birds? I'm not sure I follow.'

'No one follows Gus's line of thinking for very long,' said Mr Fuller.

'Oh stop whining, Marcus! I meant game birds. We've got a shoot on Wednesday out at my place and I wondered if Campion here fancied his luck. I'd be happy to stand you the loan of a gun and a spot of lunch afterwards. You'd be doing me a big favour by providing some intelligent company as neither of these two reprobates are any fun at all. Marcus here is frightened of loud noises and Hereward has a lawyer's natural aversion to sunlight and fresh air.'

'Not everyone shares your love of gunpowder and carnage, Gus,' said Mr Spindler prissily. 'Perhaps Mr Campion has better things to do than tramp the mud of Long Tye Farm?'

'I honestly don't know my movements for Wednesday,' said Campion, 'but if I'm still in the vicinity I wouldn't mind a pot shot at something defenceless but delicious.'

'That's the spirit! The Land Rover picks everybody up from outside Carders' Hall at eight; saves you the fag of bringing your car. If you can make it, just tell Don at the Woolpack and we'll make sure we don't leave you behind.'

'Don the barman? Does he list game-keeping among his talents?'

'Don? His only talent is for gossip,' Gus Marchant sniggered. 'We have a saying in Lindsay that there are three ways of getting a message to someone: telephone, telegram and tell-a-Don. I assure you, telling Don is the fastest.'

'Has Albert gone?' Mrs Webster asked no one in particular as she emerged from the back room of the Medley with a black linen jacket over her arm and a red chiffon scarf around her throat. Otherwise, she looked exactly the same as she had when she had left the shop a few minutes before, or at least the trio of men did not spot any difference. Only she knew how much care she had taken with her face powder, a new lipstick and a comb and brush.

'Albert is it? You're a fast worker, Clarissa, I've always known that,' said Marchant, casting an obviously admiring eye over Mrs Webster's impressive contours.

'Oh come on, Gus, you know I'm built for comfort not for speed these days.'

'I know no such thing,' Marchant spluttered. 'In fact I'm not sure I understand what you mean by that.'

'I'm sure you understand perfectly,' said Clarissa coyly, 'and since you've allowed the charming Albert to escape, you'd better make it up to me with a really expensive lunch.'

'The man said he had errands to run,' blustered Marchant. 'I didn't chase him away and I invited him shooting out at Long Tye on Wednesday; if he's still here, that is.'

'Why exactly *is* he here?' asked Marcus Fuller.

Mrs Webster examined her nail polish.

'I found him wandering like a lost soul between the Prentice House and Humble's mausoleum and I dragged him in off the street, or used my feminine charms to lure him in here, whichever you prefer.'

'I meant,' sighed Mr Fuller, 'why is he in Lindsay Carfax?'

'And just *who* is he? What line of business is he in?' echoed Marchant.

'Shouldn't you have asked that *before* you invited him to your shooting party?' sniffed Hereward Spindler who, had he been wearing pince nez, would surely have been peering over the top of them.

'Don't be such a dried-up old stick, Hereward, I was only being sociable. Campion looked a decent enough type – chap who knows when to use a fish knife and all that – and he has an honest face, so he can't be a lawyer or an estate agent.'

Mrs Webster made a cat's claw of her right hand and slashed the air with her long red nails.

'Miaow! I thought we girls were the bitchy ones! But really Gus,' Clarissa unclenched her claw and gently patted Marchant's rosy cheek, 'you ought to read a decent newspaper now and again, especially the society gossip rather than just the racing pages or the livestock prices.'

'Don't talk in riddles, woman! Are you saying this Campion is somebody in the news? Good God, he's not somebody on television is he?'

'Nothing so crass or crude, Gus,' Clarissa laughed. 'I doubt you'd ever see Mr Campion on the goggle-box, unless it was at a state occasion and even then I think he would blend into the background so you wouldn't spot him. He's a behind-the-scenes man and quite a well-connected one I'd guess, who moves in high circles.'

'So what is he doing in Lindsay Carfax?' demanded Spindler.

'Discovering all he can about the Carders,' said Mrs Webster with mischievous glee. 'I sat with him at Walker's incredibly dull lecture on Saturday and he spent the morning at Humble's and at your place, so no doubt Mrs Thornton will provide you with a detailed report. As far as I know, he's visiting his niece, Eliza Jane.'

'She's Judd's bit of stuff, isn't she?'

110

'Mind your tongue, Hereward!' Clarissa reprimanded him. 'Don't let her hear you calling her anybody's "bit of stuff". Don't let me catch you either. I know you think Ben Judd is a thug and an oik, but if Eliza Jane fancies him, that's her business. If I were her age I might make the handsome Ben my business too, but I'm not, so let them get on with it. Now, what about that lunch?'

Mr Spindler sniffed loudly.

'So you really have no idea why Campion is here?'

'None. Perhaps if you'd invited him to join us I could have wormed it out of him over coffee and Armagnac.'

'I did suggest it,' said Gus Marchant as if his manners or his honour required defending, 'but he wouldn't have any of it. Said he had to call on somebody – and then he asked directions to the Junior School.'

'Now why do you think he did that?' asked Hereward Spindler, but answer came there none.

As the machine guns opened fire, the girls screamed and ran for cover but the attack was merciless, the winged assassins swooping and diving through the massed ranks of innocent victims.

Mr Campion had quite forgotten how relentless young boys could be when they formed themselves into squadrons of Spitfires and just how loud young girls could be when they screamed, not in fear but in surprise and annoyance at having their perfectly respectable games

111

of hopscotch or skipping interrupted by aerial attack – or the next best thing as imagined by a nine-year-old with arms outstretched for wings and a constant stream of 'Takkatakkatakka...' noises which reverberated around the stone walls enclosing – at child-proof height – the playground of the Carders Junior School (Church of England affiliated).

Across the playground, the school presented itself as a smart, low Victorian building, its brick walls were faced with local flint stone and its roof was of solid Welsh slate. The main entrance, up a flight of three broad steps, was only a few strides away for an adult, but between the wall gate and the door were perhaps twenty children rushing, jostling, ducking and diving, displaying all the sense of direction to be observed in a violently disturbed ants' nest and Mr Campion hesitated before wading through such a turbulent sea of small humanity.

He was saved by the bell, or rather a bell – a Victorian wooden-handled brass school bell of which any town crier or pub landlord at closing time would be proud – being wielded with some authority by the tall, gawky and uncertain man he had been lectured by in the Carders' Hall.

Lemuel Walker raised and lowered his arm three times in rapid succession and, before the last sonorous note had faded, the skippers, hopscotchers, footballers, and even the Messerschmitt pilots had formed themselves into two orderly crocodile lines – boys on the right, girls on the left – and were preparing to march back to their classroom.

112

'Can I help you? I'm afraid we only see parents – or *grandparents* – by appointment out of school hours,' Walker called across the playground in what Campion presumed was his 'strict headmaster' voice – a voice meant to inspire and intimidate rather than inform.

Mr Campion decided that Walker must have been bullied as a child and had worked hard to get into a position where he could play the bully himself; but it was not a convincing performance.

'I do hope I am not intruding on the school day,' he said, 'and I have no wish to disrupt the curriculum. I was hoping to talk to you personally, Mr Walker, about your involvement with the Carders.'

Walker narrowed his eyes and his body stiffened to such an extent that the school bell in his right hand chimed involuntarily. Quickly he grasped the clapper with his left hand to silence it. When he said nothing, Campion persisted, leaning casually against the school yard wall so that anyone passing by would think they were merely exchanging the pleasantries of the day.

'I do not know who you are, sir, and I have no intention of talking to you in the middle of the school day.'

Walker's voice rose half an octave before it cracked.

'I am intruding,' Campion said quickly, 'and for that I apologise, as I do for my rudeness. My, name is Campion and I was present at your lecture in the Carders' Hall. I was hoping we could perhaps meet and discuss your subject further.'

113

'If you were at my lecture, then you will have heard all that I have to say on that particular subject,' said Walker, his eyes fixed not on Campion, but on the gate in the wall, as if judging the distance to it and whether he could reach it and somehow defend it if the stranger attempted to enter the playground.

Mr Campion dismissed the idea as fanciful, though he found disturbing the schoolmaster's habit of stretching his scrawny neck out of his collar and jutting his chin forward as he spoke almost as if trying to spit his words out.

'Oh, I doubt that, Mr Walker. I think you are something of an authority on local folklore and traditions and as an academic and a researcher, you must have found much more than you could shoe-horn into your Saturday night talk.'

'Whether you think that or not,' said Walker, his neck bobbing up like that of a startled ostrich, 'it does not alter the fact that I have nothing more to say on the subject. On that my mind is made up.'

'Could I ask,' Campion started his attack gently, 'just one thing?'

'And what would that be?'

'As I understand it, you were quite prepared to talk about the Carders when you agreed to give that lecture some while ago, but now you are obviously reluctant to mention them. Would your reluctance have anything to do with your recent absence – dare I say disappearance – from village society?'

Walker clearly struggled to hold his composure and apart from that hydraulic neck, his body was

114

rigid.

'If I took off for a few days, what has it got to do with you? Are you from the press?'

'I am not of the press,' said Campion firmly, 'and I believe you disappeared for nine days. You were a Nine Days' Wonder in fact, which I understand is something of a local tradition here in Lindsay, a bit like the Carders in fact.'

The Walker neck strained to its maximum height and his eyes bulged.

'I have nothing, repeat, nothing, further to say to you or anyone else. Now leave me alone!'

Thankfully, the last of the children had trooped into the school and had not witnessed their teacher's outburst but from the door where they had entered, a figure emerged to place a hand on Walker's shoulder.

'The children are ready for their dinner, Headmaster,' said Mrs Thornton, resplendent in a bright orange pinafore. 'You'd better come and say grace so they can tuck in.'

The teacher turned like an automaton and stepped back into the building. After a ten-second glare in Campion's direction, Mrs Thornton silently followed.

Mr Campion brushed a speck of dust off the sleeve of his jacket from where he had leaned over the wall and casually began to walk back towards the High Street, wondering why Mr Lemuel Walker was such a frightened man.

Eliza Jane opened the door to her cottage on Campion's second knock. She wore a paint splattered boiler suit, which had once been white but was now truly a coat of many colours, welling-ton boots and to top the ensemble, her hair was encased in a plastic shower cap.

'I knew it must be you, Uncle Dear. Everyone else in Lindsay knows not to disturb me in my lair, not while the light is with me. After about three o'clock, I lose the light thanks to the ridiculously small windows in this chocolate box house. It's like something out of Hansel and Gretel, but when I suggested putting in skylights or French windows, the Carders said not on my Nellie, as it would spoil the image of the village! Anyway, now you're here I suppose you'd better come in.' She paused for breath and opened the door wider.

'Only if you promise not to make me buy a painting,' smiled Campion, 'for I think Mrs Webster has already put my name on two, if not three, of your canvases on display at the Medley.'

'Don't worry, from here I only deal wholesale, not retail. I wouldn't dream of diddling Clarissa out of her commission. I wouldn't dare. Come on in then. I'll stop for lunch in an hour, but don't expect me to cook for you two days' running. I don't even do that for Ben.'

Mr Campion stepped over the threshold and in to what had once been a living room but now resembled the disordered paint shop of a garage in a war zone. The air shimmered with the fumes from open paint and varnish pots and bottles of turpentine and white spirit and the floor was a minefield of half-finished canvases, easels leaning at dangerous angles, sheets of rough pencil

116

drawings, half-drunk cups of tea, brushes standing in jars of dark oily liquid, scrunched up pieces of rag and at least three food-smeared plates with knives and forks neatly, if incongruously, placed together.

'I haven't wished myself on you for a free meal,' Campion said, plotting a course across the debris strewn floor, 'but I would like to use your telephone if I may.'

'Sure thing, Uncle, go through, go through. The kitchen's relatively civilised – I won't say *clean* – but it is civilised compared to this, and anyway, that's where the phone is. And you're welcome to lunch; I just won't be cooking anything. I usually pop up to Marchant's to get the fixings for a sandwich.'

'Marchant's?' queried Campion as he picked his way gingerly across the room.

'The village shop-cum-post-office. It's owned by Gus Marchant, like just about everything else around here, but it's rather nice that our village general merchant is a Marchant, if you see what I mean.'

'I met Mr Marchant this morning and he's invited me to a shoot on Wednesday.'

'My, you are a fast worker. No wonder Clarissa fancies you like mad.'

'It was at Clarissa's shop – or should that be "emporium" – that I ran into him.'

'Well you probably would; third Monday of the month is rent day, when the Carders come and demand their tithe.'

'Would you mind,' Campion said seriously, 'if we had a chat about that?'

117

They compromised and talked while Eliza Jane continued to strive to bring order to the chaos, sometimes working on two canvases at once. Mr Campion, who had promised not to light a cigarette in case of spontaneous combustion given the fume-filled air, secured a perch for himself on a high kitchen stool placed in the doorway so that he could talk to the artist's back, having first been reassured that the girl was not being rude, but she had commissions to finish. Campion in turn assured her that he had no wish to disrupt her livelihood and he was perfectly comfortable as he approved of hard work and application – and could watch it in action all day long.

Eliza Jane initiated their dialogue by asking how Campion's day as a tourist in Lindsay Carfax had gone and she laughed at her uncle's description of Mrs Thornton popping up 'like a demented Jill in the Box' at every turn, solely for the purpose of relieving him of money. (He did not, however, mention Mrs Thornton's spectral appearance on the shoulder of Lemuel Walker at the school.) And she guffawed as he recounted his kidnapping 'off the street in broad daylight' by Mrs Webster.

Almost as if it had just occurred to him, Mr Campion mentioned casually that it had been Rent Day at the Medley and no less than three rent collectors had turned up, one of whom had been Mr Marchant, who had seemed a very friendly sort of landlord – the sort who took his tenants out for expensive lunches, as well as buying them French perfume. Well that, Eliza had said over her shoulder as she painted, was

118

the magic and the mystery of the Carders: they were secretive, authoritarian, ritualistic, ruthless and cruel, but also honourable, courteous and on occasion generous to a fault. If a business couldn't pay the rent – though in fact it was more a monthly tithe than a rent – then it wasn't as if they were thrown out on to the street. As long as they kept quiet and didn't make a fuss – for the Carders hated fuss – they would find that business improved, more orders came their way, more tourists arrived or perhaps some advantageous lines of credit opened up for them. If they stuck to the unwritten rules and laws of Lindsay Carfax, then they would be alright and perfectly able and happy to pay their tithe in the future. The quid pro quo for any help they received would, of course, be that they returned the favour when asked to by the Carders, as they surely would be.

'And Gus Marchant is a Carder?' Campion asked, observing the rear view of his niece carefully.

Eliza Jane didn't miss a brushstroke.

'Of course he is and he's probably the Head Carder, or *Reichsführer,* Caesar, Worshipful Master, Lord High Executioner or First Violin or whatever they call the big cheese when they put their robes on and meet in session. Of course they'd probably cut my tongue out and bury it on a beach at high tide or some such rigmarole just for suggesting that.'

'Interesting that you should sue the word Caesar,' said Campion, 'as Mrs Webster referred to them as a triumvirate of the ruling elite.'

'Them? You mean Gus Marchant's hench-men?'

'An odd little man, who just might be human, called Fuller and a dried old stick of a lawyer called Spindler, who I believe owns the Prentice House.'

'Oh, the odious Hereward ... bought the place for a song from the batty Lady Prunella. Yes, he's one of them, and so is Marcus Fuller.'

'Marchant, Fuller and Spindler – they're all Carders?'

'Well I'd say so, though maybe not on oath as I certainly couldn't prove it, but Marchant and Fuller – Fuller Senior that is, the brother's an entirely different kettle of fish – they're as thick as thieves. As for Spindler, he fits Ben's description of the Carders' "Learned Clerk" to a T, though he'd never come out and say it was Spindler who failed so spectacularly to induct him, because *he gave his word* not to breathe a word. Sometimes I think there's too much of the Boy Scout in Ben Judd, although he hates it when they refer to him as "boy".'

'I'm still not clear why Ben was a candidate for the ranks of the Carders,' said Campion.

'Accident of birth,' said Eliza, mixing a blue to complete a wedge of skyscape, 'his mother being a Dyer and therefore – though don't ask me why – entitled to an honorary seat on the Carder Council or whatever it is.'

'There are supposed to be nine aren't there?'

'Who knows? It's part of the mystery, the legend, the myth. I think I know three – Marchant, Fuller and Spindler – isn't that enough?

Isn't three a quorum for Carders?'

'I suspect, my dear, you are thinking of Musketeers – but let me change the subject. Would you mind if I took a photograph of you?'

For the first time, Eliza Jane stopped what she was doing; in fact positively froze in her tracks apart from her head which turned slowly to face Campion.

'In *this* outfit?'

'The artist at work in her studio,' said her uncle. 'Your aunt Amanda would love it and it might become an iconic image in the future, when you are famous and your work is selling for millions at Sotheby's.'

Eliza Jane took the compliment in her stride and instinctively reverted to the professional artist within.

'If you must, but the light's not good enough in here if you're shooting colour unless you've got a flash.'

Campion lifted the camera he still carried over his shoulder and reached into his jacket pocket to produce a small, square block of black leatherette about the size of a packet of cigarettes.

'The new Olympus Trip comes with a handy flash unit,' he said with a flourish, 'which runs on tiny batteries and shoehorns on to the top of the camera in a positive trice. Flick the switch to charge it, point and click and you have pictures that would grace any fashion magazine these days – or so I'm told. Damn clever, those Japanese, when it comes to cameras.'

Eliza Jane put her paint brush between her teeth, placed her hands on her hips and turned

her upper torso towards Campion in a provoca-
tive pose.

'So you think you're David Bailey, eh?' she
said, chewing at the paintbrush. 'Well, I'm up for
it, as they say, but I insist on keeping the shower
cap on.'

'A true artist would insist on no less.'

Mr Campion pointed and clicked and his
camera did just what the manufacturer had
promised. When he was satisfied he had enough
photographic evidence of the young artist at
work, he excused himself and retired to the
kitchen – an immaculately clean and tidy kitchen
– to use the telephone.

'Give my love to Aunt Amanda,' Eliza shouted
over her shoulder.

'I'm not phoning home. I'm ringing the
police.'

'Good God, my painting's not that bad, is it?'

'Not at all. I'm ringing a friend of a friend,
based in Bury St Edmunds, to see if I can call on
him.'

Whilst Campion busied himself with the receiver, Eliza joined him and began to fill a kettle
and rinse out a teapot.

'That's me finished for the day, so it's time for
tea. Did you get hold of your friend's copper?'

'Yes I did and he'll see me tomorrow. Do you
fancy a day out in Bury? Do some shopping
perhaps?'

'I might,' said Eliza busying herself with the
tea things. 'I could do with making myself
scarce.'

She saw Mr Campion's look of concern.

'Oh don't come over all concerned and uncle-y. Tommy Tucker's claiming his share of studio time tomorrow, which means that Ben will be like a bear with a sore head – in fact quite the pig – and he'll make sure if he can't work, then I won't either.'

'The last thing I wish to do is come between temperamental lovers, but if you're free I'd be glad of the company.'

'Fair enough. Now as we've missed lunch, let's have tea and cake – it's shop bought I'm afraid.'

They took their tea in the civilised way, over inconsequential conversation about distant family relatives, the state of the art world and in particular 'pop art', music, theatre and cinema. As in the best of houses, even small two-up, two-down cottages which reeked of turpentine, the subjects of money, politics and sex were tactfully ignored.

Eventually Mr Campion consulted his wrist-watch and announced that if he slowed his normal walking pace from that of a befuddled tortoise to that of a thirsty snail, then he would make it back to the Woolpack just as the indispensable Don would be opening up the bar for the evening session. In that, however, he was wrong, for a red-faced and breathless Don was at that very moment rapping on the front door of Eliza Jane's cottage.

'Miss Fitton, I am so sorry to have to disturb you,' he exhaled in Eliza's face once she had answered his knock, 'but is Mr Campion with you?'

'Yes he is, Don, and he's been here all afternoon in case he needs an alibi.'

'Do I need an alibi, Don?' asked Campion loudly from the kitchen.

'Oh no, sir, you don't, but I reckon somebody in this village does.'

'Why, Don? Has something happened to the Woolpack?'

'Not to the Woolpack, Mr Campion, but to your car – your lovely car – which you left in our safe keeping in the residents' car park. Oooh, a car like that would have been my pride and joy, and I'm sure it was yours...'

'Has it been stolen?'

'No, much worse than that, Mr Campion, sir,' Don paused for dramatic effect. 'It's been ... *vandalised*!'

'Vandalised?'

'Yes, sir. With a hammer by the looks of it.'

Eight

A Call on an Inspector

It had been named after the sainted King Edmund who had been martyred at the hands of raiding Danes eleven hundred years ago. It had a history of enthusiasm for witch trials and had been solidly Parliamentarian during the Civil War apart, that is, for a period of rioting in 1646 when the Puritans attempted to ban Christmas. Many of those Puritans, no doubt in high dudgeon, had left to make new lives in a new world called Massachusetts. Those who chose to remain had prospered in the sugar-refining industry and in the brewing of beer, which many said was why the town smelled so sweet. These things Mr Campion knew about Bury St Edmunds, but he had no idea why someone should be following him there.

The previous evening had seen Don presiding not over his optics, ice buckets, beer taps and swizzle sticks, as was his custom at that hour, but officiating over the remains of the headlamps and indicators of Mr Campion's Jaguar in the courtyard of the Woolpack, which had once turned around mail coaches and teams of horses but now resembled a modern scrap-yard.

Mr Campion could only agree with Don's verdict – spoken with the solemnity of a mechanical coroner – that the front end of his elegant Jaguar, which had been safely parked in the bosom of the Woolpack, had been hammered into an ugly mass of torn and twisted metal. Shattered glass sprinkled the courtyard like spilled diamonds from headlights and sidelights that were now mere cavities in the bodywork from which straggled electrical wiring. There were hammer-head dents all the way up the bonnet, clearly put there out of anger or frustration, and the windscreen had 'starred' from a series of blows above the steering wheel in a clear message of eye-level hatred for the driver.

Don was profuse in his apologies that such an atrocity could take place in Lindsay Carfax, let alone in the sanctum of the Woolpack, and that the act itself must have happened in the afternoon during those dead hours when British licensed premises were forced to close as they had been since 1915 in a forlorn attempt to increase munitions production during the war with the Kaiser. The damage had only been discovered around five o'clock when the duty dinner chef – an Italian and one of the many Italian POWs who had remained in Suffolk after a later war and gone into the catering trade (Don had added unnecessarily) – had arrived on his Vespa and immediately raised the alarm, or at least dragged Don from his afternoon nap so he could.

Mr Campion was assured that the owner of the Woolpack (a Mr Augustine Marchant, no less) would strain every sinew to have the Jaguar repaired at his expense as the damage had occurred on Woolpack property. The wounded car would be taken to Sherman's Garage where it would be nursed back to roadworthiness as quickly as possible, unless of course Mr Campion wished to make other arrangements, and because of the inconvenience, should he wish to extend his stay at the Woolpack, it would be as an honoured, rather than paying, guest.

If the generosity of the hostelry and the sympathetic noises made by Eliza Jane were meant to reassure Mr Campion, they did so only until the mechanical equivalent of the Lindsay Carfax Red Cross arrived in a dirty white Bedford van fitted with a winch and towing bar and the legend *Sherman & Sons Garage & Repairs, Lindsay Carfax 293* crudely stencilled on its flanks.

Had he not been told – in a whisper from Don – that the two men in oil-stained blue overalls who approached were father and son, Campion would never have guessed, for the older man was well below average height and a positive dwarf when standing in the shadow of the younger man, who would have been a dream prop forward in any Five Nations rugby team. They introduced themselves as Shermans; the elder being Dennis and the younger, bear-sized one, Clifford. Both wore oil-stained brown overalls and both were fluent in the universal language of garage mechanics when appraising vehicles and estimating repair costs. It was a language which did not consist of words, but rather a series of tongue clicks and loud inhalations of breath over clenched teeth punctuated by a slow shaking of the head.

The two Shermans circled the damaged car like sharks scenting blood in the water and the senior one announced that repairs were certainly possible, but would be expensive and could take two to three days. Mr Campion had reluctantly accepted his fate, committed the keys of the Jaguar into the grease-stained hands of Sherman & Son and prevailed upon Eliza Jane to act as his chauffeuse for his visit to Bury St Edmunds the next morning.

They had left shortly after breakfast, crammed into Eliza's sports car, its roof firmly in place to offer protection from the elements as its driver tackled the fifteen miles of narrow lanes with attack. Within two miles, Mr Campion realised they were being followed.

'You know what they say: any friend of Superintendent Luke is just a man who hasn't bought his round yet! How is Charlie, the old scallywag?'

Detective Chief Inspector Bill Bailey had the British policeman's knack of saying ridiculous things whilst defiantly maintaining the facial expression of a vicar at the graveside or a captain going down with his ship.

'Oh, hale and hearty,' said Campion. 'In fact, irritatingly so for a man of his age. Allow me to introduce Miss Eliza Jane Fitton, my niece, guide and driver – at least for today. Eliza is a resident of Lindsay Carfax, though one shouldn't hold it against her.'

Bill Bailey took Eliza Jane's delicately offered hand and allowed a faint smile to erode his face.

'That's always been our problem here in West Suffolk Police, though by rights I should say Suffolk Police now that all the county forces are amalgamated. You see, we've never been able to hold *anything* against the residents of Lindsay Carfax – at least nothing that would stick.'

'Are we really such a nest of rogues and vagabonds in Lindsay?' Eliza Jane framed her face with her hands, palms outward, and made a large O with her mouth.

'There are one or two individuals there I wouldn't trust with the Darby and Joan Club savings fund and one or two I wouldn't believe if they told me the time by the church clock – if the church has a clock, that is. The thing – the thing which gets under the collar of every copper who's had any dealings with the place – is that there's just not enough crime there.'

Now the O of Eliza's mouth increased in diameter.

'Not *enough crime*?' she exclaimed. 'Are you blaming us for being *too* law-abiding?'

'I'm sure you're not,' said Bill Bailey, 'and I couldn't blame you for that if you were. All I mean is that for a place of that size, even buried out in the sticks, you would expect more crime to be reported: a bit of vandalism, lead going missing off the church roof, joy-riding, after-hours drinking, sheep-stealing, burning the odd haystack ... anything. Yet virtually nothing ever gets reported from Lindsay Carfax; either the place is remarkably well-behaved or it somehow takes care of its own bad apples.'

'Well, I am going to brighten your day, Chief Inspector,' grinned Campion, 'by reporting not one but two instances of malfeasance in Lindsay Carfax, thus presenting you with a positive crime wave.'

Succinctly, Campion recounted the incidents of the booby trap on Ben Judd's external staircase and the wanton damage to his prize Jaguar, to which Bill Bailey listened politely but not intently before responding:

'Disturbing, I'll grant you, but hardly requiring the Flying Squad. What I'd really like to know is what a man of your calibre, Mr Campion – a calibre vouched for by Charlie Luke – is doing in a place like Lindsay sniffing around some fairly low-level unpleasantness. Not your scene at all, I would have said.'

'I am not quite sure whether I should be flattered by that, but I will be and I will cheerfully admit that it was Superintendent Luke's descriptions of odd goings-on and Nine Day Wonders that got the nose of this old truffle hound pointed towards Lindsay Carfax. The minor mayhem which has occurred there since is probably of little consequence.'

'Little consequence?' interrupted an indignant Miss Fitton. 'I could have broken my neck on those blasted stairs!'

'Or Ben Judd could have,' said Campion softly then turned back to address the policeman. 'And there are other odd things happening. The school master there, Lemuel Walker, who recently went on a nine-day disappearing trick, is back safe and

130

mostly sound, but the man is terrified of his own shadow. Whatever happened to him scared him to the marrow.'

'Highly strung,' said Bill Bailey gruffly, 'that's his problem; far too highly strung to be a teacher if you ask me. We know all about him.'

'He was reported as a Missing Person?'

'Matter of fact he wasn't, least not by his nearest and dearest, if you count his landlady as the nearest to a dearest he's got.'

'The redoubtable Mrs Thornton. Yes, I've met her.'

'It was only after he was back in circulation that we heard about it. One of the lads stationed at Long Melford was taking his wife out for their wedding anniversary dinner and no village bobby likes to come across as the loving husband when he's on his own patch, so he took his missus over to Lindsay for scampi and chips in the basket, or whatever it is they serve in the Woolpack. Turns out that the most popular dish on the menu there is gossip and our chap kept his ears open and when I got his report I sent one of my detectives out to interview the wandering Mr Walker, but that turned out to be a waste of petrol. He just didn't want to talk. He certainly wasn't prepared to press charges against anybody and, as he hadn't asked for us to be involved, I couldn't even do him for wasting police time.'

'But there was a Nine Days' Wonder last year which wasn't a waste of police time, wasn't there?' Campion asked quietly, as if the thought had just occurred to him.

'You mean the two hippies who died?' Bill Bailey pursed his lips.

'They called them "lieabouts" in the village,' offered Eliza, 'or sometimes "the great un-washed", but I think they were just young people looking to enjoy themselves during the summer. I don't think they were hippies really, you know, not like in San Francisco, living in communes with flowers in their hair and free love and drugs.'

'There were plenty of drugs, I suspect,' Mr Bailey pronounced gravely. 'In fact it was the drugs that killed two of them and put three others in hospital. I can't speak as to the flowers and the free love, but I tend to agree with you, Miss, they weren't hippies; leastways not the ones who died. They were students, from respectable families as well. I know; I had to break the news to their mothers and fathers.'

'Students? Local ones?' Campion's tone was casual, but concerned.

'Cambridge men – well, boys, really. Archaeologists out there on a dig that summer. They'd been camping out there minding their own business for a couple of weeks and nobody noticed them until some of the peace-and-love brigade spotted their tents and thought it would be a good place to lie up for the summer. Somehow, God knows how – jungle drums probably – the word got round that some sort of event, a "happening" they call it, was ... well, happening and they started turning up from all over the place in clapped out old cars, on bikes and scooters, even a couple of gypsy caravans and an ancient

132

charabanc.'

The policeman slowly shrugged his shoulders. 'And that's when we started to get complaints from the great and good of Lindsay Carfax. Not about the drug-taking – which even that mop-headed vicar disapproved of – or the promiscuity, as it seems you really have to go some to outrage public decency in Lindsay Carfax. No, the biggest moans came from the café-owners and the souvenir shops and those picture galleries who complained that the incomers were putting off their regular tourist trade and not spending any money on knick-knacks. I don't recall the Woolpack complaining, come to think of it, as I reckon they did a roaring trade from the Four Ale Bar of take-away bottles of brown ale and barley wine.'

Mr Campion sneaked a sly glance at Eliza Jane and allowed himself a secret smile as she shuffled her feet in embarrassment.

'I had only just arrived in the village,' she said defensively, 'and the hippies I saw seemed harmless. A bit grubby perhaps, and they liked their transistors turned up loud, but they were friendly enough.'

'You'd be nearer to them in age than the average resident, I expect,' observed Bill Bailey, 'and naturally a bit more tolerant of their morals. I know for a fact that some in the village were positively gleeful when they descended on the place – that daft vicar for one, and that wandering schoolmaster for another.'

'Lemuel Walker sided with the invading lie-abouts?' Mr Campion said with mock horror.

'Whatever next? Putting the welcome mat out for Genghis Khan and his marauding Mongols?'

Bill Bailey narrowed his eyes and studied his visitor.

'Charlie Luke said you were a card. Didn't tell me you were the whole pack. Anyway, as I was saying, there were those who thought the hippies were a plague and others who didn't seem to mind them, like your schoolteacher chum. He was all for encouraging the archaeologists at first, but when they started overdosing on the drugs, then your Mr Walker ran a mile, just didn't want to know. Odd, really, because by all accounts he was an old chum of their supervisor or tutor or whatever they call the head man at Cambridge, but when the deaths occurred it was yours truly here who had to go a break the news.'

'Do you remember the name of their tutor?'

'Dr Mortimer Casson, of St Ignatius College.'

'Good Heavens, that's my old stomping ground!' exclaimed Campion.

'Now why doesn't that surprise me?' sighed Bailey. 'I suppose you know this Dr Casson personally – have sherry with him regularly or dine with him at High Table, or partner him at a May Ball, that sort of thing?'

'Actually I've never heard of him. Almost certainly wasn't born when I was swotting for my finals. Do I detect a note of antagonism towards Cambridge men?'

'Not at all, or at least no more than you'd expect from a Redbrick man, it just stuck in my gullet the way Dr Casson was when I broke the news that his students had died.'

'He was upset, of course, wasn't he?'

'Oh, he was upset they were dead. That was genuine enough. But when I told him it was drugs as the cause, he just sat there and shrugged in a "What can you do" sort of gesture. He wasn't shocked, not even surprised; just seemed to accept that students and LSD went together like ham and pickles, as we say round here. To him, drugs seemed to be part of life these days – and that's what got me about him, the casual way he accepted his students signed their own death warrants. Drug overdose? Just one of the risks of being young these days. I mean the youth of today has to question everything, don't they? Have to try everything, even if it kills them.'

Eliza Jane, Campion noticed, was earnestly studying the toes of her suede shoes, determined not to become involved in any diatribe on the younger generation.

'LSD you say? I'm no expert, but I thought "acid" was a powerful hallucinogen and not a fatal drug like some of the others can be. Of course you can go "tripping" and think you can fly and kill yourself by jumping off a bridge or such like, but I wasn't aware there was a lethal dose per se.'

'That's what the flower power people and the free thinkers would want you to believe,' said Bill Bailey with steel in his voice, 'but too much of anything can kill you, even the sugar in your tea, I reckon. Like you, Mr Campion, I don't know much about drugs, though I've got a nasty feeling that like most policemen I'm going to have to get better educated on the subject over the next few years. I'm going on what the pathologist told the coroner: the two fatalities ingested very pure, undiluted LSD in a massive quantity. Now normally, one fluid ounce of the stuff can make 30,000 doses or "tabs" as the hippies call them. We don't know for sure, but the boffins in the laboratories think the two archaeologists took doses over eighty times larger than normal – if there's anything normal about getting out of your mind like that.'

'And you're sure it was self-administered?'

'Looking for foul play? I thought that was my job. In fact, last time I looked it was and I take my job seriously, Campion. In my opinion, whoever supplied the LSD to those lads is guilty of murder – guilty as hell. But we don't know who that was and it's highly unlikely we'll ever find him. As to the administering of the drug, I'm afraid that was self-inflicted.'

'There is no doubt of that?' Campion probed.

'I'm afraid not,' the detective sighed and slumped visibly in his chair as he told the story.

'There were five of them – the archaeology students from Cambridge – and they were camped out at a place called Saxon Mills for the summer, quietly minding their own business before the hippy invasion. The must have got mixed up in this "alternative lifestyle" they're always on about, because none of them had a track record of drugs before last summer. Somehow they got hold of some LSD and decided to go on an acid trip one night. Two of them never saw the morning and the three that did saw it from a hospital bed.'

'Could I impose on you to look up the names of the two who overdosed?' asked Campion.

'Stephen Stotter and Martin Rees,' Bill Bailey snapped out the response. 'I don't have to look the names up; I had to tell their mothers what had happened to them.'

'I am so sorry about that,' said Campion genuinely. 'A policeman's lot is rarely a happy one. I presume it was one of the deceased who actually acquired the drugs?'

'It was Stotter, who was sort of the leader of the expedition. The others had no idea where he got the stuff, or who from. If they had, I'd have had the pusher bouncing off the walls of one of our cells before you could say "Peace and Love" and to hell with his civil liberties. All five of them took something that night but it seems that Master Stotter and Master Rees got the lion's share and it did for them, though I doubt they knew what they were messing with.'

'Their parents must have been devastated,' Eliza Jane said quietly. 'I feel guilty because in Lindsay their deaths hardly caused a ripple. One morning the police were all over us and suddenly all the lieabouts started to drift away.'

'We have that effect on some people,' said Bill Bailey with mock gravity.

'It didn't really sink in that somebody had actually died. We were just glad to be rid of a nuisance.'

'Don't upset yourself, my dear. What's done is done and there's nothing you could have done about it, so there's no need to beat yourself up.'

'Listen to the Chief Inspector, Eliza,' said

Campion, reaching out to place a hand on the girl's shoulder. 'Sackcloth and ashes were never a good look in any circumstances. Such a story does, however, make our little problems with the anti-social element in Lindsay Carfax hardly amount to a hill of beans, as a wise man once said.'

'But you were right to tell me, Mr Campion. There's too many things go on over there which never come to light and if you let the small crimes go unnoticed then you can't expect the big ones to be punished.' The detective paused and stroked his chin before continuing.

'The problem is, you see, that we might smell something that's gone off in Lindsay but no one there ever complains about anything. If they've got a problem they expect the Carders to take care of things, like last year with the two lads who overdosed. The story was doing the rounds that the Carders had given them nine days to get out of the village, and it was on the ninth day that they went on an acid trip from which Stotter and Rees never returned.'

'You don't put much faith in that story, do you?' asked Campion.

'Of course not; it's stuff and nonsense made up after the fact, but it adds to the legend. I don't know whether that school teacher fellow is telling the truth about his disappearing on a Nine Days' Wonder but I'll bet you won't find a soul in Lindsay who doesn't believe it was the work of the Carders. There isn't a pie in that place they don't have a finger in.'

'A chap called Marchant seems to own just

138

about everything there,' Mr Campion observed.

'Maybe not everything, but a good four-fifths,' DCI Bailey responded, 'though it doesn't make him a wrong 'un. In fact Old Gus is well known in the county and in truth he's no more dangerous than the average Rotarian – and he keeps out of politics, which is to his credit.'

'And you think he's a Carder – one of the Nine?'

'I'd be amazed if Augustine Marchant *wasn't* one of the ruling elite, and the same goes for his old mess-mate and business partner Marcus Fuller.'

'Would a lawyer-chap called Hereward Spindler make up a trio of Carders?'

'That's either clever observation, good guesswork or just a healthy dislike of lawyers, but you could be right. In fact, I've heard it said openly that Spindler is the Carders' clerk or recorder, or scribe or whatever they call it. When the Carders do good works – and they do – I can see it being useful having the local solicitor on board to sign deeds, allocate funds and so on. To be fair I don't think he makes any particular secret of the fact.'

Mr Campion stretched his long legs out in front of his chair and made circular motions with the tips of his shoes.

'What a curious place is Lindsay Carfax,' he said languidly. 'It has secret passages which are not only not secret but are openly revealed in tourist guides and on tea-towels and postcards. It is famous for the Humble Box – a secret way of forecasting the weather which, if it ever worked, was a secret which died with its inventor almost two hundred years ago – and it is said to be run by a secret society which isn't very secret. In fact we've just named three of them and we know that Ben Judd was approached to join their ranks, so that would be four.'

'But Ben didn't join them,' protested Eliza Jane.

'No he did not, but it sounds as if they had a vacancy coming up, otherwise they wouldn't be recruiting. Can Carders be fired or are older ones replaced by faster, sleeker, younger models?'

Bill Bailey allowed himself a smile. 'You might have something there, Campion, the Carders may well be looking for new blood.'

The policeman leaned forward conspiratorially.

'I always suspected that the Carder Kingpin – or Queen I should say – was a certain Lady who exchanged the calling of civic duty and life in that dusty old museum called the Prentice House for bright lights and fine wines on the French Riviera a couple of years ago.'

'You don't mean Lady Prunella, surely?'

'I surely do. Over eighty, mad as a badger, and living the life of Riley without any visible means of support.'

'Perhaps she has benefited from the exceptionally generous pension scheme for retired Queen Carders, if such she was. I'm distantly related to Lady Prunella, you know.'

'Why does that not surprise me?'

'Funny – that's exactly what Charlie Luke said. I must have that effect on policeman.' Campion smiled his Sunday-best idiot smile. 'So dear old Prunella used to live in the shrine to Esther Wickham, Victorian novelist of this parish, which now seems to have passed into the hands of Hereward Spindler, solicitor of this parish.'

'My thinking,' said Bailey, 'is that the Carders like to keep things among themselves, or at least the money-making ones, so it would make sense for one Carder to sell to another.'

Mr Campion allowed himself a frown.

'Would the sale of the Prentice House, even with its connections to the talented Miss Wickham, raise enough to allow Lady Prunella to acquire the "Riviera touch"?'

'Who knows? If there was a sale it was done privately and secretly. One day Lady Pru was swanning round the county in a 1949 Austin 10 which had seen better days – most of them before 1952 – the next, she's off to join the jet set, having given her chauffeur, cook and lady's maid the elbow.'

'I heard yesterday that she haunts the casino in Monte Carlo. She can't live alone down there, can she?'

'I believe she has employed a companion, who she insists on calling her "concierge" although she probably doesn't know what the word means. A Swiss woman called Berger and I only know that because she was driving Lady Pru around on her last visit to Lindsay about eighteen months ago when she came back for the Sherman funeral.'

Mr Campion's ears pricked up at the name.

'Sherman?'

141

'Leonard Sherman, died on New Year's Day last year, well into his seventies. He was the senior member of an old, but hardly distinguished, Lindsay family and a family which has more than its fair share of skeletons in the cupboard in my not-so-humble opinion. They run the local garage. Len's son Dennis is now in charge and he's brought in his idiot son Clifford, who is built like the wall of an outhouse and has the brains to match, if you'll pardon the colourful imagery, Miss Fitton.'

Bill Bailey waited for Eliza Jane to offer him a weak smile of forgiveness before continuing.

'We never managed to get anything on old Len when he was alive, but Dennis has previous – mostly to do with dodgy car deals, turning the mileage clock back, swapping good tyres for bald ones, stuff like that – and as for young Clifford, Clifford the gorilla, well, that boy's a long sentence just waiting to be served. Disturbing the peace, affray, drunk and disorderly – he's sampled them all, and because he doesn't know his own strength, he'll do some serious damage to something or someone one day and his cell will be waiting for him. The curious thing is that everything we ever proved against Clifford or his dad, it was always done away from Lindsay Carfax, or to people who didn't live there.

'Now I don't believe that leopards can change their spots and the Shermans, being a bunch of hooligans, are just as likely to behave badly on their home patch. Except nobody complains: it's as if Lindsay tolerates their behaviour, but if I lived there the last thing I would do is trust them with something valuable like my car.'

'Oh dear,' said Mr Campion.

They had walked to the side street where they had parked before Eliza spoke.

'You didn't tell the nice policeman we were followed here.'

'It quite slipped my mind,' said Campion airily.

'You were sure of it before,' challenged the girl.

'Just as sure as you were that the car following us came from Sherman's Garage.'

Eliza halted in mid stride and swung on her uncle, prodding him in the chest with a long red fingernail.

'I told you, Sherman's bought two new Ford Cortina saloons this year and they hire them out for weddings, funerals and so on. I've seen them around the village tons of times.'

Mr Campion caught the stabbing finger in his right hand and gently raised it to his lips.

'Without making any sudden movements or jumps for joy, is it the same Ford Cortina that's parked on the opposite side of the street about fifty yards behind me? Just peek over my shoulder, at about eleven o'clock.'

Eliza stood on tiptoe and stretched her neck whilst pretending to accept Campion's solicitations.

'I'm pretty sure it is and there's somebody in the driving seat, though I can't make him out from here.'

Mr Campion released her hand and offered his arm to escort her the last few yards to her car.

'I took a butcher's – as an old rogue I know would say – as we passed him and it's no-one I've seen before. He shrank himself down in his seat as we ambled by. Most suspicious, but I got the feeling it was you he didn't want to see him, not me.'

'So what do we do now?'

'Now? We get in your car and we speed back to Lindsay Carfax to see if we are pursued by a certain Ford Cortina. If we are, I suggest you put your pretty foot down, pull ahead and then turn into one of the many field entrances we passed on the way here. That way we can watch our friend zip by and the followed can become the follower.'

They reached the little sports car and Eliza unlocked her door and slid in. Campion took his time contorting himself through the passenger door and when comfortably seated found a pair of chunky high-heeled shoes being thrust into his lap.

'Hold on to these for me. I drive faster without shoes,' explained his niece and Mr Campion did not doubt her for a moment.

Their plan worked perfectly, with Campion only flinching twice as Eliza took left-hand bends at speed, and before they were half-way back to Lindsay she had drawn well ahead of the Cortina which was, predictably, following in their wake.

With a cry of 'Hang on' Eliza Jane swung the wheel and turned off the road into the entrance to a field where piles of harvested sugar beets awaited collection and provided more than

144

adequate cover for the low-slung sports car. Fortunately the earth beneath its wheels was firm rather than soft, which meant they did not stick there, but Campion's teeth rattled in his head as the car bumped around to face the road.

Eliza Jane cranked on the handbrake and switched off the ignition. Fifteen seconds later the Ford Cortina swept by them, the field and the small mountain of sugar beets without pausing.

'Did you get a look at the driver?' asked Campion, clutching a pair of brown suede platform-soled sandals to his chest.

'Yes I did,' said the girl grimly, turning to face her uncle. 'That's certainly one of the Sherman cars, but it wasn't a Sherman driving. It was that silly young fool Tommy Tucker who shares the studio with Ben. Now why on Earth would Tommy Tucker be following you?'

'What makes you think he was following *me*?' said Mr Campion.

Nine

Rough Shoot

The Wellington boots were a size too large and the long, padded Barbour coat would have snuggled a man of twice Campion's bulk, but the 12-bore shotgun provided fitted him perfectly. Into a metal plate on the stock was stamped the legend 'Pietro Beretta Founded in 1526' and Campion recognised the model as the Silver Hawk, a popular enough gun which, inexplicably, had been discontinued recently by its famous Italian manufacturers.

He had breakfasted by 7 a.m. and forty-five minutes later he was standing outside the main entrance of the Woolpack wearing a tweed jacket and thick brown corduroy trousers, which he hoped complied with the dress code for a morning of rough shooting in Lindsay Carfax. The previous evening, as he had performed his bar-tendering duties, the loquacious Don had assured him that boots and waterproofs would be provided by the shoot's patron, Augustine Marchant, and there would be a selection to choose from in the Land Rover arriving to collect him outside Carder's Hall at eight.

Don had offered this helpful information

without being asked, clearly and without subtlety in the hope that his gentle questioning about Campion's day in Bury St Edmunds at police headquarters would be answered in turn. Mr Campion had responded with polite inanities and retired to his room early on the grounds that he had an important Victorian novel to read and, if he had to be up with the lark, at his age he needed his full measure of beauty sleep.

As it turned out, Mr Campion found himself up not with the larks but with a brace of brewery draymen lowering liquid rations to the Woolpack through a trap door in the pavement and into the dark abyss of the inn's cellar. Standing under the timbered overhang of the Woolpack's upper floor, Mr Campion observed their well-oiled routine of transferring wooden casks and metal kegs from their flat-back lorry using ramps and ropes, finding it far more interesting, although considerably noisier, than any dawn chorus of larks ascending. What Campion found especially fascinating was the running commentary between the two burly draymen, once he had tuned his ear to their broad Suffolk accents, as they loudly discussed every detail of their task with a very British air of disparagement lest any passer-by received the impression that they actually took pride in – and enjoyed – their work.

'You got the order straight then, boy?'

'Well I reckon Oi have, but I can't speak for the bar manager. There ain't much pleases 'im.'

'Reckon you're roight there, but let's not give 'im cause to have us jumping through hoops. Check the manifest before we start droppin' off.'

'Six crates of loight ale, six of brown plus four of assorted mixers and fruit juices, one kil of bitter, a firkin of strong and a firkin of mild, two elevens of lager, one of stout and a pin of barley wine.'

'Roight, you fetch the empties up and I'll get the crates off – bloody plastic things. Oi can't stand 'em. Did Oi ever tell you why they switched to plastic an' away from good sturdy wooden crates which you could break up for kindling if you were ever caught short lighting a fire?'

'Nylons. You must've told me a dozen times or more.'

'That's roight; it was all them barmaids kept catching their stockings on the nails in 'em, causing laddering. That's no reason to go to plastic which is no use to man nor beast.'

'They be lasting longer.'

'Be that as it may, but change just for change's sake is what Oi call it. And now we've got these metal casks – aloominium – coming in instead of coopered wooden ones. You can't put a decent flower display in half a metal keg, can you? Make the allotment look loike a junk yard.'

'It's progress; you can't foight it.'

'Bugger progress, Oi say. Just leads to confusion. I mean look at these beer kegs. Why they come in "elevens" and "twenty-twos", eh?'

'That's metric system, that is.'

'It's a foreign system is what Oi say. What's wrong with the old way? You knew where you was with that. A hogshead was 54 gallons, a barrel was 36, a kilderkin is 18 and a firkin is 9 gallons. Straightforward, that was.'

'What about a pin then?'

'A pin's half a firkin, that's what that is. Four-and-a-half gallons being half of nine gallons. Bleedin' obvious as it fits in with the system.'

'System that don't make sense.'

'But it do! Fifty-four, thirty-six, eighteen, nine and then four-and-a-half. Brewers even used to sell beer in butts, which was 108 gallons, though they don't no more. Yer see the sense, don't yer? All them numbers, they's what you call multiples of nine. None of your foreign metric rubbish; everything was divided by nine, that's the tried and true way of doing it in this country.'

Mr Campion had barely filed away this nugget of rural wisdom in his cavernous but well-indexed memory, when a mud-splattered, Land Rover screeched to a halt across the street out-side Carders' Hall. A dark-haired man, as tall and rangy as Campion but perhaps thirty years younger, climbed out of the driver's door and stood in the High Street with hands on hips and feet apart, as if planted there. If there had been any traffic in the street that morning, his shout would have stopped it in its tracks.

'Are you Campion?'

It was a parade ground voice, but it had been many years since Mr Campion had felt obliged to snap to attention.

'I'm awfully afraid I am,' he replied, a vacuous grin beaming out to meet the advancing man.

'Then I'm your whipper-in, come to collect you on the orders of Mr Marchant. There's some gear for you in the Land Rover and Gus has put a gun out for you down at the farm.'

149

The younger man offered his hand in what turned out to be a remarkably strong grip. 'Name's Fuller,' he announced. 'Simon Fuller. I believe you know my brother.'

'I've met Mr Fuller,' said Campion, 'but only once and very briefly. I believe he won't be joining us, or will he?'

'No chance. Marcus is a big softy when it comes to guns and country pursuits in general which mean he misses out on what passes for the social scene around here.'

The junior Mr Fuller marched around the front of the Land Rover to the driver's side. 'Climb in, it's open.'

Once settled in the passenger seat, Campion said: 'So this shoot is on the social calendar locally?'

'Not really, it's just old Gus Marchant playing the generous land-owner to remind us poor serfs and peasants of our place. Still, that way you get a good mix of people – mostly locals and good honest sons of the Suffolk soil to boot – plus the odd outsider, or distinguished guest, such as your good self.'

'Is it a big shoot?' Campion asked as Fuller started the engine.

'No, Gus Marchant always limits the numbers on Long Tye Farm shoots.'

'So there will be nine guns this morning?'

'That's right,' said Simon Fuller. 'How did you know that?'

'Just a wild guess,' said Mr Campion gently.

Simon Fuller drove fast, flinging the Land Rover

around the corners of the narrow lanes to the north of the village with gay abandon and a cheerful disregard for any traffic coming in the opposite direction. Mr Campion braced himself as best he could against the sharp metal frame of door and dashboard, and took solace in the thought that he felt slightly safer and marginally more comfortable than he had as a passenger in Eliza Jane's sports car.

Fortunately the journey was a short one; and within a few minutes of leaving the relative metropolis of Lindsay Carfax, Fuller had turned sharply left off the lane and on to a gravel road-way lined by low hedges. Mr Campion had not flinched at the manoeuvre and had caught a fleet-ing glimpse of an old-fashioned finger-pointing signpost advertising the way 'To Long Tye Farm and Saxon Mills ONLY' – the last word in capital letters seeming to be more of a warning than a direction.

'These Saxon Mills,' said Campion casually, 'would they be wind or water power? Did the Saxons – or the Angles for that matter – have windmills? I've a feeling they came later.'

'No idea what you're talking about, I'm afraid,' said Fuller. Then, as if lecturing as platoon of fresh Territorial recruits: 'Saxon Mills isn't a mill; it's a quarry where they used to take out chalk and flints. Not even that, these days, as quarrying stopped years ago. It's just a hole in the ground of no interest to man nor beast except for maybe a few rabbits. It's still on all the maps though.'

'Wasn't Saxon Mills the epicentre of your

hippy invasion last year?'

Simon Fuller took his eyes off the road and stared at his passenger.

'Where did you hear that?'

'Actually, a very nice policeman told me,' said Campion, returning his stare.

'Well, I'd hardly call it an invasion,' Fuller said huffily, returning his concentration to his driving. 'It was just a bloody nuisance having the scruffy beasts hanging around the village. Nobody asked them to come and lie about the place, leaving litter and frightening the livestock. None of the dirty little buggers were from around here.'

'Two of them died, didn't they? From an overdose of drugs?'

'Served them right,' growled Fuller. 'I had no sympathy for them then; I have none now. If you choose to live an anti-social life, you take the consequences.'

'I rather got the impression,' Campion said, watching the face of his driver carefully, 'that your summer visitors were students on a working vacation and not really in the revolutionary vanguard trying to overthrow society.'

'You didn't have to put up with their noise and their mess and their ... *lewdness* ... if that's a proper word.'

'A perfectly good one; and Anglo-Saxon as it happens.'

Simon Fuller again concentrated on his passenger rather than the road, fortunately devoid of traffic, ahead but this time with an expression of mild puzzlement.

'I was brought up to respect my elders and be polite at all times, but I have to say, Mr Campion, that you strike me as an odd cove and not the sort that usually gets an invitation to one of Gus Marchant's shoots. What on Earth is your connection to Lindsay Carfax?'

'Slim, if not tangential. I have a wayward niece who lives here and whilst my car undergoes some serious reconstructive surgery in the local garage, my visit has been extended though not, I hope, indefinitely.'

'Your car is in the Shermans' garage for repairs?' Fuller let out a chortle as he changed down the gears and the Land Rover began to slow.

'I was given to understand it was the only garage in Lindsay,' Campion answered him.

'Oh, it is, but don't expect your car to be repaired this morning because Dennis and Clifford Sherman will be with us. All work at the garage stops when Gus Marchant has a shoot.'

'They didn't look like the country-sport types when I saw them,' said Campion as the Land Rover pulled into the cobbled yard of a long, low, three-chimney farmhouse.

'With Dennis – the father – it's a social thing. He likes to be seen with the local gentry; in fact, he thinks it's his right to be pictured alongside them, his family being a long-standing one in the village, though it didn't stop his wife running off with a travelling salesman. I've heard him, in his cups in the Woolpack, say that Sherman was just as good a name as Marchant, or Spindler, or Webster or even Fuller and I think Gus indulges

153

him. As for the son Clifford, that dumb ox just enjoys blasting away with a shotgun. I always stay upwind of him.'

The Land Rover juddered to a stop and then allowed itself several further spasms even after Fuller had turned off the ignition, as if it were a gun dog returning from a swim in a pond or river.

'It looks like we're the last ones to arrive,' said Fuller and Campion followed his gaze across the farmyard to a congregation of half-a-dozen men wearing boots, padded coats and a variety of headgear ranging from a Russian Cossack fur to an American Trapper's hat complete with ear-flaps, although the flat cap of the English country gentleman predominated. The men hovered around a trestle table on which stood a large white urn and a regiment of white china mugs, flanked by a row of gun butts and several boxes of cartridges. Slightly more disturbing than this laid-out arsenal was the fact that in among the ranks of the white mugs, which looked suspiciously like NAAFI issue crockery, stood two bottles of whisky and two of dark rum. 'Let's get your gear on,' Fuller ordered, climbing out of the vehicle and marching smartly to the rear to open the back door.

As Campion joined him, he handed him a pair of wellingtons and one Barbour waterproof, while climbing into a second for himself and pulling a folded tweed cap from its pocket.

'Everyone except me seems to have a hat,' Mr Campion simpered foolishly. 'I feel positively under-dressed.'

'Thought of that,' said Fuller reaching into the piles of clothing in the Land Rover. 'Here we are. Gus put this in for you.'

Fuller handed him a deerstalker, which Campion took with an enthusiastic grin and slapped on his head.

'How splendid! I've always wanted one of these.'

'I tried one on once, for a bet,' Fuller said dismissively, zipping his coat and turning away. 'Made me look like a simpleton.'

Mr Campion straightened his new headgear and said, quietly and to himself: 'That's just the look I was going for.'

In the throng around the gun table, Campion helped himself to a mug of coffee, which came in one flavour only – strong, stewed, sweet and filthy brown – but at least, he noted with relief, none of the shooters had succumbed to the temptation of fortifying their coffee with neat spirit. In his experience, gunpowder and alcohol rarely mixed successfully.

'Filthy stuff,' said Gus Marchant in greeting, toasting Mr Campion with his own white mug brimming with brown liquid, 'but I got used to drinking it this way, first in the army and then at interminable parish council meetings, planning meetings, Highways and Byways committees even Mothers' Union bun-fights. You'd have thought the Mothers' Union could have brewed a decent cup of coffee, but it all came out like this muck so I grinned and bore it and now find it almost palatable. I see Simon has kitted you out sartorially, though I doubt you'd ever make it as a pin-up in *Country Life*. I've put out a gun for you, one of my Berettas, so I know it won't blow up in your face.'

'That is more than kind.'

'Not at all. Actually, I prefer to have people use my guns. Some of the locals turn up with fowling pieces and blunderbusses from God knows when, which terrify me let alone the wildlife. One old farmhand once showed up with an old punt gun he could hardly lift and asked if I had some black powder and a pound of carpet tacks for ammunition!'

'It's good of you to put up with us,' Campion said politely. 'I'm sure you don't have to.'

'One has certain responsibilities and duties when one is the main landowner in a small community,' said Marchant, puffing out his chest. 'Traditions have to be upheld and things are expected of one; it comes with the territory. There's a phrase which is still used...'

'Obliging Nobbles,' chirped Mr Campion.

'What?'

'Oh pardon the schoolboy humour. It's how I was taught to translate *Noblesse Oblige* by a very irresponsible French master many, many years ago; in fact so long ago, France was probably still called Gaul and divided into three parts.'

Augustine Marchant stared at the odd, bespectacled and deerstalkered figure before him and cleared his throat loudly.

'Er ... well ... er ... yes, that's the sort of thing I mean. There are some things one just has to do in a rural community when one owns most of the land and, in any case, an organised shoot like this cuts down on the poaching.'

'Noble, worthy *and* practical,' Campion said sweetly, 'and I am truly honoured to be invited along, though I doubt I will pose much of a threat to your herd of partridges – or whatever the collective noun for partridges is.'

'Just enjoy yourself; that's the main thing, old chap. If you bag anything for the pot, that's a bonus. It's the least we can do after what happened to your car.'

'My dear Mr Marchant, you cannot possibly be blamed for the mindless vandalism of others.'

'But I take it as an affront, Campion. It took place in the heart of our village and on my property. That makes it my business; that makes it personal. Now, let's get you that gun.'

Their guns unloaded and broken open to prove it, the shooters moved off in single file down a muddy track with the farmhouse and its kitchen garden on their left and a ploughed field of dark brown earth on the right. A bird's eye view, Mr Campion thought, could mistake them for an infantry section moving up wearily to the front were it not for the cheerful banter being exchanged along the column. At its head, Gus Marchant discussed tactics over his shoul-der with Simon Fuller, whilst other voices, which Campion faintly recognised from the bar at the Wool-pack, agreed that a morning's shooting at Long Tye was infinitely preferable to a day at work, or entered into a debate on whether partridges were best hung for two or three days before cooking.

Behind Campion, the Sherman father and son marched in silence apart from the occasional unsettling giggle from the young giant Clifford at nothing in particular. At the gun table, the Shermans had acknowledged Campion's presence, though with little grace; or at least Sherman Senior had whilst his son, wearing an army surplus parka which made him look like a criminally minded grizzly bear, merely stared and grinned inanely.

'Ah, Mr Campion, your car's coming along nicely,' Dennis Sherman had greeted him. 'We're just waiting for some parts to come from Ipswich, so there's not much we can do this morning.'

'As long as things are in hand,' Campion had said neutrally.

'Oh they are, they are,' Sherman had said with something of a sneer. 'There's nothing at all for you to worry about – especially not with Gus Marchant picking up the bill.'

At his side, his son tried and failed to supress a snort of laughter.

'I would hate to think that Mr Marchant's generosity has been mistaken for a carte blanche,' Campion had replied sternly, though he felt that the deerstalker he was wearing did not exactly add to the air of gravitas he was trying to achieve.

'I'm not sure what you mean, Mr Campion.' Sherman's tone had wavered from drunken sailor belligerence to Uriah Heap humble. 'Mr

158

Marchant is a person of some importance in Lindsay Carfax.'

'Even a muddle-headed incomer such as me can see that,' Campion had grinned. 'I feel quite guilty about being taken under his wing.'

'Like you say, Mr Marchant can be generous,' Sherman had agreed. 'Many would say too generous.'

'And unless tempered with moderation, generosity can lead to ruin, as dear old Tacitus said. Or was that "candour" not "generosity"? Or was it both? I forget. My goodness, one knows when one is getting old when one forgets one's Tacitus...'

Dennis Sherman had scowled in confusion.

''E's off his head,' his son had sniggered and his father had been quick to snap: 'Clifford! You watch that mouth of yours!' Then to Campion he had said: 'Be best if we join the others now.'

Mr Campion had nodded enthusiastically.

'Oh yes, a-hunting we must go, mustn't we?'

And he had kept his face fixed in a vacant smile despite the fact that the junior Sherman's shotgun was levelled at his stomach for far longer than was comfortable; or accidental.

At a five-bar gate which gave access to another large, ploughed field of large red-brown clods of earth, the shooting party was met by two elderly gentlemen, each holding an even more ancient Labrador on a lead of baling twine. These venerable men and their venerable beasts, Marchant explained, would be their beaters for the morning and would flush out birds from the Saxon

159

Quarry – as he called it – while the guns moved south to north across the fields in fifty-yard stages. If Reuben and Zachary, their very experienced beaters, did their jobs, birds would flock across their sights from right to left in abundance and Reuben and Zachary would earn their traditional brace of bottles of Scotch (Reuben) and Navy Rum (Zachary).

As Mr Campion was a guest and new to the terrain, he was to be given poll position on the far right of the line of guns and Marchant frowned at the mutterings of the shooting party when they suggested, *sotto voce*, that the safest place behind a new gun – especially one who seemed to think he had come on a stag hunt – was not to the right or left, but behind.

The nine guns spread out across the field, automatically adopting a safe spacing between themselves; Campion on the right wing, Marchant on the far left. When satisfied that the line was in the correct position, Marchant gave a last briefing. They would hold this line and a whistle from Reuben or Zachary, now both out of sight down in the Saxon Mills quarry, would indicate that the first beat of birds was on its way. They would shoot as long as they had targets, but on no account was anyone to step out of the line to collect shot birds. Only when another whistle blew would they advance fifty yards over the field and reform the line for another beat, and so on until they had traversed the field. All kills would be collected from where they had fallen at the end of the shoot and be divided equally among the guns. Should there be birds surplus to requirements, then partridge pie would be on the menu at the Woolpack for the foreseeable future.

Campion took up his position at the far right of the shooting line and planted his feet firmly in two deep plough furrows, some twenty feet from the hawthorn hedge which formed the boundary of the field and which, he presumed, hid the mysterious Saxon Mills beyond and below. From the pocket of his borrowed Barbour, he selected two cartridges and shook them gently by his ear for the required rattle of loose birdshot, as was customary, before sliding them into the twin barrels of his shotgun and gently closing the breech. He glanced along the line of guns and saw that the others were also performing the cartridge-shaking ritual, which always reminded him for some reason of his old factotum Lugg when confronted with the task of changing a light bulb. Lugg would hold the defunct bulb to his ear and shake it until he heard the tinkle of broken filaments. Only that way would he be convinced that the bulb's illness was terminal and that it had glimmered its last.

His fond remembrance of an old and slightly cantankerous friend was interrupted by the blast of a beater's whistle, the bark of a dog and the rustle of wings beating through the undergrowth down in the quarry beyond the hedge and then a small squadron of birds appeared flying almost parallel to the line of guns and the instincts of the hunters snapped into place.

Campion's first snap shot peppered only air but his second barrel scored, sending a bird tumbling and as he broke the Beretta to reload, he ran his eye along the line as the guns crackled and the smell of cordite assaulted his nostrils. As far as he could see, Long Tye Farm's partridge population was not under threat of extinction from the shoot's combined marksmanship and, in order to blend in, when two more birds emerged from the beat directly in front of him, Campion made sure he missed both. After a third volley – one hit, one miss – the sky emptied of targets and Gus Marchant gave the order to 'break guns' and advance across the field.

After forty or more stretched paces across the wide plough furrows, the hedge to Campion's right became sparse and less tangled, offering a tantalising glimpse down into Saxon Mills which Mr Campion found impossible to resist. Another ten yards and he found himself able to peer over the edge and in to what Simon Fuller had described as a flint quarry, now overgrown and forgotten except by game birds.

The description seemed accurate for all Campion could see was scrub, brambles and thigh-high nettles covering a gentle slope down into a basin shaped depression where the ground was a reddish-grey sand in contrast to the darker loam of the ploughed field.

From across the field to his left, Marchant's voice boomed out 'Stop the line! Load!', and from down in the quarried depression to his right came another blast on a whistle and even as Campion was slotting fresh cartridges into his gun, the first birds appeared some thirty yards ahead of him.

He raised his gun and fired, deliberately making his movements jerky but not wild and unsafe, ensuring that he missed his targets and giving the impression, he hoped, of an enthusiastic but very amateur field sportsman.

Along the line the guns let loose their barrage, Campion's ears telling him that the local shooters were more than happy to take advantage of Gus Marchant's provision of free cartridges and he allowed himself to be caught up in the moment, reloading and snapping off two more shots which both brought down birds.

There seemed no shortage of targets and after a sly glance through the gun-smoke to his left showed eight barrels pointing skyward concentrating on them, Campion took two paces to his right where a gap in the hawthorn offered him an unrestricted view down into Saxon Mills. For the first time he could see the extent of the man-made depression and, at the bottom of the slope, a glimmer of light reflecting on standing water. Other than that, there was little to see; no sign of a mill, not a hint of a Saxon and no suggestion that this had been the site of a congregation of hippies seeking free love in a rural idyll the previous summer.

He had no time to take in any more information as his thought process was distracted not by the sound of the guns and their constant banging but the sense that something had disturbed the *rhythm* of the firing line.

Automatically, Campion broke his gun, ejecting the spent cartridges and fumbling in his pocket for two fresh ones. His hand was still deep in the pocket, his fingers gripping the brass rim of a 12-bore cartridge when a blast of bird-shot from an entirely different cartridge stung his legs with such force that he staggered like a drunk falling off a bus, through the gap in the hawthorn and plunged head-first over the edge.

Ten

Visiting Hours

'I really don't know which was the most embarrassing: being hauled out of an important board meeting to be told that my idiot husband has been shot in the backside, or learning that he was carried from the field of battle and transported all the way to Cambridge wearing an absolutely ridiculous deer-stalker! Really, Albert, aren't you getting rather old for such antics?'

'My darling lady, how sweet of you to come visiting; but, I assure you, it's nothing serious. Did you bring grapes? I believe it's traditional.'

Lady Amanda Campion, née Fitton, stamped the heel of a fashionably long, zippered leather boot. Though the red hair framing her heart-shaped face no longer burned quite as fiercely bright as it once had, her brown eyes positively smouldered, providing all the heat that was needed in the situation.

'You, Albert, are a fool,' breathed Amanda, 'but you're my fool, I suppose; though I feel no obligation to supply you with fruit and veg. Fortunately for you, Lugg never visits a hospital without a bunch of flowers or a pound of seedless.'

Mr Campion raised his head from his regulation hospital pillow with the speed of a jack-in-the-box.

'Lugg? Lugg is here?'

'Is that all you can say?' demanded his wife, dragging a chair towards the bedside and sitting down firmly with the air of a judge waiting to hear evidence. 'I have told the old reprobate to wait outside and annoy the nurses until I have finished my interrogation. He insisted on coming. Once he heard you'd been shot, there was no stopping him. He's convinced you did it as part of some insurance fiddle.'

'How on Earth did Lugg get to hear?'

'He knew before I did,' growled Amanda through tight lips.

'My dear, I was out cold for several hours and in no position to contact any of my legion of nearest and dearest. To be honest, I have no idea how I got here from Lindsay. It was only when a charming angel of mercy brought me a cuppa and told me that this was good old Addenbrooke's, that I twigged I was in Cambridge.'

Lady Amanda pulled off a pair of cut-away leather driving gloves and placed them with her matching clutch purse in her lap, then fixed her glowing eyes on her husband who, lying there in bed with his head encased in a broad white bandage gave the impression of a pyjama-ed sultan taking his ease.

'Let me tell you what happened after you fell down a cliff,' she said sternly, 'though how you found a cliff to fall down in the middle of Suffolk is beyond me. Then you tell me what happened *before* that. Then – and only then – will I decide whether to kiss you or not. A kiss, I may add does not necessarily imply forgiveness. *That* may require a long period of contemplation, the consumption of a large portion of humble pie and any number of grovelling apologies. Is that clear?'

'Terrifyingly,' said Campion quietly.

'Good. Now this is what I have been told.' Amanda took a deep breath and marshalled her thoughts like a general placing his reserves before she began her attack.

'It seems you were shot by person or persons unknown, your gluteus maximus being mistaken for a passing pheasant or partridge or whatever it was you were slaughtering out there. Now I am reliably informed – and informed at great length and in gruesome detail by Lugg in the car coming up here – that birdshot in the derrière is (a) not fatal and (b) not at all uncommon when ruddy-faced agricultural types tramp across ploughed fields with loaded shotguns. Particularly–'Amanda lifted her chin and narrowed her eyes imperiously '– if they have partaken of a stirrup cup or two before setting out.'

Her husband covered his heart with his right hand.

'My dear, if there had been a judge in the shooting party, I would have been the more sober,' said Campion, trying out his most engaging smile. 'And I distinctly remember thinking "Zounds! I've been shot" but after that it all goes rather dim.'

'"Zounds"? Anyone who thinks that *ought* to

be shot and "dim" is a particularly apt description for your predicament, for you chose to get yourself shot whilst standing on the lip of some sort of quarry. Quite why you didn't go the whole hog and stand on the edge of a pool of piranhas I don't know, but anyway, over you went, after a rather spectacular pirouette by all accounts and fortunately landed on your head.'

'My least vulnerable spot,' quoted Campion, only to be ignored by his wife.

'Well you landed ... eventually, after bouncing off various boulders and torpedoing through bramble bushes, finally coming to rest face down in a stagnant pool where you would probably have drowned had you not been rescued by two ancient Suffolk yeomen with Old Testament names like Jeroboam and Balthazar.'

'They would have been the beaters working for the shoot,' said Mr Campion reasonably, 'rather than large measures of champagne.'

Amanda refused to have her narrative flow diverted.

'Whoever they were, they got you to a farm – Long Tye or something like that – and the local doctor was called. If he hadn't been in the village that morning, you'd have got the local vet instead and probably been put down. Luckily, for you the doctor remembered his Hippocrates and rang for an ambulance, and somebody had the presence of mind to telephone Eliza Jane. She tried to call me, but I was on my way up to the City for my meeting, so the resourceful girl did the sensible thing and phoned the police – a chap called Bill Bailey I think. Anyway, he knew

168

Charlie Luke and knew that Charlie knew you, so he called him, only to find he wasn't at the Yard but in a meeting with a highly valued informant round at Love Lane police station. You'll never guess who the valued informant was.'

'Lugg,' groaned the invalid.

'Bullseye! And so your valued retainer and fellow *boulevardier*, who just loves the role of bearer-of-bad-tidings, volunteers to trot around to the City and force his way into the board room of an ancient private bank where I am struggling to present the benefits of a delayed and over-budget British jet engine over a much cheaper American one which they could buy off the shelf. In some ways, Lugg's interruption was a bit of a relief and it was certainly dramatic. He made quite an impression on the assembled bankers.'

'He was wearing his working outfit was he? I can see where striped jumper, black mask and a bag marked "Swag" casually draped over the shoulder might not go down too well on Threadneedle Street.'

'What are you talking about Albert? Do you have concussion or are you trying to be funny? It really is difficult to tell.'

'My dear, it was you who said that Lugg was at the Love Lane cop shop and I naturally assumed...'

'Hold your tongue, you buffoon. Lugg was perfectly well dressed. In fact, a bit too well dressed: formal black jacket, waistcoat and morning trousers plus shiny bowler, he was quite the butler coming on for the second act in a murder mystery to announce that 'is lordship 'as been 'orribly done-to-death in the library. It transpires that the old boy, who is perfectly useless at retirement, is looking for a job and hoping Charlie Luke would give him a reference, but that's by-the-by. He volunteered to come and get me out of my meeting.'

'How on Earth did Lugg know where you'd be?'

'Unlike my darling husband,' Amanda said with glee, 'some people read the financial pages of the national press, not just the cartoon strips, and take an interest in my career. Lugg knew exactly where I'd be this morning and he barged in and announced, in a voice which could have called Cerberus to heel: "Sorry to interrupt yer meeting, me lady, but yer 'usband's gorn and got hisself shot!" after which you could have heard a pin drop.'

'At which point, I assume, you got the sympathy vote and the Board agreed with whatever you were proposing?'

'Absolutely. Perhaps you should get shot more often.'

'Hmmm.'

'Well, anyway, whilst Lugg was abducting me from the Square Mile, my resourceful niece insisted on accompanying you in the ambulance all the way to Addenbrooke's. She's still here, been mooching round Petty Cury, mingling with the hippies and the artists whilst the good doctors tried not giggle as they picked birdshot out of your nether regions with rusty tweezers. I told her to go shopping and splash out on anything she fancied as you would be happy to pick up the bill. Lugg's offered to take her for tea at the Copper Kettle later.'

'Then her day will be complete,' said Campion, 'but promise me you'll get her back to Lindsay Carfax.'

'No need. Some big hairy boyfriend is driving her car over as we speak. All she had to do was whistle and he dropped everything.'

'A well-known Fitton family trait ... albeit a delightful one.'

It was Amanda's turn to frown and say: 'Hmmm. Perhaps I will let that one pass and not add it to the list of charges I intend to bring against you, but for the moment, the prosecution will rest and allow the accused to defend himself by explaining just what the devil he's been up to.'

'May I ask, dearest, are you judge or jury?'

'Both – and prosecuting counsel, bailiff, court recorder, marshal at arms, custody officer and jailer. Any questions?'

'None at all.'

'Then proceed.'

Mr Campion sat up straight in bed and cleared his throat.

'May I beg the court's indulgence, M'Lud, and request that if the dreaded Lugg is lurking in the corridor terrifying tea ladies and playing with the bedpans, could he be invited in so that I do not have to repeat my dreary monologue?'

'The court will so allow,' said Amanda grandly, bowing formally to the invalid defendant before opening the door to the corridor and switching instantly from court usher to fairground barker. 'Roll up! Roll up! Step right in here, pay merely a sixpence and see the Great Beast of Suffolk laid low by a crack squad of police marksmen!'

Mr Campion shrank into his pillows, closed his eyes and pulled his regulation hospital sheets up to hide his blushes. He emerged only when he heard a loud and pointed cough, a sound as familiar as it was fake, to find a bowler-hatted Lugg standing at the end of his bed, a brown paper bag in one hand and a green plastic cup and saucer balanced in the other. He looked for all the world like an undertaker on a tea break between deliveries.

'I say, you haven't come to bury Caesar, have you?' asked Campion nervously.

'Well I certainly 'aven't come to praise 'im,' growled Lugg, his face as mobile as an Easter Island statue. 'An' as far as I know, they don't give out medals for them that's been shot in the arse, if you'll pardon my use of medical terminology, Lady A.'

'That's quite all right, Lugg,' Amanda said graciously.

'If we're using medical terminology,' Campion proclaimed, 'then the wonderful surgical staff at Addenbrooke's removed the majority of the pellets from my upper thigh. I am sorry to disappoint you but I doubt my misfortunes will be the subject of colourful postcards sold on the promenade at Clacton-on-Sea.'

'I prefer Frinton these days,' Lugg ruminated. 'Much classier, far more genteel. Very rarely do

172

people get shot in the backside in Frinton.'

'It is not all that common in Suffolk,' said Amanda, haughtily reasserting her judicial role. 'Now find yourself a chair, Lugg, drink your tea and give Albert a grape while he tells us what happened to him.'

Reluctantly Lugg did as he was ordered, blithely ignoring the mock outrage on Mr Campion's face as he produced a near-naked stalk holding no more than three or four grapes from the brown paper bag he had been handed. When settled on a creaking wooden chair, Lugg inhaled a draught from his teacup, smacked his lips and said:

''Suppose this tepid National Health brew will have to sustain me, though if I have to listen to one of 'is nibs's fairy tales, I could do with a drop of something stronger.'

'Even in Cambridge the pubs aren't open yet,' Campion observed, 'but I'm sure I can amuse you until they are.'

And so Campion began to relate his experiences in darkest Suffolk: a tale of mischief past and present, involving secret societies and Humble Boxes, ending with a flourish by plucking the last grape and waving the empty stalk in the air like a conductor's baton.

'What a lot of ridiculous nonsense!' declared Lady Amanda. 'Secret passages which everyone knows about, secret societies which aren't very secret and people who disappear then reappear after nine days. It's all stuff and nonsense from the days of vaudeville or variety, and just as risible or it would be if my niece hadn't almost tripped to her death and somebody had belted out a drum solo with a hammer on your Jaguar.'

'And the fact that I was shot,' Campion added mildly.

'Oh well, yes, I suppose – though it probably served you right. I haven't decided on that yet; the jury's still out.'

'You sure it wasn't f'r the insurance money?' asked Lugg leaning forward inquisitorially.

'Positive, my Old China, but thank you for your concern.'

'It sounds a bit of a dangerous place, this Lindsay Carfax, if the citizenry are taking pot shots at people. It's not an 'otbed of radicalism and revolution out to topple the h'aristocracy, is it?'

'Oh please, my dear Lugg, this is Suffolk we're talking about and in any case, they have their own local aristocrat but instead of dragging her through the streets in a tumbril, they seem happy for her to enjoy exile haunting the roulette tables in the south of France. An amazing old bat by all accounts – Lady Prunella Redcar. She's a distant relative of mine.'

'There's a surprise.'

'How odd; everyone seems to think that,' said Campion, furrowing his brow.

'And you ain't got a clue who potted you in the nether regions then?'

'Not a clue, but I'm sure it wasn't me. That leaves eight possible suspects, all local residents, I suspect, so they ought not to be difficult to find.'

'Find?' gasped Amanda. 'I can't believe you are thinking of going back there.'

174

'I can't believe he thinks there's only eight people what wants to shoot him!' added Lugg unhelpfully.

'Darling, I have to go back, if only to collect the Jaguar and I may be called upon to help the local police with their enquiries. That's what decent chaps like me do cheerfully, with a smile and whilst whistling a happy tune; whereas old recidivists such as Lugg have to be dragged kicking and screaming down the High Street before they'd give a copper the correct time.'

'Albert, if I wasn't married to you, I'd swear you really had concussion. However, the nice doctors here have assured me that between that stupid deerstalker jammed on your head – jammed so tight it almost had to be removed surgically – and the natural thickness of your skull, you have probably escaped any permanent damage. Let me assure you, dearest, that unless you stay right where you are, I will personally remedy that!'

'An' if yer do go back there,' said Lugg over a jutting jaw, 'then I's comin' wiv yer.'

'Don't be ridiculous, Lugg, you're far too old for any tomfoolery.' Campion smiled, he hoped benignly. 'Your campaigning days are over and it's feet-up-and-slippers time.'

'An' I would point out that you ain't no spring chicken yourself. Plus, I still have the use of both me legs *and* I'm not the one wearing more bandages than a Hindoo fakir at a fun fair. I could slip into this Carfax place on the q.t. and blend in wiv the indigenous population, find out what's what. Shouldn't take me more than a couple of evenings in the saloon bar of the local hostelry. They do have a local hostelry, don't they?'

'Not one you'd be allowed in and if you were, you certainly wouldn't go unnoticed. I do not, however, intend revisiting Lindsay Carfax just yet.'

'I should think not,' said Amanda resuming her judicial composure.

'But I will have to return at some point.'

'I do not see why.' Amanda segued from judge into wife. 'We can have the car picked up and Eliza Jane can see to any clothes and things you've left there. Don't try and convince me you're going back to ensure Eliza's safety because she's quite clearly capable of looking after herself; in fact she's obviously far better at that than you are. And if you dare to even *think* that you want to go back just to prove you can't be scared off, then I will give you something to be really scared of.'

'I believe you implicitly, my dear, and believe me I do realise that I am getting too old for this game. In fact the idea of feet-up and slippers in a quiet snug somewhere cheating at cribbage with Lugg is quite appealing at times, though I draw the line at the two of us wrapped in tartan blankets in matching bath chairs on the seafront at Frinton.'

Amanda gave a theatrical shudder as if someone had walked over her grave.

'Those are both quite disturbing images, Albert, but there's a twinkle of old in your eye which tells me you're not going to rest until you've solved this Carfax mystery.'

176

Mr Campion straightened his back against the pillows in a forlorn attempt at dignity.

'I have a proposal,' he began earnestly. 'I will continue to investigate the mysterious and, frankly, very silly goings-on in Lindsay Carfax whilst continuing my rest and recuperation here in the peace and tranquillity of dear old Cambridge. How's that for a plea of mitigation?'

'I'll take it under advisement and with a large pinch of salt. You are proposing to investigate by remote control? By psychic power? By using a ouija-board? And all from between those crisp hospital sheets, whilst religiously obeying your doctor's orders? I was born after you, Albert, but not yesterday.'

'I am perfectly serious, dearest,' said Campion, his face a picture of angelic innocence. 'I am told the good doctors of Addenbrooke's, having had their fun picking pellets out of me, are keen to see the back of me. In fact, I hear they could give me my marching orders tomorrow if I pass inspection at morning parade. I will beg, borrow or hire a fashionable walking cane to help keep my balance and perhaps use in my famous soft-shoe shuffle routine which has earned me a good living busking in front of Queen Victoria, The Prince Regent and...'

'...many other well-known pubs,' completed Lugg in a soft growl.

Mr Campion gently bowed his bandaged head in acknowledgement.

'Thank you my friend in the one-and-nines; glad you're paying attention as your services will be required.'

'I thought you'd dismissed the idea of inflicting Lugg on Lindsay Carfax,' said Amanda curtly.

'Oh I have,' said her husband. 'Lugg's usefulness lies here in Cambridge, not out on the front line in Suffolk. Whilst I remain here in comfort like some pampered Pasha, Lugg will tootle on down to Gnats where he will present my compliments to the Master and enquire within as to the availability of one of the college's most excellent guest rooms for possibly its most distinguished alumnus.'

Lugg turned to Lady Amanda with an expression that suggested both puzzlement and indigestion. *'Gnats?* Is 'e going back to school then?'

'I'd hardly call St Ignatius college a school,' said Amanda, 'it's more a reformatory for naughty boys of good breeding and excellent manners, though few ideas. It is reputed to have an excellent wine cellar, however.'

'Now you're talking,' smiled Lugg. 'Where do I find this 'ere Master? I'm assuming he's the big cheese, right?'

'You are correct, old fruit. Cheeses don't get any bigger or riper than when they are Masters of Cambridge colleges and some of them are quite blue as well. You'll find the college just down the road, a mere hop and a skip for a man on a mission such as yourself. Go out of the hospital, turn right and stroll down Trumpington Street and up King's Parade. Avert your eyes as you pass Peterhouse, for it is an old college which has not aged well. Ignore the siren call of Corpus Christi, for its pretty courtyards are natural traps

178

for the unwary, and whatever you do, do not be fooled by the imposing facade that is King's, for it is pure Hollywood and merely a large theatrical backdrop which could blow away in a high wind. By now you will be in Trinity Street and you'll find the hallowed cloisters of St Ignatius on your right, just across the road from Trinity, which we all know has ideas well above its station, most of them decidedly left-wing. Trinity's boast is that it has produced more Nobel Prize winners than France, whereas St Ignatius modestly claims fewer than Yorkshire. Is all that clear or should I draw you a map on the side of a bedpan? Students always find lots of inventive uses for bedpans.'

'Albert, behave!' commanded his wife. 'Or I will have the doctors check you for brain damage again; and this time I'll make sure they find some. Is that the extent of your grand plan? Holing up in your old college?'

'Where better? For an investigation such as this, a detective needs massive brain power and huge research facilities. I possess neither; Cambridge has both. So you see, darling, I will do my adventuring from the safe groves of academe and facing nothing more dangerous than a poorly kept claret, but before I can embrace the life collegiate, I must ask you one vital question. It is a question on which the entire outcome of this affair could rest and which only you can answer.'

'Oh, stow the amateur dramatics. What's the big question?'

'Did you bring your cheque book, dear?' Mr Campion asked politely.

* * *

As his own cheque book and his wallet were still safely (he hoped) locked in his suitcase in an oak wardrobe big enough to double as a sentry-box in his room at the Woolpack in Lindsay Carfax, Campion admitted he was short of funds. Even the loose change he had carried in a trouser pocket – approximately six-and-ninepence he recalled – had been scattered over the slopes of the Saxon Mills quarry as he had bounced down them. Therefore he was throwing himself on the mercy of his beloved wife who would, because she was a charitable and caring soul, now take herself to the nearest bank before it closed and withdraw sufficient funds to provide him with a small war chest to cover his stay in Cambridge, and to purchase an emergency supply of socks, shirts and underwear (or 'necessaries' as he called them, loosely translating the Latin), one pair of casual, but smart, trousers and if possible a smart jacket which did not appear *too* casual.

Amanda had asked, a touch sourly, if he needed shoes to go with his new ensemble and Campion remembered that he had arrived at Addenbrooke's on a stretcher, and the feet protruding from the blanket covering him had been encased in Wellington boots. Shoes were, therefore, a necessity.

'Nothing too outlandish, mind, nothing too "trendy" if that's the word,' he had mused, 'and though I've always had a fancy for a Cuban heel, sensible black brogues will do. Definitely not brown or the dons might mistake me for an officer and gentleman.'

'You'll get what you're given,' threatened his wife. 'Just be thankful I know all your sizes better than you do yourself. I am assuming that Cambridge has an Oxfam shop.' And her husband had sighed loudly with deep affection.

Amanda consulted her watch, a twenty-year-old gold Breitling Chronomat which hung heavily on her dainty wrist but was supremely functional rather than decorative, and decided that if she was to catch the banks whilst they were still open, she would have to leave immediately. Kissing her husband briefly on the lips, leaving just enough of her perfume under his nose to keep him content, she strode purposefully from the room. Lugg levered himself from his chair to follow her but Campion signalled for him to stay, then winced as Lugg screeched his chair across the floor until it was next to the bed.

'So, what's the real score, then?' said Lugg when the door had closed behind Amanda. 'I know you won't want to upset her Ladyship, but you can tell me.'

'Tell you what, old fruit?'

'Who it was who shot you?'

'I have honestly no idea. Could have been any one of eight, though Gus Marchant, the chap whose shoot it was, was farthest away down the line so I doubt it was he. Four of the guns I'd never laid eyes on before, so I can't see why they should hold a grudge against me.'

'Were they all locals?'

'I think so.'

'And you'd been in this Lindsay Carfax for how long?'

'Since Saturday.'

'That's plenty of time for you to upset people enough for them to take a pot-shot at you. I've known villages where they've lit the torches and sharpened their pitchforks before you've got out of the car.'

'Oh, very droll; and they insist music hall is dead,' said Campion suppressing a smile. 'Now stop playing the fool and tell me what's going on.'

'What's going on where? You don't think it was me popped you, do yer? Gawd knows there have been times...'

'Of course not...'

'...lots of times. In fact, times beyond number...'

'Oh do behave, or at least shut up. I want to know what you were doing at Love Lane police station with Charlie Luke.'

Campion's eyes widened as he saw that solid old Lugg, impenetrable Lugg, was actually blushing as he concentrated his own gaze downwards to the bowler hat resting on his knees, as if daring it to move.

'I was after a job,' he said eventually.

'With the police?'

'Nah – not me!' Lugg scoffed. 'There was a position in one of the Worshipful Companies – the old London Guilds – and I was hoping Charlie would write me a reference. Coming from 'im I thought it might negate the need for anyone to look too closely into police records.'

'Sound thinking, but I'm jolly aggrieved you didn't come to me, old chum. I'm a dab hand at forging Charlie's signature and I'm sure we could have invented a couple of dukes who would swear on paper that you'd been their loyal liegeman. You might even have saved their lives or numerous occasions. But seriously, Lugg, you should be retired and taking it easy at your age.'

'My age? I'd remind you, there ain't that much daylight between the two of us. It's you who should be taking it easy; at least I haven't been shot recently. I just thought that a bit of honest work, nothing too strenuous mind, would keep the brain and body ticking over and help me diddle the undertaker out of his profit for a few more years.'

'A noble sentiment, I'm sure,' said Mr Campion. 'We should all try to make less work for the undertaker and I trust the position you were seeking was a dignified one, as befits a person of your ... er ... experience?'

'Beadle,' said Lugg enigmatically.

'Excuse me?'

'Beadle. The job going vacant was for Beadle in one of the Livery Companies. Very dignified, light duties, fur-collared robes to be supplied along with use of a tipstaff, must be prepared to say Grace and call for the loyal toast at official banquets. Bit of cleaning of silver involved and supervision of kitchen staff, but the role is mostly ceremonial, with hardly no heavy lifting.'

'Sounds ideal,' said Campion. 'I don't suppose the position is with the Worshipful Company of Carders, if there is such a thing, is it?'

'What's a Carder when it's at home?'

'That, old son, is a jolly good question.'

With a blissful disregard for official visiting hours or the peace and quiet usually insisted upon for convalescent patients, Mr Campion's hospital room and the corridor which led to it saw more human traffic that afternoon than the Brighton road on a bank holiday. In addition to the nurses and doctors who had legitimate professional duties to perform, a stream of visitors did their best to disrupt the normally smooth-flowing current of hospital life, causing the smiles on even the most placid of nurses to quiver and crack. Only when a blue-uniformed ward sister, who was unused to smiling, sternly demanded a right of way for a tea-trolley which was on a mission to provide succour and refreshment for those 'who were *entitled* to be in the hospital' did the courtiers at Mr Campion's door look to their shoes and give way.

Lady Amanda, with the most right to be there also took up the most room, laden down as she was with parcels and bags, several announcing the fact that they had come from the emporia of Messrs. Ede & Ravenscroft (outfitters), Mr T.P. Coles (bespoke tailor) or Mr Joshua Taylor's department store. Her niece Eliza Jane ran her a close second with a rainbow selection of brightly coloured bags indicating that her shopping expedition had been at the more modern and esoteric end of the retail spectrum.

Eliza Jane had returned to Addenbrooke's once she judged she had done justice to her aunt's (and her uncle's, though unwittingly) line of credit, and almost simultaneously with the arrival of Ben Judd at the wheel of her tiny sports car. Once the amorous grapplings which are such a vital show of affection between young couples who have not seen each other for several hours were complete, and Eliza Jane had retrieved the parcels she had dropped during them, the necessary introductions were made to Amanda and then again to Lugg who had at the same moment returned from his errand to St Ignatius college.

Lugg, introduced as 'an old family friend', had accepted Judd's proffered hand and returned its iron grip with neither effort nor emotion before announcing casually that there was 'beat bobby' out on Trumpington Street taking 'an unoooshually close interest' in an illegally parked sports car. As if to prove Lugg incapable of telling a lie, the said uniformed constable appeared helmet in hand, as if on cue in the already bustling corridor. The swing door had hardly swung behind him when it was pushed open again to admit a red-faced and tweed-suited Gus Marchant with, on his arm, Mrs Clarissa Webster wearing a snug, a very snug, ivory two-piece, dangerously steep white high heels and a fox fur clinging for dear life to her shoulders.

'Judd! What are you doing here?' said Marchant over the shoulder of the policeman.

'I could ask the same, Marchant,' riposted the bullish artist puffing out his chest. 'Or perhaps we should ask how you have the nerve to show your face here?'

Before the confrontation of masculine forces could spit or splutter into flame, Amanda took command of the situation.

'Gentlemen – boys – let me remind you before one of the very nice nurses has to that this is a hospital, and whilst we're all here to see the same person I believe patients are allowed no more than one visitor at a time,' she declaimed in a voice which brooked no opposition. 'As it is my husband who has managed to get himself shot, I think by canon law, common law, custom and possibly even Magna Carta, I take precedence. I suggest therefore that you all retire to the Copper Kettle, where Mr Lugg here will treat you to tea and, if you are lucky, a bun. I can inform you all that my darling Albert is alive and almost back to full idiocy. For an updated health bulletin, please return here in an hour when you can mob the invalid to your heart's content.'

Amanda paused to draw breath and gather her bags and parcels together, then remembered the policeman standing silently among them, flexing his legs gently at the knees.

'Oh I'm sorry, officer, was there something you wanted?'

The constable, recognising authority when he heard it, cleared his throat nervously.

'It's about the red sports car parked outside, ma'm...'

'That will be mine!' said Eliza Jane chirpily, raising her hand as if in school.

'I told you it was,' Clarissa Webster said to Gus Marchant, 'just as we pulled up behind it, I said "I know that sweet little car", didn't I?'

The constable, who might not have been regarded as detective material by his superiors, nonetheless recognised a confession when he heard one.

'Then I suspect,' he said with gravitas, 'that there are now *two* vehicles illegally parked outside, seriously hindering access by ambulances to what is, after all, a hospital.'

'We will move them immediately, officer,' said Marchant with good-natured bluster, 'and we apologise for any inconvenience caused.'

'I'll do my own apologising, Marchant,' snarled Judd even as he realised he was being childish and Eliza Jane had reproached him with a playful cuff to his ear, after which he added, humbly: 'But I will move the damn car.'

'That's very kind of you two gentlemen,' the constable admitted generously, 'but before I accompany you outside, could I ask the lady what she meant when she said someone had been shot?'

'A matter of overgrown schoolboys playing with popguns down on the farm,' said Amanda confidently. 'A case of stupid carelessness, that's all.'

'An "agricultural accident" according to the h'insurance company,' Lugg added unhelpfully.

The constable did not look convinced.

'What if my Inspector has a few questions about this shooting "accident"?' he asked severely.

'I am told the incident, which is really rather farcical, is being fully investigated by Chief Inspector Bailey of the Suffolk Constabulary,' said Amanda sweetly.

'Never heard of him, m'am. I'm Mid-Anglia Constabulary, not Suffolk.'

'Well then, perhaps your Inspector would like to contact Superintendent Charles Luke of the Metropolitan CID, as he can certainly answer for my wayward husband.'

'I'm afraid I've never heard of him either,' admitted the constable, 'and I doubt my Inspector has. Is there anyone in Cambridge who can vouch for your husband?'

Amanda's smile became even sweeter.

'As a matter of fact, once he leaves the hospital he will be taking sanctuary with the Master of St Ignatius college, if that's any help.'

The constable's eyes widened.

'Yes it is, ma'm, you should have said...'

'So you have heard of the Master of St Ignatius'?' Amanda could not resist.

'Oh yes, ma'm, and so has my Inspector. In fact everyone – town and gown – has heard of *him*.'

Eleven

The Professor of Nines

Mr Campion's doctors had assured him that he seemed free of any lasting damage and that none of the seventeen pellets of birdshot they had removed had damaged anything more serious than his pride. In their very professional opinions, they were unanimously agreed that after a good night's rest and a final survey for signs of infection, he could expect to be discharged the next morning. Unlike the wicked, rest was not denied Mr Campion but it was delayed until he had granted audience to a string of persistent petitioners.

Amanda, of course, came first, bearing gifts suitable for the man-of-certain-years who had been caught away from home without a change of clothing saving a hospital gown and a pair of wellington boots. As she unpacked her purchases and displayed them, Mr Campion nodded his approval and if he had any sartorial doubts or misgivings, he hid them well, apologising that he was unable to leap out of his bed and perform a fashion parade to give her the full benefit of his new wardrobe. As usual, Amanda had been thorough in ministering to her husband's needs.

She had purchased underclothes, socks and shirts, a pair of silk cravats (one lime-green with black spots, the other a vibrant orange), dark blue flannel trousers, plain black leather slip-on shoes and a jacket in narrow brown corduroy complete with leather elbow patches, as well as a wash-bag with toiletries and a razor and a cheap hold-all to contain everything.

'I thought the jacket and trousers would help you blend in with the out-of-term dons here,' she said as if considering the image in her mind's eye, 'and with one of those understated cravats you could easily pass for a visiting professor from Ruritania.'

'I doubt that,' smiled Campion. 'Oxford perhaps, but not Ruritania where I believe they still have standards.'

Amanda raised her eyebrows disapprovingly. Had she been wearing spectacles, she would have frowned over the top of them.

'I think you're rather enjoying all this attention,' she said, 'and I can't allow that. Please refrain from any high jinks whilst in Cambridge.'

'I promise all my jinks will be low ones,' said her husband, pressing his right hand over his heart. 'In fact that's the motto of dear old St Ignatius College, you know.'

'I know it is not,' his wife replied, 'and please remember that jinks of any height are pretty much out of the question at your age. Promise me.'

'I promise, darling lady. No jinks above a millimetre. In fact, I think it best if I subcontract any potential jinks to someone much younger...'

'Al ... bert...' began Amanda in a gentle warning growl.

'Where is our beloved son and heir-to-not-very-much and his beautiful new bride at the moment?'

'Rupert and Perdita are recovering from their honeymoon and working hard to renovate and modernise the flat in St Peter's Gate Square as their marital home, which is something of a Herculean task in my opinion, but their hearts are set on it. Why do you ask?'

'Because I think our love-birds could do with a second honeymoon – one can never have too many. Say ... a few days in the South of France in a very decent hotel ... with perhaps a trip to the local casino one evening...'

Mr Campion's next visitors were Gus Marchant and Clarissa Webster.

While he gushed, almost genuflecting to the sick bed, with apologies for what had happened out at Saxon Mills, she made cooing, sympathetic noises although her gaze was almost completely fixed on Lady Amanda, who was later to describe the experience as 'akin to being in an X-ray machine'.

Gus Marchant assured Campion that he should concentrate on getting better and think nothing of the items he had left in his room at the Woolpack or his car, which was still being repaired at the Shermans' garage. In fact, he was not to worry about a thing and could be sure of a warm welcome on his return to Lindsay Carfax where the entire population were anxiously awaiting news of his recovery – especially Don at the Woolpack, whose latest theory was that Mr Campion was probably an international spy and therefore a target for assassination by persons or secret services unknown.

'Please do not disabuse Don of that notion,' Mr Campion had told him, 'for it will ensure prompt service and over-generous measures on my next visit, though I don't suppose that is something I should be telling the establishment's owner.'

Mr Marchant had laughed and shaken Campion's hand and Mrs Webster had leaned over the invalid – rather too generously, Amanda thought – and planted a brief kiss on his cheek, and then the pair had left, to be replaced by Eliza Jane and Ben Judd.

Whilst Eliza Jane comforted Amanda – though an Amanda no longer in need of emotional support – Judd pumped Campion's hand and swore that vengeance and, if possible, justice would be visited on the perpetrators of the heinous crime which had resulted in his hospitalisation.

It took some time for Mr Campion to convince Judd that his injuries were minor and that he had probably been the victim of an accident rather than a crime and when Eliza Jane wisely insisted they leave Mr Campion in peace, it was as if a summer storm had blown over and left the room.

For once, the arrival of Lugg, who had patiently been waiting his turn in the corridor, provided a calming, almost pastoral, atmosphere though he would do his best to dispel it.

'I don't trust that young feller Judd, you know,'

192

he declaimed without prompting. 'Bit of a h'educated tearaway if you ask me.'

'Nobody has,' observed Mr Campion.

'Says he's an artist; which covers a multitude
of sins in my opinion.'

'An opinion unsought by anyone here,' Campion sighed.

'Well, I reckon he uses his hands as fists more
than for holding a paintbrush and he's the sort
who'd start a fight in a confessional box.'

'And there speaks one who could try the
patience of the Dalai Lama. Now please make
your report. Have you been about your master's
business?'

'Oh, very droll, I'm sure,' said Lugg over a
curled lip. 'Yes, I've been round to St Ignatius
and called on the Master. Well, strictly speaking,
I had a bit of a conflab with Mr Gildart at the
front gate. Like-minded souls we are, so it turns
out, and we sorted you out good and proper over
a glass of very fine claret from the bottle he
keeps in the First Aid box.'

Mr Lugg smacked his lips at the memory and
his expression segued from the surly to the beatific.

'Gildart?' Campion spluttered. 'Gildart the
Head Porter? That's impossible. He must have
been at least sixty when I was an undergrad –
and we never did twig where he kept that never-
ending bottle.'

'Well it just proves you don't know everything,
which I thought all Cambridge men were supposed to.'

'No,' interjected Amanda, 'they just *think*

they do.'

'I am referring,' continued Lugg, 'to *young* Mr Gildart, who inherited the position from Mr Gildart Senior, the Gildart who had you down on his Most Wanted list when he was Head Porter and you were a spotty youth, or so I hear.'

'I am flattered that my notoriety has bridged the generation of gate-keepers,' said Campion, 'but I trust I am still welcome in those hallowed precincts?'

'Surprisingly it seems you are. Mr Gildart rang the Master and mentioned your name and when the college towers did not crack nor the walls start weeping blood, it seemed as if it was safe for you to stay there. Mr Gildart said he would make all the arrangements, as it was best not to trust the Master's memory on fine detail, and to inform you that it was the Master's habit out of term to take a light lunch in an establishment called the Panton Arms, if you know where that is.'

'My dear old fruit,' grinned Mr Campion, 'that is the one thing all Cambridge men *do* know.'

'Dr Livingstone, I presume!'

'Rudolph! You promised me you would never use that salutation again, you know it vexes me greatly.'

'I apologise, Master, I simply could not resist, just as you could not resist calling me by a name I abandoned, or at least put to the back of a very dark wardrobe, some time ago.'

The Master of St Ignatius College dipped the tankard of ale he was holding in deference to the

194

new arrival in the flagged courtyard of the Panton Arms, an area universally known (or at least by members of the university and the staff of the Perse School for Girls) as 'the garden'.

'Forgive me; I must remember it should be "Albert" when you are in *mufti*. The memory's going, you know. An old man's burden: so much to remember, in so little brain. Have you settled yourself into the guests' quarters? Is Gildart looking after you?'

'Yes to both questions, Master, but I challenge the poor assessment of your mental faculties. Surely not even your enemies would describe you as having a small brain.'

'I have enemies, do I?' the Master asked with a sly grin.

'You are the Master of a Cambridge College,' said Campion firmly, 'of course you do.'

'Then I had better,' laughed Dr Jolyon Livingstone, 'recruit you as an ally by buying you a flagon of the Panton's excellent ale.'

'My loyalty comes cheap,' replied Campion graciously. 'A half-pint will suffice.'

'And will you join me in a simple luncheon of bread and cheese and pickles? I take it you are dining in hall tonight?'

'Again, two answers in the affirmative, as long as the pickles are sharp not sweet and the dinner is not formal, as I have no dinner suit with me.'

'Worry not, old boy,' said his host, rising and pointing himself towards the pub door labelled Four Ale Bar, 'dinner will be just we happy few fellows who have no homes to go to and a plain gown is all that is required for form's sake. We always have a few spare in a cupboard some-where for the unwary and unprepared, rather like ties at the Reform Club. Sit down, dear boy; pull up a pew while I see to the victuals.'

Mr Campion straddled a low wooden bench with his long legs and inched in closer to the planked wooden table until he was comfortable. He noticed that the rough oak tabletop had suffered from that curse which befalls any piece of plain wood where there are men or boys around armed with a penknife or a pen nib. On closer observation, he was delighted to detect that the most common graffiti consisted not of the traditional whereabouts of 'Kilroy' or the affairs of star-crossed lovers, but rather complex algebraic equations. He allowed himself a smile and felt reassured that in Cambridge, the vandals still had ambitions.

He was distracted by the sight of Dr Livingstone zigzagging his way slowly across the courtyard bearing, at a gravity-defying angle, a square metal tray decorated with the heraldic arms of the owning brewing company on which sat, precariously, two piled plates of food, cutlery, an empty half-pint tankard and a large glass jug containing – unless Mr Campion's practised eye deceived him – about half a gallon of foaming ale.

The Master of St Ignatius College lowered his burden on to the table in front of Campion with a resounding thump and a sigh of relief, then wriggled himself between bench and table until he was comfortably wedged.

'Shall I be mother?' he asked, lifting the jug

and offering to pour.

'I really must insist on a small one only, Master.'

'Nonsense; it's only the ordinary bitter. We don't drink the strong stuff – the Abbot's Ale – during daylight,' said Livingstone cheerfully. 'Oh, I was forgetting, you're an invalid aren't you? Just released from Addenbrooke's, I hear.'

Mr Campion sipped beer and observed Dr Livingstone over the rim of his glass.

'Your time in Intelligence wasn't wasted, Jolyon. Do you have spies everywhere?'

'I would love to say that I have, but I would be fibbing. The truth is that last night I overheard a conversation between two junior Fellows from the Engineering faculty and they could hardly contain themselves they were so excited.' Dr Livingstone refilled his own glass from the jug before adding: 'Oh, not about *you*, Albert! They had spotted Lady Amanda Fitton – the famous aeroplane designer – on Trumpington Street. Apparently, she's something of a pin-up girl among engineers. I always said you had wived well, old chap.'

If the Master of St Ignatius had indeed ever said that, Campion had been blissfully unaware and whilst he mumbled the appropriate noises of a man embarrassed by an unfair portion of good fortune, he racked his brains to try and remember if Livingstone had actually met Amanda or was merely being polite. Campion and Livingstone had shared the late years of the war doing things in Intelligence which still, twenty-five years later, were never spoken of in public and only rarely in private. With the outbreak of peace, Livingston had returned to academia as a Fellow at St Ignatius and set his sights firmly on becoming the Master. What he lacked in talent he had made up for in dogged determination, a pedantic efficiency when it came to writing the interminable minutes of a thousand dull committees, and a robust constitution which helped him outlive his rivals. Although he was ten years younger than Campion, a life devoid of unnecessary physical exertion in a college noted for its kitchens and wine cellars had hastened middle-aged spread and, coupled with premature baldness thinly disguised by two or three straggling strands combed over his pate, Livingstone could easily have been mistaken for the older man.

As they broke bread, sliced cheese, speared pickled onions and sipped beer together, Livingstone steered the conversation into calm, willowy waters as if poling a punt on the Cam.

'I would think Cambridge has seen considerable changes since your day, old chap.'

'It must have,' Campion agreed politely. 'My time as a wastrel student is so far back it should be regarded as archaeology rather than history.'

Dr Livingstone waved a pickled onion skewered on his fork.

'Students don't change in my opinion. They may be badly dressed and unwashed now compared to our day, but they are just as rambunctious. At St Ignatius of course, they have a long tradition of high spirits to live up to, not to mention high jinks.'

Mr Campion, thinking of his wife, flinched

involuntarily but Dr Livingstone did not notice.

'It is part of college folklore that a certain undergraduate, caught trying to climb the gates after midnight, spent an hour persuading the Head Porter that he was in fact a werewolf who had misjudged the waning of the full moon and had turned back into human form before he could spring over the college wall.'

Mr Campion's complexion began to take on a pinkish hue.

'I believe that same student kept a pet jackdaw named Autolycus in his rooms,' continued the Master, 'and whilst such specific behaviour may seem quaint these days, the same *joie de vivre* permeates most aspects of student life. Oh, the political ones are loud and unruly and often appear thuggish – think of that trouble when the American ambassador visited a couple of years ago – and the whole Vietnam thing has got them hot under the collar. Still, let them protest I say, just remember that the longhaired one carrying the biggest banner today is quite likely to be the chief inspector of tomorrow.'

'You may very well be right,' said Campion, relieved that the Master had wandered away from the subject of his youthful college charge sheet.

'I am sure I am, but each to his own. Let others go on protest marches while we enjoy the simple pleasures which Cambridge offers. You are familiar with the Footlights Club, of course.'

'Certainly; in my day we used to meet in a Masonic Hall.'

Dr Livingstone appeared to be surprised at

Campion's answer.

'Yes, well it's quite professional nowadays. Anyone who can sing a comic song or play the absent-minded judge in a skit gets snapped up by the West End almost immediately, or even television! Musical revue is not always to my taste, though. I myself am a jazz man and we have quite a flourishing jazz scene here, you know. Only last week I heard Dan Pawson's Artesian Hall Stompers in full flow. They almost took the roof off the Corn Exchange!'

It was Mr Campion's turn to be surprised.

'I never had you down as a cool cat, Jolyon.'

'It keeps me young, and I find the reckless rhythms positively exhilarating. Was there jazz in your day, Albert?'

'You sound as if you are quoting bad poetry,' Campion said with a broad grin. *'And was there still jazz back then, when the world was young...?* Oh yes, we knew the difference between a tuba and a tailgate trombone. Jazz was not approved of, but it was hardly proscribed.'

'Cars were, though.'

'I'm sorry?' Campion was thrown by the Master's change of tack.

'Students were not allowed to own cars, but they are now. Some things remain, some things change. Young women – they were proscribed too.'

'I don't believe there was ever a universal embargo,' Campion observed.

'But now there's talk of mixed colleges and they will come, Campion, they will come. Certain colleges – and they know who they are – are even vying to be the first to admit women as if it was some sort of race with a prize!'

'I doubt very much if it would lead to the collapse of Western civilisation, but am I to take it that St Ignatius is not in the vanguard of this particular revolution?'

'I think we shall insist on being the last to change, should change be forced upon us.'

'Forgive me if I do not join you on the barricades, Master, but I happen to believe that an injection of young female ideas might just pump some life into the place. After all, a man has walked on the Moon this year and if that was but a small step for Man, then admitting women to St Ignatius would surely not be such a giant step.'

'Good Lord, Albert, you haven't turned into one of these liberationists have you? You'll be demanding a female Master or a woman prime minister next!'

Campion pushed his plate to the side and reached into a trouser pocket. He produced two pennies and a half-crown and laid them on the table with their obverse faces uppermost.

'There is one woman in a top job, and she's being doing it very well for more than sixteen years now,' he said softly.

'Er ... quite. Of course, I was forgetting your ... er ... absolutely. Anyway, Albert, enough of my ramblings. Is there anything St Ignatius can do for you other than bed and board? Of course, that is always a pleasure...'

'I am very grateful, Master, and you are as astute as ever. There is something else. I want to pick your brains.'

Dr Livingstone finished his last morsel of bread and reached into his jacket pocket for a pipe which looked like a carbonised tree stump and a brown leather tobacco pouch.

'My dear fellow, if you can find 'em, you're welcome to pick 'em.'

'It's a question of numbers,' Campion began.

'You do realise that I have not actually taught any mathematics for nearly twenty years,' Livingstone admitted almost proudly. 'That's a young man's game and I was fortunate to discover the fact early on in my career.'

'Your career as Reader in Mathematics at St Ignatius...' Campion prompted.

'Yes, well, it was clear to me that the college needed sound administrators rather than mathematical geniuses. Let King's and Trinity take all the glory; they will claim it anyway.'

'My problem is not a mathematical one, more a question of numbers in folklore I suspect,' said Campion as the Master began to fill his pipe, using a yellow-stained thumb to tamp down tobacco as firmly as wadding in a musket.

'Folklore, eh?' The Master was not taken aback at the suggestion; in fact, he became enthused. 'You have remembered my private passion for the arcane, the mysterious, the coincidental, the pattern in the random, the cryptic repetition, the unexplained blip on the smooth surface. Oh, the big thinkers dress it up as "statistical self-similarity" or "ergodic theory" or "random transitional phenomena". There's even something called "Hadamard's Billiards" theory, though I've quite forgotten who Hadamard was.'

'I am sure I never knew,' admitted Campion, 'but I do remember you were rather good at codes once upon a time, Master, and my question is really quite simple: what does the number nine mean to you?'

'The number nine?'

'Yes, the one after eight but before ten.'

Dr Livingstone took his time finding a match, then striking it and finally, after close examination to make sure it was lit, applying it to the cauldron that was the bowl of his pipe.

'Nine, eh? In what sense?'

'Any and all. Think of it as one of those word-association tests the trick-cyclists do. I say "nine" and you tell me whatever pops into your noggin.'

Dr Livingstone puffed on his pipe for almost a minute before answering. Campion suspected he did this whether he had been asked a question on theoretical mathematics, college politics or how many sugars he required in his tea.

'Let's start with the old parlour game,' he said at last. 'A real crowd-pleaser. Roll up, roll up and be amazed at the story of the Magic Nine!'

Mr Campion summoned up all the boyish enthusiasm he could muster.

'The Magic Nine! That sounds just the ticket! Do tell all.'

'Actually, it's not all that exciting, but when multiplied by itself or any other number, the sum of the result is always 9 or divisible by 9. Let me give you an example: 9 multiplied by 9 equals 81. The result is 8 + 1, which is 9, do you see?

You try one. How about 7 times 9?'

'63,' said Campion catching on, 'which is a 6 plus a 3 which is 9.'

'Correct. How about 127 multiplied by 9?'

'1,143,' Campion answered after a diplomatic piece of mugging, 'and that's 1+ 1 + 4 + 3 which adds up to 9 again.'

'Good; now give me one.'

'444.'

'Easy enough,' said the Master. 'Multiplied by nine equals 3,996, which is 3 + 9 + 9 + 6 which adds up to 27, which can be divided by – you've guessed it – 9. Give the man a coconut. It works every time and breaks the ice at parties. Is that the sort of thing you're after?'

'Not really, but it's a good trick. Think of more folkloric connotations of nine, the more ridiculous the better.'

'You mean things like the Nine Worthies; the *Neun Gute Helden* of German myth? The Nine Good Heroes – three pagans, three Jews and three Christians. Or the Nine Muses, perhaps? You know there's a don at Magdalene who has three daughters named Calliope, Thalia and Terpsichore, though I'm not sure his wife approved.

'In many cultures nine is seen as a number symbolising perfection and totality, which I suppose stems from the accepted number of months in a pregnancy. In Hebrew, nine represents intelligence; to the Hindu it's the number of fire. According to a recent paper by a Professor Satterthwait of the University of New Mexico – yes, they have universities even there now – the Navajo Indians put great faith in healing ceremonies which last nine days. Is any of this useful to you, Albert?'

'Indirectly. It all helps to get the juices flowing. Keep going, keep going.'

'Well then, the number nine appears in scripture of course – notably in Romans Chapter 12, which reports the Nine Gifts of the Holy Spirit – and there are supposed to be nine cases of stoning in the Bible, which some would say is statistically significant. There's also the Nine Card Spread, which is a method of reading Tarot cards, or so I'm told, and Chinese and Japanese myths of fox spirits or vampire cats, both distinguished by having nine tails.

'The famous Cat O' Nine Tails was that indispensable aid to discipline employed by the Royal Navy when Jack Tars were anything but Jolly and we all know from Shakespeare that cats have nine lives. Was it not Romeo who demanded nothing from that "good king of cats" Tybalt "but one of your nine lives"?'

'I think it was Mercutio, not Romeo,' said Campion discreetly.

Dr Livingstone puffed smoked to cover his error.

'In common parlance, of course, examples abound. After all, what does a stitch in time save? And when one wants to impress in society, one always makes sure one is "dressed to the nines" which is thought to be a Victorian reference to the nine yards of cloth needed to make a good suit or the dress uniform of an officer in the 99th Lanarkshires, whichever you prefer. And when confronted by rogues, villains and cut-purses, one dials, of course, three nines.

'There is also–' Livingstone's pipe bubbled noisily for dramatic effect '–quite a well-known detective novel called *Nine Times Nine* by an American chappie called H.H. Holmes; a pseudonym, obviously. Also, one of those long-haired "pop" groups so beloved by adolescent girls made a record last year and one of the songs was called *Revolution 9*. The Dean of Music referred to it as "eight minutes of hell" but I haven't heard it myself.'

'Fascinating,' said Campion.

'But hardly illuminating, I would have thought.'

'You are being very patient with me, Master. As you will have surmised, I really have no idea what I am looking for; rather hoping for a spark which might lead to illumination. Please humour me.'

'I am the Master of a Cambridge college,' said Livingstone pushing out his chest proudly. 'It is part of my calling to humour people.'

'Then pray continue,' said Mr Campion with due deference. 'What does the phrase "Nine Days Wonder" bring to mind?'

'Why, Charles of Valois of course.'

Mr Campion had the feeling that the Master had been guarding that particular nugget of information like a gambler with one ace in the hole and another up his sleeve. He waited in silence, pleading for enlightenment, until the Master deigned to continue.

'It was Charles who wrote: *A wonder last but*

206

dayes nyne, an oold proverb is said. That is probably the earliest reference in literature to a Nine Days Wonder or, to be literal, a wonder lasting only days nine, according to a proverb that was in common parlance at the time; and that would be the 15th century of course.'

Campion, suitably vacant, waited again for Dr Livingstone to enlighten him.

'Charles of Valois, the Duc d'Orleans, a noble French knight who, at the age of about twenty-one, was wounded and captured at Agincourt in 1415 by our own, our very own, even more noble King Henry V. For some reason, Henry took against Charles and he was not put up for ransom as was the custom in those days among the warring aristocracy. Instead, poor Charles spent twenty-four years in England as a prisoner-of-war, some of it in Oxford for pity's sake! No wonder the poor man turned to writing poetry and it was remarkably good, if, that is, you appreciate a *ballade* or a *rondeau*. The debate as to whether he translated his own work into English still induces heart attacks in our medievalists I'm told, but when the poor man was eventually released and sent back to France, it was said he spoke English because he'd forgotten his French.'

'Fascinating,' breathed Campion.

'But no sudden flash of light?'

'Not yet.'

'Well then, how about a more modern reference – say, the sixteenth century?'

'That sounds positively with it.'

Dr Livingstone eyed him suspiciously, but

Campion remained the picture of an adoring audience prepared to hang on every word and that was irresistible.

'Kemp's Jig,' prompted the Master.

Campion furrowed his brow.

'Will Kemp? Shakespeare's clown?'

'Almost probably,' said Dr Livingstone enigmatically. 'He was certainly one of the Lord Chamberlain's Men and a noted comic actor in what we would call the slapstick tradition, but current thinking is that he had a bit of a bust-up with Shakespeare. He was a big draw for his time and its must have gone to his head. Well, he was an actor so one really should not expect anything else. He must have wanted to include a Morris dancing scene in *Richard III* as comic relief during the battle of Bosworth, or have a walk-on part with his wooden dog-on-wheels just as Juliet was dying for the second time; something like that. I think the modern term is "artistic differences". Kemp and Shakespeare certainly had them and Kemp was either fired or quit in a huff.

'Determined to show he was still a big star, Kemp embarked on his famous Jig in the year 1600. He told anyone who would listen that he could *dance* from London to Norwich in nine days, though why anyone should want to go to Norwich at all is a mystery lost in the mists of time. His dance, his jig, complete with bells and no doubt whistles, caught the imagination and he became a bit of a national hero. I think I remember reading something about him not going down too well in Bury St Edmunds, but then, little does. Yet, with rests along the way, Kemp did indeed reach Norwich after nine days of dancing and the city council were more or less forced to stump up some prize money for him, though what he did with it I have no idea and I do not think his career was revived by what was clearly a publicity stunt. It did, however, refresh the popular concept of a "Nine Days Wonder" and the phrase became synonymous with Kemp's nine-day jig to Norwich. Of course, nobody remembers Will Kemp nowadays; or even what his name signified.'

'His name?'

'Well it has always been a pet theory of mine that Kemp's Jig to Norwich was a publicity stunt.'

'To revive his career as a thespian, you said.'

'Oh, that was his personal motive, I'm sure. It would have been one in the eye for Shakespeare certainly, but I think the whole stunt was a put-up job by the wool merchants and I bet that was where the prize money came from.'

'I'm not exactly lost, Master, but I have wandered off your track slightly,' Campion admitted.

'Oh do wake up, Albert. What was East Anglia famous for before the industrial revolution? Wool! Wool was the source of wealth and power round here; the life blood of the economy and vitally important. Having Will Kemp, the most famous clown on the London stage, Morris-dance his way through all those wool towns and markets would have been the equivalent of having one of today's film stars saying he drank your particular brew of ale, or smoked your brand of cigarettes. There's a name for it: celebrity something-or-other.'

'Endorsement, I think,' supplied Campion.

'That's it; and my theory is that Kemp could be persuaded to do such a stunt because he clearly had family ties to the industry.'

'I'm afraid my compass is wavering and I'm wandering again, Master.'

'His name gives it away. Kemp is the term for the short hairs on a sheep's fleece; the hairs between the skin and the good wool. To have a name like that back in those days meant that his family would have been in the wool trade at some point, I'm sure of it. Have I lost you completely, Albert? If you'll forgive me, you are looking even vaguer than usual.'

Campion smiled broadly.

'Not lost at all, Master. In fact I think you've helped me see the light.'

Twelve

Digging Dirt

Mr Campion dined well in St Ignatius hall and slept soundly in a St Ignatius guest bed, to be woken at the traditional and very civilised St Ignatius breakfast hour of nine o'clock (ironically a nine the Master had forgotten to mention) by a gentle tapping on the door of his rooms. Wearing surgical-green thin cotton pyjamas, which he could only suppose that Amanda had bought for him as some form of punishment, Campion answered the knocking summons to find the Head Porter, resplendent in frock coat and top hat, standing almost to attention holding a silver tray containing a teapot, a jug of milk, a bowl of sugar cubes complete with tongs, one cup, one saucer and one teaspoon, college guests for the use of.

'My goodness, I am honoured,' gushed Campion. 'So honoured I might even swoon. Breakfast in bed – or as good as – courtesy of Mr Gildart, a courtesy never offered by your father in the three years I was here legitimately.'

Mr Gildart (?Junior) cleared his throat.

'My father always said that "legitimately" was not a word used by gentlemen, sir, because a

211

gentleman never had to.'

'And I am sure he was quite right in all particulars. He certainly taught me never to argue with a Head Porter, nor look a tea-tray in the mouth as one might a gift horse,' Campion jabbered, relieving Gildart Junior of the tray. 'Unless this is a wooden horse, as in Troy, and has been built by Greeks. Is there, perchance, an ulterior motive to your most excellent room service?'

'Yes there is, sir, very well deduced if I may say so. You're not half as vacant as they say you are. There's a policeman waiting to see you. I've put him in the Library.'

'The college has a Library?' Campion feigned horror because he simply could not resist. 'If only I had known that in my student days, it would probably have been jolly useful.'

Detective Chief Inspector Bill Bailey had, in what he regarded as his modest career, investigated crimes in churches, castles and (once) in a nunnery; had, unarmed, arrested suspects wielding knives, axes and (once) a scythe; and had interviewed knights of the realm, the occasional duke and (more than once) a marquis. Yet never could he remember feeling more socially uncomfortable than he was at that moment, having been confined in the St Ignatius Library by the head porter who acted every inch the gaoler to his prisoner.

Had he but taken a moment to run a finger over the leather-bound spines of the volumes which lined the walls of the rather small and rather gloomy windowless room, he might have felt less intimidated. His sharp policeman's eye would surely have recognised, even though the gold lettering was small and often faded, some of the works of Mr Hank Janson, Mr Harold Robbins and Miss Pauline Réage, albeit in unfamiliar rich red-leather bindings, nestling quietly between Suetonius, Herodotus, Gibbon, Thackeray and several complete sets of Dickens.

But Bill Bailey was not a book man; he heard quite enough fiction from suspects, victims, known villains and sometimes even policemen, without having to peruse dusty volumes. He settled himself in a creaking leather wing-back, stretched his legs and splayed his feet out taking comfort in the old adage that a policeman's feet should never miss an opportunity to have the weight lifted from them. He was in that contemplative position when Campion limped in.

'Chief Inspector, how delightful to see you unless, that is, my many and varied undergraduate misdemeanours have been resurrected and the Master – or more likely the head porter – has called in the long arm of the Law.'

'I can't speak for the Master of the college,' said Bailey, 'but I have met the Head Porter and he doesn't look the sort of bloke who would need any help from the Law when it comes to dealing with student misdemeanours.'

'It runs in the family,' said Campion in agreement, 'or perhaps they simply breed head porters that way, but if I'm in the clear, to what do I owe the honour of this visit?'

'Mostly for my peace of mind, Mr Campion, because if I didn't come and make sure you were

213

hale and hearty, then a certain Charles Luke of the Metropolitan Police is unlikely to give me any peace and, in any case, something has popped into my mind.'

'I am flattered by the first and intrigued by the second,' said Campion settling himself carefully into the twin of Bailey's chair. 'Please convey my best to Superintendent Luke and assure him that, as you can see, I am intact if not quite as sprightly as usual. However, I am told that after a reasonable period of rest and recuperation I will resume my punishing training schedule with a view to securing my place in the next Olympics. Munich is such a charming city.'

'Might I enquire as to which sport you would participate in?' asked the policeman drily.

'Why hopscotch of course and I think we have a real chance of a medal this time. But enough of my prattle, Chief Inspector, you said something had sprung to mind.'

'Yes, sir, it did, thanks to your niece Miss Fitton.'

'Eliza Jane is making herself useful? I'm delighted to hear it.'

'It was while she was giving us a statement about your little ... accident ... out at Long Tye Farm, or rather the Saxon Mills quarry you slipped into.'

'Slipped? I would have said "plunged" or "plummeted" was more accurate. I suspect it was quite a spectacular dying swan dive. I almost wish I could have seen it myself.'

'Well, Miss Fitton remarked that the place must be cursed.'

214

'Cursed? That's a bit dramatic even for a highly-strung temperamental artist.'

'I wouldn't say Miss Fitton struck me as highly-strung, sir, or particularly temperamental,' Bailey observed seriously.

'Of course she isn't,' said Campion, 'but she *is* an artist, which allows me to make sweeping generalisations. I take it that when Eliza Jane said "cursed" she didn't mean literally, in the sense of involving eyes of newt and tongues of frogs, numerous witches and a cat buried under the doorstep...'

Detective Chief Inspector Bailey sighed loudly.

'No, sir, not a curse as in black magic or what-have-you, she just meant an unlucky place. And by the way, sir, the old Suffolk custom of burying a dead cat under the front doorstep was supposed to keep witches and curses *out* of the family home.'

'I think I knew that,' said Mr Campion, chastised by the policeman's proud Suffolk glare, 'and I certainly did not mean to offend. That's the trouble with this Cambridge air; it frees the brain but also loosens the tongue. I will be quiet. *Persevero perpetuus*, as they say around here; though not very often.'

Mr Bailey chose to steer the safest course in the conversation by ignoring Mr Campion in the way only seasoned policeman can ignore someone sitting in the same room less than an arm's length away; that is to say, both politely and completely.

'Miss Fitton brought to our attention the fact

that the quarry pit known as Saxon Mills has been the scene of some unfortunate incidents in the past. Last year, as you know, there were two drug-related deaths of young men, archaeology students, who had been camping out at Saxon Mills.'

'But I believe you told us their bodies had been found in a local barn,' said a suddenly serious Campion.

'I did, and they were; but Miss Fitton was referring to an earlier incident – much earlier – when a body was found there back in 1937.'

'But good heavens, my dear chap, Eliza Jane wasn't even a twinkle in her father's eye back in 1937.'

'I do realise that, sir,' said Bailey patiently. 'Miss Fitton was referring to something she'd been told, about how a chap called Johnnie Sirrah had been found in the bottom of that gravel pit with his neck broken, just about where you ended up.'

'Then it is a cursed place indeed,' said Campion, 'and explains something Charlie Luke said at the outset of this business; that something had happened at Lindsay Carfax over thirty years ago which he would have treated as murder if he had been on the spot. Who was this Johnnie Sirrah fellow?'

'Can't say we know very much about him, not at this remove, but I dug out the paperwork, such as it was, on the case. It was treated as a suspicious death to begin with but the coroner eventually settled on death by misadventure given that the late Mr Sirrah was found with an almost empty half-bottle of Scotch in one jacket pocket and a full half-bottle in the other.'

'The theory being what? That he was out for a drunken stagger across a ploughed field and went head-first into a gaping quarry, bouncing all the way to the bottom just like I did?'

'Something like that, sir, yes.'

'And his tumbling act broke his neck but did not damage either of the bottles he was carrying? I'm impressed. I must try and incorporate that trick into my cheapjack carnival routine.'

Bill Bailey cleared his throat.

'Be that as it may, sir, there seems to have been enough circumstantial evidence, or gossip if you prefer, that Mr Sirrah was a bit of a dedicated reveller and fond of the odd night of heavy boozing. He had a touch of form, as we'd say these days, mostly for drunk and disorderly or causing a public nuisance but he was forgiven a lot by the Magistrates he came up against.'

'Why was that?'

'Well he had what the papers called "film-star looks" for one thing and had appeared in revue in the West End I believe, so he could put on a good show and probably scrubbed up well. He fancied himself as a literary man and even tried his hand at poetry. He was also a bit of a hero, having been one of the first to volunteer to go and fight Franco's fascists in 1936, though he earned his portion of glory as a stretcher-bearer under fire during the attack on Madrid. That made him a real heartthrob among the ladies but the experience turned him well to the left and also did for his nerves. Understandable really, he was still pretty young.

'He came back to England in '37 and took a cottage in Lindsay Carfax to rest and recuperate and found himself a girlfriend, though that didn't stop him taking up various causes: pro-trades unionism, anti-fox hunting; anti-Nazi, obviously, but pro-independence for India. Wrote a letter a week to *The Times*, including one quite famous one marked for the attention of Mr Winston Churchill, which basically said: Dear Winston, you're wrong about Gandhi but dead right about Hitler.

'A bright lad by all accounts and always ready to get involved in causes, lost or otherwise, but then he just disappeared one night and turned up dead nine days later in the gravel pit.'

'Nine days, eh? I bet the Carders claimed the credit for that,' said Campion.

'If there was any credit going, they would have,' Bill Bailey agreed, 'just as they would have avoided any blame.'

'And the police investigation?'

'Nothing to do with me, I'm happy – but not proud – to say. It started as a Missing Persons case and for a while was considered as a Suspicious Death but once the coroner decided it was almost certainly accidental with drink involved, that more or less put it to bed and nobody gave the case much of a thought until you took your dive into the quarry and ended up almost exactly where Johnnie Sirrah did.'

Mr Campion stroked his chin thoughtfully.

'In your dusty police files, was there by any chance a note of who reported Johnnie Sirrah missing?'

'Matter of fact there was: it was Mrs Clarissa Webster who I believe is a friend of your niece. Back then, of course, she was Clarissa Pinner and she was the girlfriend Sirrah had found in Lindsay Carfax.'

If he had ever given the subject much thought, which he had not, Mr Campion's ideal archaeologist would have been a tall, muscular, sunbronzed figure; a man of military bearing, with a pencil dark moustache and gleaming teeth, dressed in jodhpurs, riding boots and pith helmet. He would be fluent in at least a dozen languages – ancient and modern – of the Middle East, and be accompanied everywhere by a fiercely loyal Sikh manservant with a ruby in his turban and several curved daggers concealed about his person. He would be the sort of man who was fatherly to his army of native diggers and who would not give a fig for a Pharaoh's curse.

Dr Mortimer Casson, however, was short, skinny to the point of emaciation and had buck teeth which made him lisp when he spoke. His hair was unkempt, unwashed and unruly and Campion thought he still detected boyish curls which had survived what were clearly Dr Casson's attempts at self-barbering. At least, Mr Campion hoped the haircut has been self-inflicted; if it had been paid for, it had been a fee extorted under false pretences.

The young Dr Casson, for Campion quickly catalogued him within Eliza Jane's generation, did not look like the sort of archaeologist who would fearlessly force his way into the bowels of a pyramid or hack through jungle to find Aztec gold; in fact he looked like the sort of pale, wan and strangely loitering schoolboy who always volunteered to stay in the pavilion and do the scoring at cricket matches. Yet the Master of St Ignatius had described him as 'a coming mind' in his field and despite the tragedy of the previous year would be just the man to answer Campion's questions on the history and folklore of Lindsay Carfax. Campion had not, naturally, informed the Master that his main interest in interviewing Dr Casson was far from archaeological and did indeed concern the recent tragedy which had befallen his students.

'Come in and make yourself comfortable among the chaos, if you can,' Dr Casson had greeted him when Mr Campion had called on him and on entering the archaeologist's college rooms, he realised it had not been an empty threat.

Campion was sure there was a desk some-where in the room but it took him several min-utes to ascertain its outline, surrounded as it was by piled wooden beer crates bearing the name Bullards or Steward and Patteson, a variety of metal tools and implements leaning against it and the floor leading to it seeded with a mine-field of metal buckets full of trowels, brushes and hand-tools which looked medieval but were probably of garden origin.

As though adjusting his eyesight to rapidly-falling dusk, Campion reassured himself that the beer crates were full of pottery shards, the military ranks of weapons standing, or leaning, to attention were shovels, hoes, mattocks, a folded metal tripod, a collapsed wooden ranging staff and the buckets, trowels, brushes, scrapers and forking tools of torture were all, in fact, legitimate equipment for the practising archaeologist about town. It was just that he had never seen so much of it in such a confined space before.

'Sorry about the mess, but there is a chair in here somewhere,' Dr Casson promised. 'I have to keep all this equipment here so I can keep an eye on it. We lock our wheelbarrows in the groundsman's shed but you'd be surprised how much goes missing.'

'Student pranks, I suppose,' said Campion.

'No, Dons with wives who've taken to gardening, I'm afraid,' admitted Casson. 'I've even caught one walking off with a bucket full of *tesserae* thinking they would make a nice surround for a rose bush. Ah, here we are.'

The younger man had ploughed his way through the clutter and lifted a pile of books and papers in both arms to reveal a small wooden chair. Unceremoniously he dropped his burden to the floor and a cloud of fine dust rose around him to waist height.

'You sit here; I'll perch on the edge of the desk.' Casson snorted a laugh. 'If I can find it, that is!'

'As an archaeologist, I'm sure you are very proficient at digging up things long buried,' Campion said jovially as Casson cleared the desk top of papers, notebooks and large sheets of tracing-paper plans and maps by scooping them up by the armful and depositing them casually wherever they fell. It reminded Campion of a man frantically trying to bail out a sinking rowing boat with a colander.

Eventually Dr Casson decided he had cleared sufficient space at one corner and settled his rump there but as he had made no attempt to clear away the long-handled tools leaning against the edge of the desk, only his head was clearly visible to his visitor, giving the impression that he was peering over some rude battlement or ancient wooden fortification which, Mr Campion thought, was probably quite an apt state of affairs for an archaeologist.

'Now what can I do for you, Professor Campion?'

'You flatter me, Dr Casson. I am not a professor and the only chair I hold is the one I am sitting upon temporarily.'

'But the Master described you as a Distinguished Visitor...'

'You clearly heard capital letters where none were intended, or indeed deserved. I like to think I may be distinguished in some things, though none of them have any bearing on our meeting today, but I am only a visitor to Cambridge in a general sense, though now I am here I simply had to see you.'

'Me? What have I done?'

'Nothing illegal, as far as I know,' said Campion affably, 'but I was hoping you could help me.'

'With what?' Dr Casson remained outwardly

calm, but his voice had risen a tone.

'About what happened at Lindsay Carfax.'

'Oh, *Christus*, not again. I wish I'd never heard of that damned place.'

'I appreciate you must have been asked before...'

'By the police, by the Dean, by the Faculty, by the press, by the parents ... the parents, that was the worst.'

'The parents of the two students who died?' Campion prompted gently.

Dr Casson nodded his drooping head.

'Stephen Stotter and Martin Rees – both of them good guys and good diggers – and neither deserved what happened to them.'

'Can you tell me the background to their deaths? I assure you I do not ask out of morbid curiosity, but I do have an interest in things unexplained in Lindsay Carfax.' As if on cue, Mr Campion felt a twinge in his thigh which was still tender after the ministrations of Addenbrooke's surgeons. 'In fact you might say I have a vested interest in events there which may or may not be connected.'

'Connected? Steve and Marty died a year ago.'

'I get the feeling that some things fester in Lindsay Carfax for far longer than a year,' said Campion soberly. 'I think that what happened to your students could be just one piece of a rather strange jigsaw puzzle. I would greatly appreciate it if you could tell me what happened.'

'Very well, as long as I don't have to go to that awful place myself I don't suppose it can do any harm – or any more harm – and the Master has

told me I should assist you, so I suppose I must.'
Dr Casson's hands plunged into the pockets of
his jacket and he produced a pack of cigarettes
and a cheap French stick lighter. Nervously he lit
a cigarette and was returning the pack to his
pocket when he seemed to remember his manners. 'Oh, sorry; did you want a gasper?'

'No thank you. My doctor told me I could extend my life if I stopped smoking and my wife
guaranteed me the opposite if I did not.'

'We all have our vices,' said Casson, rather
primly.

'We do indeed,' agreed Mr Campion, 'and
mine is curiosity. I am keen to know why you
dispatched your diggers to Lindsay Carfax in the
first place.'

Dr Casson wearily exhaled a cloud of smoke.

'Saxon Mills seemed like the ideal place for
the usual training dig for first year undergrads. It
should have been. It was not a difficult site
archaeologically, it wasn't that far away and it
was a safe place to dig.'

'Safe?' Campion queried.

'The site was on agricultural land, away from
busy roads, fast-flowing water and falling rocks,
that sort of thing, though of course the place
didn't turn out to be safe for Steve and Marty.'

'What were they expecting to find there?'

'Frankly, nothing we did not already know was
there, which, that is to say, nothing much. The
name Saxon Mills goes back to Domesday but if
there ever was actually a mill there, it was probably long gone by the time the land was given to
the monks of Lindsay Carfax so they could build

224

an abbey. Along came Henry VIII with his Re-formation and bang went the abbey – probably quite literally. Most of the stone would have been robbed to use in buildings elsewhere and quarrying in the 19th century finished the job, but there are still traces of the place if you know where and how to look for them. As I say, a perfect place for a training dig; no difficult strati-fication, no complex plans to draw, and the chance to practice digging and recording small features with little risk of damaging anything archaeologically important. There was also the chance of small finds, mostly pottery but perhaps a coin or a metal spoon, which is always good for morale and keeps the diggers keen.'

'And you were supervising them?'

'In Cambridge I was their academic super-visor, but out at Saxon Mills, Steve Stotter was the site supervisor.'

'A first-year undergraduate?' Campion failed to suppress the surprise in his voice.

'That's perfectly usual on a training dig in this country and at Cambridge we believe in giving our students responsibility. In any case, Steve had been going on digs since he was a school-boy. He was a natural at it.'

'And he was in charge of...?'

'There were four others, all first-years, but they were level-headed and I had complete faith in all of them – as diggers, that is.'

Dr Casson stared mournfully at his knees for a moment, then at the cigarette in his hand and then he began casting around for somewhere to extinguish it, finally deciding on a metal bucket which bloomed with trowels and metal hand-shovels.

'Just out of interest,' Campion asked, 'did they find anything?'

'Not a sausage – well not a sausage of any interest. They even went over the entire site with the mine detector.'

'Mine detector?'

'That's what the policeman who returned it called it. He gave me quite a lecture on how he'd used one at El Alamein or somewhere and couldn't understand why we should have one with *Property of St Ignatius College* stamped on it. It's a metal detector of course, but it works on much the same principles as the old wartime ones; in fact the detector and the telescopic level were just about the only bits of equipment we got back. Of course metal detecting on site is frowned upon by the purists, but archaeologists have been using them since 1929 when Mussolini ordered the excavation of Caligula's Imperial sailing barges from the bottom of Lake Nemi.'

'But no Imperial metals detected at Saxon Mills, I suppose?'

'Ha-bloody-hah!' Casson scoffed loudly. 'Fat chance! The only thing they found – and very carefully excavated – was a starting handle!'

Mr Campion raised an eyebrow.

'So would that be a Saxon, or a Tudor, starting handle?'

'Oh never fear, we did all the jokes. It turned out to be the starting handle from a 1935 Austin 7. Several of the older Dons identified it straight away. Some of them are still driving their Austin

226

7s with pride and all of them seemed to have owned one at one time.'

'So the dig was not a success?'

'As a training exercise it seemed to be going very well, and then the hippies turned up and things got out of hand. That's when it turned into a disaster.'

Campion felt a wave of sympathy for the young archaeologist, for it was clear that conjuring memories of Saxon Mills was distressing him.

'Would you tell me what happened?'

Dr Casson fumbled for another cigarette and when he could hide behind a cloud of exhaled smoke he said:

'As much as I can. I wasn't there of course, not after the first day. I drove them over to Lindsay Carfax in one of the college vans with their gear. It was almost as if they were going on a camping holiday; they were all singing and cracking jokes in the back of the van – couldn't have been happier. We were met at Long Tye Farm and we unloaded...'

'Met by whom?' Campion interrupted gently.

'We had written permission from the land owner, Gus Marchant, of course, but we were met by a chap called Fuller.'

'The young one or the old one?'

'This one was fairly young, about my age I'd say. He looked like the Territorial type and was a bit snooty when it came to my students. Said he thought a bit of hard digging and a few weeks under canvas would do them good. He made it quite clear he thought we were a bunch of softies. I helped carry the equipment down into Saxon Mills and when they'd got their tents up and a couple of jerry cans of fresh water from the farm, I agreed with Steve Stotter the areas to be excavated. Then we all walked into Carfax, so they could see where the shop was and buy some provisions and I went to meet an old friend for a pint in the local pub.'

'May I ask who your friend was?'

'A chap I was at school with, name of Lemmy Walker. He's the local schoolteacher out there and he offered to keep an eye on my students!' Dr Casson's voice now betrayed a hint of bitterness. 'But I can't blame Lemmy for what happened. He was devastated by it, but then he always was a bit of an innocent when it came to drugs.'

'Isn't that the best way to be?'

'I suppose so, if you're a village schoolteacher, but I'm afraid we have to accept them as a fact of life among the student population. We've had the "summer of love", flower power and psychedelic music blasting out of our televisions and wirelesses. It should not come as a surprise that young people want to experiment with mind-altering substances.'

'*Illegal* substances,' Campion said softly but firmly.

'The law is being used – what was the famous phrase – to break a butterfly upon a wheel? It is the knee-jerk response of reactionary governments who fear a social revolution where the young guard replaces the old.'

'The phrase is a quote from Alexander Pope,

but you have given it the ring of a line from a manifesto; a simplistic, naïve and unintelligent manifesto at that. May I be so bold as to suggest it is a slogan you have heard and that you repeat without necessarily understanding or believing?'

The younger man seemed surprised to be addressed in such a way, but at least had the decency to blush a deep crimson and to avoid meeting Mr Campion's gaze, which by now had a steely quality.

'It was something Lemmy used to say,' Casson said hesitantly. 'He was a great believer in free spiritism among young people.'

'Free spiritism?' Campion snapped. 'That's not even a word let alone a philosophy.'

'Well Lemmy was sincere – or he was back then. He believed that it was possible to free the artistic spirit through hallucinogenic drugs and that freedom acted as a drug in itself. It was the genie let out of the bottle. Once the mind had been liberated, the conventions of a creaking and hypocritical society could no longer repress and suffocate the dynamism of youth.'

'You sound as if you are quoting again,' Campion pressed him, 'and although I am of a generation whose opinions no longer matter a fig, allow me to say you are quoting piffle and your attitude seems to condone not only the illegal but the very, very dangerous. Lethal as it turned out.'

'I was not responsible for what happened last year!' Casson squeaked, retreating into the persona of a guilty schoolboy.

'Then who was?'

'I don't know! Whoever supplied them with

the LSD, I suppose.' Now the schoolboy was sulking. 'They knew what they were doing, it wasn't their first time. For goodness sake, think how many drink-drivers die every year.'

'We now have strict laws about that too,' said Campion severely, 'but one irresponsible action does not excuse another. The fact is that two of your students died at Lindsay Carfax and three were taken to hospital and I do not believe they did know what they were doing. As I understand it, they took massive overdoses.'

'Then it was a stupid accident. Whoever supplied them didn't know what they were doing. Nobody would deliberately take an overdose and no supplier would sell a dangerous overdose. Suppliers like repeat customers, not dead ones.'

Mr Campion took a deep breath and held it, eventually breathing out slowly in order to calm himself. He thought of the surprisingly large number of occasions in the past when he had heard that somebody-or-other 'deserved a damn good thrashing' and he had promised himself that he would never allow advanced age, dishonest politicians or the rate of income tax to persuade him to apply the phrase sincerely. He had kept his promise so far, but with the emotionally withered Mortimer Casson it was going to be a close run thing.

'Do you have any idea who the supplier was?' he inquired calmly.

'Somebody in Lindsay Carfax,' the archaeologist said defiantly. 'Probably the hippies who set up camp there.'

'Could they not have taken the drugs with

them?' Campion asked casually, trying not to sound like a policeman.

'They didn't have them when we left Cambridge. I told you, I drove them there in the van. They wouldn't have been "carrying" because if anything had been found on them – if we'd been stopped by the police for any reason – then I would have been in trouble with the college.'

'You would have been acting *in loco parentis* I suppose.'

Dr Casson allowed himself a wry smile which verged on a sneer.

'That particular doctrine is under legal review in America, I believe. The times, as they say, are a-changing. I was more worried about the insurance policy for the van – and also losing my driver's privileges if there was trouble. There are few enough in the archaeology department who can drive as it is. As a breed we don't seem to take to modern things.'

'Apart from fashionable drugs it seems,' Campion was unable to resist, 'but you're sure they obtained them in Lindsay Carfax?'

'They must have. I brought the van back to Cambridge so they were more or less stuck there for the duration. They'd been there about a week when the hippy convoy arrived and set up their camp next to my chaps' tents. I'm sure one of them was a dealer – the supplier – and so was Lemmy Walker, who tried to befriend them, though the locals called them everything from "lie-abouts" to "dirty gyppoes" and couldn't wait to set the police on them.'

'Too late to help your diggers, though.'

'Yes, they disappeared quick enough when Stephen and Martin died and I never heard if the police questioned any of them seriously. Lemmy was so upset by the whole business that he sort of ... well, blanked it out.'

It was not, Mr Campion knew, the only thing that Lemuel Walker had deliberately forgotten, but he kept that to himself.

'What happened to the three students who were hospitalised?' he asked.

'They were sent down of course,' said Casson coldly, 'and no doubt their parents gave them hell. I've not seen them since the day I drove them over there.'

'And you never saw Stephen Stotter or Martin Rees again?'

'Obviously not. I drove them all there and left them. I've never been back to the damned place'

'But did you not say that they had found a starting handle from a car?'

'Yes I did and yes, they did. So what?'

'How did you know about that?'

Campion pulled out a handkerchief (a brand new one, courtesy of Amanda-who-thinks-of-everything), removed his spectacles and began to polish them.

'It was Lemmy Walker who brought it over one weekend. I've still got it somewhere here.' Dr Casson waved his cigarette vaguely over the chaos of his room. 'Lemmy had been out at Saxon Mills talking to the hippies and showing an interest in the dig and Steve had shown it to him, making a big joke of it, thinking it might make a good trophy for the common room.

232

Lemmy said he would give it to me the next time he saw me and that's exactly what he did. Except of course by then, the joke had gone a bit sour. Is it important?'

'Probably not,' said Campion, 'but there is one thing that might be and I should have asked a nice policeman but to be honest, I forgot. When your party of diggers took the drugs they did, irrespective of how they obtained them, were they in their camp at Saxon Mills?'

'No they weren't,' said Casson indifferently. 'Does it matter?'

Campion waved a hand dismissively and said, 'I can always ask a policeman.'

'I don't know why, but they had left their tents and equipment – equipment which still hasn't been returned to the department, by the way – and gone into Lindsay Carfax.'

'To buy the LSD?'

'Perhaps. I have no idea. All I know is that they were found the next morning in some sort of barn or warehouse just off the main street. Lemmy told me it was an old storehouse somewhere near the village garage and behind the shop, near a studio run by some loud-mouthed bully of a painter who thinks he's an artist.'

Thirteen

The Student of Owling

After his adventure with the emotionless archaeologist as he thought of it, though that did strike him as a chapter heading out of a John Buchan story, Mr Campion felt in need of both a bath and a strong drink. St Ignatius, true to its principle of satisfying the body before ever troubling the mind, provided both and by the time he was be-gowned and striding down to hall, he was refreshed and looking forward to his companion at High Table, assuming that the Master had remembered to invite him.

Fortunately, Dr Livingstone's memory had not failed him; or it had been nudged by the imperious Gildart, who officiated at college dinners even out of term and was probably secretly delighted to have another diner to look down upon or scowl at should he pass the port the wrong way or use the wrong cutlery. Even though both scenarios were highly unlikely, Gildart (?Junior) struck Campion as having his father's dedication to waiting patiently for years, if not decades, to pounce on someone committing such a flagrant breach of etiquette.

It was the Head Porter who, with silent dignity,

234

pulled back a chair so that Campion could be placed next to a small, rotund, ancient frog of a man with long, unkempt white hair seated next to the Master, twirling an empty sherry glass between finger and thumb.

'You must be Campion,' said the benign amphibian. 'I'm Christmas at King's.'

Mr Campion's face cracked into a huge grin.

'Do you know, I'm not quite sure what to say to that?'

'Don't rise to the bait, Albert,' said the Master. 'Casper does that just to get his retaliation in first, rather like me introducing myself as "I am the Dr Livingstone you presumed". To be absolutely accurate–'

'Or as pedantic as usual,' interjected the squat visitor.

'–allow me to introduce Professor Casper Christmas *of* King's College, an establishment you will find by turning left out the college gates and after a few yards its rather ostentatious architecture will present itself on the opposite side of the street.'

'I've just remembered why I visit St Ignatius so rarely,' said Professor Christmas, with a well-practised wrinkling of his brow. 'The food is passable, the wine cellar excellent and the staff are–' Here he flounced his long white mane and winked at the statuesque Gildart standing to attention in the wings. '– impeccable, dedicated and notoriously underpaid. But, my dear chap, the Fellows ... Suffice it to say *they* leave an awful lot to be desired. I believe you had the misfortune to be an undergraduate here?'

235

Mr Campion settled into his chair, and into the game.

'My parents knew from the cradle that I was not clever enough for King's,' he said, putting on what Amanda called his "innocent owl" expression, 'and of course, Oxford was out of the question...'

'Naturally.'

'...and then someone suggested St Ignatius as the nearest thing to a respectable Borstal and they took me in out of charity and sheltered me for three years, but were less successful when it came to reforming me.'

'Sir Evelyn Ruggles-Brise,' the Professor announced.

'I beg your pardon?'

'The chap who invented the Borstal system, formalised in the Prevention of Crime Act of 1908.'

'I'm sorry I did not know that,' Campion chuckled.

'Don't apologise, my boy. I'm the historian here. It's my job to know such things and more.'

'Really, Casper, you are such a show-off,' said the Master, signalling Gildart to approach, for the table was now as occupied as it was going to be.

'Does the Master require wine?' the Head Porter enquired in sepulchral tones.

'Yes!' answered three voices in unison.

'The Master tells me you are not only the best historian currently at this table,' Campion charmed, 'but possibly the best in Cambridge.'

Professor Christmas turned his head like a

236

slowly revolving globe towards Dr Livingstone.

'Only "possibly", eh, Jolyon? Well I'm certainly the oldest, so *de facto* I am the historian with the most history. Shall I tell you how I acquired my *sobriquet*?' he asked, using the modern French pronunciation.

'Tell Campion if you must,' said the Master raising his eyebrows, 'but I've heard the story a thousand times. In fact, I've heard all your stories a thousand times.'

The Professor ignored him and rotated his head back towards Mr Campion.

'I became known as "Christmas at King's" partly because of my surname of course, which is a perfectly common-place surname in certain parts of Essex and Sussex. Nowhere else though, oddly enough. Must be down to East and South Saxons converting to Christianity at the time of St Augustine or thereabouts. Ruggles-Brise, the chap who invented Borstals, he was an Essex man like me; his family are still prominent in the county. But I digress.'

Inwardly, Mr Campion agreed.

'When I settled in Cambridge, the temptation was for my students to call me "Merry" or even "Mary", but that didn't last long. The young bucks didn't poke fun at a decorated major who had been in charge of a machine-gun battalion, or they didn't do it more than once, and those who had been in the trenches had more respect. But the year I arrived at King's was the first time the Nine Lessons and Carols service was held in the Chapel and "Christmas at King's" became a facet of Cambridge life in more ways than one.

The Christmas Eve service is still going and, of course, so am I.'

'So you came up in ... that would be 1918?' Campion ventured.

'As a junior fellow, yes. I was an undergraduate before the war, of course. In fact, my first book was published the day that poor Archduke got himself shot in Sarajevo, though nobody remembers it now. My book, that is, not the Sarajevo thing.'

'And dear old Caspar has never left,' said the Master.

'Why should I go anywhere? I had been a student at King's and knew that it was the place for me. I had done enough travelling and seen far too much of life – and death – during the war to last me a lifetime, so coming back to Cambridge in 1918 suited me just fine.'

'And you've never been tempted to leave?' Campion asked politely.

'Got as far as Sawston once; when some fool of a woman tried to get me interested in bicycling, but didn't like it much.'

'I'm sorry, I thought we were talking about you not leaving King's ... for some other university,' stuttered Mr Campion. 'I didn't realise ... Have you really not left Cambridge in over fifty years?'

'No need for it. Finest minds, finest library and finest publisher, all within strolling distance. Oh, I know that *modern* historians are falling over themselves to get on the wireless or, even worse, the television, but they're mostly Oxford men and in any case it would require travelling down to London – quite an appalling prospect. No, I am perfectly happy here in Cambridge. An awful lot of interesting people come here, so I don't have to go anywhere. You, for instance, Campion; you are quite interesting.'

'I am?'

'Of course you are. I know your background well enough to refer to you as Albert Campion and that use of any of your many real names would likely result in me being sent to the Tower via Traitor's Gate.'

'Which would be terribly inconvenient,' Campion chuckled, 'as it would involve leaving Cambridge.'

'Damned inconvenient, intolerable in fact; that's why I mind my p's and q's in polite company whenever your name crops up.'

'My burning ears radar must be failing. Does my name really crop up?'

'Only occasionally; and not so often these days. When it did I used to say "That's the nephew of the Bishop of Devizes, isn't it?" and that seemed to stifle all further conversation.'

'I often have that effect on people.'

'I remember you were talked about quite a bit during that Faraday affair before the war. That would be the second war, of course. Terrible business that; mind you, so was the war. I knew Caroline Faraday of course, everyone in Cambridge did. She was, after all the widow of a previous Master of St Ignatius, although quite a distinguished one for a change.'

'Do behave, Casper,' growled Dr Livingstone.

'I even knew her odious nephew Andrew

Seeley, the one who got himself dead in the river, and I was a nodding acquaintance of her son William, the one who went on to write *The Memoirs of an Old Buffer*, which was quite a humorous read. It was turned into a West End musical I believe, but I never saw it. That would have...'

'Required a trip to London?' Campion supplied.

'Quite, although there were several charabanc trips from Cambridge to see it. I never knew that *quite* so many Dons were interested in the musical theatre ... still, I don't for a moment think you got Livingstone here to invite me to table in order to hear my reminiscences, did you?'

'No Professor, I did not, though it would be delightful to hear them all one evening.'

'You would have to set aside more than an evening for that, Albert,' chimed Dr Livingstone. 'Casper could reminisce for a month of Sundays without pausing for breath.'

'Unlike most of your guests at high Table,' sparred the Professor raising an empty glass, 'who usually die of thirst.'

The Master signalled the impassive Gildart.

'Point taken, Casper. St Ignatius has a proud tradition of offering hospitality unquestioningly to urchins, vagrants, weary travellers, pilgrims, the poor – both deserving and undeserving – the lame, blind and lost; and even Fellows of King's.'

'I can second that,' said Mr Campion.

Professor Christmas narrowed his eyes and asked, 'And which category do you come in?'

240

'Initially, in this instance, the lame, for I threw myself upon the charity of the college when the hospitallers of Addenbrooke's had had enough of me. I remain here as a pilgrim of sorts, seeking enlightenment.'

'From me?' whispered Professor Christmas, shrinking coyly back in his seat and widening his eyes in mock surprise.

'The very fount of all knowledge, I am assured.'

'Well, dear boy, I always try and help the younger generation when they seek enlightenment.'

'I would hardly call myself the younger generation,' Campion smiled.

'You are to me! I will be ninety on my next birthday, which makes me old enough to be your father.'

'Casper, please!' exclaimed the Master, flapping at his distinguished guest with his napkin, but the Professor had set himself on a course of mischief.

'Of course, I'm not saying I *am* ... but...' he turned to Campion and winked lewdly '...was your mother in Colchester in September 1899 by any chance?'

'Casper! How very rude; and quite possibly treasonous!' Dr Livingstone shouted in exasperation, his face the colour of beetroot.

Campion held up the palms of his hands to calm the Master and kept the smile fixed on his face.

'I'm pretty sure she wasn't,' he said to Christmas, 'but extrapolated, that was a jolly good

241

guess at the date of my conception.'

'I'm a historian,' said the Professor drily, 'I don't guess; I look things up. I looked you up. Still have no idea what you want with me, though.'

'If you'd let the poor man get a word in edge-wise, Casper,' said Livingstone waspishly, 'you might find out. If you listen, you might learn, though I do realise that is futile advice to give to anyone from King's.'

As the two Dons glared at each other, Mr Campion took the initiative.

'I need enlightenment on the history of the wool trade in general and, if at all possible, on a place called Lindsay Carfax in Suffolk.'

Christmas at King's inflated his body with a loud and long intake of breath.

'In the late 12th and early 13th centuries,' he began, ignoring the soft groan from the Master of St Ignatius on his right, 'Suffolk was one of the mostly densely populated areas of England. That population survived on the backs of sheep; quite literally. The wool on their backs became "the jewel in the realm" and by the time of Henry VII, woollen cloth made up 90% of England's exports. The Speaker of the House of Lords doesn't sit on a woolsack for nothing, you know; and Henry Tudor was a shrewd man. He knew the value of English wool and he supported the merchants. All in all, he's underrated as kings go and it would be a terrible shame if all he was ever remembered for was denying Richard III a horse, a horse at Bosworth and stealing the crown out of a thorn bush. He was one of the

242

only monarchs we've had who actually left the country in the black rather than the red. He could teach today's politicians quite a bit about the balance of trade and export drives!'

'Does enlightenment have to come,' queried Dr Livingstone, 'in the form of a lecture as long as the Enlightenment itself?'

'Wisdom is the daughter of experience, Jolyon, and impatience is the mother of ignorance,' the Professor declaimed, 'though I bet there isn't a St Ignatius man alive who can tell me who I'm paraphrasing.'

Dr Livingstone dropped his head and stared silently into his glass.

'Leonardo da Vinci,' said Campion quietly. 'Now pray continue, Professor.'

Christmas granted Campion a gracious but almost imperceptible bow and then said: 'Where was I?'

'Still in the fifteenth century,' breathed the Master, only to be ignored.

'Yes, well, in the *sixteenth* century the fashion changed to lighter weights of wool cloth than those normally produced in Suffolk, but wool was still a very big business and when Henry VIII dissolved the monasteries he made sure that the best grazing lands – and the biggest flocks – went to his closest friends. One such case in point was the lands of the Abbey of Lindsay Carfax, which were reckoned, acre for acre, to be some of the richest sheep country in England.

'The wealth of Lindsay Carfax, indeed its very existence, depended on wool. If the church there is old enough, I'll wager you'll find an inscription somewhere saying something along the lines of: *I thank God and ever shall, it was sheep that paid for all.* There are wool churches all over Suffolk and Norfolk, huge things that now seem completely out of proportion to the size of the congregations they attract.

'Of course it all changed with the industrial revolution. Suffolk has no fast-running water, or coal mines, and the wool trade moved to where the machines could dominate – the mill towns up north. Lindsay Carfax declined just like dozens of other wool towns in East Anglia, though it did have one last flurry of woollen notoriety in the 1740s when it was named a centre of owling.'

The Professor, like all good professors, waited for his student to catch up.

'Owling? That sounds as if it could be quite fun,' said Campion, tilting his head to one side and adopted what his wife called his Idiot-in-Search-of-a-Village expression.

'It wasn't fun if you were caught,' lectured the Professor. 'The traditional punishment for owling was to have the left hand cut off and nailed in a public place, which just shows how highly sheep were valued.'

'So owling is sheep stealing, or should that be rustling?'

'Technically, owling is sheep smuggling, traditionally to France or Holland, where English wool was highly prized and prized even more if you could avoid taxes and duties and the attentions of the revenue men. The traditional centre for owling was Rye in Sussex, but Ipswich was a very useful port if you were owling to Holland

and many of the sheep that were "owled" came from Lindsay Carfax, a place which seemed untroubled by the forces of law and order in the eighteenth century.'

'Some would say that tradition still continues,' noted Campion and the Professor snorted a snort to show that such an idea did not surprise him.

'A report to the house of Lords in ... 1741, I think, called for measures to prevent the "pernicious practice or smuggling, running or owling wool" and proposed a public registry which would keep a tally of all bales of wool and cloth and fleeces. It was especially sensitive at that time because of trade embargoes imposed by the war.'

The Professor paused in his lecture and looked at his pupil expectantly. Mr Campion allowed the moment to hang in the air before saying:

'That would be the War of Jenkins' Ear, I presume?'

'Well done,' beamed Christmas. 'Not all hope is yet lost for St Ignatius.'

Dr Livingstone objected by snorting loudly whilst Campion smiled an embarrassed smile.

'I think I learned that at school, I'm afraid. I mean, it's not the sort of thing one forgets, is it? Going to war over a Welshman's ear being sliced off by the dastardly Spanish whilst on the High Seas; that's just the sort of history lesson which sticks in the mind of a spotty schoolboy, but I can't recall any mention of owling. Was it relevant to Captain Jenkins' unfortunate surgery?'

'Not directly, but a war – any war – disrupts trade. Wool was a valuable export, much in demand and in those circumstances, owling flourished. You have, I presume, guessed why it was called owling?'

'Because it was always done at night and the smugglers communicated by owl hoots?'

'Good boy. At least St Ignatius gave you a suspicious mind, which is always useful to a scholar – or a policeman.'

'I have neither the application nor the talent to be either,' said Campion, 'but let me pretend to be both and press you further. Was Lindsay Carfax known to be a hotbed of crime, or perhaps a nest of owlers?'

'Certainly. The local sheep farmers would have profited from it, the local magistrates, who were probably also sheep farmers, would have turned a blind eye and the Revenue Men were too few and too far between to do anything about it. There were questions asked in parliament – in the Lords, that is – and I'm sure the name of Lindsay Carfax would have been mentioned, as it would have been in the flurry of pamphleteering which took place at the time.'

'Pamphlets?'

'Oh, in the 1730s it positively rained pamphlets on the scourge of owling! The pamphlet was the cheap and easily distributed form of mass propaganda long before Goebbels showed how one could twist the wireless to evil ends, or Hollywood and now television showed how to keep the masses happy on a diet of mindless pap.'

'That's rather a sweeping generalisation, isn't it, Casper?' muttered Dr Livingstone.

'You think so, Jolyon?'

'Perhaps ... perhaps not ... I wasn't really listening.'

Now it was Professor Christmas's turn to snort in disgust, before he warmed, once again, to his theme.

'I remember – and you must realise, my boy, that I am speaking without the benefit of notes – some famous ones were printed around 1739, anonymously of course. Most of them were; to avoid prosecution for sedition. One pamphleteer signed himself "A Sussex Farmer" and called for favourable treatment of wool imported from Ireland, in order to stop Irish wool being "owled" to France and Holland. The whole subject was highly political, you see, because such a lot of money was involved. People made fortunes by smuggling in those days. Today, the income-tax Gestapo are far better resourced, unfortunately.

'Another propagandist called for the total abolition of duties, basically saying leave the wool trade alone for the good of the national economy, but I doubt too many people took it seriously as it purported to come from a Mr Webber.'

'You mean it wasn't taken seriously because it wasn't anonymous?' asked Campion, confused.

'No, dear boy, the anonymous ones were the most seditious as a rule. Putting the name Webber to a pamphlet indicated it was either an inside job, or a put-up job.'

'Really, why?'

'It would be like getting a letter asking you to

leave your front door unlocked at night, signed "A. Burglar". It's all in the name. Webber is actually Old English for "weaver", which is a dead giveaway for somebody involved in the wool trade. Surnames, or their origins, can tell us a lot about people. Take yours for instance.'

'Mine?'

'Tread carefully, Casper,' said Dr Livingstone softly.

'Well, the name you adopted – Campion. It comes from the Old French "champiun" meaning a professional fighter who could be employed to stand in for you in a trial-by-combat. Almost certainly came over with William the Conqueror, in fact I'm pretty sure I've seen the name William Le Champiun on a roll for Suffolk in 1220 or thereabouts. No relation, I suppose?'

'I very much doubt it,' grinned Campion, 'but I'll certainly check, just in case he left me anything in his will. Your theory on surnames is fascinating, though, and bears out something useful the Master told me.'

'You were taught something useful in St Ignatius?'

'It was not surprising that I was taught, only that I learned. The Master and I were discussing Will Kemp and his nine-day jig to Norwich and I learned that Kemp was also a name associated with the wool trade.'

'Well obviously,' sniffed the Professor. 'It's Old English again, a kempster was one who combed out the short, coarse hairs on a fleece and Kempster is not an uncommon surname today, neither is Shearer, who sheared sheep, or

Packer, someone who packed wool into sacks, or Walker, someone who walked over wet fleeces to thicken the wool, which I think was more or less the same job as a Fuller, and that's another common surname. You'd be surprised how many modern English surnames, or variations of them, are derived from occupations connected to the wool trade, especially here in East Anglia.'

'Actually, Professor,' Campion said politely, 'I don't think I would.'

Fourteen

That Riviera Touch

'The hotel is beautiful, but I do wish we hadn't arrived in a hearse.' Perdita stepped out of the dress which had fallen around her ankles with a sigh and stretched her arms upwards to the sun pouring through the open windows, adopting a pose of which her husband thoroughly approved.

'It wasn't a hearse, my love, it was a Citroën,' replied Rupert, his hands clasped behind his head as he lay supine on the bed watching his wife change out of her travelling clothes, 'admittedly rather a large one.'

'It was bigger than the Caravelle we flew in on. I could have parked my little Mini in its boot.' Perdita chose a cotton top with wide blue hoops from her suitcase shook out the creases and pulled it over her head.

'Technically, I don't think the Safari has a boot, as it's an estate car,' said her husband, his eyes registering every contour of her body, 'though the French don't call it a Safari, they call it a Break or something. Still, it was jolly nice of Monsieur Bouilleau to send it to meet us at the airport.'

'Who is Monsieur Bouilleau?' asked Perdita

demurely as she stepped into a pair of very short crisp white shorts.

'The manager of the hotel, or perhaps the deputy manager or the under-manager, I'm not actually sure, but he is a personage of some importance and an old friend of my father who has been told to take us under his wing.'

'Told?'

'Asked.'

'That's better. I would hate to think we'd been foistered on anyone in order to do your father's skulduggery.'

'He assured me that no skulduggery was involved,' said Rupert, concentrating with admiration as his new wife slipped her feet into a pair of white leather sandals and bent over to adjust the straps, 'or at least very little.'

In fact, it had been Rupert's mother Lady Amanda who had given the assurance that no skulduggery was involved – because she had declared there had better not be – and that Mr Campion's offer of a second honeymoon for the couple came with only two conditions: that they stay at the luxurious Hotel de Paris in Monte Carlo, which would naturally involve a visit to the nearby casino, and that, whilst there, they pass on Campion's best wishes to a distant relative, Lady Prunella Redcar.

Rupert and Perdita, who had first met less than two years before as minor players (walk-on parts only) in a piece of skulduggery at a Gothic pile with literary pretensions called Inglewood Turrets, both had ambitions of the thespian persuasion. After fifteen months of having them thwarted, both singly and as a double-act, they had decided that two unemployed Equity members could starve as cheaply as one and had decided to marry. The offer of a second honeymoon – the first having proved the old adage that the Scottish Highlands really were the wettest place in the United Kingdom – was a chance to catch some late summer Riviera sun and to extend their repertoires.

The offer of the trip to Monte Carlo had come at such short notice that the couple had little chance to choose or rehearse the roles they imagined themselves playing until they were already aboard the Air France Caravelle to Nice. To the consternation of the other passengers they had initially plumped to be a Bonnie and Clyde couple on the run from the law and living off their ill-gotten loot. When they tired of that scenario, Perdita suggested she played the youngest of four daughters from an impoverished aristocratic family who had, unwisely, eloped with the chauffeur's son and the last scraps of family silver to have avoided the pawnbroker. That, Rupert had said, was 'far too Austen-tacious' for which he had received a punch on the arm. His own preference, given that one of the conditions of their free holiday was that they had to visit a casino, was that he should assume the mantle of a debonair secret agent sent to the Riviera to expose a vile enemy by besting him at whist, or snap, or Happy Families, or whatever card game it was they played for ludicrously high stakes. For that suggestion, he took another blow on his arm as Perdita pointed out that he had not packed a tuxedo, or at least she certainly hoped he hadn't, and the stakes involved in casino-visiting would be anything but high given their budget.

As their jetliner began its approach to Nice airport, they had plumped to be an ambitious young Hollywood starlet ('typecast again,' Perdita had sighed) accompanied by her rather shady theatrical agent who was probably of Hungarian stock judging by the accent Rupert adopted with gusto. Yet it very quickly became clear to them that the staff of Nice airport and possibly the entire native population of the Riviera were not the sort to be impressed by Hollywood starlets – however pretty – or oily agents, however atrociously they mangled the French language.

By the time they had been greeted by a small, round Frenchman with a goatee beard and a square of white card on which was written CAMPIUN and deduced, in halting French, that he had been sent from the hotel to collect them, they had tired of the film star life. Once she had seen the large black Citroen estate car in the airport car park, Perdita had assumed the identity of an abducted and rather dim virgin, constantly referring to Rupert as 'Mr Snodgrass' and wondering why her father always referred to him as (deep gruff voice) 'that damned lounge lizard from Accounts'. Rupert, holding his giggles in check, played his part and unctuously reassured 'Miss Trim' that they were now far away from her ferocious father's prying eyes and after to-night he hoped that she would allow him to use her Christian name, Boadicea, for the very sound of it excited him, he confided, twirling the ends of an imaginary moustache. Perdita was already too good an actress to allow herself to giggle – or 'corpse' as it is known in the trade – or even blush at the liberties Mr Snodgrass was taking or hoping to take and she threatened to swoon if Mr Snodgrass made any salacious suggestions about putting his slippers under her bed. Such a thing, proclaimed Miss Boadicea Trim primly, could scar a young chambermaid for life.

Their ad-lib performance had its run cut short rather smartly by their driver when he turned in his seat to assure his passengers, in perfect English, that the staff of the Hôtel de Paris were very understanding, and that lots of important men took their mistresses there. This was France, after all, a country where mistresses were appreciated. Perdita was later, much later, to say that after that, auditions held no fear for her. The rest of their journey into Monte Carlo, though, was conducted in silence.

Monsieur Bouilleau snapped his fingers and a waiter, seemingly poised and ready for the starting gun, shimmered across the Terrace bearing a tray of tall flutes of *Kir Royale*.

'I insist you join me in an *aperitif* before you join me for dinner, *Madame et M'sieur Campion.*'

'I would certainly enjoy a drink, but I do not think I am suitably dressed for dinner,' Perdita said graciously.

'Pah!' breathed M. Bouilleau in the way only a

Frenchman can. 'We are very informal here in the hotel and you would be perfectly lovely however you dressed. That particular ensemble is *très chic* for the Riviera – perhaps a little more St Tropez than Monte Carlo this season, but no one here – absolutely no one – would be rude enough to point that out. Already three of my staff have decided you are a famous Hollywood star holidaying under an assumed name...'

'Her name is perfectly legal,' said Rupert rather coldly.

M. Bouilleau turned and appraised him for the first time.

'I meant nothing untoward,' said the Frenchman with a polite bow. 'We often have movie stars staying here under assumed names. Yours is not only a legal name, it is a very honourable one and one which I will not have abused in my hotel; I owe your father much more than I can repay in one lifetime.'

'Is that why we were able to obtain reservations at such short notice – and why you sent a car to the airport for us?' asked Rupert, his tone warming.

'I am neither embarrassed nor ashamed to say that this hotel, as long as I am in charge, will provide preferential treatment for honoured guests. If that offends any democratic or socialist principles you may have, then I will apologise, but it will not change things. You are my guests and I mean that literally; you will not be required to pay for anything at all whilst you are here on the Cote d'Azur.'

'I assure you, M'sieur,' said Perdita huskily,

patting the Frenchman on the back of his hand, 'we have absolutely no political or moral principles worth offending.'

'You must forgive my wife, Monsieur Bouilleau,' said Rupert in his version of French which, whilst better than Perdita's, would not have outshone a third-form schoolboy, 'but we are not seeking charity.'

'There is nothing to forgive, my young Campion,' the hotelier replied in perfect English, 'and charity does not enter into it when a debt of honour is being repaid.'

'A debt of honour?'

'Quite so, and I am not being overly dramatic, though I suspect you think that, being French, I must be. I learned my English during the war in England to which I escaped as a very young man in order to fight alongside Général de Gaulle.' M. Bouilleau placed his right hand briefly over his heart. 'It is difficult to believe that he is no longer our President and perhaps it is not a popular thing to admit one still admires him, but I do. So too, I think, did your father, for on many occasions his war work was done in alliance with the Free French forces and the Resistance operating within Occupied France.'

'My father rarely talks of his wartime activities.'

'He was asked not to. There are ... reasons ... and your father would have given his word and I respect that. All I can say is that your father extended the hand of friendship and the shield of protection to a foolish French boy who would have got himself killed five times over had it not

256

been for having an angel on his shoulder. I can never repay that debt in kind, but I beg you, do not refuse the little I can do for my guardian angel's son – and, of course, for his charming and beautiful wife.'

'It would be churlish to refuse,' Perdita smiled sweetly and this time her hand patted M. Bouilleau's knee, a gesture he seemed all too comfortable with.

Rupert, determined not to show that he was far from comfortable, took a long swig of his *Kir* and asked: 'So my father has been in touch with you?'

'But of course; by telephone and telex. Indeed, he asked that I make our telex machine available to you, which of course I agreed to do.'

'Why should we need a telex?' asked Rupert, then to his wife: 'Do you know how to send a telex?'

Perdita sat back in her seat, crossed her long bare legs and bobbed her blonde hair with her right hand, before stretching out her arm and examining the back of her hand, fingers splayed.

'Ah'm shoo-er,' she drawled in a voice reserved for Tennessee Williams productions, 'Ah could never operate one of those infernal machines. Why, they play merry hell with a girl's nails, don't yer know?'

M. Bouilleau smiled at Perdita's performance and clapped his hands softly, though it appeared to Rupert that the smiling Frenchman was applauding his wife's legs.

'The hotel machinist will, naturally, be at your disposal. All you need to do is write your reports

257

in English and he will transmit them to M. Campion at his Cambridge college, where he says he has discovered they have a telex machine they did not know they possessed.'

'Forgive me, M'sieur, but what reports?'

M. Bouilleau looked surprised.

'Why, your daily progress reports of course. He said something about a daily report being far preferable to a postcard which only arrives after your return.'

'I knew there'd be a catch,' Rupert sighed.

'Well, I don't mind in the slightest,' said his wife, preening herself. 'After all, we film stars sometimes have to suffer for our art.'

Telex to: 8955509 SNTIG C
For: Mr Albert Campion
Dearly beloved Pa-in-Law,
I am doing report duty because your grumpy-pants son is having difficulty fitting in to the Riviera lifestyle. I, on the other hand, am being treated like the Hollywood star I will surely become and enjoying every minute of it. We have been royally greeted and treated by M. Bouilleau, who sends his regards and who has arranged for us to meet the local casino manager (I know that makes him sound like the neighbourhood postman) in the morning. He's called (I think) Joseph Fleurey and has promised to show us something called 'The Redcar Twist', which sounds intriguing. I hope M. Fleurey is a friend of yours like M. Bouilleau, as that way we might get free chips for the casino as well as free board and lodging! And that is really all I have to report

for our first day here. We're off to dinner now –
ten courses of haute cuisine at least. If not, I shall
demand your money back!

All love and please try not to get shot again,
Perdita. X.
(and, I suppose, Rupert.)

Wrapped in her glittering starlet persona and
sedated by a superb dinner without the slightest
worry about paying the bill, Perdita did not give
a moment's thought to the telex she had dispatched, via a clunking machine which resembled an overweight typewriter and a role of tape
peppered with lines of neat but meaningless
holes. After an excellent night's sleep and a
breakfast (in bed) of freshly-squeezed orange
juice, strong and pungent coffee and croissants
as light as angels' feathers, nothing could have
been further from her mind.

By mid-morning, as she and Rupert, suitably
dressed (for film stars travelling incognito)
strolled over to the casino across from the hotel,
a whisper of a memory of something about 'free
chips' did perhaps ring a tiny bell in her brain,
but if it did it faded as quickly as it had arrived.

Until, that was, the moment when the dash-
ingly smart M. Fleurey, in the process of showing them around the main floor of the casino,
happened to mention, in a manner which suggested that such things were perfectly routine,
that 'a sufficiency' of gambling chips had been
lodged for their use with the cashier and they
could collect them at their convenience.

'Excuse me?' exclaimed Perdita stopping dead

in her dainty tracks and squeezing her husband's hand with enough violence to provoke a loud intake of breath. 'Did you just say that we get to gamble for free?'

M. Fleurey was both puzzled and apologetic.

'Did I not make myself clear, Madame Campion? I know my English is not as good as that of Charles Bouilleau and you must feel liberated to correct me when I make a mistake.'

'Your English is so superior to our French, we would presume to do no such thing,' said Rupert, flexing his crushed hand and glaring at his spouse. 'I think you gave my wife a surprise, albeit a very pleasant one. May I ask if you have had some communication with my father?'

'But naturally. Monsieur Albert arranged everything a long time ago. I see you are still bemused – that is not an insulting word I hope – and perhaps you would step into my office so that I may provide clarification.'

The couple followed M. Fleurey, Perdita with a definite skip in her step, through the obstacle course of tables offering roulette, baccarat and chemin-de-fer and chairs, all empty as the Casino had not yet officially opened for the day. No gamblers, tourists or envious sightseers were in evidence, only a platoon of cleaning ladies in smart black maids' uniforms polishing and dusting with a determination which could only be explained by the manager being 'on the floor'.

M. Fleurey lead the way, first to a glass-and-wire construction the size of a telephone box which was the domain of the *Cassiers*, the cashiers, who were, he assured his guests, 'the most important people in the house' as he made Rupert and Perdita stand in front of the cash window so that their faces could be imprinted on the mind of the man on duty behind the armoured glass. The man on duty registered Rupert's face in two seconds, spent considerably longer on Perdita's, then, without a word to either of them, went back to sorting round and oblong coloured chips into piles.

They then followed, at his very polite request, up an ornate, winding staircase to the first floor and it became clear, as he mounted the stairs two at a time, that this was an energetic, athletic Frenchman, the very opposite of the languid M. Bouilleau at the hotel. Panting slightly, they stood at the top of the staircase and surveyed the scene below them. Although empty save for the cleaners bustling between the gaming tables, it was still an impressive sight.

'The view is even better from my office,' M. Fleurey assured them.

And it was, because one entire wall of it was in fact made of tinted glass and offered a panoramic view over the whole of the floor below.

The junior Campions stared open-mouthed as if confronted by an impossible magic trick which, in a way, they had.

'You did not notice my window on the world as you ascended the stairs, did you, my friends?'

'There was a mirror...' Perdita said hesitantly '...but not this big.'

'Madame is correct. It is a large two-way mirror but much of the mirror side is disguised by coatings of lacquer and a curved surface so that it reflects the bright lights from the casino floor and appears, from below, to be much smaller than it is. Do not ask me to explain the physics or the chemistry of it, for I could not in my own language let alone English, but this window allows me to see everything which goes on in the casino below.'

'Oh but I would so want to be down there where the action is!' gushed Perdita with girlish enthusiasm.

'I do not think Madame would,' said M. Fleurey. 'Believe me, at three o'clock in the morning, the atmosphere down on the floor can be quite sickening, with the smoke and the sweat ... and sometimes the winners perspire more than the losers! I prefer my air-conditioned office and from here, you will see what you came to see.' He consulted an expensive, gold wristwatch. 'And perhaps very soon; we may just have time to take coffee.'

A button on M. Fleurey's desk was pressed and three large *cappuccino* coffees arrived, complete with grated chocolate sprinkled on their frothy domes. Perdita exclaimed 'What a treat!' and dived into hers headfirst, emerging unselfconsciously with a large dot of foamed milk on the end of her nose which she removed with the end of an impressive, and distinctly feline, tongue.

As they sat and sipped their coffee, M. Fleurey begged the permission of his two English guests to be allowed to explain his position to which the pair politely agreed, although Perdita asked quietly: 'But we still get the free chips to gamble with?' for which she received a scathing look from her husband.

M. Fleurey, who insisted they call him Joseph whilst in his office (though not, if they did not mind, in front of the casino staff?), reassured them that a certain amount of chips were available for their use instantly. This had been due to the foresight of M. Albert Campion who, after an all-too-brief visit to the casino some four years before, had not taken his modest winnings in cash, but left them in the safe keeping of the casino, to be called upon at some future date. It had been almost as if M'sieur Albert had known that the British government would introduce currency restrictions which allowed travellers a mere £25 of 'pocket money' – if that was the correct expression.

'Is that legal?' Rupert asked him, avoiding an ankle-swipe from his wife.

'In France it is not *illegal* to keep an account in credit. Unusual, yes, but not illegal. If it contradicts British travel laws in some way, then I would suggest your best course of action is not to win too much!'

'I for one will try and disappoint you, M'sieur Fleurey,' Perdita said with a sweet smile and a flutter of eyelids.

'That would be impossible, Madame, unless you refuse to call me Joseph...'

'Were you also a friend of my father's in the war, Joseph?' Rupert said, determined to change the subject.

'Oh, I was far too young to do anything in the war except take chocolate from American

263

soldiers when they finally arrived. It was my father, Étienne, who knew M. Campion and that was before the war. He was the manager of the Hôtel Beauregard in Menton, along the coast. Do you know it?'

'I'm afraid not.'

'It is very famous with the English, for one of your national heroes is buried there.'

'Really? Which one?'

'William Webb Ellis of course, which is why the rugby football is popular in this area. We even have a team named after him in Menton. You must try and spectate a game.'

'I doubt we will have time, Joseph,' said Rupert rather glad to see that Perdita's eyes had wandered from the handsome Frenchman and back to the viewing panel of the eyrie that was the office. 'We are not really here as tourists.'

'Of course, forgive me. You are here to see the famous Redcar Twist Method in action.' As he spoke, Joseph Fleurey's eyes sparkled with amusement.

'What the dickens is a Redcar Twist?' Perdita giggled. 'Is it done to music?'

'It is performed almost every morning at Roulette Table Number One,' said Fleurey, 'between the hours of eleven and twelve and it is quite, quite ridiculous. But see for yourself, for the Duchess of Lindsay Carfax has just entered the premises.'

Telex to: 8955509 SNTIG C
  For: Mr Albert Campion
  From your Special Correspondent lounging on

the Riviera.

All the splendid hospitality shown by your French connections – M. Bouilleau for his most comfortable bed and excellent board and Joseph Fleurey for his close attention to Perdita's every whim – did not prepare us for the first sight of the target you assigned us.

Lady Prunella – who is said locally to pass herself off as the Duchess of Lindsay Carfax! – made a distinctly regal entrance into the casino here this morning. We are told she does this every morning and it has become – as has she – something of a regular attraction on the Riviera tourist trail by which you could set your fob watch. (I think you still have one.)

Lady P. is accompanied everywhere by a fierce assistant-driver-bodyguard called Frau Ulla Berger, who is thought to be Swiss. When Lady P. plays the roulette table, Frau Berger stands one pace behind her holding the royal handbag – presumably for the transportation of all Lady P.'s winnings.

Everyone here seems to know them and knows that Lady P. plays to a system which has something to do with betting on a column of numbers and doubling the stake until she wins. (Joseph Fleurey will supply technical details if required.) Some days she wins, others she loses, but the stakes are never very high. Her daily visits to the casino seem to be more to do with ritual than income.

Her method of betting has become known as The Redcar Twist. This has nothing to do with odds or strategies or set sequences of numbers. It is simply because when Lady P. wants to double her stake, she shouts (and I do mean shouts) 'Twist' and when she wants to stop playing she yells 'Stick'.

The French think she is eccentric but harmless – in other words, English. The German, Italian and American visitors think she is quite mad and I am beginning to side with the majority voice.

So far we have only observed her from a safe distance. Tomorrow we will move in closer.

Wish us luck,

Rupert.

P.S.: Please make enquiries regarding prospective membership of Gamblers Anonymous for Perdita.

'Campion? Did you say Campion? I knew a Campion once. That wasn't his name of course. Haven't seen him for years, though I could be related to him. I might even be his godmother. I'm not your godmother am I? Albert, did you say?'

I am talking to Lady Bracknell, thought Rupert. No, I am being lectured by Lady Bracknell. Her fashion sense may not be Victorian, for she wore steel-rimmed glasses rather than lorgnettes and did not carry a handbag, but it *was* Lady Bracknell, or at least a very good actress on her way to an audition.

'Albert Campion is my father, Lady Prunella. My name is Rupert and this is my wife Perdita.'

'I am sure I am delighted to meet you. Was I expecting you?' Lady Prunella offered a gracious hand encased in a pink silk glove.

Rupert seemed at a loss as to whether to kiss or shake it and whether to bow whilst doing either. Perdita rode to the rescue.

'We are here on honeymoon,' she beamed. 'Our second honeymoon actually, even though we haven't been married long.'

'In my day,' said Lady Prunella sternly, 'one honeymoon per marriage was thought excessive. Did I send anything to the wedding?'

'That is not of consequence, Lady Prunella...'

'Of course it is. That silly girl Ulla must have forgotten to remind me. Where is the girl?'

The silly girl in question was in fact parking an ancient but spotless blue Panhard saloon in a side street, having stopped at the doors to the casino in order to allow Lady Prunella time to compose herself before joining her for their ritual grand entrance, despite there being no audience to appreciate the spectacle at that time in the morning.

Joseph Fleurey had fully briefed Rupert and Perdita on this daily routine and pointed out that Lady Prunella's 'silly girl' was a forty-year-old Swiss-German with a muscle tone which suggested she was an accomplished downhill skier and a temperament that suggested she might be referred to as an assistant, a secretary or a companion but never – never – a servant. His father, said M. Fleurey, would have referred to Frau Berger as a *Sergent-Chef-Major*, though the rank no longer existed in the French army; not an officer, but a personage whom those of lower rank called 'Sir' and often so did the officers.

The junior Campions had followed Joseph's

advice in choreographing their first encounter with their prey, choosing the one small window of time when it was possible to approach Lady Prunella without Frau Berger peering over her shoulder. They had dressed in smart, casual clothes – she in a yellow knee-length summer frock and he in white shirt and navy blue blazer – as befitted the climate, the setting and a young English couple on holiday, having resisted the temptation to indulge in any of the many dramatic roles they had been rehearsing.

Their ambush, though initially successful, did not secure as long a private audience with Lady Prunella as they might have wished, but luckily the Campions' bumbling introductions had struck the right note.

'Ah, here's Frau Berger now. I don't know what I'd do without her. Well of course I *do*, but one has to say these things, doesn't one?'

Despite very sensible low-heeled shoes, which did nothing to disguise her height, Frau Berger reminded Rupert of the stewardesses he had seen on brash cinema adverts for trans-Atlantic airline companies, dressed as she was in a pink twin-set complete with white gloves and a double strand of fake pearls resting on a granite-firm bosom. She wore her blonde hair piled in a beehive and large, square sunglasses. She carried a white leather bag large enough to conceal a small machine gun and gave off the air of someone who knew how to use one.

'Here you are at last, Ulla. Where have you been?'

'Parking the car, Lady Redcar,' said the taller

woman crisply, though her sunglasses were trained firmly on the two interlopers. 'And who are zeese?'

'*These*,' corrected Lady Prunella, 'are young people from England and very probably distant relatives of mine. They have been recently married and you seem to have forgotten to remind me to send a wedding gift. I thought you Swiss-Germans were supposed to be efficient.'

Frau Berger did not flinch, merely cocked her head to one side in mild curiosity.

'If mine is the fault, then I apologise. What was the name, please?'

'There is no fault on anyone's part,' said Rupert with a gentle bow. 'My name is Rupert Campion and this is my wife Perdita.'

Frau Berger offered a gloved hand to each of them in turn as Lady Prunella looked on as imperiously as a judge.

'Perdita ... that is a Shakespearean name, is it not? *The Winter's Tale*, ja? It is one of my favourite comedies. I particularly like the scene with the bear. And your name before marriage was Browning, was it not? Like the poet.'

'You are correct,' said Perdita putting on her best head girl smile, 'but I cannot claim any connection with either Shakespeare or Robert Browning, other than being an admirer of their works. May I ask how you know me?'

'I do not know you, but I read *The Times* of London, even though we receive it two days late here, and I remember the announcement of your wedding, because Perdita is not a common name.'

'If you saw the announcement, why didn't you bring it to my attention you silly girl?' Lady Prunella demanded.

'I had no idea you knew either the Campions or the Brownings. I am not psychic.'

'What a pity, I was sure I included that in the job description.'

Rupert tightened his stomach muscles to stifle a laugh as Perdita said cheerfully: 'A psychic would come in awfully handy in a casino.'

'How right you are, my dear,' said Lady Prunella, peering over the tops of her spectacles as if realising her presence for the first time, 'but as we do not have one to hand, I will have to make do, as usual, with a prayer to the Old Bones. Will you join me in a spin of the wheel, my dear?'

'I most certainly will,' said Perdita with far too much enthusiasm for Rupert's liking.

Lady Prunella offered her arm, which Perdita took with alacrity and the four of them progressed like a stately galleon out of the sunshine and into the welcoming cool of the casino.

Telex to: 8955509 SNTIG C
  For: Mr Albert Campion
  From Rupert
  Who the Devil is Austin Bones????

Fifteen

The Man Who Hardly Troubled the Bank at Monte Carlo

It quickly became clear that Lady Prunella Redcar's daily appointment with the roulette wheel was not a matter of obsessional behaviour or economic necessity. Nor was it any sort of public or social statement, for she indulged her habit almost in private, preferring to play at a time when serious gamblers were still sleeping off their losses from the night before and casual tourists were more interested in selecting a restaurant for lunch. The casino staff of croupiers, waiters and even cleaners still not quite finished with their dusting and polishing were her only audience, should she be in need of an audience, apart from Frau Berger. Whether she won or lost on the roulette, the employees of the casino displayed a professional and unemotional impartiality. So too did Frau Berger, who remained impassive standing at Lady Prunella's shoulder, her eyes hidden behind her sunglasses even in the dimly-lit casino, clutching the large Redcar handbag to her bosom. When Lady Prunella required chips from the cashier, the handbag would be popped open and she would reach in to extract

271

a gloved fist full of francs. When the handbag was safely closed, the wad of bank notes was pressed into Frau Berger's hand and she was directed to the cashier's glass fortress.

Rupert and Perdita, in their roles as young newly-weds whose meeting with Lady Prunella was pure serendipity, were careful to maintain an air of innocence. They entered the casino as part of the Redcar royal progress with expressions of wide-eyed wonder, even though Joseph Fleurey had given them a personal guided tour the previous evening, during which Perdita had found baccarat unfathomable and roulette slightly addictive.

As Rupert positioned himself next to Lady Prunella at the edge of Roulette Table 1, Perdita followed Frau Berger to the cashier's window and observed her negotiations for some brightly coloured plastic markers in exchange for the French francs she clutched. Perdita estimated that the Swiss woman had bought little more than £10 worth of chips and when it was her turn to stand in front of the Cashier all she said was 'S'il vous plait' with a quiet nod which the Cashier answered with a sly wink as he slid the chips towards her without any money changing hands.

The two couples were the only players at Table 1, it being not quite 11.30 a.m. and the duty croupier still with flecks of pastry from his *petit déjeuner* on his bow tie and the lapels of his black jacket. In fact, they were the only gamblers in the casino; something on which Lady Prunella decided she had to comment.

'I much prefer to indulge my little passion for roulette without an audience; and even though my visits here have made me what I believe is called a "fixture" in this casino, I do so hate being gawked at by people.'

'I hope we are not intruding, Lady Prunella,' said Rupert politely.

'Don't be foolish. If you're a Campion you are probably family. Was your mother a Fitton, from Suffolk?'

'She still is,' affirmed the dutiful son.

Lady Prunella paused in the middle of forming her chips into equal piles on the edge of the green roulette 'layout' cloth.

'Didn't I read somewhere that she had to take a job – something in engineering? No, surely I must have dreamt that.'

'Lady Amanda is actually a well-known aircraft designer and consultant,' said Perdita, leaping to her mother-in-law's defence.

'So she chose a *career,* did she?' If Lady Prunella did not actually inject disdain into the word, she used it as if it was unfamiliar and possibly unknown to her. 'It was always said that the Fittons were unconventional and headstrong, and of course she is much younger than your father who is, I believe, a Victorian, as I am. Girls today seem to want – no, demand – to do everything. What do you do, my dear?'

'I'm am actress.'

'Of course you are. Shall we place our bets?'

Lady Prunella reached over the table and carefully placed three circular chips in a neat pile at the bottom of the first column, just under the

273

number 34. Perdita offered her handful of chips to her husband, but Rupert shook his head, deferring to her enthusiasm if not her skill, and offered her the freedom of the table. With a look of deep concentration on her face, a concentration indicated by the tip of her tongue poking through tightly closed lips, Perdita took a single chip and slowly waved it over a large area of the layout before opting to cover the single square occupied by the number 12.

'*Rien ne va plus, mesdames,*' said the croupier in a quietly bored voice which was almost a yawn and spun the wheel, the small white ball rattling loudly in the empty casino.

Perdita's right hand reached out for Rupert's left and she grasped it tightly, a gesture which somehow reassured the both of them and reassurance became necessary and their grip tightened jointly as Lady Prunella began to quietly intone what they first thought was a Gregorian chant.

'*Bones ... Old Bones ... come on, Bones ... share the luck...*'

Rupert could not help but stare at the old woman standing next to him and was about to ask if she required a glass of water, or a chair, or whatever it was elderly ladies needed when an attack of the vapours – whatever they were – seemed imminent. He then noticed his own concerned reflection in the sunglasses worn by Frau Berger who was staring at him, her face impassive, telepathically defying him to intervene or comment on the strange behaviour of her octogenarian companion.

'*Bones ... Old Bones ... share the luck...*'

The little white ball of chance gave a final death rattle and settled into a slot on the roulette wheel.

'*Dix-huit, rouge, pair,*' announced the croupier.

'Damn!' said Perdita.

'Twist!' exclaimed Lady Prunella.

The croupier gave a loud sigh, the sort of sigh that middle-aged French waiters with fallen arches specialised in, and extended his rake to sweep in the two losing bets.

Lady Prunella replaced her lost chip with a new one and then added a second to the bottom of the first column.

'Well, my birthday wasn't lucky, so I'll try yours,' said Perdita, placing a chip on number 20.

'If you bet on single numbers, you face very long odds,' advised Rupert.

'But much bigger winnings,' said his wife in a voice which brooked no argument.

'*Come on, Old Bones ... spread the luck,*' Lady Prunella chanted softly and the wheel spun.

'*Vingt-et-un, rouge, impair,*' intoned the croupier, extending his rake.

'Blast!' snapped Perdita.

'Twist!' snapped Lady Prunella.

'Oh well done me!' laughed Rupert, scooping up the two chips the croupier had shovelled his way.

'What did you do for that?' asked his wife, narrowing her eyes.

'I played it safe, darling. You bet on a red number, so I bet on black. The odds are only evens, but by doing the opposite of you I felt I turned them in my favour.'

Perdita's nostrils flared and she turned back to the layout, placing a small tower of chips on red 18, saying firmly: 'Shall we see how lucky our wedding anniversary is then?'

Lady Prunella, seemingly oblivious to the marital discord taking place at her side, piled four chips at the base of the first column and began her quiet mantra as the croupier spun the wheel again.

'This time Bones ... spread the wealth, Old Bones...'

As the white ball rattled its death rattle and Lady Prunella chanted, the croupier's face – had anyone around the table been looking at it – showed emotion for the first time and the emotion was one of great relief.

'Trente-et-un, noir, impair.'

'Damn and blast!' snarled Perdita.

'Yippee!' shouted Rupert, although he shouted very quietly.

'Good Old Bones!' exclaimed Lady Prunella.

The croupier's rake flashed, dragging Perdita's chips away and then delivering one to Rupert and eight to Lady Prunella.

'What just happened?' Perdita asked her husband.

'You bet on a red number so I bet on black. Lady P. did a column bet and 31 black is in the first column. I won at Evens, she won at odds of 2:1. You lost.'

'Don't take it too badly, my dear,' Lady Prunella comforted her. 'Roulette is a cruel game of chance and to win, one needs a guardian angel looking over one's shoulder.'

The junior Campions automatically looked towards Frau Berger who seemed an unlikely candidate for the role of angel.

'Oh, I don't mean Ulla,' Lady Prunella snorted. 'My guardian angel really is an angel, a wonderful man called Austin, who I just know is looking down and smiling on me.'

There was a slight religious pause broken by the croupier coughing discreetly and asking the ladies and the gentleman if they would care to place their bets.

'Come on, Old Bones, onward and upward!' Lady Prunella said gleefully clapping her hands twice before placing a single chip on the layout, this time at the foot of the middle column and mouthing 'Old Bones, good Old Bones'.

Perdita gritted her teeth and place a chip on black 13. Rupert slid a chip quietly on to the red quadrant.

'Quatorze, rouge et pair.'

'Good Old Bones!' chirped Lady Prunella.

'Dammit! I was only one away!' moaned Perdita.

Rupert said nothing.

With two more spins of the wheel, Perdita was out of chips and sulkily refused to accept charity from Rupert's modest winnings. Lady Prunella stayed on the middle column, shouting 'Twist' when she lost and thanking 'Old Bones' whenever she won. She moved on to the third column and lost three spins in a row, despite demanding to 'Twist!' twice. After the third spin, as the croupier raked away her stake, Lady Prunella slapped the table and said loudly: 'Stick!'

Frau Berger, taking her cue, swept up Lady Prunella's remaining chips and made a beeline for the Cashier, giving just enough time for the eagle-eyed Perdita to estimate that the Redcar coffers, unlike the Campions', were in small profit for that morning's work.

'Are you staying long in Monte?' Lady Prunella asked, tugging her gloves tighter.

'A few days only,' answered Rupert, collecting the few chips his cautious gambling had won.

'Perhaps we'll meet again at the tables.'

'We are not really the gaming type,' said Rupert and almost bit his tongue for sounding too priggish.

'Neither am I, but one has certain obligations ... debts ... to the past, which I know is a terribly unfashionable attitude these days. Still, perhaps you would come and have tea with us?'

Rupert exchanged glances with his wife but before he could formulate an answer, Frau Berger had returned to stand at Lady Prunella's side.

'You have forgotten, my lady; the furniture restorers are expected tomorrow and we will be in no position to entertain guests.'

'Ah yes, Ulla is quite right – she often is. I have some antique furniture you see, just a few pieces I brought with me from Lindsay Carfax. Nothing terribly rare or valuable, except to myself for sentimental reasons; but the climate here does not agree with some of it and sadly the insect life does, so occasionally we have to get professionals in to look after it. It means that we simply cannot cope with visitors, which is a shame. If I do not see you again, do give my regards to your father, if he remembers me. I am almost certain I remember him.'

Rupert did not have to wait long for the answer to the rather cryptic question he had immediately sent to his father in Cambridge by Telex, for M. Joseph Fleurey supplied the answer that afternoon. He and Perdita had lunched at the hotel at M. Bouilleau's insistence and, M. Bouilleau being French and in command of a brigade of highly trained chefs, luncheon had lasted a good three hours. To recover, the junior Campions had gone in search of sea air and mild exercise and after a strenuous walk and a bout of standing, staring and sighing enviously at the luxury yachts tinkling at their moorings in the harbour, they made their way back to the casino where they asked to see M. Fleurey if he had a few moments to spare.

M. Fleurey did indeed, and they were shown up to his office with its panoramic view of the casino floor below where the afternoon 'tourist crowd' were shuffling aimlessly between the tables almost being tempted into a wager, but never quite summoning the courage. When they were seated comfortably, Fleurey asked if they would like a glass of tea, which they both refused rather too quickly, being conditioned by the historic English prejudice that no other nation was capable of producing afternoon tea properly.

'We have met the Lady Prunella,' Rupert

279

began, 'and played her at her own game – or rather one of your games.'

'I know,' said Fleurey pointing to the glass-mirror wall, 'I watched you. Please do not be offended by that but it is my job to observe all our patrons, and in truth I could not resist.'

'We are not offended,' said Perdita with her sweetest smile, 'we were only hoping you could tell us what was going on down there.'

'But you were there, Madame Campion, standing next to her. You saw what was going on. I assure you there was no collusion or impropriety on the part of the casino. The roulette wheel is a game of chance, we do not – cannot – control which numbers come up.'

'I was suggesting no such thing, my dear M'sieur Fleurey. We are looking for an explanation for Lady Redcar's behaviour.'

'Behaviour? She comes to the casino every morning and she always plays her own system, betting on each column in turn. Sometimes she wins, sometimes she loses; then she stops, always after nine bets.'

'Nine?'

'Always. She always places nine bets. Did you not notice?'

'We were rather distracted,' said Rupert, 'by her singing *D'em bones, d'em bones, d'em dry bones* in that tuneless drone of hers. It's a good job you don't have many other customers that time of the morning. I think serious gamblers would find that most distracting.'

M. Fleurey smiled a wry smile.

'Lady Redcar is not, as you suspect, a serious

gambler. It matters not to her whether she wins or loses. She plays for low stakes on the safest of bets and she has something no true gambler has – the ability to say "Stop!" before things go too far.'

'Or "Stick!" in her case,' observed Perdita.

'Precisely. She places her nine bets and then stops. Every day it is the same. But you are wrong about her singing, *M'sieur*. She is not singing the Negro spiritual, she is chanting a prayer.'

'A prayer? For luck?'

'No, not, I think, for luck but out of remembrance.'

'But she was asking "the old bones" to share the luck,' said Perdita.

'She is *remembering* "Old Bones" and the luck he had. I do not think she prays *to* him – that would be heretical, would it not, even in England? I think she prays *for* him or at least for his soul for he is surely no longer with us.'

'Do you know who Austin Bones is ... was?' asked Rupert.

'But naturally, although his name was Bonus, not Bones and his story is a legend in the world of the casino here on the Riviera.'

'Don't tell me,' Perdita gasped gleefully, rubbing her hands together and breaking into song, 'Austin Bones was ... *the Man Who Broke the Bank at Monte Carlo!*'

Joseph Fleurey threw back his head and laughed.

'I would say that he was the man who hardly troubled the bank at Monte Carlo, even though

281

he was a winner and caused quite the scene when he won. There are many stories about famous winners and losers, even losers who sadly went on to commit the suicide,' Joseph Fleurey gave a dramatic shudder to emphasise his point, 'but Austin Bonus was a man who could not have been happier. He even sang that awful song about breaking the bank at Monte Carlo – which nobody ever has – even though he did not come close, though his winnings would have been a considerable sum in his day, perhaps ten thousand English pounds.'

Perdita let out a long low whistle and said, 'I wouldn't mind winning that today if you could arrange it, darling Joseph.'

M. Fleurey showed her the palms of his hands indicating that he was powerless in such matters.

'When was this, Joseph?' Rupert steered the conversation away from his wife's charming cupidity.

'It was before the first war ... 1910, that was it.'

'And was this Austin Bonus a regular visitor to the casino?'

'Not at all; no one knew him, no one knew where he came from or where he stayed. No one had seen him before and no one saw him again. When he collected his winnings, he left a receipt which the manager of the time had framed. In addition to his signature, he had written a line from Madame Campion's favourite song: *"I to Monte Carlo went, just to raise my winter's rent."*'

'I'm afraid I only know the chorus,' confessed Perdita. 'Is that significant?'

'No, just an example of the English sense of humour, yes?'

'So this Austin Bonus was definitely an Englishman?' Rupert pressed on.

'*Most* definitely, but then we have always been popular with the English.'

'But you said his story was legendary. What made him a legend?'

'Two things,' said Joseph, linking his fingers across his shirt front and leaning back in his chair. 'Firstly, his system of playing roulette: he did not have one; it was as if he had never seen a roulette wheel before that night. I am paraphrasing from the diaries left by the manger here in 1910, you understand. He carried a bag of money with him, what I think was called the Gladstone bag, perhaps. Once he saw the roulette wheel, he watched the other players for a few moments then he attempted to put the bag on the layout cloth, which caused quite a stir. The croupier explained that he had to buy chips from the cashier before he could play, and so he did. He emptied the bag into the cashier's window, all of it, which amounted to a little over 4,000 Francs, and he exchanged it for four 1000 Franc chips. He returned to the table and some said they heard him say a short prayer and then...' M. Fleurey showed that he knew how to use a dramatic pause with a captive audience '...he placed all his chips on one number and that number came up! The odds paid were 35:1 and this on his first bet! It was also his *only* bet, as he collected his winnings and left the table.'

'And that is why Austin Bonus is a legend?

Because he made one incredibly lucky bet at roulette?'

'In terms of time spent at the table, it was a remarkable achievement and no one could remember seeing anything like it before, but then no one had seen a gambler quite like Austin Bonus before. I said there were two things which made up the legend of Austin Bonus. It was not simply that he was a remarkably lucky winner, it was that he was the most unlikely person to be on the floor of the casino in the first place. You see, he was dirty and ... what is the word? ... dishevelled, yes that's it, and unshaven as if he had travelled a long way, which of course he had, and he had not eaten for several days. He came through the doors of the casino just before midnight and all the other guests and players were in evening dress, so his appearance was even more ... incongruous, yes?'

'He sounds like what we might call a tramp,' said Rupert. 'I'm surprised he was let in.'

M. Fleurey shrugged a Gallic shrug.

'Normally, he would not have been, but our doormen were caught off guard by the fact that he was a priest.'

'Excuse me?'

'A priest, or a vicar, as you call them in England.' Fleurey put a hand to his throat to hide his bow-tie. 'Complete with – how you say? – *faux-col d'ecclésiastique.*'

'Dog collar.'

'Exactly. He was the vicar of a place called Lindsay Carfax, which I believe is where Lady Redcar lived before she moved to the Riviera.

Perhaps he was her priest – vicar – though it was all sixty years ago and I do not think Lady Redcar is so old.'

'Do not be such a gentleman, Joseph,' smiled Perdita. 'Lady Prunella is quite old enough. She is proud to be a Victorian.'

'How long has Lady Redcar lived in Monte?' asked Rupert.

'Three years I think, but she does not live in Monte Carlo, she has a small house in the village of Gorbio in the hills towards the Italian border. It is not far, perhaps fifteen kilometres. Do you intend to visit her, if you can get beyond her Swiss guard dog?'

Rupert chuckled. 'I know what you mean. Frau Berger is rather formidable. We were sort of invited for tea I think, but the guard-dog said it wasn't convenient; something to do with furniture repairers.'

'Bof!' said Joseph Fleurey, which is not a word in any language except French. 'That woman and her furniture; you would think there were no craftsmen in France the way she sends her things back to England for the slightest repair and it is not as if she has a collection of valuable antiques. People who have visited her say that she has but a few pieces of any age, which she brought with her, and those are of inferior quality. They cannot be worth the cost of shipping them to England and back two or three times a year. It is curious, but then she is a curious woman, is she not?'

'Yes, she is,' agreed Rupert, 'and I am mildly curious to see where she lives. Could you give us directions?'

'Of course. Gorbio is not far from my home town of Menton and it is not a big place; but you will need a car. I am sure Charles Bouilleau at the hotel can arrange one. It is a beautiful drive, very *panoramique*.'

'How about it, darling?' Rupert appealed to his wife. 'A nice drive into the hills from where we can watch the sunset over the coast.'

'Well, I thought we might...' Perdita began to pout, but Rupert quickly spotted the warning signs.

'We could be there and back in time for a late supper and then I thought we might come back here to the casino to try our luck if, that is, we have any credit left.'

Joseph Fleurey waved a magnanimous hand indicating that their account was still in the black.

'In that case, it's a wonderful idea,' enthused Perdita, leaping to her feet. 'But there is one thing I must know, Joseph.'

'Yes Madame?'

'Do you know which number it was that Austin Bonus bet on?'

M. Fleurey smiled to himself.

'Ah, if only I had one of your English pounds for every time I have been asked that question. The legend is that Austin Bones staked everything he had on number nine.'

Sixteen

As a Thief in the Night

The car was not anywhere near as big as the 'hearse they arrived in', Rupert had insisted, but Perdita remained unconvinced. It was, he conceded, a Citroën and possessed the same hydraulic suspension which dealt so effectively with uneven French roads but which made unwary English passengers seasick. It was a Citroën DS which, if you said it French, was *Déesse* or 'Goddess'; but Perdita was one goddess who remained unappeased.

M. Bouilleau the hotel manager had arranged the car for them on condition that it was returned more or less in one piece – the odd scratch and scrape being acceptable for the driver would, after all, be English – as it belonged to the hotel's best pastry chef and good pastry chefs were easy to offend and difficult to replace.

With great care and some skill – though not enough to pacify his wife who was finding driving on the 'wrong' side of the road disconcerting – Rupert negotiated the Citroën along the coast road to Menton and found with little difficulty the minor road which twisted inland and up into the hills to the medieval village of Gorbio. Apart from excellent directions, M. Fleurey and M. Bouilleau had between them supplied the additional knowledge that Gorbio had a population of less than seven hundred souls, no decent restaurants, a passably attractive fountain in the village square where one could water one's mules and donkeys if one so desired, and an ancient elm tree supposedly planted in 1713 though no one could remember why. They had also provided the very useful advice that once in Gorbio, the junior Campions should not attempt to negotiate the narrow streets in a strange car but park in the village square and explore on foot, for it was not a big place and they would easily find the Rue Garibaldi, where the eccentric Lady Redcar lived at Number 9.

There it was again, Rupert thought: Austin Bones' lucky red nine on the roulette wheel, Lady Prunella's nine bets and now her address. What was it about the number nine? His father had not mentioned that it had any significance when he had asked Rupert and Perdita to 'go and brace the old she-wolf in her lair' but then Mr Campion Senior had always regarded vagueness as a legitimate modus operandi and had not exactly given them a detailed brief. He had asked them to make contact with Lady Prunella, to pass on his regards and to report back on the venerable lady's health, sanity and wellbeing. He had not specified how the junior Campions were to quantify or interpret their findings, nor to what purpose they would be put. He had, however, said that he wanted Rupert and Perdita to act as 'neutral observers' and they were in no way to think of themselves 'as detectives'. Well, they had tried observing neutrally and all they had discovered was a slightly batty old English lady who had a fixation with an eccentric Edwardian vicar and the number nine. Surely a bit of practical detective work would flesh out their next report, justifying their travel and hotel expenses, not to mention Perdita's gambling habit.

Gorbio, in the quiet of an early evening when the sun still gave an artist's light but little heat, was a picturesque settlement of pink stucco houses with red-tiled roofs, narrow cobbled streets and arched passageways. It was impossible to miss the village square with its fountain (mules and donkeys for the use of?) and the famous ancient elm tree of 1713. The only other tourist attraction seemed to be a shop, closed for the day, called *La Cave de Gorbio,* which sold artisan local pottery and poorly but enthusiastically executed watercolours of local views.

Rupert followed the advice he had been given and parked the Citroën in the square after executing a flamboyant three-point turn so that the car was facing towards the road down to the coast.

'Always secure the means of a quick exit,' he told Perdita when she queried his actions. 'It's the one piece of paternal advice I tend to follow.'

'Are we expecting to have to make a quick exit?' asked Perdita, unperturbed.

'Better to be safe than sorry. Come on, let's explore on foot and find out where the old bat roosts before the sun goes down.'

'You make her sound like a vampire.'

'She's a Victorian Englishwoman – that's far scarier than a vampire!'

'Lead on, then, Van Helsing.'

They spotted a sign, half-way up the wall of a stone-built house, saying Rue Garibaldi as soon as they reached the edge of the square.

'It's a good job we didn't have to ask directions,' Perdita observed as she looked around at the deserted streets and the empty square, silent except for the tinkling of water in the fountain. 'The local inhabitants seem to have taken cover. Wait–' She sniffed the air loudly, turning in a circle '–I'm getting thyme, garlic and crushed basil ... it must be dinner time.'

'It almost always is in France,' said Rupert, 'and jolly civilised it is too.'

'Now don't go native on me, husband. Let's get detecting before it gets dark and the vampires and the English gentlewomen come out.'

Holding hands, as any recently married couple still would, they walked slowly down the Rue Garibaldi which curved around to their left and sloped gently downhill. The houses were of a similar design and age, stone built into the hillside, of two storeys with front doors straight off the narrow street and firmly shuttered windows, each separated from its neighbour by a patch of land to the side which was guarded by a stone wall at least seven feet in height containing wooden gates wide enough – just – to accept a vehicle.

It was impossible to tell whether the space enclosed by the walls was used as a garden or a parking space or something more suspicious, for their height and the ubiquitous signs saying *Attention au chien* ensured a considerable degree of privacy. And the citizens of Gorbio seemed to value their privacy to the extent that only the occasional whiff of cooking or the muffled rattle of pots and pans escaping through ground-floor shutters suggested that the town was inhabited at all.

The flickering glow of a television screen through a net curtain was, in this medieval context, quite startling.

'Is French television as bad as they say?' Perdita had asked, peering rudely, but vainly, into the curtained window.

'Worse,' said Rupert pulling her away. 'A circus every night and the rest is all politics, makes you really appreciate the BBC.'

Hand in hand, they continued carefully down the street, picking their way over the cobbles which were playing havoc with Perdita's unwise choice of lemon-yellow high-heeled shoes. She was at the point of cursing her entire choice of wardrobe – the wispy yellow summer frock and the thin pink cardigan – which might have fitted the image of a tourist promenading through Monte Carlo but which made her feel like a clumsy sunflower in the narrow, shady streets of the ghost village of Gorbio. It was noticeably cooler now, the twilight coming on quickly, causing Perdita to shiver involuntarily.

'Remind me, dearest, what exactly are we doing here?' she sighed.

'Just looking,' said Rupert. 'Just looking and reporting back to the Old Man.'

Perdita was about to ask 'Looking for what?' when Rupert pulled down hard on her hand causing her to stumble into his shoulder and he stopped abruptly and pressed himself back against the wall of the nearest house. The street had curved sharply to their left and around the corner, perhaps thirty yards away, parked in the street and occupying more than its fair share of it, was the rear end of a white Bedford commercial van with British number plates and an oval GB sticker.

'The furniture removers,' whispered Rupert.

'Restorers,' muttered Perdita, rubbing her arm.

The Bedford was parked tight up against the garden wall of the house displaying a 9 on its traditional blue and white enamel plaque. The green wooden gates in the wall were open offering a slit of a view of a shadowy, shrub-filled garden. There was no sign of life in or around the van or the gate, but an upstairs light had been turned on in the house.

Rupert slipped his arm around Perdita's waist.

'Come on, let's just saunter casually down the street and see if we can spot anything.'

'What if Lady P. spots *us*?' Perdita hissed, but made no attempt to remove his arm.

'Then we act utterly surprised and go into our "Fancy bumping into you here, Lady Redcar – were you out for an evening promenade too?" routine. You can improvise on that.'

'I'm much better with a script and rehearsal time. I never saw the sense of those lessons where we had to be a cat scenting danger or a train. I mean, what was the point? When would we ever get jobs in a theatre playing a cat or a steam engine? The *legitimate* theatre, that is.'

Rupert gave her a gentle squeeze. 'Then I'll be the rich playboy who is actually the Riviera's most notorious jewel thief and I have seduced you, the humble peasant girl who does the village laundry, and you're out taking the evening air with me while I case the local houses for rich old widows who wouldn't miss the odd diamond necklace. How's that?'

'I think I'll stick with surprised but extremely polite English girl saddled with an idiot husband who has got them both lost.'

'If you're comfortable with that...'

With the idiot husband's arm around the polite English girl's waist, they sauntered down the street having eyes only for each other in case they were being observed, until they reached the rear door of the Bedford and the garden gates kept open with thick wooden wedges at the bottom corners, at which point they both did an eyes-left as they slowly passed by. All that could be seen was a rectangular garden and patio with shrubs and small trees planted in earthenware pots the size of beer barrels, and a set of open French windows which gave access into the house. Despite the open gates and windows, the place seemed deserted and because the gates and windows were open, it also seemed suspicious.

And then there came a thump from the interior of Rue Garibaldi 9, as if someone had missed a step on the stairs or dropped a log on an uncarpeted floor and a muffled curse which could have been in one of several languages, but was undoubtedly masculine in timbre.

The courting couple froze in their tracks, clutching each other tightly. There was no pretence now of casually passing by and they leaned in to the gateway, straining their necks and eyes towards the open French windows.

When they heard a second thud and a second and then third curse, they involuntarily found themselves stepping into the garden.

'What *was* that?' Perdita breathed into Rupert's ear.

'I don't know but I think it's coming from upstairs.'

'Is the old girl being burgled, or worse?'

'It would take a brave burglar,' whispered Rupert. 'You keep back, while I take a look.'

'For goodness sake, be careful,' said Perdita releasing her grip on her husband and taking a step backwards into the potted shrubbery.

'I will,' he promised.

Rupert took a tentative step across the threshold of the open French windows and into the empty room, which with the approaching dusk and no other source of natural light was cool and already gloomy. Rupert detected the scent of stale 'black' French tobacco in the room's still air, mixed with a woman's perfume which he made no pretence of recognising. It was clearly a living or sitting room, with armchairs positioned under standard lamps with fringed shades, a sideboard on which perched an ancient Bakelite radio and a low coffee table on which sat a silver tray with a decanter half-full of brown liquid, a soda syphon and a single empty glass. Across the room was an open door through which he could see the foot of a staircase and it became instantly apparent that the staircase was the source of the bumps and grunts.

Rupert distinctly heard the heavy – very heavy – tread of feet clumping down the creaking stairs and then a jarring scraping sound followed by an angry exchange in ripe but clear English.

'Bleedin' 'ell watch it, you dozy ape, you'll damage the damn' thing.'

'I thought it be supposed to be damaged – an' don't going calling me names or Oi'll rip your bloody ears off.'

'I'll call you what I like, you lumbering ox, if you wake the old coot up with your row.'

'Stop arguing!' commanded a third voice. 'And don't worry the old lady; she will sleep until morning after one of my special nightcaps.'

The third voice was female and easily identifiable as belonging to Frau Berger.

Rupert's eyes shot towards the empty glass on the tray on the coffee table and then urgently back towards the staircase in response to the sound of descending footsteps. He stepped back out into the courtyard garden pulling the French windows closed as he went and he half-turned his head and hissed loudly: 'Hide! Quick!'

But the French windows did not want to close, at least not without a struggle and then a very loud snap.

Through the thick glass panes, Rupert saw a large figure enter the living room, a very large figure, entering slowly and laboriously – and backwards. He heard a voice raised in surprise, which could only have been in response to the noise he had made closing the windows, but he did not wait for clarification.

Rupert turned on his heels and ran for the gate. He had completed two long strides when his foot connected with the thick wooden wedge keeping the nearest gate open and he tumbled, base-over-apex as his old rugby master would have said, landing painfully on his back and rolling out into the cobbled street. His one thought as he performed his inelegant and involuntary somersault was *Where the hell is Perdita?*

Perdita was later to say (often and to anyone who would listen) that if her husband had any future at all in the theatre it would not be as a director or a playwright for his stage directions were worse than useless.

For as long as they remained married, which would be a long time, Perdita always maintained that Rupert's hissed warning to 'Hide! Quick!' on being almost discovered trespassing at Rue Garibaldi 9 was nowhere near as helpful as the instruction 'Run for it!' would have been. In fact, standing as he had been in the French windows, what he ought to have done was brazen it out by striding into the room swishing an imaginary racquet and intoning 'Anyone for tennis?' as he had done many times in preparation for a career in regional rep.

Perdita, sensing but not seeing the source of tension which had affected Rupert, did what all young wives do – or pretend to do – and instantly obeyed her husband, by hiding quickly. As she was in a garden of sorts, albeit a garden of potted plants, tomboy instinct from a childhood spent with three older brothers told her to climb a tree. Unfortunately, in small walled patio gardens in hillside villages in the south of France, trees were in short supply and so Perdita improvised. In the corner of the garden were two substantial bay plants which had been confined to large earthenware pots for many years and had grown as luxuriant bushes, as thick as a good privet hedge and over five feet tall. The possibility of climbing up either of them would have daunted an agile cat, but their thick green foliage provided the perfect hiding place, at least for someone willing to dive behind them and then clamber on to rims of their pots so that their feet did not show.

It was positioned thus, her arms outstretched around the two neighbouring bushes as if hugging a portly uncle, and her yellow high-heeled shoes each balanced on the edge of a pot rim, that Perdita saw, through the tiny gap in in the bay leaves she had made with her nose, her husband make his spectacular exit from the courtyard, pursued a few seconds later not by the *Winter's Tale* bear (a creature known to all in the acting profession) but by two men she had never seen before in her life, and then one woman she had met only that morning.

But that morning, the woman had not been carrying a small automatic pistol.

'There's nobody here,' said Frau Berger, 'you must be imagining things.'

'Oi'm sure I pulled them windows open wide.'

'You couldn't be sure you'd tied your bootlaces unless somebody double-checked for you.'

'An' you could find one of my bootlaces tight round your scrawny neck if you ain't careful, boy.'

'Be quiet, both of you!' snapped Frau Berger. 'Check the street.'

The two men, dressed in blue overalls, were a Laurel and Hardy pair but what they lacked in charm and humour they more than made up for in swaggering menace. The smaller of the two was all quick rat-like movements, whilst his much larger colleague walked with a lumbering gait that probably required a brick wall to bring it to a halt.

It was the larger, hulking, one who had – to Perdita in her fragrant evergreen hiding place – a definite East Anglian accent. She was sure of that as it was an accent she had mastered for the paltry three lines she had once been allowed as a parlour maid in a forgettable country house murder mystery which ran for a week at the Theatre Royal, Norwich. (Her character, the maid, was not specifically identified in the script as a Norfolk lass but the producers had insisted as their local audience would feel more at home.)

The two overalled thugs – Perdita was sure they were thugs as neither had shown any surprise that Frau Berger was waving a pistol about – did as they were ordered and marched out of the gate to check the street for their suspected intruder and where they would almost certainly find Rupert lying in the gutter having knocked himself unconscious.

Incredibly, the two thugs reappeared in the garden shrugging their shoulders.

'Nothing out there – the street's empty. Nothing moving, not even a mouse,' the smaller one reported.

'Then lock the gates and fetch the box and try not to break anything else on the way,' instructed Frau Berger, slipping the pistol into the pocket of her cardigan. 'As soon as it's dark, I will transfer the goods.'

'Why do you have to do it out here in the dark?' whined the small thin man, his companion behind him looming over him like a cliff.

'Because, *dummkopfen*, in the dark we cannot be observed from the houses further up the hillside which look down on us.' Frau Berger's tone made it clear that not only houses could look down on people. 'And we do it out here in the garden because I cannot risk spillages inside the house. The police have dogs with clever noses and they could become suspicious if they ever came to call.'

'You reckon they'd notice that gun you've been flaunting then?' growled the second, big-as-an-ogre, man.

Frau Berger was not in the least intimidated and shrugged off the question.

'Pah! In Switzerland, every house with a man has to have a rifle by law, as all men are in the militia. Here in France, handguns are permitted in houses to protect against burglaries. Here in this garden I could shoot you dead as an intruder and the police would thank me for saving their time.'

In the bay trees, clinging to the shrubbery and convinced that spiders were nesting in her hair, Perdita's mouth went very dry very quickly.

Where the hell was Rupert?

Perdita had read, in one of the lowbrow Sunday newspapers, stories of Japanese soldiers marooned on Pacific atolls who were unaware that their war had ended more than twenty years before. The stories, she knew, were almost certainly invented on slow news days, but as she shivered in the dark and the foliage, she could empathise with the terror felt by those abandoned soldiers who peered out from their jungle hideaways and watched a strange world pass before their eyes.

Dusk had rapidly turned into night and this reassured her, for even though a bright, almost full moon was rising, the walled garden with its potted bushes offered another layer of darkness to mask outlines and aid her concealment. She felt confident that if she could resist moving suddenly to uncramp her tortured leg muscles and if the bay leaves stopped tickling her nose and she fought back the urge to sneeze, she could remain undetected. *Why did she have to think about sneezing?* She should concentrate on what was happening in front of her, less than thirty feet away through the bay leaves. *Thirty feet! Good Lord, how could they not have seen her or sensed her presence?* Although the night was cooling fast, she knew she was sweating profusely and for a moment was convinced that the liberal application of her roll-on underarm deodorant (she hated the new-fangled aerosols) that morning would not be enough to protect her. Even the fattest, laziest, over-fed French restaurant dog would surely have sniffed her out by now. *Oh God, what if they had a dog?*

This way lies madness, thought Perdita, steadying herself. She would simply pretend she was not there in that garden at all, but her uncomfortable perch on the rims of adjacent plant pots would be her seat in the stalls and the sharp, brittle leaves of the bay trees would be the curtain through which she could peep at the dramatic action on the moonlit stage thirty feet in front of her.

After securing the gate, the assembled *dramatis personae* had retreated into the house and for a split second Perdita thought she had a chance of escape, but she knew the garden walls were too high to scale and before she could register crushing disappointing, the players re-emerged for the next act, entering from stage slightly right as she viewed it.

The two henchmen – should that be *spear carriers*? – appeared first, though they were not carrying spears. Between them they were manhandling what looked at first, in the dark with the only backlighting a single lamp in the house, like a trunk or a small coffin. But as Perdita concentrated, she discerned that the object had a leg at each corner and as the henchmen set down their load in the garden and stepped back, the outline of the thing reminded her of the small electronic organs she had encountered in run-

301

down provincial theatres and church halls used as rehearsal rooms.

Was she about to be serenaded or treated to a recital? Were the henchmen in reality frustrated musicians who had to resort to performing in secluded French gardens after dark? Clearly, Perdita's imagination was wandering and needed to be calmed by a stiff drink or the arrival of her husband riding to the rescue; and neither seemed probable.

For a moment she was convinced her hallucination was solidifying when the smaller of the henchmen lifted a lid on the organ/trunk/ coffin and propped it open. If the giant one had produced a stool for him to sit on and held sheet music for him to follow, she would not have been surprised, but the two men – she had now labelled them in her racing brain as Giant Thug and Scrawny Thug – were merely part of the chorus there to support the diva.

Frau Berger made her entrance on the al fresco stage through the French windows with a small torch in one hand and a dark Gladstone or doctor's bag in the other. She set the bag down next to the whatever-it-was-on-legs and shone the torch, which had a thin pencil-like beam, on it. Then she gave orders to Scrawny Thug to which he responded, then sank to his knees and opened the bag in the torchlight.

They had not, Perdita realised (more slowly than she would later admit), been speaking English or French or, as far as she knew, any of the four languages in official use in Switzerland. And though she would never admit it, her vague

302

suspicions were only confirmed by Giant Thug, who complained loudly: 'Oi've told you before Oi don't loike you speaking foreign.'

Frau Berger and Scrawny Thug had a further exchange in 'foreign' and both found whatever was said highly amusing as they laughed, much to the annoyance of Giant Thug.

'Don't you mock me. Oi don't loike it when Oi'm mocked.'

'Nobody's mocking you, you big goon,' said Scrawny Thug, though his voice betrayed a stifled laugh. 'We're just talking business.'

'And I suggest we get on with it,' said Frau Berger with authority.

Perdita was unable to see clearly what that 'business' involved, but she heard it and it involved much clinking of glass and things being removed from the coffin/organ and replaced by other things from Frau Berger's Gladstone bag. When it was finished, the lid on the whatever-it-was was closed and Frau Berger shone her torch into Scrawny Thug's face.

'Now get that into the van and make sure it's secure.'

'We always take care of the merchandise,' Scrawny Thug answered her. 'We've got blankets and rope in the van.'

'When you've done that, bring me my money and you can have a drink while I count it.'

'Now you're talking,' enthused Giant Thug. 'A bit of hospitality wouldn't go amiss.'

'Just one drink,' said Frau Berger sternly. 'You've got a long drive ahead of you and if you're going to have an accident, I would be happier if it was in England.'

She unlocked the wall gate and the two hench-men picked up the thing-on-legs and carried it out into the street.

Perdita calculated her chances on making a freedom dash for the street. Her legs were cramped, she would have to force her way through, or knock over, two substantial potted bay trees, and then sprint past Frau Berger who, as far as she knew, still had an automatic pistol in her pocket. It did not sound like much of a plan and the opportunity to put it into action quickly passed.

She heard her two Thugs open the door of the van over the wall on the street and a succession of bumps and thumps, some muffled swearing and finally the slamming of a metal door and the rattle of a handle checking to make absolutely sure it was locked, an action which only the male of the species seems compelled to perform.

Then Scrawny and Giant came back into view, Scrawny holding a large thick envelope or parcel which he handed to Frau Berger, who again spoke to him in a language Perdita did not recog-nise, but conscious that Giant Thug, right behind him, had started growling, he answered her in English.

'No, no problems. British Customs are only really interested in what we bring back in. They asked at Dover if we knew about the currency regulations and we said we just had the regu-lation £25. They didn't bother to search us. I mean, we don't look the sort to be carrying that much cash, do we? And the French only glanced at our passports. I doubt they'll even do that on the return journey.'

'Good. Shall we now count it just to make sure none has ... evaporated?'

She led them into the house, closed the French windows, turned on the main lights and drew the curtains, ending the second act of the private performance they had given to an audience of one.

Perdita was sure there would be a third act but had no intention of staying to watch. She raised herself up to stretch her aching legs but even standing on the rims of the bay tree pots, the garden wall seemed impossibly high and unconquerable. Perhaps Frau Berger's Swiss efficiency had momentarily lapsed and she had left the key in the lock of the garden gate. Failing that, the gate might offer a foothold or two which the wall did not. Gingerly she dismounted from her perch and quietly eased her way through the underbrush, conscious of the fact that she was walking bandy-legged as if she had just completed a long, cold journey on the pillion of a motorbike.

The first thing she would do – once she had avoided detection by Frau Berger and her thugs, clambered over the gate, found her way back to that bouncy Citroën and somehow got it started without keys – would be to search the streets of Gorbio for her heartless, cowardly husband and give him a good solid clout around the ears. But finding and clouting Runaway Rupert, drat him, would have to wait until she had escaped from the walled garden.

'Perdita, darling! Up here, my love!'

And there was the dratted Rupert, lying on his stomach on top of the wall, dangling two helping hands and arms as a lifeline.

'Where have *you* been?' Perdita hissed up at him.

'Hiding under their van; they never looked there. Now I'm lying mostly on the roof of their van and I'd rather not be here when they drive off, so jump and grab my hands and I'll pull you up.'

Perdita took a deep breath and was about to say something cutting and possibly blasphemous, but suddenly thought that it could, along with the clouting, wait.

'This won't be dignified,' she warned her husband and her eyes flashed like a tiger's in the night. 'Thank God I'm wearing sensible knickers!'

She kicked off her yellow high heels, picked them up and jammed them in among the bay leaves, then rucked up the hem of her frock and stuffed it into her pants front and back. She took a three step run-up and leaped into the arms of her husband.

Telex to: 8955509 SNTIG C

For: Mr Albert Campion

Much to report, though best done in person or by phone. However, highlights include:

a) Strange goings-on chez Lady Redcar;

b) Lady R's companion Frau Ulla Berger certainly warrants further investigation;

c) Lots of drama tonight around visit of re-

306

moval men from England. From their accents, one is certainly from darkest East Anglia, the other spoke Dutch as well as English. Don't know if that means anything;

d) Removal van containing suspicious furniture now en route England, possibly Calais-Dover crossing. May be worth tipping off those in the know to look out for white Bedford van. Signage on side reads: Sherman & Sons, Garage & Repairs, Lindsay Carfax 293;

e) Darling Perdita bet all remaining expenses money on red 9 on the roulette wheel. Lost the lot. She says you also owe her a new pair of shoes.

Awaiting instructions. Alternatively will hitch-hike home tomorrow.

Rupert.

Seventeen

Detectives No Longer Required

'Albert Campion, you are a barefaced liar!'

Mr Campion removed the telephone receiver from his ear and held it at a safer distance.

'Amanda, darling, I assure you I speak with an unforked tongue and if my face is bare it is with shock at your staggering mistrust of me.'

'I'm married to you, you fool; of course I mistrust you, it comes with the job description.'

'But what, dearest lady, have I done to ferment such mistrust?'

'Repeat what you just told me when I asked if you were sure you were taking it easy,' Amanda ordered down the line. 'Go on: word for word, exactly what you said a minute ago.'

'I said – as far as I can recall, for I wasn't really listening to myself – that I had been involved in absolutely no jiggery-pokery or engaged in jinks high or low during my stay here in Cambridge.'

'Go on.'

'Then I think I said that I was doing nothing more than sitting snugly in the bowels of St Ignatius being fed and pampered by the staff so much I must have put on a stone in weight and that...'

'There you are! Liar! You haven't put on a troy

ounce in weight since I first met you. Having less fat on you than a butcher's pencil is possibly your most irritating feature. Now tell me honestly what you've been up to.'

Mr Campion smiled into the telephone and suspected that, more than fifty miles away down the line, his wife was smiling too.

'Nothing strenuous, please believe me, though I'm really quite mobile now and have a very fashionable stick which gives me the air of a *boulevardier* as I stroll down King's Parade. I did search high and low for a swordstick, but none of the emporia in Cambridge seem to stock them any longer.'

'Idiot! Get back to answering the question.'

'Very well, light of my life, would you believe me if I told you that in the last few days I have been closeted with a mathematician, an archaeologist, several historians, a clutch of librarians, more bibliophiles than you could shake a sword stick at, two Professors of Law because I required at least sixteen different legal opinions on the law of copyright, a chemist and the odd local policeman? All our meetings were very amiable – apart from the archaeologist who was a sour young man – and all highly productive. And I've done all that without straying more than a quarter mile from the college kitchens, and the staff here really are trying to fatten me up. In fact, I think I hear Gildart approaching stealthily with afternoon tea, toast, crumpets and fairy cakes.'

'Well good luck to them with that,' said Amanda primly, 'but what about our son and our beautiful daughter-in-law?'

'Rupert and Perdita seem to have had a jolly enough time on the Riviera. They landed just after lunch and Rupert telephoned from the airport to fill me in.'

'I know,' said Amanda with a touch of menace, 'I've spoken to Perdita and she told me all the exciting adventures they had playing detective on your behalf. I'm taking them out to dinner tonight to help them recover from their holiday. You, of course, will be paying.'

'I insist upon it,' said Mr Campion sincerely.

'So you should, and over our *expensive* dinner I will inform the children that they must never again agree to do anything you suggest without asking my permission, which will naturally be denied.'

'I say, Amanda, that's a trifle harsh isn't it? After all they're jolly grown up now.'

'Yes, Albert, but you're not. I'm not suggesting you are ready for bingo and basket-weaving quite yet, but at your age you really must start to take things easy.'

'At my age, darling, Winston Churchill was Prime Minister.'

'And that might be a nice quiet job for you to consider in your retirement, my dear, because we must talk about that when you come home, and I do mean seriously. Am I making myself clear?'

'Absolutely, my dearest, and you have my blessing to kill the fatted calf, or the fatted pig or the fatted chicken, or whatever we have in the larder, as I intend to be home the day after to-morrow.'

'Shall I drive up and collect you?'

'That won't be necessary but it is sweet of you to offer, my love.'

'You're not going back to Lindsay Carfax, are you? When you call me your "love" you're always hiding something from me.'

Mr Campion smiled into the receiver again, comforted and proud that his wife knew him so well, but also glad she was not there to see the smile.

'Only to pick up the Jaguar, my love, that's all.'

'You are sure that's your only reason?' his wife asked suspiciously. 'You're not likely to get shot again, are you?'

'I certainly don't intend to and I will have Eliza-Jane with me as a bodyguard. If there are any bullets flying about, I expect her to throw herself in front of them.'

'Do not joke about things like that, Albert, and don't you dare put my niece in harm's way by stirring things up as you usually do.'

'Stirring? Dearest, I thought I had made it clear. All snooping necessary has been done from the comfort of High Table here at Gnats or by the children down on the Riviera.'

'So no more snooping around Lindsay Carfax?'

'No further snooping necessary in Lindsay Carfax. Detectives no longer required there.'

'Honest Injun?'

'Absolutely.'

'And there's nothing else I need to know, or worry about?'

311

'Nothing springs to mind, my dear.'

'Then tell me one thing, darling: why do we owe Perdita a new pair of shoes?'

It took Mr Campion far longer than was dignified to fit his long legs and his silver-topped cane into the well of the passenger seat of Eliza Jane's sports car and his contortions were accompanied by involuntary grunts of pain and sighs of resignation.

'Are you sure you're all right, Uncle?' asked Eliza Jane as she slid, easily and decoratively, behind the steering wheel.

'I'm fine, my dear. Any peculiar sounds you may hear are merely the creaking of my old bones.' As he spoke, Mr Campion allowed himself a soft chuckle, which brought a quizzical stare from his driver as she reached for the ignition key.

'Don't mind me, Eliza, I've just reminded myself of something Rupert told me about old bones.'

'Something medical, or just downright comical?' Eliza Jane asked drily but politely.

'Neither. Something ecumenical if anything, though there is a comic side to it.'

'Are you *sure* you feel all right? No headaches or dizzy spells or anything?' Eliza sounded genuinely concerned.

'After several days being wined and dined in a Cambridge college, even one as humble as St Ignatius, a certain amount of headaches and dizziness are to be expected; in fact without them one would feel positively short-changed. When I

312

referred to my old, aching bones, it put me in mind of "Old Bones" Austin Bonus, the fabled vicar of Lindsay Carfax. You know who I mean, don't you?'

'Of course, everybody who lives in Lindsay knows the story of the mad vicar who disappeared with the Old Folks' Christmas Fund and turned up nine days later claiming a miracle, or something like that. I forget the details and it all happened so long ago it's almost ancient history. It was back in 1850s I think, or thereabouts.'

'It was 1910, which is hardly ancient history, young lady,' said Campion with mock severity. 'I was at prep school and we were all jolly excited at the news of those magnificent men in their flying machines. Perhaps you're right, though, it is history and I must be ancient.'

'Oh, I won't allow any wallowing in self-pity. You may be a man of distinguished years, but they seem to have been quite exciting ones.' Eliza-Jane started the engine and pressed the accelerator until it growled throatily before selecting a gear. 'After all, how many men half your age get picked up on the street by a fantastically attractive dolly bird in a sports car?'

'You have a point,' conceded Mr Campion. 'I should just sit back and enjoy it.'

In fact, he sat back in his seat rather more suddenly than he had expected as Eliza Jane released the handbrake and the car tore down Trinity Street, much to the consternation of several Dons and cyclists too numerous to count. It was only when they were clear of Cambridge and he was amused, as he always was, to see the fingerpost signs pointing the way to the communities of Frog End and Six Mile Bottom, that he relaxed enough to request a briefing from his niece.

'So what's new in Lindsay Carfax?'

'As usual, absolutely nothing,' replied Eliza Jane, her eyes fixed (Campion was relieved to notice) on a severe upcoming bend in the road.

'How disappointing. Has no one missed me?'

'Oh I think your presence has been missed, for the place has been deathly quiet without you stirring things up.'

'There I go again, stirring things up without knowing it. What stirring did I do this time?'

'Well, you upset our rather tragic schoolmaster Lemmy Walker – though as he's very highly strung, that's not difficult to do; your very expensive car managed to get smashed up whilst safely parked and not even moving; and then you get yourself shot. Quite honestly, Lindsay hasn't had so much free entertainment since a wayward barrage balloon floated over from Ipswich during the war and the entire population ran across the fields trying to catch one of the guy ropes. Lord knows what would have happened if anyone had; they might have been dragged across the border into Norfolk, which would have been terrible for them as none of them have passports!'

'Now, now,' cautioned Campion, 'don't be so disparaging of the good folk of Suffolk. They have, after all, taken you to their bosom.'

'And speaking of bosoms,' Eliza Jane pounced, 'you were certainly missed by Clarissa. She's been mooning around the place like a sick heifer, nagging away at poor Gus Marchant to drive her over to Cambridge to visit you in your sick bed.'

'I am grateful that you defended my honour by dissuading her.'

'Oh don't thank me, thank Gus Marchant. He refused to drive her, saying "the poor fellow's been shot – hasn't he suffered enough?" but not saying it when Clarissa was in range.'

'Well at least somebody was thinking of me...'

'I suspect a lot of us were. Ben – my Ben – was itching to go and crack a few heads to find out which idiot it was who loosed off at you on that shoot. Not that he needs much of an excuse to pick a fight with Simon Fuller; those two have been like cats in a bag ever since they first met, and he would have had a go at the Shermans, father and son, because he thinks they're crooks. Fortunately the son, Clifford, the one built like King Kong, seems to have disappeared or at least he's not been seen around Lindsay for a couple of days, which is just as well as he's huge and would probably have massacred my Ben.'

'Yes, he did strike me as the sort of chap one shouldn't provoke. The junior Sherman, that is, not your Ben.'

'Oh Ben's got just as short a fuse as Clifford. They're both hairy gorillas beating their chests in the jungle, but at least Ben tries to be civilised most of the time. Clifford, I am sure, is sub-human.'

'That is not,' said Campion seriously, 'an expression I approve of. In fact, the last people I knew who used it all wore smart uniforms and shiny jackboots and some of us sub-humans had to do something about them.'

'I didn't mean it like that, Uncle,' said Eliza-Jane contritely. 'It's just he's uncouth and boorish – and I know Ben can be at times – but Clifford is a bully and a thug and probably a crook. It does run in the family, after all.'

'What are you suggesting, young lady: an organised crime family here in the depths of rural Suffolk? This isn't the East End you know.'

'I'm not suggesting the Shermans are anything like those awful Kray twins who went to prison this year, but Sherman *père,* Dennis, has a reputation as a dodgy character and *his* father, Leonard, who died last year, was the worst of the bunch by all accounts.'

'By *all* accounts?' Campion asked quizzically.

'Well according to the best gossip money, or at least a discount for cash on any sale item in The Medley, can buy in Lindsay Carfax. Sherman *grand-père,* the late Leonard, was the fat spider at the centre of quite a web of intrigue and blackmail when he was at the height of his powers.'

'Blackmail? Isn't that a bit strong, young lady? Draw it mild, draw it mild, as we used to say.'

'Perhaps it is,' conceded Eliza Jane, 'but Leonard Sherman seemed to have a hold over a lot of people in the village and a lot of fingers in a lot of pies. He started off as a poacher and odd-job man around the village, specialising in helping out aged widows, and getting left a surprising number of valuables in their wills. Leonard did well enough out of that sordid little game to set his son up in the garage business.'

316

She glanced across to catch the look of distaste on Campion's face.

'Oh, he didn't murder them in their beds or anything, or at least I've not heard that suggested. He just frightened them into thinking they couldn't manage without him. By all accounts – sorry about that – he had an entrée into every house in Lindsay, whether he was invited or not and always seemed to be around, offering to help, if there was bad news to be broken or a death in the family. It was a creepy sort of helpfulness which no one quite trusted but nobody had the courage to tell him to bugger off and mind his own business.'

'Shades of Uriah Heap perhaps?'

'Who?' chirped Eliza Jane cheekily.

Campion sighed loudly.

'My dear, your education really needs to be brought to book, as well as your rather modern language.'

'Cool it, Uncle, don't have a heart attack,' grinned the girl. 'I was kidding. I know full well who Uriah Heap was – and that he was always "very 'umble" but that's not something one could ever say about Leonard Sherman, from what I hear, and certainly not to his son and grandson. *That* I can testify to, but if you want a character reference for the late Leonard Sherman, ask your number one fan Clarissa. She thought him a first-rate bad 'un and she was genuinely scared of him. She says that his funeral was a great relief for the whole village. Ben is convinced it was a Sherman – Dennis or Clifford – who shot you out at Long Tye Farm.'

'Does your Ben have a theory as to why either one should do such a thing?'

'Well Clifford might, just because he would think it was funny, but I don't think Dennis would – not as long as your Jaguar was being repaired in his garage. I mean, that would be bad business, wouldn't it, and with Dennis, business always comes first. I can't see him taking a pot shot at you until your garage bill had been settled.'

'So there's one person who will be glad to see me back in Lindsay,' said Mr Campion.

'Two,' corrected Eliza Jane. 'Don't forget Don the barman at The Woolpack. He has been so deprived of good gossip; he's been pining at the moon for your return.'

If he had been expecting bunting, a brass band, a token Morris dance and a welcoming committee with speeches from local worthies, then Mr Campion was disappointed (though he disguised it well) as Eliza Jane's sports car coasted down the deserted High Street of Lindsay Carfax and with a gentle squeak of brakes, halted at the door to her cottage.

'Oh God, my secret admirer has been to call, again. I wonder what it is this time.'

Mr Campion's eyes followed the girl's pointing finger and focussed on a polythene bag sitting on the doorstep.

'You're sure it's not a bomb, my dear? My secret admirers always send me bombs on high days and holidays.'

'It will be something sickly and quite ghastly if

past form is anything to go by.'

'You've had love tokens before?'

'Love tokens? That sounds awfully quaint, Uncle.'

'I'm considered a very quaint character in some circles,' admitted Mr Campion, 'but love tokens have a long and distinguished history. Convicts being transported to Australia used to engrave a little rhyme on coins or bits of scrimshaw for the loved ones they'd left behind: *When this you see, remember me*. I suspect the same principle holds good even if the art of engraving has been forgotten.'

'Well, I wish my secret – and unwanted – admirer would go to Australia and bloody well forget where I lived!'

Campion peered over the rims of his spectacles as Eliza Jane drummed the steering wheel with her fingers.

'I take it that Ben Judd is not the phantom present-giver, then?' he said.

'God, no! He would go berserk if he found out. Thankfully, these anonymous little presents turn up when Ben's away or locked in his studio working. Come on; let's go see what the pest has left me this time.'

If it was possible to flounce out of a small, low-slung sports car, then Eliza Jane flounced athletically and strode around to the passenger door to help her uncle with his far more laborious exit. When Campion had stretched and bent his back, rather like a cat preparing for its morning patrol in search of breakfast, he reached back into the car for his silver-tipped walking cane

319

which had managed to get itself wedged behind the gear stick.

'Can't go without my pilgrim's staff,' he said jovially. 'I could give that bag a poke with it, you know, just in case it is a bomb.'

'It won't be anything as interesting as a bomb,' said Eliza Jane cynically. 'It will be chocolates, or a houseplant in a grubby pot, or a horrid vase or cheap perfume. Once, I swear, it was a badly-stuffed teddy bear straight off a fairground rifle range.'

They approached the bag together and without hesitating, the girl scooped it up, thrust a hand inside and withdrew a bottle shape wrapped in tissue paper.

'Things may be looking up,' she said, 'this might be something we can drink and not something to be donated to the White Elephant stall at the church fête – anonymously of course.' But as she tore at the tissue wrapping, her expression changed. 'Oh no, we can forget that! It's a Barsac. Ben says that's the wine stupid women drink with dinner because Babycham and Blue Nun are thought common!'

'Tell him not to be such a snob,' Mr Campion chided her. 'Barsac is next door to Sauternes and they are both very respectable Bordeaux wines.'

'Dessert wines,' moaned Eliza Jane, 'why do men always think girls only like sweet drinks? Port and lemon, rum and blackcurrant, gin and that awful orange squash stuff, whisky and lime cordial ... Sometimes I feel like storming into the Woolpack and demanding a pint of best bitter!'

'I'm not sure Don the barman is a supporter of

Drinkers' Liberation, let alone Women's Lib and you might just induce a heart attack. You should be grateful, that's quite an expensive bottle you've got there, judging by the price written on the label in French francs. Has your secret admirer been across the Channel recently?'

'How would I know?' the girl replied crossly, thrusting the bottle towards Campion. 'Here, take the damned thing, I daren't let Ben find it here as he'll know I didn't buy it. He's very insistent, quite fierce really, that he alone buys our wine. Anyway, the only people I know who've been to France recently are old man Marchant and old man Fuller and they always bring presents for Clarissa, but not for little ole me.'

'So who is your furtive present-giver?'

'I honestly haven't a clue,' said Eliza Jane firmly.

'Really?' said Campion softly. 'I have.'

Mr Campion refused to elaborate there on the doorstep but hinted that he might if Miss Fitton would accept dinner at the Woolpack in recompense for her duties as a chauffeuse. Miss Fitton performed a mock curtsy, attempting Georgian deference despite the shortness of her skirt, and informed her kind suitor that she would be delighted to accompany him to said hostelry but only after she had bathed and changed. They arranged to meet at the inn at eight o'clock, by which time Campion would have reclaimed his room and belongings and have been debriefed by Don.

Campion took the holdall Amanda had bought him from the boot of the sports car and watched as Eliza locked the car and then unlocked her front door. Again, she asked him to take charge of the bottle of Barsac – 'in case Ben pops round and spots it' – and before he could agree she had thrust it into the holdall, burying it in folds of green flannel pyjama.

'Taking alcohol into a public house?' observed Campion with a smile. 'It positively reeks of Prohibition and speakeasies in the America of my youth, or perhaps coals-to-Newcastle is the phrase I'm looking for.'

'I'll see you later,' said Eliza Jane, kissing him lightly on the cheek. 'Don't let Don stand you too many drinks before I get there.'

'I will do my very best to resist his generosity.'

With his hold-all in his left hand and his 'pilgrim's staff' in the other, Mr Campion stretched his long legs and strode up the High Street, wincing slightly as the tender muscles in his right thigh reminded him of walking-wounded status. But he did not go to the Woolpack directly. As soon as the inn's ornate frontage came into sight around the bend of the street, he crossed to the other side of the road and continued up the slight hill. Passing the house and museum of Josiah Humble on his left (now fortunately closed for the day, though Campion mentally reached for his wallet), he turned his face to the windows as though absorbing every historical detail. Thus he hoped to be, if not unobserved, at least unrecognised by any prying eyes from the bar of the Woolpack opposite.

He continued past Humble's as the street curved to the left of the Carders' Hall which sat in raised isolation, grandly allowing the High Street to flow down either side of its imperious timbers like an island in the stream. In a flight of whimsy, Campion imagined the view from the air would remind him of the Ile de la Cité in Paris with the High Street playing the part of the Seine and the Hall doubling as Notre Dame.

Now hidden from the Woolpack by the regal bulk of the Hall, the flint and stone solidity of St Catherine and St Blaise loomed ahead of him like a jutting architectural jaw offended at the proximity of the Hall with its warm, intricately carved wooden features. But before reaching the church, Campion turned smartly left and through a broken wooden gate which guarded a weed-and-gravel path and bore a pokerwork oak sign announcing 'The Vicarage'.

It was a cold, plain, grey stone and slate-tiled building with dark windows, seemingly built by Victorians determined to establish a plain counterpoint to the medieval and Tudor richness of the village. The present incumbent was clearly no gardener and, judging by the state of the window frames and front door, no particular fan of do-it-yourself either.

Mr Campion paused on the stoop and briefly turned his head to look behind him; not to see if he was being followed, for he was sure he was not, but to judge the distance from the vicarage to the Carders Hall. Satisfied with his mental calculations, he raised his cane and rapped severely three times. After a minute of muffled thumps and the rattling of a surprising number of bolts and locks, the door was opened by a wide-eyed and rather dishevelled vicar.

'Good heavens!' exclaimed the Rev Leslie Trump as he scanned his visitor from shoes to spectacles.

'I feel that would be more your department,' Mr Campion said cheerfully. 'I would like a quick word on something more earthly, if I'm not intruding of course.'

The Rev Trump was dressed in jeans, brown leather sandals (and grey socks) and his uniform white polo-neck and black pullover, tucked into the front of which was a blue-and-white striped tea towel employed as a napkin.

'No, not intruding...' he started hesitantly '...I was just having some cold cuts for my tea and my housekeeper, Mrs Duck, has the evening off. We were not expecting guests...'

Mr Campion moved the holdall slightly behind his legs.

'Please do not be alarmed by the luggage. I am en route to the Woolpack – which is where we first met.'

'We did?'

'You were emerging from one of the famous Lindsay secret passages, in hot pursuit of a suspected intruder, I believe,' Campion reminded him.

'Oh yes ... yes, of course. You're Albert Campion. I heard you'd been shot.'

'A popular rumour, I'm sure, though I assure you I stand before you in fairly rude health and I seek only a brief audience in order to pick your brains on a point of local history.'

The Rev Trump's face, which was that of a cherub with a permanent hangover, brightened with surprise.

'I have little interest in history, local or otherwise, but to be asked an opinion on any subject in this parish is an irresistible appeal to my vanity. Come in, come in.'

Campion followed the diminutive Trump down a short corridor and into the vicarage kitchen where a bare pine table displayed a half-consumed plate of thick slices of meat of unidentifiable origin surrounded by dollops of pickled red cabbage, a pickled egg and several pickled onions the size of golf balls. Next to the plate and its knife and fork akimbo, was a pint mug of cooling tea and a book – *Trout Fishing in America* by Richard Brautigan, which Campion knew had little to do with matters piscatorial.

'Can I get you anything?' the vicar offered, sweeping an arm towards the huge enamel kitchen range without the slightest conviction that he knew how any of it worked.

'Thank you, but no,' said Campion, 'but I will take a seat to rest my leg, if I may.'

Trump scurried to pull out a plain pine dining chair for him and as he settled on it Campion said, 'Do continue with your meal. Please accept my apologies for interrupting and I do promise to be brief.'

Once Trump was seated again and had speared a forkful of meat and pickles, he looked at Campion expectantly. 'How can I help you?'

'It's about one of your predecessors – a long

time before your time – the Reverend Austin Bonus. I was wondering if you knew the real story.'

'Everyone in the village does,' said Trump between chews. 'He was the vicar here before the Great War and did a disappearing act for nine days, but came back and did great things for the church and the school.'

'When we first met,' Campion said smoothly, 'you implied that you thought Bonus had some sort of hold over that other local institution, the Carders.'

'Did I?' Trump swallowed heavily and his face blushed pink. 'I don't remember.'

'I do. You distinctly implied that the Rev Bonus had threatened to make a stink about the Carders and in return for his silence, the church got a new roof and a new organ.' Mr Campion used the flat of his right hand on the silver tip of his stick to make slow circling movements, an activity which seemed to hypnotise Leslie Trump. 'But I think you got it the wrong way round,' he continued quietly. 'Austin Bonus didn't threaten the Carders; they protected him. You might almost say they saved him from himself.'

Leslie Trump had dropped his arms on to the table as if the knife and fork he held had suddenly increased greatly in weight.

'I don't know what you're getting at, Mr Campion, or why you think I know anything except the local legend about Austin Bonus. The poor man was dead long before I was born.'

'But you have access to the church accounts

326

and if you were diligent in your duties, which I am sure you are, you will have looked at them if only for insurance purposes. I think you are well aware of the massive injection of capital which your church received just before the Great War thanks to Austin Bonus and I also suspect you know where it came from. It certainly wasn't raised by jumble sales and whist drives – not in a village well past the prosperity it had once enjoyed nor from a shrinking congregation.'

'You appear to have given this matter considerable thought,' said Trump, narrowing his eyes in a poor attempt at defiance.

'I have had surplus thinking time recently,' said Campion, 'which many say is always dangerous for a man of little brain. Shall I tell you what I think really happened?'

'I can see you want to,' the small man said petulantly.

'Forgive the vanity of old age,' Campion deferred. 'I suspect the Rev Bonus to have been something of a highly-strung fellow, though his heart was in the right place. He is supposed to have had plans to set up a home here for waifs and strays from the East End but there was clearly no money for such project, not with the church in disrepair and the parish no longer rich. This vicarage, which I suspect was built – around 1880?'

Campion paused as Trump nodded in silent agreement.

'Well, with the best will in the world, it's hardly a lavish building, is it? Very basic by Victorian standards but all the parish could afford at the time. It hardly matches the splendour of the fantastic wool church next door, and I know such things should not matter in a perfect world but I suspect the lack of church funds played on Austin Bonus's mind, perhaps even snapped it.

'Something certainly did, or perhaps he had a revelation or an epiphany. He took a desperate gamble, literally. He seized whatever church funds he could and guided by a shining light or a voice in his head, he made his way to Monte Carlo where he made one spectacular, and spectacularly lucky, bet on the roulette wheel. He returned to Lindsay Carfax with his winnings – a considerable sum in those days – and as he travelled by the cheapest means, I surmise that the round trip took him nine days and thus was a legend born.

'If the Carders – whoever they were at the time – had any influence on the wayward vicar, it was probably that they helped cover up that initial misappropriation of church funds and kept the story out of the newspapers. It was probable too that Austin Bonus's conscience was pricking him, once he realised he had behaved quite outrageously. I do not pretend to know what the Bible says about gambling, but Old Bones would have known.'

'It says surprisingly little,' volunteered Trump. 'In Timothy we have "Love of money is the root of all evil" which is a verse most people know but misquote and then in Proverbs it says "Wealth gained hastily will dissolve", though neither specifically mentions gambling.'

'I bow to your knowledge of Scripture but I

think the Reverend Bonus was a decent man who, at the very least knew he had betrayed the trust of his parishioners. I also think the Carders reminded him of the fact that if his escapades made the popular press, his Bishop would come down on him like the proverbial ton of loose roof slates. The money he had won, however, could be wisely spent on the church, a new organ and improvements at the Carders School, all credit, of course, going to the Carders. The true source of the money – Bonus's bonus if you like – was kept quiet and because the vicar had been missing for nine days, somebody called it a "Nine Days' Wonder" and it became a sort of trade mark of the Carders, or so they were happy to let people think.'

'I always assumed it was an old tradition for the Carders to deal in units of nine,' Trump commented in a disinterested way.

'My sources – impeccable when it comes to folklore and humbuggery – can find no reference to a "Nine Days Wonder" specific to Lindsay Carfax before the tale of Austin Bonus and as far as we know, he never told anyone his story. Do you know what happened to him?'

'Only that he left the living of Lindsay in 1915.'

'He did indeed,' Campion said, stabbing the point of his cane into the floor. 'He joined the 5th Battalion of the Suffolk Regiment Territorials as a chaplain and went to Gallipoli with them in 1915. He did not return, but the Regimental war diary speaks highly of his courage and compassion under fire.'

'You say that in a way which indicates you expect me to feel guilty about something, Mr Campion. Just what is your interest in this matter?'

'A little bit of guilt is surely good for us all,' replied Campion without humour, 'and my interest in Austin Bonus is purely academic, simply a piece of wood to be cut away so I may see the trees.'

'And the trees are the Carders?'

'Some of them, perhaps not all.'

'Well, if you fancy your chances as a lumberjack, I'll help you lop off a few of their odious branches.' The small man jutted his jaw pugnaciously, but he still reminded Mr Campion of a consumptive cherub.

'I do not need your help, Vicar, merely your permission.'

'Permission to do what?'

'To burgle your vicarage sometime tonight or tomorrow. It would be awfully helpful if you left the front door unlocked.'

Eighteen

Centre of the Web

On leaving the vicarage, and a slightly bemused Leslie Trump, Mr Campion embraced the gathering dusk and decided to take the longer way back to the Woolpack by circumnavigating the large traffic island on which sat the Carders Hall. He passed the looming church and crossed the road before risking the edge of the village pond, which brought him to the north-east corner of the Carders Hall and opposite the frontage of The Medley where, although closed to commerce, a few low-wattage bulbs had been left on to display the shop's motley wares to any insomniac art-loving customers. In the distance, down the slope of the street to his left, he could see the lights on in Sherman's Garage and a vehicle pulling up to its pumps, but Campion turned to his right and, tapping his Pilgrim's Staff as he went, walked the semi-circle around the Hall, passing the dark and closed up Prentice House, until he was greeted by the warm glow of the Woolpack. Now, perhaps, there would be bunting and brass bands.

He settled for a large gin and tonic 'on the house of course' from Don the barman, who seemed genuinely pleased to see the return of his most valuable – in gossip terms – resident, though the bar being almost empty he lacked a suitable audience for his largesse.

'Your room's just as you left it, Mr C.,' Don announced, 'barring the necessary hoovering of course, nothing's been touched, and here's your key.'

Don pressed a room key on to the bar next to the drink he had just presented. Campion looked at it quizzically.

'Mr Marchant handed it in after your ... er ... accident,' Don supplied.

Campion made a show of being relieved, as if the loss of the key had weighed heavily on his mind. In truth he was mildly amused that some-one had gone through his pockets whilst un-conscious, but now that Don had provided the opening...

'Talking of keys, old chap,' beamed Campion, 'you offered me a key to your secret passage when I arrived. Is there any chance I could take you up on the offer now? I fancy a little snoop down there before I leave Lindsay.'

Don raised an eyebrow, noting another gem of gossip, and placed a second key on the bar.

'You'll be dining with us tonight, Mr C.?'

'Absolutely, and with a very attractive young lady,' Campion teased.

'Miss Fitton will be joining you then?' Don smirked.

'I'm sure my secret is safe with you, Don.' Campion tapped the side of his nose conspira-torially.

332

'Your other guest is already here.' Don nodded towards the rear corner of the bar where Campion had sat only to be disturbed by the Rev Trump emerging from the panelling. At the table there, nursing a half of bitter, his shoulders hunched, sat Lemuel Walker.

'I don't think he will be joining us for dinner,' said Campion pocketing the two keys and making his way over to the waiting schoolmaster.

'Thank you for seeing me, Mr Walker.'

'I only came because Mortimer asked me to,' said the seated man.

'I asked Dr Casson to ring you because our last meeting was rather strained and I need your help.'

Campion placed his glass on the table and pulled out a chair, lowering himself gently and wincing as he did so, though Lemuel Walker offered not a shred of sympathy for the invalid.

'I am not prepared to speak about the Carders. I have said everything I had to say on that subject. I believe you were there at my lecture.'

'Indeed I was, but I was more interested in what you did *after* the lecture.'

'I have no idea what you mean,' said Walker, but he said it far too quickly.

'I think you disappeared into the woodwork that night, quite literally: using the not-very-secret secret passages that radiate from the Carders Hall.'

'What if I did? I was merely waiting for the audience to disperse, having made it clear I would not answer any more foolish questions.'

'And in your subterranean peregrinations, did

333

you stumble in to the passageway that leads to the Vicarage?'

'What's your interest in all this, Campion? Just who are you and what are you trying to prove?'

Campion took off his spectacles, produced his handkerchief and with flourishes began to polish the lenses.

'My trouble, Mr Walker, is that I have a compulsion to tie off loose threads wherever I find them and there seem to be an awful lot lying about in Lindsay Carfax. Moreover, I think they are silken threads from a rather old and dusty spider's web at the centre of which is something really unpleasant. Oh, not you; you are, I feel, very much on the fringe of things. But if you won't confirm your movements, would you at least describe the underground network in Lindsay for me? That makes it sound a bit like the Piccadilly Line, doesn't it?'

Lemuel Walker studied Campion intently. Here sat a figure Walker was unfamiliar with: a man who didn't mind appearing ineffectual if not a bit of an idiot – in fact he seemed to revel in that persona. Walker had not encountered anyone like Campion before, but he was intelligent enough to recognise the steely resolve beneath the casual surface.

'You can read about the "Carfax Passages", as the tour guides call them, in any decent guide book. I don't see why you need...'

'Please indulge an old man.' Campion's tone suggested an order, not a request.

'Very well, there is little mystery or secrecy about them,' Walker said reluctantly. 'They were probably dug in the early eighteenth century and used to hide smuggled goods including woollen fleeces and even live sheep, at a time when...'

Mr Campion put up a hand, as a schoolboy would.

'Please sir, if you don't mind, I consider myself to be something of an expert on the ancient crime of "owling" – or at least more of an expert than I was this time last week. Could we skip the history and stick to the geography, please?'

'Very, well, I'll make it short and sweet. If you imagine the Carders Hall as the centre of a wheel, then the four spokes, or passages, run to the Humble Museum, the shrine to Ester Wickham that is the Prentice House, here to the Woolpack and, yes, the Vicarage.'

'The Vicarage is a relatively modern building, though.'

'True, but it was built on the site of a much older house which had fallen down. The Victorians didn't try and replicate the Tudor architecture or craftsmanship, more's the pity, but they made the passage entrance part of a cellar rather than block it off.'

'I see. And the passages are reasonably passable?'

'Oh yes. You need a torch of course and they are quite low and they twist and turn somewhat, but they rarely flood and one sees relatively few rats down there.'

Mr Campion rapped a knuckle on the wall panelling beside him.

'So, if I was to use the Woolpack passage, I could get straight into the cellar of the Vicarage without passing "Go" or collecting £200?'

'You could, as long as you knew the right exit passage.'

'Please explain,' Campion said, all flippancy gone.

'The Woolpack passage is your entrance passage That takes you to the Carders Hall, or rather the cellars under it. Actually, it is one big cellar, rather like a catacomb and it is the hub for the other passages, from the Vicarage, Humble's and the Prentice House. As long as you pick the right passage, you come up at the right destination, but it is very dark and disorientating down there. Very dark...'

Campion watched the schoolmaster's face intently.

'Is that where they kept you?'

Lemuel Walker's eyes widened in horror and the hand holding his glass shook so violently that beer splashed out; but his reaction had not been triggered by Campion's comment, rather by what the schoolmaster had seen over Campion's shoulder.

'I have to go,' said Walker as he jerked himself upright, shaking the table.

Speechless, Campion watched him scurry to the doorway where, with head down and without a word, he pushed through the small crowd of patrons who had just entered rather loudly and were already calling out their orders to Don.

Campion recognised them all: Gus Marchant, wallet already in hand, Clarissa Webster strategically placed with Marcus Fuller on one arm and his son Simon on the other, and bringing up the rear at a more sedate pace, the sepulchral figure of Hereward Spindler, lawyer of this parish. Mr Campion wondered which one of them had frightened Walker so much and so suddenly.

Perhaps all of them.

They may not have been playing brass instruments and there was no sign of any bunting, but Mr Campion's official welcoming committee had finally arrived. Gus Marchant clapped his hands on Campion's shoulders and called loudly for drinks all round. Clarissa Webster, on tiptoes, leaned in far closer than was necessary to kiss him on both cheeks then demanded that Marchant ordered champagne. Marcus Fuller offered a claw to shake and his son Simon, straight faced, nodded politely in curt military fashion. Hereward Spindler said, to no one in particular, that he would much prefer a dry sherry and looked as if he would rather be anywhere else in the world.

Mr Campion restored order to the adoring throng by refusing their hospitality on the grounds that he had to yet to check into his room ('Number 8 isn't it, Don?' to which the barman, now part of the throng, nodded in agreement), have a wash, find a clean shirt and get back down to treat his niece to a splendid dinner. After that, however, he would be in party mood and quite willing to demonstrate that his recent injury did not impair his ability to do the Charleston or the Black Bottom, though the Twist might be beyond him.

'Oh, you must have one drink with us,' vamped

Mrs Webster, 'so we can welcome you back to the village.'

'I will, dear lady, I will, but I have promised Eliza Jane dinner and you would all be welcome to join us were it not that we had family affairs to discuss. If you will allow me to fulfil that obligation, then I will be all yours. In fact, your being here has saved me the trouble of gathering you all together in the library later for a demonstration of my amazing deductive powers.'

'What the devil are you talking about?' demanded Gus Marchant.

'What library? We don't have a library,' added Mrs Webster.

'I know you don't,' said Campion with a broad smile, 'but I just couldn't resist. I've always wanted to gather all the suspects in a library.'

'Suspects?' said Marcus Fuller, close to bluster.

'Did I say "suspects"? I do apologise, I meant Carders, and I suppose it would be only polite to wait for the other two to join us.'

There was a stunned silence in the bar. The atmosphere of bubbling enthusiasm had been replaced by cool uncertainty.

Campion himself broke the silence by picking up his holdall and, using his cane to full effect, limping dramatically towards the staircase which led to the inn's rooms. As he did so, he called out 'Toodles!' without looking back.

In his room, Campion threw his cane and holdall on to the bed and did a rapid inventory of his possessions. Nothing was missing and he was touched to see that a shirt had been washed and ironed, a pair of trousers pressed and his shoes shined. He washed, shaved and changed, revelling in the comfort of familiar clothes, though he would never have criticized Amanda's choices in the provision of his emergency wardrobe.

Once his tie was neatly knotted and his faithful hairbrush had done its best to bring order to his white locks – still luxuriant enough to be a source of envy among his peers – he took his Olympus camera from its case and checked that he had sufficient film and that his flash unit was in full 'Watch the Birdy!' working mode. Then he slung the camera case over his shoulder, grabbed the spurned bottle of Barsac from his hold-all and the copy of Esther Wickham's *The Face of Diligence* from his bedside table, and made his way back down to the bar.

The five people he had left in the bar were still there and had been joined by a sixth, Dennis Sherman, and all were fully armed with drinks. As Campion entered, all eyes fixed upon him and he grinned inanely at them in return as he eased his way through them, acknowledging only Don the barman who announced that Miss Fitton was awaiting him in the dining room. As if that was a pre-arranged signal, (and it was), Campion set his course for the dining room, determined not to be diverted or delayed.

To Gus Marchant's demand that he now – finally – join them for a drink, he merely shook his head. To Mrs Webster's plea that, surely, he had time for her now, he smiled his Sunday best smile and strode on. Only when Dennis Sherman, wearing an immaculate sports jacket over brown, oil-stained overalls, said 'Your Jaguar's all fixed, good as new, Mr Campion, whenever you're ready to leave' did Campion pause and acknowledge the garage owner with a polite nod.

He was approaching the entrance to the dining room when he heard two of the male voices say in stage whispers: 'Damned odd behaviour' and then 'Bloody rude if you ask me' and he stopped in his tracks.

There was an embarrassed silence, the sort of guilty silence usually reserved for when a class-room misdemeanour is about to be publicly revealed, as Mr Campion turned towards the six faces frowning at him. But he spoke only to the sixth face, that of Don behind the bar, which remained professionally inexpressive.

'I almost forgot,' said Campion as if he and Don had the bar to themselves, 'do you have such a thing as an ice-bucket?'

'Of course we do,' said Don proudly.

'And do you have ice?'

'I'll see what I can find in the kitchen fridge,' said Don less confidently.

'Good man. Put this in it, would you?' Campion handed over the bottle of Barsac he had been clutching. 'Just leave it on the bar, please. We'll be out as soon as we have finished dinner.'

'I don't believe it! I think you've managed to snub the entire village in one fell swoop.'

Mr Campion smiled benignly at his niece and said: 'Not the *entire* village, only the Carders – or most of them.'

'Did you arrange for them to be here?'

'Not exactly; I simply made sure that Don knew I was meeting Lemuel Walker here earlier and consequently I attracted quite a crowd. Now let's enjoy our dinner. I see it's mutton on the menu tonight – how apt for an inn called the Woolpack – and as we eat it must seem as if we are deep in conspiratorial conversation.'

Eliza Jane bit her bottom lip until a maternal waitress, who enquired politely after Mr Campion's 'accident' (and was assured that he was now 'fighting fit'), had served them with oxtail soup and bread rolls which had seen better days, none of them today. With a spoon delicately poised halfway to her mouth, she whispered, 'You do realise they're all watching us from the bar, don't you?'

'I should jolly well hope so, I want them straining with curiosity,' replied Campion, 'and although it is not good manners, I have a book I wish you to read, or at least look at, whilst you eat.'

From his jacket pocket he produced *The Face of Diligence* and laid it next to Eliza's soup plate so that their waitress could not fail to see the title.

'Is this charade absolutely necessary?'

'Possibly not, but isn't it fun to discomfit one's enemies?'

'Enemies? That lot?'

'Well, perhaps not all of them, but they all have something to hide.'

'What?'

'Perhaps we'll find out when the second act

starts.'

'And when does the curtain go up on that?'

'As soon as we've finished dinner and joined our friends, or enemies, in the bar when you will have your own starring role, as long as you are happy to go through with it.'

'Are you sure he'll come?'

'Oh, I think we've given the jungle drums enough time to get the message out. Are you sure Ben Judd *won't* come?'

'I gave him his orders,' said Eliza Jane firmly, 'and I hope to God he sticks to them, because if he turns up here, he'll blow his top and thump somebody and that's a certainty. As certain as the fact that the oxtail soup came out of a packet.'

'Yes, Ben is a bit of a loose cannon,' said Campion thoughtfully, 'but if he sticks to the plan, there will be a bit of excitement in it for him later on. Just remember, the objective to-night is to lull the Carders into a false sense of security.'

'Which of them are Carders?' the girl returned to whispering mode whilst sneaking a furtive glance towards the bar.

'Why, all of them,' said Campion in his normal voice, 'except Don of course.'

'It was always fairly obvious, wasn't it?'

As Campion and Eliza Jane tucked in to their dinner, seemingly in intimate and occasionally animated conversation as they did so, the noise level in the bar resembled a continuous rumble if not a soft growl.

'What is the man up to?'

'If the man's got something to say to us, why doesn't he come out and say it?'

'We might not want to hear it.'

'Oh for goodness' sake, don't start with the sackcloth and ashes. We've done nothing wrong.'

'Or illegal.'

'Others might put a different interpretation on events.'

'Don't you start getting cold feet...'

'Cold feet about what? What have we got to worry about?'

'Nothing, if we remember our oath and that what we have done has always been to "contribute to the common area".'

'And *that* covers a multitude of sins.'

'What do you mean by that?'

'Please don't play the innocent; it simply does not cut the mustard.'

'Look! He's got the book.'

'What book?'

'One of the Wickham's.'

'So what?'

'Oh dear, you really don't know, do you?'

'Know what?'

'Shut up. Campion knows nothing. He can't. He's bluffing.'

'Bluffing? To what end?'

'To get a reaction from us. If we all keep our nerve and keep quiet, how can he hurt us?'

'I don't know, but I think we're about to find out. Here he comes.'

Mr Campion settled himself in a captain's chair,

stretched out his right leg with a suitably martyred sigh of suffering, placed the tip of his walking stick between his knees and rested both hands on its silver top. Eliza Jane had, as they had agreed, perched on a bar stool and after a brief struggle to retain as much modesty as possible given the shortness of her skirt, had crossed her legs and anchored herself to the bar with an elbow. Don, without prompting, placed an ice bucket advertising tonic water but containing the bottle of Barsac on the bar in front of her and at her nodded command, set to opening it.

Gus Marchant, feeling the need to exert seniority if not authority, was the first to break the uncomfortable silence.

'Now what's all this about, Campion? I feel as we have all been summoned to the headmaster's study.'

'That was sort of the atmosphere I was aiming for,' replied Campion, blinking innocently behind his spectacles, 'but I see we are not all gathered in yet.'

'What do you mean by that?'

'I see only six Carders before me. One cannot be with us and one is not in this country, but that still leaves us one shy. Where is Tommy Tucker?'

Marchant's face contorted in surprise, then shock, as Clarissa Webster thrust a chair behind his knees.

'Sit down before you fall down, Gus,' she ordered, then to Campion she said: 'He's in the public bar. I saw him sneak in there just after the charming Eliza arrived, strangely enough.'

344

Mr Campion attempted to decipher the look Mrs Webster gave his niece, but quickly accepted defeat.

'Would you ask Mr Tucker to join us, Don?' he suggested and the barman, eager to please, disappeared as smoothly as a carnival conjurer's trick.

Moments later, a short, thin young man with long, greasy black hair and a face showing the scars of a losing battle with acne, entered and surveyed the assembled throng with a sneer and a swagger of bony shoulders inside a leather jacket far too big for his frame. Until, that is, he saw Eliza Jane on her bar stool and his expression softened to a simper as he sidled up to lean on the bar.

'Ah, Mr Tucker, we haven't met before,' said Campion making no move to stand or even spare the younger man a second glance, 'but I have seen you around and have heard quite a lot about you.'

'If we are all assembled to your satisfaction, Albert,' Clarissa Webster scolded, 'would you mind awfully saying what you are clearly bursting to get off your mind so that we can enjoy the rest of our lives?'

'Which I am sure you all will, once you have allowed me to indulge myself.'

'Are you accusing us – singly or collectively – of something? I should remind you that I am a practising solicitor,' said Hereward Spindler gravely.

'He wouldn't bloody dare!' snapped Simon Fuller with venom.

'Marcus, kindly ask your brother to button his lip,' commanded Marchant, 'so that Campion can crack on with whatever it is he's got to say.'

'Thank you,' said Campion politely. 'Crack on I will. I do not intend to make any specific accusations, but I would like to give you a little lecture, so please pay attention, for there may be questions at the end.

'First of all, I have to say that I came to Lindsay Carfax in a state of blissful ignorance. However, certain unfortunate incidents, involving potential danger to my niece and other members of my family, plus actual bodily harm to a valued motor car and to a sensitive area of my own person – which may not be valuable, but is valued – have led me to take an interest in the place. You might say an academic interest and I would like to share my new-found knowledge with you.'

'He talks a lot, don't he?'

Several heads turned towards the bar where Tommy Tucker leaned as if auditioning for the role of 'insolent motorcycle tearaway' in a bad second feature. It was only an ice-cold glare from Eliza Jane which prevented further outbursts.

'I was intrigued to hear of a secret sect called the Carders,' Campion continued, 'and even more intrigued to discover that it wasn't all that secret. In fact, I discovered that I had been introduced to most of them. Now do tell me if I am wildly off the mark in any particular, but I am assuming that the current membership list of the Carders contains Mr Marchant, the two Fullers, my learned friend Mr Spindler, Mr Sherman, the

charming Mrs Webster–' (Here Campion allowed himself a smile and a nod in Clarissa's direction) '– and Mr Tucker, who has now joined us.
That makes seven, but there should be nine – that
mystical number nine. So, *in absentia,* let me
acknowledge Lady Prunella Redcar and the late
Leonard Sherman, whose death last year left the
Carders numbering eight, which is a lucky number in China, but not, it seems, in Suffolk.

'You see, lady and gentlemen, it was your un-
successful attempt to recruit Ben Judd to bring
your numbers back to the traditional nine which
made it all clear to these old and failing eyes.
Ben was approached by virtue of the fact that his
mother's maiden name was Dyer. There was the
link and the clue even I could not ignore. To be
entitled to be a Carder, by history and tradition,
one had to have a surname connected with the
wool trade, from which the Carders drew their
original power and wealth. A Dyer was, clearly,
someone involved in the dyeing of woollen
cloth. A Marchant, or Merchant, was someone
who sold wool; a Sherman, or *shear*-man was
someone who sheared sheep; Fullers, Spindlers
and Websters – or Weavers – were all trades of
the wool industry. As were Pinners, which I
believe was Mrs Webster's maiden name. Ironically, a "Walker" as in Lemuel Walker is also a
surname connected to the wool trade as in walking the sheep to market, but poor Lemuel was an
outsider, his family was not from around here, as
I believe they say in the more rural parts of
America, or perhaps Norfolk.

'For a while, I was stumped by Mr Tucker, or

347

rather by his name, until I remembered that in Dutch, it would be spelled T-u-k-k-e-r which derives from the occupation of towel-maker, towels being made from wool and the wool trade in Breda in Holland having historic ties to the industry here in Suffolk. Indeed I am reliably informed that Breda and Ipswich were notorious centres of "owling" at one time, though that may be a story for which the world is not quite ready. The point is that I believe Mr Tucker's family to be of Dutch origin and that he himself actually speaks Dutch, Not bad, eh? Considering I have only just met him ... but please don't applaud just yet.

'Lady Prunella Redcar's status as a Carder took a bit more detective work. Not by me, I hasten to add, but some of the finest minds in Cambridge. Historically, the most important figure in the Carder hierarchy was the Abbot of Lindsay Carfax, who controlled the vast wealth represented by all the sheep the Abbey owned. When jolly old Henry VIII decided to call time on the Abbey, the wealth and property of the place devolved to a series of non-religious landowners, merchants and farmers. Whoever owned a piece of the old Abbey lands could, however, be appointed as one of the Nine Carders as a representative of the old Abbot. By the early nineteenth century, that privilege, even though it was by then an honorary position, had fallen to a certain Esther Wickham, spinster of this parish and, as it turned out, prolific novelist.'

Campion paused, stretched his back and held up his copy of *The Face of Diligence*.

'I am sure you all know this book, though you probably have not read it. I cannot blame you for that, as it is fairly dull and unimaginative stylistically, a bit like Thomas Hardy without the jokes, the gunfights and the cliff-hanger endings, but I digress.

'Esther Wickham died without heirs and her property was acquired by the Redcar family around 1873. By default, they also acquired the right to Carder membership thanks to the Abbot of Lindsay connection, though I suspect that by then the Carder sect was pretty moribund and almost penniless. Lady Prunella, the last of the Redcars, sold the Prentice House to Mr Spindler here, which not only kept things in the Carder family, but also helped to finance her move to the south of France and a more leisurely life. However...'

Campion paused for dramatic effect and held up the book again.

'...the physical property of Esther Wickham was only part of her estate. Apart from the house, some good grazing land and probably a few sheep, Esther Wickham also left a considerable amount of intellectual property, if I might call it that, in her books and poems. Interestingly – my associates in Cambridge used the word "incredibly" – Esther Wickham's literary works have remained in print for more than one hundred years. Now I am not suggesting that we are talking about best-selling books on the scale of, say, Mrs Christie, who I believe is still quite popular, but nonetheless reissues of the Wickham canon over time would have provided a steady income for someone – someone not too worried about the law of copyright.'

'Are you accusing me?' Hereward Spindler intoned in his best undertaker voice.

'I am accusing no one – individually. I believe the Carders, your predecessors that is, acted in concert and in the best secret society traditions. They kept quiet and discouraged anyone from asking questions, easing their consciences by doing the occasional charitable work for the good of "the common area" as their ancient oath specified. And round about 1910 the Carders had something of a windfall with the Rev. Austin Bonus who not only provided them with a lump sum he was too ashamed to own up to publicly, but by pure chance he provided a wonderful piece of mythology.

'The Rev Bonus's nine-day trip to the flesh-pots of Monte Carlo was the beginning of the Lindsay Carfax "nine days' wonder" legend. Thereafter, anything which was to the advantage of the Carders and which involved – I think the modern term is "putting the squeeze on" – some-one, took a magical nine days. Of course in reality it rarely did, but when the legend works better than the fact, here in the eastern marches, they stick to the legend. Most recently, of course, your schoolmaster Lemmy Walker was subjected to a bit of a going-over, partly I think because of his friendship with the students and hippies who invaded Lindsay Carfax last year and partly because he was looking for something. What? I have no idea. He certainly would not tell me, but his snooping was enough for the Carders to put the frighteners on him and to keep him out of public view for the regulation nine days.'

Mr Campion looked at each of the expectant faces looking at him.

'How am I doing so far?' he asked his rapt audience. 'Have I besmirched the good Carder name? Brought shame on Lindsay Carfax? Have I told you anything you did not know?'

When his rhetorical questions were greeted with a rhetorical silence, he continued. 'I thought not, but now perhaps I will. More than thirty years ago, when the world and I were much younger, there was a rather fatal nine days' wonder here in Lindsay. A bright young chap called Johnnie Sirrah...'

For the first time Campion was interrupted; by a loud gasp from Clarissa Webster.

'...who disappeared for the statutory nine days before being found dead at the bottom of Saxon Mills quarry, with which I recently became personally familiar. A distinguished policeman of my acquaintance, Charles Luke by name, is convinced that Johnnie's death was no accident yet could not come up with a motive, but I think I might have.

'Among the many fascinating people I talked to in Cambridge was an ancient professor of history – as opposed to a professor of ancient history – who actually remembered the name Johnnie Sirrah. It appears that Mr Sirrah, who was something of a man of letters, had written several times to the University Library asking for information on the copyright position on the works of Esther Wickham and what the penalties

351

were for unauthorised editions.

'Was it possible that Johnnie Sirrah was getting close to uncovering a rather shady source of Carder income and so had to be taught the traditional nine-day lesson? Only something went badly wrong and Johnnie ended up with his neck broken. The question is was it broken *before* he went over the edge of that quarry?'

'That is an outrageous suggestion,' boomed Gus Marchant, 'for which you have absolutely no proof!'

'I may not be able to prove anything at this distance in time, but I am convinced in my mind that the murder weapon came to light last year.'

'Pure fantasy!' snapped Marcus Fuller.

'The man's talking utter tommy-rot. He's either drunk or brain-damaged,' his brother joined in.

'Shut up, the lot of you!' shouted Mrs Webster, and she was instantly obeyed. 'I want to hear this. Go on, Albert.'

Mr Campion met Clarissa's fixed stare but retained his neutral expression.

'Do the names Stephen Stotter and Martin Rees mean anything to anyone?'

'Of course,' said Gus Marchant gruffly, 'we are neither ignorant nor heartless. Those were the two student boys who died here last summer.'

'Indeed they were. They were archaeologists on a training dig in the ruins of Lindsay Abbey, or what's left of it. They didn't find anything of interest, at least not from Tudor times, but they turned up something odd with their metal detector: the starting handle from a Ford 7 dating from about 1935 rather than 1535. Now I am not saying that we could prove this was a murder weapon but if, as young Mr Fuller suggests, someone was "brain damaged" out at Saxon Mills all those years ago, then it might be significant.'

'Don't put words into my mouth,' snarled Simon Fuller, 'I wasn't born when Sirrah died.'

'That seems a perfectly reasonable alibi to my non-legal mind and I repeat, I am not accusing any individual of anything.'

'But you are accusing the Carders *en masse* of something,' stated Hereward Spindler in a dry monotone.

'Mostly of being secretive simply for the sake of secrecy. There are some secrets which do not deserve to be kept and some which have no right to be secret. And on that enigmatic note: here endeth the lesson. I have no more to say except "Good Night", at least for the moment.'

With the aid of his cane, Mr Campion levered himself to his feet as his audience watched him in open-mouthed silence, but only for a few seconds.

'You're leaving?'

'Where the hell do you think you're going?'

'What intolerable behaviour!'

'Bloody rude!'

'You'll have to forgive me, but I'm only following doctor's orders,' said Campion, rapping the top of his cane on a table in a call for order. 'I am under instruction to exercise my recent injury by walking briskly for at least thirty minutes. As it is a fine, bright night, almost a full moon I believe, I will enjoy a final stroll around

Lindsay Carfax before I take my leave of it tomorrow.'

Campion slung his camera case over his shoulder and buttoned his jacket.

'I am sure Don here is anxious to serve you all with the drinks you look as if you are in need of. If you are still here when I return from my stroll, I will join you for proper farewells, should you feel like giving them. If, however, I am waylaid by Carders lurking in a dark alley and do not return for a period of nine days, I will know I have struck a nerve.'

Nineteen

Humble Pie

As soon as Mr Campion left the Woolpack he seemed, mysteriously, to be less in need of his cane as an aid to walking. If anything, his stride lengthened and his pace quickened as he took the right fork of the road running around the Carders' Hall, passing the Prentice House and The Medley again and aimed himself down the deserted High Street like a confident *boulevardier*.

Lindsay Carfax did not run to street-lighting, presumably on the grounds that it was unnecessary for the legitimate driving of sheep to market and a positive disadvantage to 'owling' activities. (Perhaps, Campion mused, it was something the Carders should consider as a project 'for the common area'.) Bright moonlight served well enough, however, and Campion heard no sound of a mass exit from the Woolpack behind him and saw no sign of roadblock or ambush ahead. The night was clear and cool with more than a hint of autumn and the faint scent of burning coal from domestic fires. The population of Lindsay seemed content to remain indoors, behind drawn curtains, basking in the warm glow of flickering television sets.

Down the slope, Campion crossed the road to the post office and village shop and then, with a final glance over his shoulder, he turned sharply left down the un-named side street which would take him to the converted barn where Ben Judd had his first-floor sleeping accommodation and his ground-floor studio.

Keeping to the left hand edge of the street, which was little more than a thinly metalled track, Campion paused for a moment to observe Sherman's Garage opposite. Although an outside light illuminated the forecourt and petrol pumps, the business was clearly closed and the place seemed deserted of all life save for the fact that someone had parked a dull white Bedford van with its rear doors snug up against the wooden doors of the garage's workshop.

'No, one thing at a time,' Campion said aloud and concentrated on finding his way down the dark lane without stumbling into the ditch he knew was to his left.

Sherman's Garage, like Ben Judd's studio-cum-flat, had started life as a weatherboard and brick barn. The third barn along the track had not been modernised as far as Campion knew and its silhouette loomed out of the moonlight to his left as the lights of Ben's studio came into sight, for which Campion felt relieved. He knew that even though remarkably fit for a man of his age, he was not spry enough to go investigating old agricultural buildings in the dark. Was it not said that more people were killed in agricultural accidents than road accidents? The very thought reminded him of the soreness in his rump and thigh and convinced him that surviving one agricultural accident per month was to be his limit.

Ben Judd snatched open the door of his studio before Campion's cane had rapped its third rap.

'You made it. I'd almost given up on you,' was his greeting.

'So many have in the past,' said Campion cheerfully. 'Did you get Eliza Jane's message about the torches?'

'All present and correct,' said Ben, leaving Campion in the doorway as he picked a duffel coat off the floor and put it on.

'And the right tools? So that we can, as the police would say, go out equipped for burglary?'

'I've even done a recce and all we need is a screwdriver. We can be in there in a jiffy, without having to blow the bloody doors off.'

'Oh good,' said Mr Campion, 'I was hoping for stealth and discretion rather than explosions and alarums.'

Ben Judd handed him a long, heavy rubber cased torch, the double of the one he held and which, with a click of rubber button, he shone full into Campion's face.

'You're a queer old stick, Campion, but I never had you down for a bit of breaking-and-entering.'

'Oh, I assure you,' Campion replied turning on his torch and holding it like a footlight to Judd's face, 'in my youth I was quite the recidivist, though always in a good cause I like to think. Shall we be about our shady business?'

In unison they clicked off their torches and were at the wooden doors of the unconverted barn before they switched them on again even though, as far as Campion could tell, the only eyes likely to be trained on them in that moonlit lane were those of rodents or their predators.

As Judd had reported, the doors were secured with a simple padlock and hasp and it was a matter of a minute for Ben to loosen and remove the four screws which held the hasp and ease the right hand door outwards, the padlock and hasp dangling from its metal hook on the left door.

Using the torches together as the headlights of a car, they illuminated the dry, dusty interior, sweeping the beams over a seemingly random collection of old agricultural tools, empty fertilizer sacks, unidentifiable bits of machinery, oil drums, empty and crushed petrol cans, lengths of rusting chain and saw blades, thick piles of damp and curling copies of *Farmer's Weekly* bound up with baling twine and any number of old tyres orphaned from their wheels. A blackened oak work bench complete with rusting vices stood against one wall and above it was fixed a tool rack displaying a fearsome arsenal of chisels, files, hand-saws and planes, all coated in cobwebs and a thick layer of rusty dust. Mr Campion suspected that the scene before them could be replicated in a thousand rural outbuildings in Suffolk, let alone the rest of the country.

'This is just junk,' said Judd. 'What exactly are we supposed to be looking for?'

'Something which may look like junk, but isn't.'

'That's not very helpful, old boy. Can't you be a bit more specific?'

'Canvas tents, camping stoves, sleeping bags, buckets, trowels, mattocks and what will look like a long piece of wood about three or four inches wide with numbers painted on it and metal clamps on the side.'

Judd grunted as if disgusted with the whole business but handed Campion his torch and set to with a noisy will, pulling aside an empty oil drum, some tyres and what appeared to be an ancient tea-chest stuffed with oil-soaked shreds of wool 'shoddy' – the waste product of the woollen trade put to use to mop up the oil spillages of a modern garage. Even the rubbish in Lindsay Carfax, Campion thought, was connected to the wool trade.

'Is this the sort of thing you're after?' Judd asked, manhandling a large painted metal sign advertising Shell petrol out of the way to reveal a pile of canvas and cloth weighted down with buckets and three mattocks. 'They look like tents and from the smell something's living in them right now. Want me to pull them out?'

'No,' said Campion, directing the two torches beyond the heap, 'don't disturb the local wildlife. That's what we're after.'

'I still don't know what the hell that is, or why you wanted it.'

It had taken Ben only a few minutes to re-screw the hasp of the lock to the door so that it appeared that the barn remained securely locked and unviolated and now he and Campion stood at the foot of the outside staircase which ran up the side of his studio. Ben held the torches and shone them full on to a blinking Campion who held the curious length of white wood with numbered gradations in both hands, as if he were holding a rifle at 'port arms'.

'When the two archaeologists died here last summer, all their gear was moved from Saxon Mills and stored in that barn, which I presume is owned by Mr Marchant.'

'Fuller,' corrected Judd with distaste. 'That old pedant Fuller owns most of the village; at least it was the Fullers I bought my place off.'

'It probably doesn't matter,' said Campion. 'My point is that the only two items of equipment which were returned to the university were the metal detector and the level used to record the depths of any archaeological features. But to take levels, you need a staff with the heights marked on. One chap looks through the sight on the level – a bit like a surveyor's theodolite – whilst the unlucky one climbs into a pit or a ditch and holds this levelling staff up until his mate gets a reading from these numbers painted on the face.'

Judd blew air from inflated cheeks and shook his head.

'Call me thick, Campion, but you've lost me.'

Mr Campion smiled and the torchlight caught the twinkle in his eyes.

'Allow me to demonstrate.'

With the dexterity of a stage magician, Campion began to extend the staff by pulling out the sections, each new section slightly thinner than the previous snapping into place like the 'pulls' of a telescope, until he was struggling to hold a narrowing wooden pole over twelve feet in length. With less dexterity, he adjusted his feet and carefully swung the staff in an arc over Ben's head until he was positioned at the foot of the studio's external staircase with the staff held out before him like a jousting lance.

'Lights,' said Campion and Judd raised the torches to light the staircase, 'camera, action!'

The torch beams followed the tip of the staff as Campion slowly raised it up and strained to hold it steady with arms outstretched until the end was positioned in the centre of the door to Judd's living quarters. When satisfied he was in position, he swung the staff out from the door and then returned it, producing a series of short raps in a *Da-Da-DaDa* pattern.

'Well I'll be damned,' said Judd, 'that's how he did it! How did you figure that out?'

'An educated guess,' said Mr Campion, lowering the staff and laying it flat on the ground. 'And if one cannot have educated guesses in Cambridge, where can one? I guessed it must be here somewhere and a policeman told me that when the bodies of the poor students had been removed, their things had been brought to this barn where they died and no one had thought to collect them. An extendable levelling staff struck me as the ideal way to knock on a door high up in the air and run away before it opened.'

'Leaving a nasty little booby trap which could have broken Liza's neck.' As Judd spoke, the torch beams wavered in his shaking hands.

'I think it was meant for you, not Eliza Jane,' said Campion.

'It was Tommy-Bloody-Tucker, wasn't it? He's the only person who uses that barn, calls it his workshop. It's where he knocks out fake Humble Boxes for Clarissa Webster.' Judd was breathing deeply and loudly, his hand shaking even more, making the torchlight dance. 'By God, if he was here now I'd make him answer for it!'

'I think young Mr Tucker has more to answer for than an unrequited infatuation with my niece, but that has served a purpose tonight.'

'What do you mean by that?' snapped Judd.

'I wanted Tommy out of the way tonight, so we could do our burglary. Eliza Jane agreed to be our decoy. She's keeping an eagle eye on all the Carders down at the Woolpack where they are all having a jolly good think about their future, I hope.'

'Tucker is with Liza? Now?'

'It's not as if she's alone with him and I doubt if the atmosphere is even remotely conducive to...'

But Ben Judd had turned on his heels and was charging down the lane, bellowing like a wounded stag, the two torches he still held weaving insane patterns of light and shadow to each side of his body, giving his disappearing figure an unearthly outline.

Mr Campion threw down the levelling staff and set off in pursuit, knowing that it was hopeless.

If he had been forty years younger and as fit as he had been when he went up to Cambridge as an undergraduate, Campion doubted he could have caught the rampaging figure of Ben Judd. As a man of advancing (if not 'pipe and slippers' just yet) years who had recently had a handful of shotgun pellets removed from his leg and thigh, he would be lucky to keep him in sight. Only the dread thought that he would be responsible for what would inevitably happen spurred him on. Lugg had been right not to trust Judd – Lugg, of all people! Lugg had spotted that Judd 'could start a fight in a confessional' and now Campion had pointed him in the right direction and lit the blue touch paper.

By the time he reached the end of the lane by Sherman's Garage, Ben Judd was pounding up the slope of the High Street and half way to the Carders' Hall. His chest already heaving and his right leg burning with pain, Campion set off in pursuit, realising that he had left his walking stick behind outside Judd's studio. Not that it would have been of much use at the hobbling pace he was trying to maintain. He even thought of throwing away the camera case which swung wildly around his neck from its leather strap, determined to strangle him.

Bizarrely, Judd still held a lit torch in each hand, the beams flashing out to either side of his running figure like the navigation lights on the wing-tips of an aircraft. As he dashed on, the effect of the light flickering across the frontage of The Medley and then the Prentice House reminded Campion – still some distance behind and breathing heavily – of the opening titles of a Hammer horror biography of Jack the Ripper. And then Judd's spectral figure disappeared as he rounded the curve of the Carders' Hall, leaving only a shard of torchlight like a silent flash of lightning in the night.

Campion slowed his stumbling pace to a more dignified walk, fumbled for his handkerchief and mopped his brow, then with a loud sigh continued his fruitless pursuit.

He knew he was going to be too late. He was a man who could no longer keep up with his allies, let alone chase his enemies.

He was too slow.

He was too old.

'He'll pay for any damage!'

Campion's ears recognised Eliza Jane's voice as soon as he pushed open the door to the bar of the Woolpack, but the scene which met his astonished eyes was anything but familiar.

Tables, bar stools and chairs had been overturned; angular wooden bodies on a battlefield. Glasses and bottles had been smashed. A wall-mounted light fitting dangled from its wire. The floor was awash with spilled drink in which ice cubes twinkled frostily and upturned plastic ashtrays floated like small but menacing icebergs which left a trail of cigarette stubs and grey ash in their wake. Yet the physical disarray of the room was only half as shocking as the state of its human inhabitants. Both furniture and people resembled a living museum exhibit showing Londoners in the immediate aftermath of an air raid during the Blitz.

Campion did a quick head count. All the people he had left in the bar were still present, though in a considerably dishevelled state. Clarissa Webster, clutching a broken string of cosmetic pearls to her throat in a futile attempt to stop them dripping off her to bounce on the floor and roll away among the flotsam, was being comforted in the embracing arms of Gus Marchant. The pair of them leaned against the far wall underneath the obligatory print of Constable's *Haywain* which had been disturbed by the recent hurricane and now hung at a precarious angle. With only a fleeting glance, Campion registered that Mrs Webster was clutching her protector perhaps closer than was absolutely necessary to her ample bosom and had made no attempt to correct the hemline of her dress which had risen above the knee by the currently fashionable four inches, although usually on much younger women. She seemed uninjured and in no immediate danger of swooning; or at least unintentionally.

The others in the room showed definite signs of distress.

The shrivelled figure of Marcus Fuller looked the frailest of them all, even though he had adopted the role of nursing angel – or perhaps combat surgeon – and was ministering to his brother, who was seated in one of the few chairs still upright, his legs splayed out in front of him, holding a blood-soaked handkerchief to a split lip and nursing his left arm across his chest.

Dennis Sherman was similarly providing first aid to the battered and dishevelled figure of Tommy Tucker who was slumped, his eyes closed, on the floor, his back to the wall. His shirtfront had been pulled open, revealing a distinctly grubby string vest on to which blood was dripping from his bleeding nose and dark bruises were already forming on his forehead and upper cheek bones. He would, thought Campion, be sporting one if not two black eyes come the morning.

The stick-like Hereward Spindler was leaning with both forearms propped on the bar. In other circumstances he could have resembled an over-familiar, and over-relaxed, customer seeking to confide in the barman were it not for the fact that his legs – in fact his whole body – was quivering with shock and fright. On the professional side of the bar Don was doing what professional bar-men do and providing his own brand of solace and medication, or in this case, a well-known brand of cognac, which he was offering towards Spindler's open mouth in a large balloon glass.

Centre stage, however, was the tableau on the floor, directly in front of the bar. It wasn't exactly a *pose plastique* as there was movement in the scene: an empty ice bucket and an empty bottle of Barsac rolled across the floor before finally coming to rest against the main display, the inert figure of Ben Judd lying prone on the floor, parallel to the bar in the place where, in several venerable London pubs of Campion's acquaintance, there would be a sturdy brass foot rail.

Ben Judd's body was not being used for the support of a brown brogue or a black boot, though. Rather, his muscular frame had been pressed into service as some sort of ad hoc *chaise longue* by Eliza Jane, who sat imperiously on his shoulders, one arm behind her pressing his head face-first into the floor, her legs stretched down his back, occasionally using her high-heel-ed shoes as spurs into his flanks.

'He'll pay for any damage!' she said again.

Those involved in or who had witnessed the events in the Woolpack bar were divided on what to do with Ben Judd, and it was as if Campion's arrival was a cue for them to make a decision despite Mr Campion not having said a word.

Hereward Spindler was, true to his profession, a stickler when it came to others adhering to the letter of the law citing assault, battery, wilful destruction of property and disturbing the peace as preliminary grounds for calling the police. Both Fullers agreed completely with the solicitor's analysis, Marcus Fuller stating that the maniac should be locked up but Simon going further and suggesting he be given a good sound beating before cell doors were slammed and keys thrown away. Clarissa Webster, between bosom-heaving sobs (which seemed to grow in the heaving department with the presence of Mr Campion), declared that the 'poor boy' should not be judged too harshly, for his judgement had been clouded by the green-eyed demon of jealousy, which happens when a man is in love.

Gus Marchant, trying to support that heaving bosom and at the same time establish his authority, declared that not even a lovesick rogue elephant would behave as badly and thuggish violence needed to be nipped in the bud; or in this case, as soon as possible. The police should be called immediately, if Don would be so kind. Don, respecting the wishes of the owner of the Woolpack who was *de facto*, his employer, agreed to do so with alacrity.

It was only when Mr Campion, speaking for the first time, suggested that as Simon Fuller seemed to be nursing a broken arm and Tommy Tucker could well be suffering from concussion, perhaps the first 999 request by Don should be for an ambulance. There was a short, embarrassed silence followed by a begrudging but general murmur of agreement and Don, after receiving an encouraging nod from Gus Marchant, dissolved from the bar in the way only experienced barmen can.

'Whilst we await the arrival of the emergency services,' said Campion calmly, 'might I suggest that we retire to the dining room and persuade Don to serve us drinks in there?'

With care he stepped over broken glass and ice cubes, his shoes making squelching noises in the sodden carpet. Then, with the smooth skill of a gunfighter, he drew his Olympus Trip from the case hanging round his neck and as the assemble crowd watched in amazement, he coolly took the flash attachment form his pocket and shoehorned it on to the camera.

Bending slightly at the knees, as he had seen fashion photographers do in arty films, he took three flash pictures in rapid succession of his niece (who actually smiled sweetly into the lens) sitting astride her felled lover.

'Now that I have photographic evidence of Mr

Judd's rather embarrassing predicament, I am sure it is safe to allow him to regain his dignity, Eliza.'

He held out a hand which the girl took and pulled herself upright, carefully placing her feet on the floor rather than Ben Judd, who let out a loud moan of relief.

'If Mr Judd promises to remain silent – by which I mean that he says not one word – then he may join us in the dining room if he sits quietly in a corner. Alternatively, he could bolt for the door and escape into the night, in which case we would all co-operate in the hue-and-cry which the police would no doubt initiate. I do not think he would get far and it would add another charge to his growing list of indictments.'

Campion looked around the wrecked bar. He did not need a police enquiry to tell him what had happened. The enraged Ben Judd has burst in to see his beloved Eliza Jane seemingly in flirtatious mode with the despised Tommy Tucker; behaviour which was being accepted, if not actively encouraged, by the great and good of Lindsay Carfax, in fact the very hierarchy of the Carders he so disdained. He had no doubt bellowed something obscene and threatening in a fairly accurate impersonation of a bull seal protecting his harem at which point Simon Fuller, Campion guessed, had stepped forward to remonstrate with him and perhaps it was then that the furniture had started to go over.

Judd had lashed out at anything which stood between him and his imagined rival in love and had probably forgotten that he still gripped a heavy torch in each hand. Thus his swinging blows had caused far more damage than his bare fists would have, resulting in broken bones and broken heads.

In the general melee, which would have been messier, quicker and far less dramatic than an over-choreographed saloon fight in a Hollywood western, Judd had been stopped in his tracks before homicide could be committed and somehow laid low.

Eliza Jane was later to cheerfully admit to the attending police officers: 'Oh that would have been me. I smashed him round the head with the ice bucket. When he's in that sort of mood, it's the only way of reasoning with him.'

'The Great Woolpack Brawl' as it would become known in local legend, was investigated by the local police force of Sergeant James and PC Wilson, both of solid Suffolk stock. Their arrival coincided with that of an ambulance and so the forces of law, order and medicine combined to restore order to chaos.

Statements were taken; injuries examined and diagnosed. Tommy Tucker was indeed suspected of having concussion and Simon Fuller had definitely acquired a broken arm. In the eyes of the law, that constituted bodily harm, possibly grievously, and Mr Judd (who himself sported numerous cuts and bruises to his face) would be accompanying them to the police cells in Bury St Edmunds where he would spend the rest of the night.

Mr Campion, noting that his presence seemed

to make all the Carders determined to be seen to be upright and law-abiding citizens, wondered idly if the boorish behaviour of Ben Judd would have been treated differently had Judd agreed to join the ranks of the Carders. In his own mind, Campion was sure that had that been the case, the public version of the Woolpack's bar-room rumpus would have been quite different.

The ambulance men claimed Tucker and the younger Fuller, insisting that they needed hospital treatment. Marcus Fuller demanded to accompany his brother and Dennis Sherman volunteered to accompany Tommy Tucker, offering to drive Fuller in the wake of the ambulance. Sergeant Jones said loudly and correctly that he hoped Mr Sherman had not been drinking over the limit, for their police car was equipped with a generous supply of the new breathalyser kits.

When the injured and the arrested had vacated the bar, Campion announced that he had had quite sufficient excitement for one evening and would walk Eliza Jane to her cottage before retiring. Don, who had produced a long-handled brush and was sweeping up broken glass, said that he would not lock up until Campion returned. Hereward Spindler straightened his jacket and, straight-backed, left without a word to anyone. Gus Marchant, his arm around Mrs Webster's shoulders guided her to the door, giving Campion a brief nod of acknowledgement. Clarissa Webster turned more dramatically and stretched out an imploring hand towards Eliza Jane.

'Try and forgive him, my dear,' she said with a

quiver in her voice, 'the poor boy is totally besotted you know and love like that makes a man's blood boil over.'

As Campion walked his niece down the High Street to her cottage, he was less generous in his assessment.

'I am so, so sorry to have put you in that situation, Eliza. I had no idea Ben would go storming in there in the way he did.'

'Don't worry, Uncle dear, it's not your fault that Ben can't control himself. I knew he had a temper, I just didn't realise it was so volcanic. For a moment I thought he was going to kill Tommy Tucker.'

'It was a good job you slugged him then, but you should never have been put in that position.'

'Nonsense,' laughed the girl, 'it was quite a liberating experience and the looks on their faces...! All those big tough Carders and me – the little dolly bird as they would say – the only one willing to stand up to the raging homicidal maniac.'

'Your boyfriend the homicidal maniac,' Campion pointed out.

'Yes, well the jury's out on that one for the moment. Still, I made sure none of the Carders left the Woolpack while you were up to no good. How did that go?'

They had halted in the moonlit street outside Eliza Jane's cottage as she fumbled in her handbag for her keys.

'Part One of the plan went ... well, to plan,' Campion began hesitantly, 'in that we discovered how your phantom knocker-on-doors did the trick.'

'And we're sure it was Tommy, are we?'

'As sure as we can be until he owns up to it, but I think he heard the two of you arguing and decided to teach Ben a lesson, so he strung his tripwire and rapped on the door using an extendable surveyor's staff, something the archaeologists left behind last summer. It was all the proof Ben needed and when I stupidly let slip that you and he were in the Woolpack, he was off like a rocket and these old legs simply couldn't keep up.'

Eliza Jane sensed the old man's hesitation.

'So what was Part Two of the plan?'

'That was supposed to have been me making an ostentatious departure from Lindsay Carfax tomorrow and then Ben helping me sneak back under cover of darkness to clear up one last Carder mystery, but his rather foolish action this evening means he will be in custody and I will have to rethink.'

'I don't see why,' said his niece, 'I can drive and I've proved I can handle myself in a rough house. Look no further for a trusted sidekick, Uncle.'

Campion smiled with genuine affection.

'I could not allow it, my dear. It could be unpleasant and possibly dangerous.'

'Danger? There could be danger involved?' Eliza Jane threw up her hands and feigned shocked horror; feigned it rather well. 'In that case, you've got me whether you want me or not. I know you like to come across as a bit of an old fogey, Uncle, but since you turned up things have got quite interesting around here. If you're going, I want to be there to make sure you go out with a bang.'

'Preferably not too loud a bang,' said Campion gently.

Twenty

Mole Run

Breakfast at the Woolpack the next morning was served with a determined air of 'business as usual' although the portions of Suffolk ham were more generous than normal and the waitresses pathetically grateful for the smallest morsel of gossip in return. Mr Campion maintained a cheerful but slightly aloof air, as if the broken furniture, the molehills of swept-up smashed glass and the spongy carpets underfoot were all part of the standard fittings and fitments.

His bag packed, he presented himself at the Regency drum table in the entrance lobby, which served as a reception desk for the inn. To his surprise, it was Don wearing a large green apron, who appeared to relieve him of his room key. The barman explained that he had volunteered for extra duty to help 'clear up the fracas' of the night before, but Campion suspected that Don simply did not want to miss any new developments. Information is always valuable, but in a Lindsay Carfax it is sometimes priceless.

There was, of course, no bill to be settled as Mr Marchant had taken care of all that and Mr Campion would also be pleased to know that

Dennis Sherman had delivered his fully-repaired Jaguar to the inn's car park first thing that morning so that Mr Campion would not have the bother of walking to the garage to collect it. Naturally, the cost of all repairs had been covered by Mr Marchant.

Campion expressed his gratitude to the citizens of Lindsay Carfax in fulsome prose bordering on the gushing, which Don could and would quote in the winter evenings ahead. To cement Don's impression of him as 'a real gent' he produced a £5 note from his wallet, which he palmed to him during their final handshake. A tip, Don said, was absolutely unnecessary but the note disappeared into his apron pocket with alacrity.

Reunited with his car, Campion examined the repaired bodywork with grudging admiration then locked his bag in the boot, along with one of Ben Judd's torches which he had borrowed when walking Eliza Jane home and had 'forgotten' to return. Then, in full tourist mode, he did a final leisurely promenade around the sights of Lindsay Carfax, choosing the clockwise route around the Carders' Hall for a final view of the Humble Museum, the church and the pond before taking a deep breath and crossing the road to The Medley.

Despite the alarms and excursions of the previous night Mrs Webster was open for business and Mr Campion was welcomed like a warrior lover home from a long war far away. But this Penelope seemed more interested in seeing Odysseus's cheque book rather than Odysseus himself.

'Albert my dear, I knew you'd call in before you left,' she gushed, planting a wet kiss on each side of his face with enthusiasm if not accuracy.

'I thought I should take a proper farewell,' said Campion, glad that no one was present to see his blushes, 'so as not to leave the village on last night's unpleasantness.'

'And to collect your paintings, of course,' said Clarissa, the businesswoman in her winning out over the flirt.

'My paintings?' Campion asked vaguely.

'By Eliza Jane, of course. You asked me to put a pair aside, but I couldn't make my mind up, so I've selected three. They're all packed and wrapped in the back room for you. They are all, shall we say, Constable-esque in execution – one of the church and the village pond, one of Carders' Hall and one of the High Street – and I am sure that family sentiment will make allowances for any artistic failings.'

Mr Campion knew when to submit to moral blackmail and produced his cheque book with a sigh. When a price – with which he dare not disagree – had been suggested, he began to write but then paused as if inspiration had struck. Rather than take the pictures now, would it be possible to have them sent (an extra £10 covering the cost of delivery) to St Ignatius College in Cambridge, marked for the attention of Mr Gildart?

It would, of course, be perfectly possible and Mrs Webster even agreed to Campion's request that Eliza Jane never be told the identity of the purchaser. Even though Clarissa Webster insisted on sealing their bargain with another damp peck on the cheek as he left the shop, Mr Campion had the distinct feeling that he had somehow got off lightly.

He strolled by the Prentice House and made a point of staring through the windows into the Victorian parlour interior only to discover its guardian Mrs Thornton staring back at him. He gave her a cheery wave which she did not return.

Outside the front of the Carders' Hall, Campion stood in the middle of the High Street and took a handful of photographs of its ornate façade despite the hooting of car horns and the ringing of bicycle bells telling him to get out of the road. As he framed a final shot of the steps the hall's frontage, the viewfinder of his Olympus Trip filled with figures all peering down the lens at the photographer.

Campion dropped the camera from his face and raised a hand to the full size figures of Messrs Marchant, Fuller and Spindler standing on the steps of the hall, framed by its open oaken doors. A trio of Carders, he thought, and none of them seemingly pleased to see him. They might, however, be pleased to see him go.

'Gentlemen, good morning to you,' Campion called out cheerfully, regretting he was not wearing a hat, for he would have raised it to them, 'just taking a few snapshots to remind me of dear old Lindsay. Sorry if I'm diddling you out of commission on the official postcard trade.'

He raised his camera quickly and snapped a shot of them before they could object.

'I was hoping to be able to say goodbye to you

all,' Campion said, fussily putting the camera back in its case. 'How is Simon, Mr Fuller?'

'He has an arm in plaster thanks to that damned painter!' snarled Marcus Fuller. 'The maniac ought to be locked up.'

'I assumed he had been,' Campion said innocently.

'He will probably be released on bail today, more's the pity,' said Hereward Spindler the solicitor, offering free legal advice for once, 'but I am certain that charges will be pressed.'

'And young Mr Tucker? How does he fare?'

'Not well,' said Gus Marchant. 'The hospital's keeping him in for observation. I'm sorry you had to see Lindsay Carfax at its worst, Campion. We don't all behave as badly as Ben Judd and I hope we haven't left you with a bad impression.'

Campion bit his tongue and instead of what he was thinking, he said: 'At my age, gentlemen, one quickly forgets bad impressions. In fact it is easy to forget most things. Some days I count it a victory for sanity if I remember to put trousers on before shoes.'

Campion was delighted to hear the throaty purr of the Jaguar once more and he drove quickly but not recklessly along the twisted lanes out of Lindsay Carfax until he joined the Bury St Edmunds road, just to get the feel of the car back. On the outskirts of Bury he found a shop which offered 'filled baps' and much more besides. He bought four (ham, ham and cheese, ham and tomato and ham and pickled onion), two bars of chocolate, a large bottle of lemonade and the latest edition of the *Bury Free Press*. Once he had his purchases carefully stowed on the passenger seat, he turned the Jaguar around and drove slowly back towards Lindsay Carfax, pulling off the road several miles shy of the village, to park out of sight of the road in the open beet field where he and Eliza had waited for Tommy Tucker to overtake them. Campion treated himself to a filled bap (closing his eyes and choosing at random to add surprise to his lunch), opened his newspaper and settled down to wait.

By the time Eliza Jane's sports car bounced into the field, Campion had long finished his newspaper and been forced to resort to his copy of Esther Wickham's *The Face of Diligence*. The sight of his niece picking her way over plough furrows from her car to his was a welcome one, even though in her brightly coloured flower-print top with its voluminous sleeves, bright red flared trousers and wide-brimmed white hat with paper flowers pinned to the brim, she seemed inappropriately dressed for a field in Suffolk unless, he fancied, there was a festival of music and free love planned for later on.

'How's my dolly, dolly spy?' asked Campion holding the passenger door of the Jaguar open for her.

Eliza Jane flashed him a look.

'No one has called me a dolly bird to my face before. I'm not sure I like it.'

'But you did remember to be a spy, didn't you?'

'Of course,' she said, settling into the seat. 'My ears having been flapping like an elephant's and

380

my eyes have been on stalks all day. Of course I could have saved myself the strain on my facial muscles simply by asking Don at the Woolpack what was going on. He's in his element, you know, after last night and has no doubt cast me in the role of scarlet woman. It's a career I may pursue if I don't make it as a painter.'

'Or a spy; a spy who reports promptly and succinctly.' Campion closed the door, walked round the Jaguar and reclaimed his place behind the steering wheel.

'Right then, I have spent most of the day re-assuring people that you really have gone, even those who saw you drive away. Most of Lindsay now seems to be glad to see the back of you, apart from Clarissa that is. She's probably incon-solable, at least until the next coach-load of suckers – I mean visitors – can be lured into The Medley.' She caught Campion peering at her over his spectacles. 'Oh, don't worry, Uncle, I didn't forget to check Sherman's garage; I even called in to fill up with petrol. The van's still there all right, backed up against the workshop so no one can see what's inside it. I don't think it's moved for the last two days.'

'But I think it will tonight,' said Campion, 'when it gets dark.'

It was the night of the full moon and therefore nowhere near as dark as Campion would have liked, but the High Street of Lindsay Carfax was deserted, indicating that behind the curtained windows, there was something good on tele-vision. Eliza Jane had, as Campion had suggested, taken a tortuous route through winding lanes and dark woods, to approach Lindsay from the south and once in the village she drove slowly, on sidelights, only past her own cottage and up the gentle hill to ease left by the darkened Humble Museum. Once the Hall shielded her car from any prying eyes in the Woolpack, she braked and Campion reached for the handle of the passenger door, climbing out and slinging the Olympus in its case over his shoulder.

'Be careful,' whispered Eliza Jane.

'I always try to be,' hissed Campion and he closed the car door as quietly as he could.

Campion watched the red dots of the sports car's rear lights diminish down the hill until Eliza Jane indicated left and turned down the track to Judd's studio. He was standing by the lych gate which guarded the path to the church and from the orange glow in the windows it seemed that the church was occupied. The Rev Trump, thinking he might at some point need an alibi, had clearly decided he had urgent business in the church and had carelessly, if anyone should later ask, left the vicarage unlocked.

In the hallway of the vicarage, Campion switched on the torch that had been spoiling the cut of his jacket pocket rather than turning on the lights, and made his way into the kitchen where it took no great feat of deduction to discover the door which revealed a dozen stone steps leading down to the cellar. Here he did reach for the light switch and a single 40-watt bulb illuminated an old washing tub, washboard and mangle, a tin bath and two old bookcases pressed into service

382

as shelving displayed a leaking bag of flour, half a dozen tins of soup, a large tin of black treacle, a basket of clothes pegs and, ominously, several mouse traps all unbaited and all sprung.

There was also a small wooden door, kept shut only by the rusting wash tub which Campion pulled aside with some effort as he discovered it to be half full of water. Pulling the door open his senses were met by a damp, earthy staleness and the beam of his torch showed a cobweb-lined tunnel sloping away into complete darkness. Taking a deep breath of cold, dead air he stepped inside.

The passage was large enough for Campion to stand in, but only just, as his hair was doing a passable job of sweeping the tunnel's roof clear of cobwebs. Yet within ten unsteady paces, Campion regretted not bringing a ball of twine for the not-so-secret passages of Lindsay Carfax were as disorientating as a Cretan maze. Campion reassured himself that a few feet above his head a twentieth-century village was settling down to its twentieth-century creature comforts and the likelihood of him encountering a Minotaur down here was remote.

When the vicarage passage broadened out into a much wider, darker, echoing space, Campion realised he must be under the Carders' Hall and a sweep with his torch showed three other dark passageways leading off it. Instinctively, he tightened his grip on the torch and pressed the off button. The blackness was complete and even though Campion had been expecting it, he felt a wave of panic welling in his chest. Summoning all his nerve, he counted aloud up to ten before switching his torch back on, then breathing a loud sigh of relief at the reappearance of the thin yellow beam. Few lighthouses had been welcomed so warmly by sailors in a storm, for the darkness had been complete and disorientating.

Taking his bearings, he deduced that the passage yawning darkly ahead of him would be the one leading to the bar of the Woolpack, whereas the one to his right should lead to the Humble Museum and one somewhere over to his left in the darkness would be the tunnel to the Prentice House. Four rat-runs, but leading to a nest or away from it? The nest would surely be the Carders' Hall, but where was the entrance – or should that be exit?

By making circular sweeps of his torch beam – which induced a distinct feeling of sea-sickness – Campion determined that one area of darkness was not *quite* so dark; not black but not quite grey, there was definitely contrast. What was the old French proverb about all dogs being wolves in the dark? Was there really such a proverb? Why was he worrying about that when he should be worrying about how to find his way out of this catacomb? Was that a rat brushing against his shoe?

He had to pull himself together; this was ridiculous. All he was doing was crossing a road in a quaint country village, from the vicarage to the pub. It was just that he was doing it underground in passageways which had been used for two hundred years and the tamped-down dirt floors were not littered with the skeletons of sheep, or tourists, though many of both had passed this way. Had he not been told that parties of school children were shown around the passages in order to learn of their ancestors' skill in 'owling'? Was he really now just a frail old man frightened of the dark?

He put his best foot forward – when in doubt, stick to the old maxims – and almost immediately felt the ground slope upwards. Another step confirmed his feet were not playing tricks on him and his torch showed that he had, without realising it, found the passage which led to the Carders' Hall. Holding his left arm outstretched so that his fingertips brushed the cold but surprisingly dry surface of earth and flints, he strode on confidently, stooping slightly as the headroom decreased, until his torch illuminated a solid wooden door set in a solid wooden frame which completely blocked the passageway in front of him.

Solid was definitely the word. This oak – if it was oak – had been firmly sported and there seemed no obvious mechanism for opening it from this side, which did not in itself surprise or disturb Campion. After all, the Carders meeting in full ritual session above would not have wanted their proceedings disturbed by owlers herding tax-free sheep pursued by irate Revenue Men. Perhaps the door was only opened on state occasions, or if it was raining and the Carders wanted to keep dry as they repaired to the Woolpack.

Which reminded Campion that he had Don's key to the passage door in the bar. Perhaps he should return it in spectacular fashion by bursting in and demanding to know why they were all talking about him. If nothing else, he might be able to eavesdrop on the Woolpack crowd just to see if he was still the subject of gossip. If he was not, and the locals were more concerned with the price of wool or hot under the collar about the cost of winter silage, then he would naturally be disappointed and would creep away into the night. Or rather, back into the dark of the empty subterranean maze.

Except it was no longer empty and Campion was no longer alone down there.

Before he saw or heard anything, he sensed a change in the still, earthy air and turned off his torch again, this time without hesitation. He was as blind as a mole and strained every fibre or muscle and nerve to prevent himself making any movement. He felt as one does in dream when the hole opens up in front of the dreamer, but there the fatal step off the edge usually jerks the sleeper awake. Mr Campion was not asleep; he was very awake and more conscious than ever that he was in a maze and would have to retrace his steps to the centre of it before finding any avenue of escape, assuming the Minotaur let him pass.

In the complete darkness, he placed the torch into his right jacket pocket and adjusted the camera case so that it hung from his neck and rested on his chest, leaving both arms free to reach out to the sides of the passage. His hands would be his navigation aids and his stabilisers, but even so his first few steps down the gentle incline induced dizziness and a nausea he struggled to contain.

When the palms of his hands told him that he had reached the end of the passage, he halted his shuffling gait. Before him, he knew, there was the wider space where all the passages converged, the place Lemmy Walker had called a 'catacomb' but Campion preferred to think of it in more mundane terms as a crossroads or a traffic roundabout. However he visualised it in his blindness, he knew he would have to switch on his torch now, or stay rooted to the spot quivering in the dark, before he could find an exit.

He took the torch from his pocket and grasped it tightly but still hesitated before switching it on. Something prevented him from that small, life-enhancing action of pressing a tiny button and bringing light into his world of blackness. But those secondary senses which had advised caution were proved right even as his thumb wavered over the on button.

From somewhere to his right – yes, it was definitely to his right – there came a *thud*, a distinct grunt and then a heavy footfall. As his eyes were of no use, Campion strained to listen for further sound and like an animal, sniffed the air. Yes, there was difference, a mustiness – a musk – which hadn't been there before; and then there were more footsteps and a strange *creaking* wooden noise and then a very loud *thump* with a faint echo of – could it be? – tinkling glass. Whatever it was, it was *near* and all the more frightening when the noises stopped entirely and the darkness became silence once more.

In his head, Campion counted to one hundred until he was convinced that whoever had been in front of him – and surely some *human* action must have been involved – had gone, retreating into one of the other passages. He dismissed the thought, which sprang unbidden into his favoured imagination, that a Minotaur would do exactly the same: hide in another part of the maze to lure his victim into the open.

Taking a deep breath, Campion pushed his shaking right leg forward and flicked on the torch. The sight which met his blinking eyes made him exhale in surprise and stumble forward off balance. He brought himself to attention and sprayed the torch beam in an arc, still not quite believing what he saw.

Less than ten feet from where he had been standing (hiding?), there had appeared on the tamped earth floor of the central 'catacomb' area where it was as out-of-place as a 'No Spitting' sign in the State Landau, a Humble Box, standing on its six wooden legs.

Campion stared at it in the torchlight, its squat, spinet-like shape framed by dark shadows. Should he take a photograph of it? Otherwise, who would believe that a two-hundred-year-old piece of adequate carpentry but dubious scientific equipment (if indeed it was a genuine one) had suddenly materialised in a sheep smuggler's tunnel. Perhaps it was a common enough occurrence when there was a full moon over Suffolk. Perhaps Campion should stop his mind from wandering and concentrate on *why* this ridiculous piece of furniture should have been placed where it had, in a central, unmissable position for anyone trying to navigate the passages.

Did the Cretan Minotaur leave bait to entice and trap those brave enough to enter the maze? He would be able to ask the question out loud soon, for he could hear the Minotaur coming.

'Was that what you were snooping for, Mr Nosey Parker?' said the Minotaur in a rich Suffolk lilt.

'I was hoping to see a Humble Box tonight – one recently arrived from the south of France in fact – but I didn't expect it to come looking for me. However, when Mohammed can't make it to the mountain, it is jolly decent of the mountain to pop underground,' Campion chirped, slowly raising his torch.

'Oi said you was off your bloody head, didn't Oi?' said the Minotaur.

Campion focussed on the voice. It had come not from the vicarage passage, but from the next black hole along to the left as Campion stood, which would, if his mental map of Lindsay's underground system was accurate, be the passage leading to and from the Humble Museum. To confirm his theory, the shadows in that passage shifted as the torch beam teased them. The shadows moved quickly, and were very large.

Campion decided he would feel safer if he continued talking; a thesis his wife would never have supported.

'Is this the Humble Box from the Museum or the one sent for repair by Lady Prunella? Or should that be Frau Berger? Lady Pru, bless her, probably has little idea what's going on.'

'You just love your snooping, don't you?' said the Minotaur from the darkness. 'You loike stirring things up, and that ain't roight. Not roight at all. You an' that Ben Judd, you're both troublers. Real stirrers you are, just like them stoodents last year, just like that schoolmaster, Walker.'

'There have always been "troublers", haven't there, Clifford? It is Clifford, isn't it?' Campion's question was met with total silence and his torch showed that the Minotaur had retreated out of its range. 'Stirrers like Johnnie Sirrah and Austin Bonus.'

There was a silence, a frighteningly long silence, before the Minotaur replied.

'We took care of that Sirrah feller alroight. He didn't make no more trouble.'

'What are you saying, Clifford?' Campion flashed the torch across the passage entrance. 'You weren't born when Johnnie Sirrah died. Your father couldn't have been much more than a boy.'

'He was twelve, he was, but he saw it all. Saw how Grandad Leonard settled his hash with a starting handle.'

'I rather wish you hadn't told me that, Clifford.' Campion moved to his left trying to judge where the passageway to the Woolpack lay in the Stygian gloom, without taking the torch beam away from the Humble Museum passage, as light seemed to be the only thing which deterred the Minotaur.

'You can't touch me for it, nor my dad,' said the voice in the dark. 'Anyway, what you gonna

390

do about it? We can keep you down here for nine days. That'll cure you of being nosey, boy!'

Campion stepped up to the Humble Box and ran his left hand over its wooden lid, whilst his eyes scanned the edges of the pool of torchlight to locate the passage which would lead to the Woolpack; or so he hoped.

'Well before I'm cured of my curiosity, I might as well see the goods, mightn't I?' he called out to the figure in the dark. 'This is how you bring them into the country, isn't it? I understand that quite a lot of Lysergic Acid Diethylamide is now manufactured in Switzerland and Frau Berger is Swiss, is she not?'

Campion lifted the wooden lid and lit up the interior with his torch. The flasks and vials, the scientific 'guts' of the box, were all full of liquid; a liquid which in no way aided in the forecasting of the weather.

'This must be the most valuable Humble Box ever,' said Campion. 'I have no idea of the "street value" as I think it is called, but I am told that one ounce of LSD can make 30,000 doses when diluted and taken on sugar cubes or tiny squares of blotting paper. What happened, Clifford? Did you sell some undiluted Acid to get those students high last year? They weren't used to such a concentration, were they? No one would be, it was eighty times stronger than usual – it was a lethal dose.'

There was no answer from the Minotaur's lair.

'That's a high price to pay for a high, Clifford. Too high.'

Campion raised the torch and brought it down

391

viciously into the workings of the Humble Box. He was rewarded with the satisfying sound of breaking glass; and almost immediately chilled to the marrow by a loud and angry scream as the Minotaur, head down, charged out of the dark towards him.

Clifford Sherman was a bull of a man in daylight. In the dark, narrow tunnels of Lindsay Carfax, he was gargantuan – and he was frighteningly fast on his feet. Its beam swinging wildly as Campion used the torch as a club to wreck damage on the vials of liquid, made the whole scene appear as if it were the ragged end of a broken film running through a projector.

Campion had no more than two seconds to take evasive action, which he spectacularly failed to do. Whether Clifford Sherman launched himself to attack Campion or to protect the Humble Box will never be known. Effectively he tackled both together with ham-sized fists flying, sending the older man crashing winded to the earthen floor and depositing his own considerable weight with considerable force on to the wooden box, which cracked loudly and crumpled under the impact. Campion saw little else, for as his back connected painfully with the ground, the torch flew out of his hand, bounced off a wall and went out, rolling away into the complete darkness.

Flat on his back, Campion instinctively used his heels, shoulders and elbows to inch away from the wreckage of the Humble Box and his assailant, whose location he had no difficulty in gauging from the his heavy breathing and the crackling of wooden splinters and the tinkling of crushed glass as he attempted to stand up. If he stayed low – and he could not get much lower – and kept quiet, then he might, just might, be able to put a safe amount of darkness between himself and his attacker. The disadvantages to this plan were that he had no idea in which direction he was back-crawling, though as long as it was away from the sound of Clifford Sherman crunching wood and glass underfoot, it would be the right direction, and that he had no idea how long he could keep up the activity. He had taken a fist to the chest and the burning sensation he felt suggested that a rib could be cracked or broken, and when Sherman's charge had knocked him off his feet, he had landed on his right thigh, inflaming the nerves and muscles so recently shot at then poked and prodded by doctors. But at least if he bit his lip and ignored the pain which came with every inch of ground covered, he could use the darkness to his advantage.

'Oi bet Oi can see better in the dark than you can, old feller,' said the Minotaur quietly.

Campion froze, determined not to make a sound but straining to hear any which may give away his enemy's proximity.

'Oi've been crawling round these tunnels since I were a nipper. There ain't no way you's going to get by me.'

Was the voice nearer? Feet away, or merely inches?

'An' you ain't getting out, not now you've gone and smashed up the goods. They was worth

393

a lot of money them goods, in places loike Cambridge an' Lunnun.'

Campion heard a piece of grass crack followed by a snort of pain. Perhaps the Minotaur was on all-fours and had injured a paw; when the monster had boasted about 'crawling these tunnels' had he perhaps been speaking literally?

'Oi ain't taking the blame for losing them goods. You're going to answer for that, you old snooper.'

Campion dug his elbows and heels into the ground and hauled himself away from the threats, making his escape in six-inch spurts. He was wriggling on his back like a frightened worm, but dignity was the least of his worries. He knew that if he tried to stand and run or even turn over on to his knees and crawl like a baby, the beast in the dark would hear his ancient bones slowly creak or somehow detect his movement, and then strike. At least on his back, he could see the *coup de grâce* coming ... if only he had light.

'You can't get away, you old booger.'

The Minotaur was so close now. Campion was sure he could smell him: a faint whiff of sweat, tobacco and motor oil and an underlying scent of poorly-washed woollen clothing. His enemy was very close, but at least he smelled human – and what was grasping at Campion's ankle as he squirmed backwards was definitely a hand, not a paw or a claw.

Campion kicked out with his left foot and felt a brushing contact with something; he could not tell what.

'You're a slippery old sod, ain't yer? Well, Oi got all noight an' you ain't going nowhere.'

The voice in the dark was sneering now and Campion sobbed silently in frustration. He was going to be hurt, possibly killed, down here in the black earth; put in a grave before the decency of death, scrabbling in the dirt to postpone the inevitable without even the satisfaction of looking his killer in the eye or spitting in his face. If only he had light!

But he had; it was hanging around his neck trying to choke him.

As he felt hands grabbing at his feet again, he used his own bruised and bloodied fingers to fumble open the camera case lying on his chest and remove the Olympus and its flash. By touch alone – and the luck of a desperate man – he slotted home the flash into its shoe fitting on top of the camera and flicked the on switch with a thumb. The normally faint electric whine of the flash unit charging up seemed to be amplified in the confines of the tunnels and it produced a loud grunt of surprise for the Minotaur, followed by an angry – and successful – grab for Campion's right foot.

'Got yer, grandad!'

Campion was jerked along the passage floor, pain flashing up his right leg and thigh but worse pain followed immediately as a hammer blow from a clenched fist piled into his ribcage.

Campion felt tears behind his useless spectacles and was sure that the next blow might see his end: a weak, frightened, old man crying in the dark and the dirt. Yet somehow he had kept hold of the Olympus and thrusting both arms straight out before him, he screwed his eyes closed and pressed the shutter.

Behind his wet eyelids he registered a red light as the flash fired. The effect on Clifford Sherman, who took the white light with eyes wide open at a range of only a few inches, was spectacular; he screamed in shock and released Campion's foot to put both hands over his eyes.

Campion, still blind but not blinded like his opponent, drew up his knees and shot out both feet in what he was sure would not be a recognised move in the French *Savate* school of street fighting. Nonetheless, the effect was satisfying as the soles of his shoes connected with some part – it did not matter which – of Clifford Sherman, who toppled away with a grunt and the sound of more glass being crushed under him.

Now Campion rolled on to his right side and with considerable discomfort and an unnerving amount of swaying, pulled himself to his feet and thrust out an arm until he found a solid wall to lean against. He had no idea which wall of which passage it was, or where Clifford Sherman was, but he still held, miraculously, the Olympus and had automatically thumbed the wind-on mechanism to load the camera for another shot.

Somehow he had managed to wound the Minotaur, judging by the gasps and grunts the animal was now emitting and though he knew himself to be close to fainting, he realised that the two of them could not remain in close proximity in that dungeon. He had a weapon, of sorts, and he had to use it. Aiming for the thrashing sounds Clifford was making, Campion held up his camera, averted his eyes, and pressed the shutter.

His man-made lightning lit up a scene worthy of a Murnau piece of expressionism. Clifford Sherman was on his knees amidst the wreckage of the Humble Box, his huge fists twisting violently in his own eyes, his mouth open and emitting a low, animal howl of distress.

Campion stepped away from the moaning beast, which was clearly wounded, though he could not work out how. But as wounded animals can still be dangerous, he thumbed the mechanism of the Olympus and flashed off three more lightning bolts as he moved away, keeping his back to the tunnel wall. He did not know or care which direction he was moving, only that it was away from Clifford, for the flashes bouncing off the passage sides and roof, had disorientated him as much as his victim. It was only at the third flash that he registered that his victim was no longer where he had been.

Campion sank into a crouch, sitting on his heels, pressing his back into the earth wall and listened for the sound of footsteps. He heard something – a shuffling sound and then a loud thudding noise and a yelp of pain – and then the silence returned to the darkness and he allowed himself to exhale.

To his surprise he saw the outline of his torch lying only inches from his feet, but it was several seconds before his brain informed him that the really surprising thing was that he could see it because there was now light entering the passage.

Automatically, Campion reached up under his glasses and wiped away the tears to help him focus. The source of the light was, he determined, the passage which led to the Carders' Hall where he had first hidden; the passage that had ended in a locked door. Now light was flooding in from there like the incoming tide and there were sounds – muffled, but unmistakably human, voices and the slap-slap of hurried footsteps.

Wearily, Campion let go of one weapon, the camera, and reached for his dropped torch, though he doubted that he had the strength to swing it in anger. Just the effort of reaching out for it had unbalanced him and he had slumped on to his backside.

'Never mind him, bring more light down here,' ordered a voice Campion vaguely recognised and then there was, again, the crunch of breaking glass and wood as whoever was coming out of the passage trod in the remains of the Humble Box.

'Good God, what sort of devilry has been going on down here?' said Gus Marchant.

'Quite a bit,' said Mr Campion turning on the torch and holding it under his chin so the weak beam lit his face from below in the way Boy Scouts frighten themselves when telling ghost stories around the campfire. 'Welcome to hell.'

Twenty-One

Board Meeting

'Aunt Amanda is going to kill me, but only after she's finished killing you!'

Campion was in no state, or position, to argue with his niece. Her right arm was around his waist, his left drooping over her shoulder whilst his right side was ably supported by the sturdy Gus Marchant, whose jacket smelled comfortingly of pipe tobacco, rum and Brylcreem – or perhaps Campion's senses were as exhausted and confused as the rest of him.

Eliza Jane had followed Marchant out of the passage clutching a bicycle lamp. She had surveyed the scene before her, let out a short, sharp scream and rushed to her uncle's aid. She and Marchant lifted and then half carried, half dragged Campion into the passage and the light now flooding through the open door from Carders' Hall.

As they trod on wood and glass, Marchant grunted: 'What the hell is this underfoot?'

'The remains of a Humble Box,' said Campion wearily. 'A very valuable one.' Then, as they neared the doorway, he saw Dennis Sherman kneeling by the inert body of his son, who was in a crumpled position resembling a beached and sleeping walrus, and said, 'What happened?'

'We think Clifford shot up the passage in a blue funk,' said Marchant without a hint of sympathy, 'and ran head first into the door and knocked himself out, the idiot. You must have scared the living daylights out of him down there in the dark.'

'My Clifford weren't never scared of the dark,' growled the senior Sherman. 'He's been scurrying around down here without a torch since 'e was a nipper. There must be sumfink else wrong with 'im.'

'I assure you Clifford was not the one who was scared; but I believe you are right,' said Campion, 'there is something wrong with him. I suggest we get him up into the Hall and summon an ambulance urgently.'

'You look as if you need an ambulance more than he does,' snapped Marchant. 'Clifford only bashed his head whereas you look like you've gone through the ringer.'

'I'll be fine, just get me out into the daylight and I'll be fine.'

'Daylight? Moonlight more like it.'

'I seem to have lost track of time,' sighed Campion.

'It's not yet nine o'clock,' said Marchant grumpily. 'I had only just sat down to a bit of supper when this spitfire of a niece of yours drags me away from hearth and home on a matter of life and death, or so she said.'

'She was very nearly right,' said Campion, feeling his legs buckle slightly. 'I really would like to get out into the fresh air, if you don't

400

mind, but not until someone has telephoned for an ambulance for Clifford.'

'Clifford don't need no ambulance,' snarled Dennis Sherman, cradling his son's torso, which was beginning to twitch and spasm. 'He's as strong as a Large Black boar. He'll come round in a minute.'

'I don't think he will, I'm afraid. I insist you call an ambulance. I have an awful feeling that Clifford may have taken a large dose of the hippy's favourite drug, LSD and possibly in a dangerous concentration.'

'My Clifford don't do drugs!' yelled Sherman *père*.

'I'm sure he doesn't, but he does sell them and tonight I think he managed to get some into his eyes. It is, I am told by people who sadly know these things, an accepted method of ingestion for some users, though not in the undiluted strength to which Clifford was exposed. Is there a telephone here?'

'Yes there is,' said Eliza Jane, 'in the office at the back of the stage.'

'I will do it,' said a new voice.

Campion turned his heavy head and squinted into the light coming down a short flight of steps from the Hall. The angular figure of Hereward Spindler came into focus.

'I rang Hereward and told him to meet us here,' said Marchant, clearing his throat in embarrassment. 'I thought we might need a solicitor.'

'Oh yes,' agreed Campion, 'I rather think you might.'

Eliza Jane held on tightly to her uncle's hands as they sat on the steps of the Carders' Hall looking down the empty High Street by the light of the fat, full, harvest moon.

'You're filthy, your clothes are torn and your hair seems to be full of cobwebs, spiders and probably earwigs. In short, I'm glad we don't run to street lighting in Lindsay – you're a sight I wouldn't be seen with.'

'Thank you for your support, my dear,' Campion said with a smile.

'Support? I was trying to be rude!'

'Ah, the family trait. You Fittons try to be rude but it never quite comes off.'

'I'll tell Aunt Amanda that!'

'I'd rather you didn't. What I meant – genuinely – was thank you for your help in this rather unpleasant business.'

The girl allowed herself a snort of derision.

'Unpleasant? That's drawing it mild, isn't it? Trapped underground in the dark with that thug Sherman trying to kill you is a bit more than "unpleasant" surely. When does "unpleasant" become "downright dangerous" in your book?'

'From now on,' said Campion firmly. 'I am far too old for this sort of thing.'

'I'm delighted to hear that. It's just what Aunt Amanda said on the phone.'

'You rang Amanda?'

'Of course. I rang her this afternoon, before I came to pick you up. She asked what you were planning and I said you were photographing some evidence and then you were on your way home – all fairly straightforward. She said nothing involving you is ever straightforward and unless I wanted to incur the wrath of Fittons past, present and future, I was to keep an eye out for you. Just after I dropped you off at the vicarage, the Shermans' van passed me coming the other way. I turned off my lights and watched it in my mirror. It stopped outside the Humble Museum and that gorilla Clifford got out, unloaded something with a horse blanket over it and carried it inside. I didn't know what to do and I panicked a bit and charged out to Gus Marchant's place, screaming blue murder.'

The pair heard a footstep behind them and turned to see Gus Marchant holding out a china teacup.

'Only water, I'm afraid,' he said as he offered the cup, 'but it's the best we can do. The Hall isn't licensed, you see, but I could always nip over to the Woolpack for a bottle of medicinal brandy.'

Campion took the cup.

'This is fine, thank you. I think I swallowed half a pound of dirt and cobwebs down there. How's Clifford?'

'We got him out up the steps with a bit of an effort and we've laid him out on a sofa in the reading room. He's out to the world, quietly burbling away to himself and seems harmless. Dennis is watching over him and Hereward is watching over Dennis. An ambulance is on its way.'

'I hope it arrives in time,' said Campion soberly.

'You think this LSD stuff is serious?'

'It was for those two Cambridge boys last year.'

'Look here, Campion, what exactly is going on?' Marchant sat down on the cold stone step next to Eliza Jane. 'I really am uncomfortable at the thought of dangerous drugs being freely available in my village.'

'I doubt they were ever free,' said Campion laconically, 'but Lindsay Carfax seems to have become a centre for the importation of every-one's favourite hallucinogen, LSD or "Acid", which I am told is the popular choice of pop stars, film stars and artists, not to mention the young people who copy their every fad and fashion.'

Campion drained the cup of water and met Marchant's eyes.

'Your distinguished fellow Carder, Lady Red-car, provides – probably unwittingly – the source of the LSD and the mechanism for transporting it to England in those curious and quite insane valves and flasks that are the guts of a Humble Box. As no one on Earth understands how a Humble Box works, or indeed cares, the chance of one being taken to pieces by an over-zealous customs officer is fairly remote. Lady Prunella is an eccentric English lady with eccentric pieces of English furniture who insists – eccentrically – on them being transported back to England when they need repair. Every time one is returned here fully loaded with LSD, it is quietly exchanged – using the not-so-secret passages – for one of the boxes in the Museum, the Prentice House or the

Vicarage. I understand there is a reproduction one in The Medley, but the shop was never on the underground passage network. The innocent box is sent back to the south of France for replenishment whilst the box sloshing with Acid is hidden in plain sight on show in the village until a buyer is found, the drug removed – probably down in the passages – and diluted to a non-lethal concentration for retail sale to students, hippies, flower children ... whoever is foolish enough to want an out-of-mind experience.'

'But that's outrageous!'

'Yes it is.' Campion allowed himself a soft chuckle. 'To think: you Carders were charging tourists to look at the wonderfully quaint invention of Josiah Humble, but in fact they were admiring the raw materials for a drug factory.'

'I hope you are not making accusations of illegality, Campion.' Hereward Spindler had materialised from the Hall, standing over them rather like an emaciated ghost.

Campion looked up at the solicitor and gave him a beatific smile.

'I'm not, but I think the police will. It is, however, perfectly possible that you as the owner of the Prentice House had no idea what your Humble Box may have contained at certain times, just as I am fairly sure that the Rev Trump never bothered to examine his specimen too closely.' He raised his empty teacup, 'pinky' finger extended, as if to celebrate the arrival of a new idea. 'In fact, I think Lemmy Walker was on to the scheme and took every chance he got to use the passages for a bit of snooping. The vicar almost caught him at it the night he gave his unbelievably dull lecture on the Carders, despite his Nine Days' Wonder disappearance. That was meant to put him off snooping and certainly nine days underground with Clifford and Tommy Tucker as dungeon masters would have curtailed my snooping instincts.'

Eliza Jane reached out a hand and patted Campion on the dirt-covered knees of his trousers.

'Perhaps that wouldn't have been a completely bad thing, Uncle.'

'You *have* been talking to your aunt, haven't you? Still, although that particular cure does not appeal in the slightest, I think she may have a point somewhere in that pretty head of hers.'

Eliza Jane's affectionate pat turned into a gentle smack.

'Don't be patronising!'

'I'm very old,' Campion riposted. 'I'm allowed!'

'Excuse me,' growled Marchant, 'but this is a damned serious business. Are you saying that Clifford and that Teddy Boy Tucker, whom I've never liked, cooked up this whole business between them?'

'No, I am not,' said Campion, serious again. 'They were the hired help, there to do the heavy lifting and the driving. The brains belonged to someone else.'

'Do you know who?' Marchant leaned in closer and even Hereward Spindler could not resist stooping to hear.

'I'm pretty sure, thanks to my niece here.'

'What? What have I said?'

'It was you who pointed out that Clifford delivered the now-destroyed Humble Box to the Humble Museum tonight. Where did he get the keys?'

'Not from the Fullers!' exploded Gus Marchant. 'I mean, Marcus owns the place, but Marcus wouldn't...'

He stopped mid-breath when he realised Campion was staring intently down the High Street at the headlights of a fast-approaching vehicle.

'I don't think that's the ambulance,' he said.

'It will be Marcus,' said Hereward Spindler behind them. 'This sounded like Carder business, so I rang him and told him to meet us here. Can't think what kept him.'

Mr Campion said nothing, but got carefully to his feet and positioned himself in front of Eliza Jane as the Land Rover pulled up in front of them and Marcus Fuller got out of the driver's seat and walked towards them.

He was holding a shotgun.

If in daylight Marcus Fuller gave the impression of a scrawny and bedraggled bird ready to peck at any crumb in the dust, in the moonlight, wearing a dark raincoat over a white wool pullover and carrying a shotgun, he presented a much more menacing image; a jackdaw or a magpie perhaps, stalking arrogantly across a newly cut field of wheat searching for small and defenceless rodents.

Gus Marchant jumped to his feet with an energy Campion envied and also placed himself

407

protectively in front of Eliza Jane, who was all-too-aware that Hereward Spindler had edged himself safely *behind* her.

'There might be a poacher's moon, tonight, Marcus,' Marchant boomed jovially, 'but the High Street's hardly the place is it, old boy?'

Marcus Fuller looked at him bemused and then down at the shotgun in his hands, which he seemed to notice he was carrying for the first time.

'Oh I am no poacher, Gus. This is for Campion.'

Before any of his astonished audience on the Hall steps could say anything, Mr Fuller took two paces towards them and held out the shotgun with both hands as an offering to Mr Campion.

'Don't worry, it's not loaded,' he said calmly, 'and I don't know if it can be used by the police in their ... what are they called? Forensic science, that's it. Or you might like to keep it as a trophy, as it's the gun that shot you out at Saxon Mills.'

Mr Campion took the proffered weapon and nodded in polite but silent thanks.

'Have you lost your marbles, Marcus? You weren't at the Long Tye shoot and you've never liked guns.'

'Oh it's not mine, Gus, my old friend,' said Fuller, stepping back around the Land Rover and striding to the other side. 'It's Simon's.'

Fuller pulled open the passenger door to reveal his brother sitting there wearing a sheepish expression and a large white sling bandage which nursed his plastered arm. He winced as his elder sibling ordered him to get out, as painfully as if he had been gripped and dragged by the ear like a recalcitrant schoolboy being pushed into the headmaster's study, or in this case made to stand before the judicial-looking Campion and Marchant, with Spindler and Eliza Jane acting as a jury.

'I know you're the family solicitor, Hereward, and you're probably going to advise Simon not to say anything which might incriminate him,' Marcus Fuller announced in a voice which did not expect either contradiction or answer. 'Well, you're too late. He's told me quite enough to incriminate himself and I intend to make sure the police know everything, for the sake of the family name and for the sake of the Carders. If it means the end of us, then so be it. At least we will go out with a clear conscience.'

Hereward Spindler cleared his throat in the official and sepulchral way that only officers of the court or undertakers can master. 'Are you saying, Marcus, that Simon has confessed to some form of crime?'

Fuller nudged his brother with a finger like a pistol in the small of the back. The downcast younger man shuffled forward until he was no more than a yard from Campion, but his eyes remained fixed on his shoes.

'Simon has confessed to several crimes, including popping off a load of buckshot in the direction of Mr Campion during the shoot on Gus's farm. That I regard as cowardly and despicable behaviour for someone who is both a Fuller and a Carder. Campion here is perfectly entitled to press charges and I would be happy to appear for the prosecution.'

'I would advise caution, Marcus. You are allowing your emotions to run away with you.'

'Oh shut up, Hereward. We all know you don't have any emotions, so please don't lecture me.' Fuller prodded his son in the back again. 'Well, Simon, aren't you going to apologise to Mr Campion?'

'I would prefer an explanation to an apology,' said Campion relaxing and speaking for the first time since the Fullers had arrived on the scene. When all eyes turned on the younger man, Campion surreptitiously broke the action of the shotgun and glanced down to check that it really was unloaded.

'I wanted to scare you out of Lindsay because we had a shipment coming in,' said Simon Fuller, meeting Campion's eyes, 'and you were the last person we wanted hanging round the village when that happened. Tommy and Clifford thought smashing your car up would work, but that was stupid because it just stranded you here.'

His chin sank back down into his chest.

'You've got Tommy Tucker to thank for me hanging around,' said Campion. 'If he hadn't set a booby trap for Ben Judd which nobbled my niece, I would have happily seen the sights, bought a few postcards and driven off into the sunset, leaving local law and order to the Carders. They seem to have been taking care of that themselves for quite a few years now, although the fact that no one in Lindsay seemed remotely concerned about, or particularly interested in, dear Eliza's accident made me suspect that it must have been an inside job, done by a Carder. Anyone else would surely have disappeared for nine days and had the fear of God put into them.'

'Tommy was besotted with her,' said Simon Fuller, 'from the moment she arrived here. He still is. The fact that she fell for that boorish pig Ben Judd drove him mad.'

Eliza Jane snorted quietly and whispered into her uncle's ear, 'I knew it would somehow be all my fault.'

'It was Judd's rather impetuous actions last night which rendered both you and Tommy Tucker *hors de combat*, leaving poor Clifford to unload the latest consignment alone once darkness fell,' said Campion, 'and it's nicely ironic that the angry but innocent young artist is in police custody whilst our gang of drug dealers roam free, though I suspect not for long.'

The younger Fuller nursed his plastered arm with his working one.

'I knew it was a mistake to trust Clifford to do anything on his own,' he said without emotion. 'He's not all there, you know, never was. Even as a kid, he was a bit slow on the uptake and all the other kids teased him at school until he got so big and strong that nobody dared. I had no idea – honestly – that he would give those students the LSD concentrate last summer. I didn't think he even knew what it was.'

'Clearly he did not know enough to dilute a fatal dose,' said Campion but got no further as he was interrupted by Dennis Sherman hurrying out of the Hall and staring at the group on the steps

411

in disbelief.

'What the bloody hell is going on? Where's that ambulance?' he demanded gesticulating wildly at the empty, moonlit High Street.

'Calm down, Dennis,' said Marchant. 'Hereward rang 999. I'm sure they're on their way.'

Eliza Jane leaned into Campion and whispered, 'So did I.'

'Excuse me?' Campion hissed back out of the corner of his mouth.

'Well I left a message for Inspector Bailey in Bury this afternoon before I drove out to pick you up and smuggle you back into Lindsay. Aunt Amanda suggested it. "Insurance" she called it.'

'She's a wise woman,' whispered Campion, 'but never tell her I said that.'

'I still want to know what the hell is going on,' shouted Dennis Sherman. 'Is this a town meeting or something?'

'It looks more like a trial to me. An *al fresco* trial by moonlight, which sounds rather romantic. Why wasn't I invited?'

The gathering on the steps turned as one to identify the intrusive new voice, which was loud and slightly shrill, distinctly feminine and definitely lubricated with alcohol. Mrs Webster had emerged from the oaken heart of The Woolpack across the curve of the road. Her knee-length coat was open to reveal a far from knee-length skirt and a frothy white blouse. In one hand she held a lit cigarette and, rather precariously, a glass of red wine in the other.

'Clarissa, my dear!' said Gus Marchant, more with resignation than enthusiasm. 'Do join us;

412

we had no intention of excluding you and I suppose you really should know what is going on.'

'I wish someone would tell me,' muttered Dennis Sherman as Mrs Webster put one somewhat unsteady high heel in front of the other and stepped off the pavement.

'Now we have a quorum,' Campion said softly to Eliza Jane. 'There are nine of us, if you count Clifford.'

'Oh, I get it,' said the girl, 'this is Carder business.'

'Perhaps the final assembly of the Carders; keep an eye on Clarissa.'

'So what am I missing?' asked Mrs Webster taking a sip from her glass as if standing in the middle of the street at night drinking was her natural habitat. 'And why is Albert holding a gun?'

'Purely for decoration, I assure you,' smiled Campion. 'Perhaps Mr Marchant would prefer to chair this unofficial board meeting?'

'No, no, Campion, you're doing splendidly.'

Mr Campion shrugged his shoulders. 'If there are no objections then, I suppose I can play the Learned Clerk although that role properly belongs to Mr Spindler, I believe.'

'Are the Carders on trial?' Mrs Webster giggled. 'Do I plead guilty now or will you cross-examine me, Albert? I do hope I get the third degree, though I'm not sure what that means.'

'This is serious, Clarissa,' Mr Spindler chided.

'Oh pish, Hereward, you old killjoy.'

'It really *is* a serious matter,' said Marcus Fuller grasping Clarissa's arm to steady her, 'you

413

should listen to Campion.'

Mrs Webster shook off Fuller's hand, thrust out her bosom and fluttered her eyelids at Campion.

'I am all ears,' she said coquettishly.

Campion ignored her, just as he ignored the niece quivering at his side desperately trying to contain an outburst of laughter.

'Mrs Webster does have a point. The Carders may well be on trial. Individual Carders certainly will be in due course: young Mr Tucker and the younger Mr Fuller will be charged with smuggling and purveying illegal substances, as will Clifford Sherman, who may also be charged with the manslaughter of Stephen Stotter and Martin Rees, the young archaeology students who found the starting handle which killed Johnnie Sirrah back in 1937.'

'You can't know that!' Dennis Sherman blurted angrily.

'I didn't,' said Campion fixing him with a steely stare and speaking through gritted teeth, 'not for sure, until Clifford told me down there in the tunnels.'

'That's ridiculous,' said Gus Marchant. 'How could Clifford know that? He wasn't born when Johnnie Sirrah died.'

Of the group, only Campion registered Mrs Webster's lower lip begin to wobble as she said 'Johnnie' quietly to herself.

'No, he was not,' said Mr Campion, 'but his father was a boy of, I suspect, eleven or twelve when he saw *his* father, Leonard, do the deed out at Saxon Mills. It was, from what I've heard, quite in character for Leonard Sherman, who

414

was – and this is pure guesswork – quite a ruthless leader of the Carders.'

'Things have changed a lot since Leonard's day,' said Marchant, his voice squirming in embarrassment.

'Johnnie...' breathed Mrs Webster again.

'But not quickly enough,' Campion continued. 'You Carders continue to profit from your manipulation of Esther Wickham's estate' – he turned his head to glare at Hereward Spindler – 'and above all from the fog of secrecy with which you surround Lindsay Carfax. Anyone who questions you is intimidated or shunned. Just ask Lemmy Walker or the Rev. Trump. You people were so obsessed with your secret rituals, your meagre tithes and rents which were little more than protection money, and the airs and graces you had given yourself that you never realised how corrupt you had become, despite the odd act of charity.'

'Steady on, Campion,' said Hereward Spindler.

'I think that you, as a lawyer,' Campion replied, 'deserve the lion's share of my opprobrium, though none of you are innocent. You are all guilty because not one of you said "Enough" or "This has gone too far", did you? I think it is time the Carders seriously considered their future; if the Carders have a future, that is.'

There was a silence broken only by Mrs Webster, who dropped her cigarette on to the road and ground it out with the sole of her shoe and elaborate twists of quite a lot of shapely leg, before stepping up to Campion, close enough for him to inhale her perfume as it was wafted towards him by her fluttering eyelashes.

'You can't think I'm guilty of anything, can you?' she said in a rich caramel voice.

'Other than by association with the Carder ethos, it is possible you are a complete innocent,' Campion admitted.

'Oh, I'd never say that...'

Mrs Webster smiled sweetly at Mr Campion, then at Gus Marchant and then at Marcus Fuller as she moved into the throng of bodies on the steps. Simon Fuller and Dennis Sherman she ignored. She and Eliza Jane exchanged a furtive glance and the younger woman took a step to the side to allow Mrs Webster to stand directly in front of Hereward Spindler.

'You knew Johnnie Sirrah,' she told the solicitor in a low and deliberate voice, 'and I think you knew what happened to him. You and Leonard Sherman were thick as thieves, weren't you?'

'I had nothing to do with Johnnie's death,' said Spindler drawing himself up to his full height to tower over his accuser.

'I'm sure you wouldn't have the guts to do the deed – you haven't got any guts, or marrow or blood in that stick you call a body – but evil old Leonard wouldn't think twice before bashing somebody's head in; somebody who was asking too many questions about your little Esther Wickham scam, for instance.'

Eliza Jane clutched at Campion's hand for reassurance and found her grip returned as Mrs Webster's voice rose to a scream.

'You knew what happened though, and you didn't say a word. You *knew*, you desiccated old

416

prune, you *knew*!'

With a short-range jabbing motion of her left hand, Clarissa Webster hurled the contents of the wine glass she was holding at the solicitor's shirt front where a dark stain instantly appeared as if he had been shot.

Hereward Spindler reacted instinctively by bending at the neck to look down at his soaked chest. At that point he brought his face down well within range of Mrs Webster's clenched right first which delivered a perfectly timed hay-maker to his jaw.

Spindler fell as if pole-axed, which he probably felt he had been, his body crumpling like a marionette after the strings had been cut.

Mrs Webster kissed the knuckles of her fist and turned to Campion, all sweetness and light.

'Not so innocent now, am I?'

Twenty-Two

Moonglow

The ambulance arrived and its crew did brisk business whilst muttering that if Lindsay Carfax was going to call on their services every night, they might have to build the hospital nearer, the price of petrol being what it was. They grumbled under the weight of Clifford Sherman on a stretcher and asked aloud how he had got so drunk, what with the pubs not being shut yet. They were even more appalled that an 'elderly gentleman of some standing in the community' (for they recognised the supine Mr Spindler) could get himself into a fist fight resulting in several lost teeth and a bloody nose, no doubt whilst inebriated and in public! And him a solicitor, too!

The police were hot on their heels, in three cars which had barrelled down the High Street with blue lamps flashing but thankfully no sirens, bells or whistles, which might – just might – have dragged some of the residents of Lindsay Carfax away from their television sets. As it was, not a curtain twitched and no door opened even a crack. When Carder business was being conducted out in the middle of the street, it was

418

perhaps wiser to stay indoors.

Chief Inspector Bill Bailey and a uniformed sergeant climbed out of the first car and two uniformed constables emerged from each of the other two. All six officers of the law approached the steps of the Carders' Hall and surveyed the chaotic scene before them. Even the experienced Bailey seemed unsure of what the next move should be or who should make it.

Mr Campion, his face, hair and torn clothes begrimed with dirt, and with a broken shotgun over his arm, did a sprightly tap-and-heel step towards the policemen and took command.

Using a winning smile and short, precise sentences, he explained who was in need of medical help (Clifford Sherman and Hereward Spindler), who was in need of arrest (Clifford Sherman, again, Simon Fuller and, *in absentia*, Tommy Tucker), those from whom a statement really should be taken (just about everyone?), who was in need of a shoulder to cry on and some strong coffee (Mrs Webster), and who was in desperate need of a good night's sleep in his own bed (himself?).

Bill Bailey relieved Campion of the shotgun and after ordering his men to start taking names and addresses, drew him to the side of a police car for a more private briefing.

'I don't normally attend minor public disturbances with three cars and five men, you know,' said the policeman, 'but as you were involved, I was persuaded to make an exception. It looks as if I should have brought a couple of Black Marias as well.'

'I'm very grateful,' said Campion, 'and ask for indulgence if my niece pestered you mercilessly, but she was only concerned for her frail and ancient uncle.'

'It wasn't just your niece, though she did pester supremely well on your behalf; hers was only one of several phone calls I've had today. That's partly the reason I didn't get here until whatever riot you managed to spark seems to have fizzled out.'

'It was hardly a riot,' Campion demurred.

'More than three people gathered on the street at night under a full moon is either a riot or a witches' coven in rural Suffolk in the opinion of some of our magistrates, and Lady Amanda warned me that if you were involved, I could rule out neither.'

'My wife?'

'Quite clearly she is, and someone I have no intention of letting down. She told me you were due home today and if that wasn't going to be possible, I had to promise to put you up at my house or in a police cell until the morning and then escort you to London in irons.'

'Ah, well, yes, perhaps I did promise something of the sort, but events in the Woolpack last night...'

'The bar brawl,' scolded Bailey.

'...er, yes ... that rather threw my timetable out of kilter, though it did work out well in the end.'

'I'd hate to be around you when things go badly, Campion, but I have to admit you have quite a gang of guardian angels watching over you. Your niece, Lady Amanda – who even

420

roped in the Chief Constable as the Fitton name still carries weight in Suffolk – and then there was Charlie Luke, who was on the phone as well, not to mention Her Majesty's Customs and Excise. In fact, I was at a meeting with them in Ipswich this afternoon, discussing certain aspects of the Dangerous Drugs Act when the phones started ringing. Customs at Dover had had a tip-off about a Bedford van, a van registered in Suffolk and a van, unless I'm much mistaken, very similar to that one parked up the street there by the Museum.'

'The very same,' Campion agreed, 'though I'm afraid its illegal, contents are scattered over the secret passages under the Carders' Hall. There should be enough sweepings to use as evidence though, not to mention poor Clifford Sherman.'

'Young Clifford's in a bit of a state, isn't he? One of the ambulance chaps tells me he's taken LSD *through his eyes*, for God's sake. I didn't know that was possible.'

'A chemistry graduate in Cambridge told me that using an eye-dropper is a perfectly accepted way of getting a high, as he called it,' said Campion seriously. 'It was the most depressing thing I learned on my recent return to my *Alma Mater*.'

Bill Bailey shook his head slowly.

'What a world, eh?'

'Not mine, any more,' confessed Mr Campion.

'And this was all Carder business?'

'Let us say it was a bit of private enterprise by a few of the Carder mob, but I have a feeling that all Carder activity is about to be wound up and consigned to the history books.'

'Not before time in my opinion,' said the Chief Inspector.

'It is a course of action worth considering in other ways too,' said Mr Campion thoughtfully.

Gus Marchant had supplied the friendly shoulder needed by Clarissa Webster and from somewhere Eliza Jane had found a lacy square of handkerchief for her to dab delicately at her nose and eyes.

'I've made a complete fool of myself, haven't I?' sobbed Mrs Webster.

Marchant and Eliza Jane murmured 'Not at all' and 'There, there' in equal proportions.

'And in public, too.' The sob was in danger of becoming a wail.

'I don't think you have anything to worry about, Mrs Webster,' Campion reassured her as he reached the three figures seated on the Hall steps like naughty children.

'Clarissa,' the woman corrected him with a sniff and a quick look up from under her fringe.

'You've nothing to worry about, Clarissa. You were, in a sense, among friends or at least Carders. No one here tonight has anything to gain by spreading gossip.'

'Don at the Woolpack will have seen everything. He can see through walls, that man. He won't be able to resist. Gossip is currency to him.'

Eliza Jane nodded her head in silent agreement.

'I doubt it. If Don saw you floor Hereward

422

Spindler with that fantastic right hook of yours, then I think he'll keep his peace. If he knows what's good for him, of course. If he doesn't, there's always the threat that he could be the next Nine Days' Wonder of Lindsay Carfax.'

'There will be no more of *that*!' snapped Gus Marchant rising to his feet and helping Mrs Webster to hers. 'You've forced us to see the error of our ways, Campion. The Carders started off with good intentions to "contribute to the common area" but through time became corrupted and allowed awful things to happen to people. The Carders should be no more than a charitable trust – a real, open one for once – with trustees and auditors. Everything else, every racket, every bit of privilege, must stop. I know Marcus will go along with me and the Shermans and Spindler don't really have a say in things as far as I'm concerned. If you're with me Clarissa, that gives us a quorum, should anyone dispute matters.'

'I seriously doubt anyone will,' observed Campion.

'I think that's a splendid idea, Gus,' said Mrs Webster, her eyes shining. 'Let's put all this behind us and start a new life.'

'Er ... yes ... precisely. Now, we'd better talk to Bill Bailey. He's a good sort and I'm sure he'll give us a sympathetic hearing. Then I'll walk you home.'

If he had not known better, Mr Campion would have put Clarissa's sudden weakness at the knees and consequent stumbling into Marchant's manly chest down to shock, but he was sure Mrs Webster was not the swooning type.

423

'We owe you our thanks, Campion,' said Gus who had suddenly found himself holding Clarissa's hand. 'Do stay and let us buy you a good dinner or two. I'll make your room at the Woolpack available for as long as you want.'

Mr Campion clasped his hands in front of him as if in prayer, and performed a small bow of humility.

'You are too kind, but I have left Lindsay Carfax too many times already. I must make a final exit tonight or I will face severe penalties domestically. There may, however, be a way in which you could express your gratitude, if I may be so bold.'

'Name it, and if I can provide it, it's yours.'

'You own the Woolpack and several other public houses do you not?'

'Certainly I do. I also have shares in several restaurants and two golf clubs.'

'And these business activities – totally legitimate ones of course – bring you into contact with the brewing trade?'

Marchant looked surprised, but said, 'Naturally. My late wife, who did not approve of licensed victualing, used to say I was the brewers' best customer. That would be wholesale, of course, not retail.'

Campion smiled. 'I was wondering if you had any contacts with bodies such as the Brewers' Society or the Brewers' Company in London.'

'As a matter of fact I do. We sell London bottled beers in Suffolk; they take Suffolk ales and barley wines in London, not to mention our malted barley. What are you after, Campion? A

424

couple of barrels for a party or for the Christmas feast?'

'No, nothing like that. I would like you to use what influence you have to get someone I know a position in Brewers' Hall in the City.'

'Well, I'll put in a word if you think it will help.' Marchant raised an eyebrow. 'Though I'm not sure if I approve of nepotism...'

'It's not nepotism; not really, it's more a public service by keeping an undesirable off the streets. You see there's a vacancy at Brewers' Hall for a Beadle and an old mess-mate of mine called Lugg would fit right in.'

'Are you sure you won't stay over, Uncle? You really do look shattered.'

'No, my dear, my mind has been made up for me. I must keep my promise to leave Lindsay Carfax and get home. Bill Bailey has kindly offered to give me a lift in a police car and one of his boys in blue will pick up the Jaguar before the local farmers use it as a scarecrow. I'll grab forty winks in a police cell in Bury, which will no doubt be good for my soul, then a hearty breakfast in the police canteen and I'll be back in London in time for morning coffee and severe reprimands.'

Uncle and niece walked slowly down the High Street in the bright moonlight. Very occasionally a curtain now did twitch and a front door open and then quickly close; the comings and goings of so many vehicles so late in the evening finally proving irresistible. Not one of the villagers, however, came out to enquire what was going on.

'There's obviously something better on television,' said Eliza Jane, reading Campion's mind.

'Let the good people of Lindsay sleep through the revolution. When they rise with the dawn it will be to a life without Carders.'

'Will they notice?'

'Probably not; though that's not necessarily a bad thing,' said Campion reasonably, 'and there will be something else on telly tomorrow night.'

'And what about the Carders themselves?'

'They will dissolve into folklore, all except Lady Prunella Redcar, who is already a thing of legend. She will retain her life of splendid and pampered ignorance in Monte Carlo because Gus Marchant is a kind man and will continue to provide whatever Carder pension she draws. Though she will be troubled by frequent visits from the French police and Interpol and will have to advertise for a new companion-housekeeper.'

'Monte Carlo, eh?' said the girl impishly. 'I might apply for the post.'

'You should have a word with my daughter-in-law Perdita first,' said Mr Campion. 'On second thoughts, I think it might be dangerous if you two got together and hit it off.'

'Dangerous for whom?'

'Mankind in general, I would have thought. And speaking of dangers to man, I dropped my rather splendid walking stick, my pilgrim's staff, down by the studio last night. If it's still there in the grass, do give it to Clarissa as a keepsake, or as stock for The Medley.'

'I'm not sure I'll be spending much time at the studio in the future.'

'Really? I'm so sorry to hear that.'

'Sorry, but not surprised?'

Mr Campion slowed his gait and studied his niece's face, revelling in the familiar Fitton features.

'I must be careful what I say, but I have always thought you had your aunt's impeccable taste in men. With Ben Judd, you just forgot it for a while.'

'That's the most arrogant, immodest thing I've ever heard!' Eliza Jane snapped, stamping a foot, but her fury was transient. 'It's also sadly very true. I was besotted with Ben. Perhaps I thought I could tame him but after the way he behaved last night, I think that's an impossible dream and I would go mad in the attempt.'

'Not only beautiful, but wise,' said Campion fondly, 'which is the Fitton family motto, or it ought to be.'

They walked a few more paces in silence until they arrived at Eliza Jane's cottage.

'Are you sure you'll be all right?' asked the girl.

'Of course I will, I'm being taken into custody and a night in the cells in Bury St Edmunds will be a new adventure for me.' Campion smiled his most owlish smile.

'Haven't you had enough adventures? Shouldn't you be taking it easy?'

'At my age, you mean? You might be right; in fact I think you are.'

'Steady on, Uncle, don't go all serious on me.'

'I hope I'll never do that,' said Campion, taking her hand in his, 'but recent events have been rather wearying and I am no longer as young as most people think I am.'

Eliza Jane tugged on his arm to acknowledge the joke.

'Look up there,' said Campion, pointing his spectacles to the billowing full moon above.

'Beautiful, isn't it.'

'It certainly is, but my point is that a man walked on that earlier this year.'

'And one day a woman will.'

'Of that I have no doubt, but when I was born men – and women – were still some years away from even flying. Now we send men to the Moon and watch it on television from the comfort of our own homes. It is a very different world now from the one I was brought in to and I think it is a world getting harsher and more ruthless.'

'You mean the drugs scene?'

'Not just that, though that is unpleasant and will undoubtedly become more of a problem. It is the speed of change – progress, if you like – which is leaving people like me behind. It is the way of the world and I am not making any special pleading, but I don't have to like it and I think it better for all concerned, myself, my family and my friends, if I accept that I can no longer keep up the pace. I've had many a jolly adventure, been lucky in life and very lucky in love. Hopefully I have the wisdom to know when it is time to retire gracefully from the scene.'

Eliza Jane squeezed her uncle's hand, the gesture expressing an affection she would have found hard to put into words.

'I came to Lindsay Carfax,' said Mr Campion, 'because I was intrigued by what sounded to be a really *old-fashioned* mystery, the sort of mystery that required an old fashioned adventurer.'

Mr Campion smiled his gentlest smile.

'It was; and I am. And both of us have had our day.'

Albert Campion will return in Mr Campion's Fox